W9-CGP-582

LIFE AFTER GENIUS

LIFE AFTER GENIUS

M. ANN JACOBY

GRAND CENTRAL PUBLISHING

NEW YORK BOSTON

This book is a work of fiction. Names, characters, places, and incidents are the product of the author's imagination or are used fictitiously. Any resemblance to actual events, locales, or persons, living or dead, is coincidental.

Grand Central Publishing
Hachette Book Group USA
237 Park Avenue
New York, NY 10017

Visit our Web site at www.HachetteBookGroupUSA.com.

Printed in the United States of America

First Edition: October 2008
10 9 8 7 6 5 4 3 2 1

Grand Central Publishing is a division of Hachette Book Group USA, Inc.
The Grand Central Publishing name and logo is a trademark of Hachette Book Group USA, Inc.

Library of Congress Cataloging-in-Publication Data
Jacoby, M. Ann.
Life after genius / M. Ann Jacoby. — 1st ed.
p. cm.
ISBN-13: 978-0-446-19971-1
ISBN-10: 0-446-19971-0
1. Gifted persons—Fiction. 2. Self-actualization (Psychology)—Fiction. 3. Family-owned business enterprises—Fiction. 4. Eccentrics and eccentricities—Fiction. 5. Riemann hypothesis—Fiction. 6. Embalming—Fiction. 7. Psychological fiction. I. Title.
PS3610.A35683L54 2008
813'.6—dc22

2008012629

To my father
for his sense of humor
and to my mother
for her sense of family

LIFE AFTER GENIUS

"Each generation finds itself obligated to begin the act of living almost as if no one had ever done it before."

—JOSÉ ORTEGA Y GASSET

1

UNDERAGE DRINKING

High Grove, Illinois
Eight Days Before Graduation

BEFORE MEAD BOARDS THE TRAIN in Chicago's Union Station bound for Alton, Illinois, he sells his brand-new CD player and several barely listened-to discs to Forsbeck, his roommate, to raise cash for the ticket. He then holes up in their room, sitting by the window until Herman leaves the dorm and heads off across campus for his final exam. Even then Mead is terrified that the guy will double back and follow him, suddenly materializing in the train seat across the aisle. "Where're you going, Fegley?" Herman will say. "It's not like you to ditch school. Could it be that I misjudged you?"

Even after detraining, six hours and twenty-two minutes later, Mead remains uneasy, nervously scanning the platform. He picks up his green-and-blue plaid suitcase in his left hand and lugs it clumsily over to the taxi stand, his right hand wrapped in an Ace bandage. He knows he is being paranoid but cannot help it. What will Herman do when he finds out Mead is gone? Will he go to the dean and rat him out? Or will he hold off in hopes that his well-laid plans can still come to fruition? Mead is betting on the latter. He believes that he knows Herman better than he knows himself. A shining example of humanity, Herman is. The type of person who brings into question the whole notion of man as the superior species on the planet.

The cab driver is skeptical when Mead gives his destination. "High Grove," the guy says. "Why, that must be thirty miles from here." He stares at Mead's bandaged hand. But he relents when Mead promises to make it worth his while. And Mead is surprised just how easily the driver gives in, how willing this stranger is to take him at his word. It's something Mead would not have even considered doing a year ago—or even a week ago—getting into a cab with barely a dollar in his pocket and having only a vague notion of how to pay for the ride at the other end. He wishes the driver would throw him out on his ass. Tell him to get lost. Tell him to find another sucker. Because then the world would seem right again, the stars aligning with the planets, or whatever.

Outside of the cab, the sun is setting behind a recently planted field of corn. It isn't a spectacular dusk but rather dull. There are no clouds to catch the last rays of light, only a small circle of orange on the horizon, which, like the dying embers of a fire, snuffs out before Mead's eyes. A perfect metaphor for what his life has suddenly become.

"Right here," Mead says, and the driver pulls to a stop in front of a one-story brick house. The lights are on inside, the dining room curtains glowing yellow. His parents have probably just sat down to supper. If there was a funeral today, his father will be sipping a martini and discussing the ceremony. If not, he will settle for a Coke and talk about furniture. Perhaps they will even spend a little time on the subject of next week: when they will leave, what hotel they will stay in, and where they would like to take their son to celebrate the big event of his graduation from college. At the age of eighteen, no less. Thoughts that make Mead's stomach churn.

He rings the front doorbell, and a moment later, the porch light comes on, throwing him into the spotlight. Mead's tempted to lift his suitcase and smash the bulb. To remain in the dark. To slip into the house through the back door and down the hall to his bedroom unnoticed. But there is the small matter of the taxi driver.

If there is any saving grace in any of this, it is that his father is the one who opens the door. His face is a mask of neutrality. This is a man accustomed to dealing with tragedy on a day-to-day basis. A man who knows that, in his line of business, there is no room for getting emotionally involved. A man inured to shock. "Teddy," he says. "What're you doing here?"

"I owe the cab driver a hundred dollars."

His father looks past him to the curb.

"I haven't broken any laws or done anything wrong. Beyond that, I have nothing to tell. I just want to be left alone to deal with this in my own way, all right?"

His father doesn't answer, just looks at the waiting cab as if it might contain some explanation as to this sudden change in events.

THE PHONE RINGS, WAKING MEAD UP. A ringing phone can mean only one of two things: either someone has died, or it is the dean. Mead hopes that it is the former, that someone has died. He sits up in bed and glances at his watch, but there isn't enough light in the room to see, so he steps over to the window and cracks open the blinds to let in a sliver of morning sun. It's 8:40. Three hours and twenty minutes to showtime. Only the star of the show is nowhere to be found, vanished from his dorm room and from the face of the campus for the second time in three months. He releases the blinds and the slats snap closed like an eyelid. Mead crawls back into bed.

Footsteps come down the hall. *Click-clack, click-clack.* The sound of bad news. They stop outside his bedroom door—more bad news—and Mead braces himself for what he knows is about to come.

The door opens and his mother sticks her head inside. A perfectly coiffed head with powdered cheeks and glossy lips. It is easy to picture her lying in a casket. She will look just as she does now, only with her eyes closed and her mouth stitched shut. He would give anything to have her mouth stitched shut right now.

"It's Dean Falconia," she says. "He wants to speak with you."

"Tell him I'm not here."

"I will do no such thing. He knows you're here. For god's sake, the least you could do is have the decency to speak with him, to offer up an explanation."

Mead rolls over so that his back is to his mother. He does not want to talk to the dean—or to anyone else for that matter—because he does not know what to say. Where he would start. How to explain the stupid things he has done. Once he opens his mouth, he will have lost the only advantage he has and he cannot afford to let Herman get the upper hand. Not this time.

"Whatever it is that has happened," his mother says, "it can't be worth throwing away a college degree. Worth ruining your life." Her voice falters. But whether she is choking up with tears or anger, it is hard to say. Probably a little of both. And Mead cannot blame her. He would probably feel the same way if he were in her shoes. But he isn't.

She leaves the door open, her heels *click-clacking* back down the hall. "Give me a couple of days to get to the bottom of this," Mead hears his mother say to the dean before clamping the bed pillow over his ears.

THE SIX-LEGGED CREATURE IS CROUCHING behind Mead. He cannot see it, but he can hear it breathing in and out. In and out.

Waiting for just the right moment to pounce. It has been shadowing Mead since seventh grade, ever since he brought home that C on his report card. The creature is insatiable. Always hungering for more, more, more. Mead thought it would stay behind when he boarded the train north to Chicago for his freshman year of college. He saw neither hide nor hair of it for several weeks. Then one evening in the library, a week before final exams, it reappeared, breathing down the back of his neck. Mead was so shocked that he scooped up his books and ran all the way back to the dorm. But it followed him and then hung around for several days—straight through finals week—before disappearing again. After that, it started showing up more and more often until, once again, it had become a constant presence in his life. It was almost as if Mead had never left home at all.

It was not until he came back to High Grove—last night—that he realized how weakened the six-legged creature had been up there in Chicago. Not until he returned to its nest was he reminded of just how powerful the beast can be when it is on its home turf.

"I'm not budging until you tell me what this is all about," it says.

Two hours, thirty-six minutes, and seventeen seconds. Eighteen seconds. Nineteen seconds. That's how long the creature has been crouching behind him. And in all that time, Mead hasn't moved a muscle. But he's starting to wonder how long he's going to be able to keep this up. Lying motionless. His mattress, which started out feeling soft and comfortable, has turned into a bed of jagged rocks that are poking into his hips and thighs, making it almost unbearable to remain still. But Mead is afraid that if he moves, even an inch, the creature will sense weakness and be fortified in its resolve to sit him out.

The phone rings for the second time this morning, followed

by a different pair of feet coming down the hall, the footsteps this time around less punishing to the ear. They stop outside Mead's open bedroom door.

"That was the coroner," his father says. "I have to go out."

Mead rolls over and comes face-to-face with the six-legged creature: his mother sitting on a straight-backed kitchen chair, her arms crossed over her chest, staring at him. Standing directly behind her is Mead's father: a tall, thin man in a black suit who could easily be mistaken for the beast's shadow. Mead looks past the creature, as if it isn't there, and says to its shadow, "I'll go with you."

As they drive across town, Mead unwraps the Ace bandage from around his right hand and flexes his fingers. The pain is far less intense than it was just twenty-four hours ago and the swelling has gone way down. It's amazing to Mead how quickly the body repairs itself. Bounces back and keeps going. The brain, on the other hand, is a little slower on the rebound.

"How did you hurt your hand?" his father asks.

"I let my emotions get the better of me."

"You hit someone?"

Mead flexes his fingers and flinches at the memory. "Don't worry, Dad, I've got them under control now."

The black hearse pulls to a stop in front of a white colonial with green shutters. A lawn stretches out before it, as relaxed as a sleeping cat. Daffodils smile up at the sun. The house itself seems to breathe with life. It's not hard to imagine a kitchen filled with fragrant smells, laughter floating down the stairs, a dog sleeping by the fireplace.

"Are you sure this is the right address?" Mead asks.

His father shuts off the engine. "You don't have to come inside, you know. You can stay right here. I'll be back in a minute."

Mead considers his father's offer. Considers the fact that he is under no obligation whatsoever to go inside. After all, he's not even supposed to be here. He's supposed to be at Chicago University, standing behind the lectern in Epps Hall before an auditorium full of mathematicians, chalk in hand, discussing the significance of the spacings between the zeros of the zeta function. Which is precisely why he has to go inside, because he isn't in that auditorium. He's here. In the passenger seat of his father's hearse.

"No," Mead says. "I'll go." And he proceeds to climb out.

A couple of girls come down the street on bicycles, beach towels stuffed into their handlebar baskets. Talking and laughing. Until they spot Mead's dad unloading the gurney. Pushing it up the front walk. They stare at the bed-on-wheels as if a dead person were already on it and come within inches of colliding with each other.

"I'm here to pick up Delia Winslow," Mead's father says to the dry-eyed woman who answers the front door. She nods, and Mead helps him maneuver the gurney up the steps and into the front hall. It's a long hall lined with photographs, like an art gallery. Cocktails will be served from three until five. Please leave all charitable donations in the candy dish by the front door.

"That's her right there," the dry-eyed woman says to Mead and points to a black-and-white photograph of three young women. "The one in the middle."

"Her who?" Mead asks.

"My mother-in-law. Delia. Of course, she was much younger back then. That picture must've been taken over fifty years ago."

Mead leans in for a closer look. All three women are wearing gingham dresses trimmed in white eyelet collars as if they sense a barn dance in their near futures. And each one is holding a fruit pie in her left hand and a prize-ribbon in her right. The sun must have been bright that day because they're all squinting into the camera.

"That was the year Delia won first place in the County Fair Bake-Off," her daughter-in-law says. "She made the best cherry pies in the whole state of Illinois. Really. Delia was a genius in the kitchen."

Genius. Mead flinches at the sound of the word, having never before associated it with pastry. A self-important word. It brings to mind an imaginary photograph, one not hanging on the Winslow's wall. A black-and-white snapshot of Mead standing next to the twenty-five-year-old Delia, she holding her blue-ribbon pie, he a stack of textbooks. The two geniuses of Grove County.

"Did she win the blue ribbon again the following year?" Mead asks.

"Oh, no. Delia never entered the contest again. She'd had her moment in the sun and wanted to give other women a chance at theirs."

Or she discovered that she didn't like it. Being a genius. Didn't like being separated from the rest of the herd. A target for not only praise but also jealousy. Mead wishes he had met the curly-haired woman with chipmunk cheeks when she was still alive. He feels as if he knows her, or at least understands the ambiguity she must have felt about her genius. He would have liked to have spoken with her. He might have learned a thing or two from Delia about how to handle living life as a genius. Pastry or otherwise.

Which is perhaps why it comes as such a shock when Mead turns the corner at the end of the hall and comes face-to-face with the present-day Delia: a seventy-five-year-old woman with thinning white hair, sunken cheeks, and skin that looks several sizes too large for its occupant. A man is sitting next to Delia's bed. He stands when Mead and his father enter the room, introduces himself as Samuel, son of the deceased, and apologizes for the stench. “We did our best to clean up my mother before you arrived.”

“No need to apologize,” Mead’s father says. “This kind of thing happens all the time.” Pulling two pairs of latex gloves out of his back pocket, he hands one to Mead. “Put these on,” he says and dons the other pair himself. The gloves are lined with talcum powder and fit Mead like a second layer of skin, but pulling the right one on over his still-sore hand hurts like hell. Through this haze of pain, he watches as his father turns down the bedsheets—and almost gags.

Mead now wishes he had taken his father up on that offer to stay in the hearse. It’s not that Mead hasn’t seen a dead body before. He’s seen plenty of them. But those were the sanitized version of dead, already bathed and preserved. This is different. This is a little old lady in her soiled nightgown. Mead tries to take a breath and chokes. If he’d actually eaten anything in the past twenty-four hours, he’d be heaving it up all over the deceased right now. But lucky for Mead, he hasn’t had any appetite at all since his last conversation with Herman.

“Why don’t you open a window?” Mead’s father says to him as if it was hot in the room and a cool breeze might be welcome. Mr. Calm-Under-Pressure. Mr. Never-Let-Them-See-You-Sweat. Mead would like to tell his father that it isn’t necessary. That he is man enough to take it. But it is necessary and he isn’t man enough. And so Mead throws open the sash and sticks his head out into the backyard, startling the pet dog who isn’t sleeping by the fireplace but watering an azalea bush. A little dog that starts barking its head off when it sees Mead. *Yip, yip, yip, yip.* The damned thing is no bigger than a cat. *Yip, yip, yip, yip.* Reminds Mead of Dr. Kustrup, the chairman of the math department, a man who confuses quantity with quality when it comes to the use of his vocal chords. *Yip, yip, yip, yip.* Mead sticks his tongue out at the dog. *Yip, yip, yip, yip.* The smaller they are, the bigger they try to sound. Seems to go for both dogs and men.

By the time Mead pulls his head back inside, Delia has been transferred from her bed to the gurney and covered with the ubiquitous white sheet. Samuel apologizes again and offers Mead a glass of water. Mead turns it down because of the look on his father's face. It isn't a look of disapproval—Mead only gets those from his mother—but of embarrassment. Mead knows what his father is thinking: The family of the deceased has enough on their minds and shouldn't have to deal with the undertaker's weak-stomached son.

THE RIDE BACK INTO TOWN IS SILENT. Mead stares out the window of the hearse at the passing houses but sees instead an auditorium full of mathematicians and visiting professors squirming in their seats. Glancing at their watches. Talking among themselves. Wondering where the key speaker is. Why the damned presentation has not yet gotten under way. Mead sees a man walking on the sidewalk but pictures instead Herman, pacing up and down the hall outside of the auditorium, watching his master plan crumble to pieces before his eyes. Mead sees Dean Falconia stride purposefully past Herman and into the auditorium, eyes to the floor, head shaking, trying to figure out what he is going to say to the scholars in the audience who made a special trip to Chicago just so they could witness—with their own eyes—the overwhelming statistical evidence that Mead has gathered that points to the veracity of the Riemann Hypothesis. Important men. He sees Herman walk up to the dean and ask where Mead is. Sees shock register on the young man's face as it begins to dawn on Herman that there was a third possible scenario to his plan. One that he had not foreseen.

Mead's father turns onto Main Street and drives past a row of mom-and-pop stores. A pharmacy. A grocer. A hardware store. A five-and-dime. Welcome to lovely downtown High Grove, a mere six hours and three decades away from Chicago. A hop, skip, and a jump into the past. The hearse then passes in front of the largest storefront in town, in front of a row of plate glass windows behind which are displayed a tall chest of drawers, a floor lamp, and a sofa. And hanging above these windows is a sign that reads: FEGLEY BROTHERS INC. FURNITURE. CARPETS. UNDERTAKERS. The hand-painted sign has hung there for a couple of generations. Mead's father turns into the alley just beyond these windows and parks in the lot behind the store where Mead's uncle Martin is waiting.

Mead slides down in his seat. Shit. He had forgotten all about his uncle, something about which he is not at all proud. Another indication of just how messed up his life has become in the past twenty-four hours.

"It's all right, Teddy," his father says, peering down at Mead from on high, "I told him you were home." But this only makes Mead feel worse.

He slides back up, peers out the window, and smiles at his uncle, but the man does not smile back. Instead, his uncle looks straight through him, as if Mead doesn't even exist. He opens the back of the hearse and pulls out the gurney. Mead's father and uncle lock heads to discuss the deceased—time of death, age, approximate weight—then roll Delia onto the freight elevator. After another short conversation, Mead's father walks back to the hearse, peers in at his son, and says, "He'd like you to join him downstairs."

Shit. Mead would rather his uncle find another way to get back at him. Like screaming in his face and calling him an ungrateful, self-centered, egotistical spoiled brat. At least Mead could take that, knowing that he has it coming. But this, this is beyond the realm of getting back; this is pure cruelty. "I can't, Dad. Sorry, but I just can't."

His father walks back over to the elevator to relay the message. Uncle Martin stares at Mead with hate in his eyes, then the elevator door closes and he is gone. Only then does Mead get out of the hearse and follow his father through the rear entrance into the store, stepping abruptly back in time to his childhood.

Ten thousand square feet of sofas and coffee tables and dining room suites, of bed frames and mattresses and dressers and rockers, of floor lamps and carpets and caskets, distributed over three floors. That's Fegley Brothers. Unchanged from as far back as Mead can remember. When he started elementary school, fitted with his first pair of prescription glasses, Mead used to pretend the store was a castle and that he was the young prince who would one day inherit it. On the first floor, he would crouch behind bookcases and entertainment centers, pretending they were trees and that the forest was filled with bandits. He'd pop up from behind sofas brandishing a yardstick as if it were a sword and fight them off. On the second floor, he would jump from bed to bed, pretending that he was leaping over rivers filled with jaw-snapping alligators, then he would ascend to the third floor where the king kept all his riches, where closed caskets sat on raised platforms under klieg lights and looked to the young Teddy Fegley like treasure chests filled with gold. The only place he did not play was in the basement. The dungeon. The place where the king kept his prisoners chained to the walls and fed them only water and gruel. The place where the young Teddy Fegley's imagination really soared. This was where he consigned the boy in first grade who tripped him in the hall, laughed, and said, "Can you see the floor, Theodore?" And the girl who gave him, on Valentine's Day, a shoebox containing the corpse of a bird. "Is it dead, Ted?" she said, and then ran off to join her coterie of tittering friends. But the king had the last word and he sent to the dungeon all those who dared betray the trust of the young prince.

Floorboards creak under Mead's feet as he now crosses through the back office and peers out onto the showroom floor. Standing in the middle of the showroom, talking to a customer, is Lenny, a balding, middle-aged man of indistinct features. A fixture at Fegley Brothers as permanent as those klieg lights on the third floor. Mead realizes, with a bit of a shock, that he doesn't know the man's last name. He has always referred to him simply as Lenny. A man of many talents: salesperson, deliveryman, pallbearer, gravedigger. If something needs doing, Lenny is the guy who will get it done.

"So how does it work?" Mead asks his father.

"How does what work?"

"The store. How does it work?"

"Well, customers come in, select a piece of furniture, and we deliver it to them the following day."

Mead gives his father a sidelong glance. "Thanks, Dad, for that illuminating description."

"I'm sorry," he answers back. "Was that a serious question?"

Mead gazes at a display of six walnut chairs seated around a matching dining room table but sees instead the dean, standing at the podium. He sees him tap a piece of chalk against the lectern until the auditorium quiets. He hears him apologize to the assembled mathematicians and then make up some excuse as to why today's much-anticipated presentation has been called off. Mead sees the attendees rise from their seats and head for the exits. Some of them are angry, some are merely disappointed. One of them is utterly surprised. Then the auditorium is empty.

Quiet enough to hear a pin drop as the end of one life gives birth to the next.

"Yes," Mead says. "Yes, it is a serious question."

His father starts him off with the accounting books, with lists and lists of incoming and outgoing merchandise. With columns of numbers that need to be added and subtracted, multiplied and divided. After running through the basics, Mead's father hands him a pile of balance sheets and asks if he wouldn't mind looking them over and checking for errors. "After all," his father says, "you're the mathematician."

Mead is offended. Is this what his father thinks he was doing up there in college all this time? Adding and subtracting simple columns of numbers? Well, he couldn't be more wrong. Mead spent most of his time thinking in the fourth dimension, a concept around which he doubts his father could even begin to wrap his mind. But then Mead catches himself with the realization that he is directing his anger at the wrong person—again—that his father has not a clue that his request is insulting, because all he knows is this store, that furniture out there, these columns of numbers in this ledger book. And they mean as much to him as the zeros of the zeta function mean to Mead.

Meant.

"Sure, Dad," he says. "I'd love to." And the thing is, it actually ends up being kind of fun. Playing with numbers. Like hanging out with old and trusted friends. Everything else in Mead's head—all thoughts of the dean and Herman Weinstein and the presentation that never quite happened—empty out to make room for those numbers. And before Mead knows it, two hours have passed and he has found a dozen mistakes that add up to over two thousand dollars' worth of outstanding moneys owed to Fegley Brothers Inc.

"Well, would you look at that," his father says, holding up the ledger book so Mead's uncle can see it with his own two eyes, the man having just emerged from the basement where he spent the better part of the morning with Delia Winslow. His eyes are blurry and unfocused like a mole's; his body ripe with a mixture of sweat and formaldehyde. "Look, Martin, at what Teddy did."

"That's great," Uncle Martin says. But he barely gives the ledger book a glance. Pushes past Mead into the bathroom behind the office to take a shower. Slams the door shut.

ON HIS FATHER'S SUGGESTION, Mead heads over to the five-and-dime to pick up sandwiches at the lunch counter. As if saving the family business two thousand dollars on his first day on the job isn't enough. As if fetching food might better salve his uncle's still-open wounds.

His first day on the job. That's sort of what this is, isn't it? The first day of the rest of Mead's life and all that crap. Wow. This is not at all how Mead thought his life would turn out—and it most certainly isn't what his mother had planned for her genius son—but it's okay. There are a lot worse things in this world a person could be than a furniture salesperson slash undertaker. Like for example, a parasite. As defined on page 965 of the College Edition Dictionary: par•a•site (párə sīt), n. 1. Herman Weinstein. That's what it says. Swear to god. Or at least it will in the next edition, because Mead intends to submit it.

The counterman recognizes the sandwich order Mead places and says, "Hey, I know who you are. You're Lynn Fegley's son, Teddy."

Not in the mood for idle chitchat, Mead says, "Yes, and if you know that you probably also know how testy my uncle gets after an embalming."

"I sure do," the counterman says. "Your order will be right up."

Mead gazes out the window to avoid further conversation. It's a habit he picked up in junior high, after he got promoted from fifth grade to seventh, as a way to ignore the spitballs and rubber bands that flew past his head or pinged off his eyeglasses. A way to pretend that he did not hear his peers saying things like, "Do you still wet the bed, Ted?" He has found that people tend to leave him alone when he is gazing out a window, as if they are afraid to interrupt his train of thought, as if the young Theodore Mead Fegley might be on the brink of making some earth-shattering discovery. Or at least this is what Mead tells himself when he is studying alone in the library on yet another Saturday night.

Someone is chaining a green Schwinn to a bicycle rack across the street from the five-and-dime, someone with a gray ponytail hanging halfway down his back, someone who closely resembles Mead's math professor Dr. Alexander. What did the man do, ride his bicycle all the way down here from Chicago? He must be worried, that must be it. He came to High Grove to make sure Mead is all right. To find out why he left. Mead steps over to the plate glass window and raps it with his knuckle. "Hey," he yells, but the professor doesn't turn around. "Hey," he yells again and raps harder, then opens the front door and steps out onto the sidewalk. "Hey! Dr. Alexander! It's me! Mead!" Finally, the old man hears him and turns around. Only it isn't Mead's math professor, it's a middle-aged lady in trousers and a work shirt. Mead drops his arm. But of course it isn't Dr. Alexander. How silly of Mead to have thought that it might be. After all, the professor is probably just now finding out that Mead not only skipped the presentation but skipped out of town altogether.

Disappointed, Mead steps back into the five-and-dime, letting the door swing closed behind him. He looks up and sees everyone seated at the lunch counter staring at him.

"Friend of yours?" the counterman says.

"No," Mead says, embarrassed to have been caught making a public spectacle of himself. He snatches up the two brown paper bags on the counter and hands over the twenty-dollar bill his father gave him to pay for lunch. The counterman rings up the order and says, "Aren't you supposed to be a genius of some kind?"

"Ex-genius," Mead says. "I converted back to Catholicism a month ago."

"Excuse me?"

"Keep the change," Mead says and hurries out of the store before the counterman can ask any more questions.

NOTHING SOOTHES THE SOUL of the savage beast like food. Whoever said that has obviously never met Martin Fegley. Not only does the man appear ungrateful that Mead got the sandwiches, he seems downright pissed off about it. Like the more Mead tries to please him, the angrier he is going to get. Uncle Martin unwraps his roast beef sandwich and peers between the slices of bread as if hoping to find a dead cockroach in there, something he can add to the growing list of demerits he is compiling against his sorry-assed nephew.

"So how did it go?" Mead's father asks Martin.

"Not too bad," he says, smelling like a mixture of Ivory soap and formaldehyde. He leans back in his chair and sets his feet up on the desk.

Lenny has also joined them for lunch. He's sitting in a chair next to the window that separates the back office from the showroom floor, so he can keep an eye out in case a customer should come in.

"I got to her before rigor mortis had a chance to set in," Martin says as he chews on his sandwich, "so I didn't have to do too much massaging of the extremities. She was a little stiff around the knees and ankles, though, due to arthritis." He takes another bite out of his sandwich, chews and swallows. "But I tell you, I'm always amazed how much blood comes out of these little old ladies. It's as if they've been hoarding it, like cat food, for a rainy day."

"I helped, you know," Mead says. "I didn't just sit in the car. I helped transport the body to the hearse."

Martin takes another bite and washes it down with some soda. "The other thing about little old ladies is that few of them have any teeth left. If they come to me without dentures, then I've got to stuff their mouths full of cotton before stitching their lips shut. So they'll look good, you know, at the funeral."

"All right, Martin," Mead's dad says. "That's enough."

"Cotton. It's an embalmer's best friend. Yup. Nothing plugs up the ol' anus better than a good wad of cotton."

Mead knows what's going on here: His uncle is trying to gross him out. And as much as he hates to admit it, the man is succeeding. In spades. Mead throws down his sandwich and storms out of the office. Pulls open the back door and steps out into the parking lot, fuming. He considers walking back to the house—after all, it's only seven blocks away—but decides against it because the only thing waiting for him back there is the six-legged creature. Then he considers his other options and realizes that he has none. Not a one. Because of Herman.

The back door opens and Lenny steps out. "I thought I might join you for a breath of fresh air," he says. "You mind?"

Mead doesn't answer, instead he sits down on the parking lot bench. Why there's a bench in the rear parking lot, he has no idea. Perhaps it is here for this very reason: to blow off steam whenever Uncle Martin starts acting like an ass. How many times has Mead's dad come out here to do the exact same thing?

Not that he ever needs to blow off steam. Not Mead's father. Everything just rolls right off that man's back. It's some set of parents Mead got. On the one hand, there's his father with his calm, cool reserve; and on the other, there's his mother with her high academic expectations. Shit. Between the two of them, Mead has no wiggle room to be human at all.

"So what're you doing?" Lenny says.

"Trying to stay out of my uncle's way."

Lenny sits down on the bench next to Mead. "No, I mean what're you doing here in High Grove? Ain't you supposed to graduate next week?"

"Birds are supposed to fly south for the winter," Mead says, "and flowers are supposed to bloom in the spring. Days are supposed to be long in summer and corn is supposed to be harvested in the fall. But I am neither a bird nor a flower nor a day of the week nor an ear of corn."

Lenny smiles, the kind of smile someone wears when he hasn't understood a word of what has just been said but thinks he should have. And he won't ask Mead to repeat it because he's afraid it will make him look stupid. It's another habit Mead picked up in school—talking in metaphor—to deflect questions he did not wish to answer, like whether or not he had a date for the senior prom.

"You're right," Lenny says. "It ain't none of my business." And hands Mead the sandwich he left half-eaten inside.

Mead takes a bite out of it and chews angrily. "Does Uncle Martin always talk like that at lunch or was this a special performance for my benefit?"

"He has his good days and his bad."

"Please tell me this is one of his bad days."

Lenny stands up. "Time heals all wounds."

"Where'd you read that, in a fortune cookie?"

Lenny smiles, then heads back into the store.

Now why did Mead have to go and say that? After all, he isn't mad at Lenny. Shit, Mead is acting more and more like the insensitive, self-centered prick his uncle thinks he is. And he isn't. Really, he isn't.

SAMUEL WINSLOW IS STANDING on the sidewalk in front of Fegley Brothers holding a navy blue dress up to the plate glass window and knocking on the door, which has been locked since the close of business half an hour ago. Mead's father crosses the showroom to let him in and Samuel hands over the dress, saying that he'd like his mother to wear it at her funeral. The two men then head up to the third floor to select a casket. Lenny is busy pushing a broom around the showroom floor and Uncle Martin has already gone home, so for the first time all day Mead is alone.

He sits down in his father's chair and leans back. If he were still up in Chicago, Mead would just be getting back to his dorm room, the biggest day of his life behind him. And lying there, on the other bed, would be Forsbeck, his roommate. Sound asleep at six o'clock in the evening. Getting a little shut-eye before heading out to spend the evening with a dozen or so of his best friends. Mead glances at the phone on his father's desk and thinks about calling his room at the dorm. About waking up Forsbeck to ask if the swelling under his eye — where Mead punched him — has gone down. Or maybe he will call Dr. Alexander instead. He could tell the professor how he thought he saw him on Main Street in High Grove with his bicycle. How Mead momentarily forgot that the professor was still limping around with one leg in a cast. He'd like to ask the professor if he is disappointed in Mead for skipping out on the presentation. Or angry. Or worse.

Lenny knocks on the office door. "I'm taking off now," he says. "You gonna be around tomorrow, Teddy?"

"I don't have anywhere else to go."

"Then I guess I'll see you in the morning." He leaves by the back door.

Mead continues to stare at the phone but doesn't make any calls. Because questions would be asked. Questions Mead does not want to answer.

On the way home in the car, Mead's dad suggests they stop at the Elks Lodge for supper and Mead jumps at the opportunity, happy to avoid what would have otherwise been an uncomfortable evening spent in the presence of the six-legged creature. The Lodge is nestled inside a grove of trees on the north edge of town, a log cabin whose parking lot is more brightly lit than its rooms. Mead follows his father through a lobby decorated with rifles into a smoky dining hall ripe with the smell of sweaty bodies and malt liquor. A room full of men celebrating the end of yet another workweek, escaping from the demands of their lives at least for a few hours. It is a concept Mead is all too eager to embrace: escape. Not just from the past week, but from the past month. Past year. Past decade. Oh hell, Mead would like to escape from his whole frigging life, to go back to day one and just start all over again. Maybe next time he won't worry so much about pleasing his mother. Maybe next time he'll refuse to skip third and then sixth and then tenth grades, because next time he'll know better. Next time he'll know that being the kid with all the right answers means being the kid with no friends. If only somebody had told him this before, then Mead could have saved himself a whole lot of grief.

Four people are sitting at the table to which his father has led him. Three strangers and Uncle Martin. Shit. Mead cannot believe his father did this. Tricked him. If the man had told Mead ahead of time that his uncle was going to be here, he wouldn't have come. No way. As a matter of fact, he can still leave. No one is stopping him. He can just turn around and walk back out the front door. After all, the Lodge is only about a mile from his house. It's completely doable. He could just leave right now, walk home, and eat supper with the six-legged creature.

Mead pulls out a chair and sits down.

"Well, well, well, would you look who's here," his uncle says. "Surprised you could make it, Teddy boy." The man's got one hand wrapped around a beer mug, the other around a fork, a combination that strikes Mead as downright dangerous.

"Does everyone know who this is?" Martin says and gazes around the table at his companions. "Why, this here is the infamous Fegley genius. The family jewel. A freak of nature. So tell me, Teddy, to what do we owe this great honor?"

Mead's uncle is drunk, so everybody ignores him. Instead Mead's father introduces Mead to the strangers. Sitting beside Martin is Mr. Sammons, a broad man with the body of a superhero, only older and softer in the middle. Next to him is the missus. She looks like an ex–beauty queen, her face and hair all made up as if she's planning to attend a pageant after knocking back a few frosty brews. And seated next to the missus is this pretty blond girl, Hayley. The daughter. She looks like what her mother probably looked like before age and time took its toll, only without all the makeup.

"I know who you are," Hayley says. "I remember you from first grade."

"I was never in first grade," Mead says.

"Yes, you were. I gave you a shoebox with a dead bird in it for Valentine's Day. You know, because your dad's an undertaker. It was a pretty awful thing to do but I was only six. I hope you can forgive me."

Great. Of all the people in all of High Grove that Mead has to end up sitting next to on the worst day of his life is the girl who was responsible for the second worst day of his life. "I'm afraid you'll have to be more specific," he says. "I got a lot of dead birds that year. Was it the robin, the blue jay, or the wren?"

"I never heard this story before," Mead's father says.

"And you didn't hear it just now either, Dad. She's making it up. Or maybe she's thinking of somebody else."

"Teddy's right," Martin says. "She probably gave it to the other undertaker's son. You know, to Percy."

Not a single person sitting at the table believes that Hayley gave a dead bird to Percy for Valentine's Day. Not a one. He just wasn't the kind of kid to whom other kids gave dead birds. He would much more likely have been the kid who handed them out. Besides, Percy wasn't even in first grade the year Hayley and Mead were. He was in fourth grade.

"Congratulations on your recent graduation," Mrs. Sammons says and reaches across the table to pat Mead's hand. "I saw the announcement in the local paper."

"What announcement?" Mead says and looks at his father.

"Your mother sent one in to the *Grove Press*," he says. "They weren't supposed to publish it until next week."

"Phi Beta Kappa," Mr. Sammons says. "That's pretty impressive."

"And yet you don't look a day over sixteen," the missus adds.

"He's eighteen, Mother," Hayley says. "Like me."

"Hayley just graduated from high school," Mr. Sammons says. "Last week."

Everyone in the dining hall is shouting to be heard above everyone else and all the yelling is beginning to give Mead a headache. That and the cigarette smoke. A waitress drops by the table to take a drink order and Martin asks for a pitcher of beer but it is unclear to Mead whether he is ordering it for the whole table or just for himself. Mrs. Sammons orders a gin and tonic. Hayley asks for a Pepsi. Mead looks up at the waitress and says, "Two Tylenol, please." She thinks she has heard wrong and asks him to repeat his order. He motions to his glass, using international sign language to say, "I'll just have water." But when the waitress comes back, she places a frosted mug in front of Mead and fills it with beer. "I'm underage," he says and tries to hand it back to her. "I don't drink alcoholic beverages."

"If I was you," Mr. Sammons shouts above the din, "I'd learn how."

THE ROAST BEEF IS CHEWY and the string beans are mushy and bland—just like in the university cafeteria—so Mead has no trouble at all swallowing them down. What he does have a hard time swallowing is the sight of his uncle, hunched over his dinner plate as if the weight of the whole world rests solely on his shoulders, as if he has cornered the market on bad things happening to good people. But it simply isn't true. Shitty stuff happens to good people every day. Okay, so maybe Mead wouldn't have believed that a week ago. A week ago he would have thought that people bring bad stuff upon themselves. A week ago, if you had told Mead that everything he has worked so hard for was going to add up to squat, he would have dismissed your words out of hand. He would have thought you jealous or delusional or worse. But he would have been wrong. Mead does not mean to take anything away from his uncle. The man has a damned good reason to be angry—he really does—but so does Mead. The difference being that Mead is not wearing his heart on his sleeve, because he does not find it to be a very attractive look. He prefers to suck it up and move on. The way he did in junior high when his so-called peers Super-Glued his desktop shut. And when his father missed his fourth, fifth, and sixth birthdays in a row because of deaths in other people's families. Mead is simply going to look upon this latest unfortunate turn of events in his life the way he has looked upon all the others: as an opportunity for personal growth. And so he resolves, as of this very moment, to change things up. To live out the rest of his life as the other half is living theirs—or, according to his SAT scores, the other ninety-nine percentile—and if that means trying new things, things Mead would never have even dreamed of trying before, well then, that is exactly what he is going to do.

Mead looks across the table at Mr. Sammons, who has locked heads with Uncle Martin to talk baseball statistics. Last week Mead probably would've seen an overweight individual with ruddy cheeks, suggesting a man who suffers from high blood pressure, high cholesterol, the beginning stages of heart disease, and probably a little cirrhosis of the liver too. But now he sees a sanguine fellow, wise to the ways of the world. And so he lifts the beer mug to his lips and gets a first taste of his new life at 5.2% alcohol per volume.

MEAD'S DAD EXCUSES HIMSELF to go say hello to the people at the next table. He spends about five minutes or so talking to them, then moves on to a second table. And then a third and a fourth and a fifth table, hell-bent on making his way around the entire dining hall. The man probably knows every person in this place—and on a first-name basis no less. Mead wonders how he does it, how he memorizes a whole town's worth of names. He pictures his father sitting up in bed late at night, surrounded by dozens of high school yearbooks and the telephone directory. The man opens the directory and flips to the *L*'s. Runs his finger down the page until he finds the name he is looking for: Brad Lastfogel. Then he reaches for the 1969 edition of the High Grove High School yearbook and turns to the section titled MUSIC. The caption below a black-and-white photograph of eight boys and one girl reads: BAND: BACK ROW: E. JOHNSON, C. THOMPSON, R. KELLEY, AND B. LASTFOGEL. Bingo! Brad doesn't have as much hair anymore, and he has put on a few pounds, but the impish grin and square jaw line are still intact. Under the phrase, WHAT I WANT TO BE WHEN I GROW UP, it says *astronaut or doctor.* Mead's father crosses that out and writes in its place: Manager and Pharmacist of Lastfogel's Drugs.

MR. AND MRS. SAMMONS'S DAUGHTER leans across the table and says to Mead, "You doing anything tomorrow?"

"Yes," he says. "Getting on with my life."

"Well, how would you like to get on with your life out at Snell's Quarry?"

"I have personal obligations," Mead says, "which must be met before I can indulge in the ordinary frivolities of life."

"Excuse me?"

"I can't, I have to work at my father's store."

"How about after that then?"

"That won't work either."

"Why not?"

Mead is suspicious. Any boy in High Grove with a pair of working eyes would jump at the opportunity to go swimming with Hayley Sammons, so why is she asking him? Unless her plan is to lure him out there and then laugh at him with all her friends because he actually showed up.

"Don't worry, Theodore. I'm not going to make fun of you or anything."

"I didn't think you were."

"Then it's all set. I'll pick you up at your father's store at five."

Shit.

* * *

Martin sits down in the chair next to Mead. Oh boy, here it comes. His uncle has been waiting for this opportunity all day: to be alone with his nephew. Without Mead's shield (i.e., his father) around to protect him. Uncle Martin has downed three beers—that Mead knows of—and god knows how many more before Mead and his dad arrived. Picking up the pitcher the waitress has just set on the table, Martin refills Mead's empty mug and tops off his own. "To homecomings," he says and holds up his beer for a toast. Mead taps his mug against his uncle's and then knocks back half the contents in one gulp, as fortification against what he knows is about to come next.

"Thanks for inviting me to your graduation, Teddy."

Mead looks over at Mr. and Mrs. Sammons, hoping for a rescue. But they have fallen into deep discussion with their daughter, the three of them with their heads together, thick as thieves, like secretaries around a water cooler. "I didn't graduate, Uncle Martin."

"I know. What the hell is the matter with you? Do you have any idea how much it cost your father to pay for four years of college? And this is how you show your appreciation? By walking out a week before graduation?"

"Three years, Uncle Martin. I completed all my credit requirements in three years."

"Three, four. That's not the point, Teddy; the point is you're an overeducated, underachieving momma's boy with no care or concern for anyone except yourself."

These words fall upon Mead in a shower of spit. Placing his hand over his beer mug, Mead glances at the Sammonses once more. They have come out of their huddle and are staring at Martin with pity in their eyes, even though he is the one doing all of the name-calling. "I'm sorry, Uncle Martin," Mead says. "I didn't miss Percy's funeral on purpose."

"Funeral? There wouldn't have even been a funeral if you had been where you were supposed to be when he drove up there to visit you."

Suddenly sick to his stomach, Mead stands up. Fresh air. He needs some fresh air now. The floor begins to tilt beneath his feet, his brain comes loose from its moor and sloshes around inside of his skull, and between the floor and his brain Mead is finding it hard to walk. He grabs on to the backs of chairs as if they were railings on a ship at sea and makes his way across the dining hall toward the lobby. A buck's head is mounted above the men's room door, a doe's head hangs over the ladies' room. The two stuffed deer gaze down upon Mead with indignation in their glass eyes. He pictures his own head, mounted above the door to Herman's bedroom. Dust collects on his nose and in his hair and, once a year, a maid takes him down to vacuum him off. But the rest of the time Mead hangs there all but forgotten, Herman's interest in him lost as soon as he was bagged.

Mead staggers into the bathroom and throws up. Maybe he shouldn't have come home. Maybe he should have just accepted Herman's proposition, graduated with honors, and continued on with his life. No one would ever have to know just how dishonorable it really was. No one, that is, except Mead.

2

MUSIC TO THE EARS

Chicago
Four Months Before Graduation

SOMEONE KNOCKS ON THE DOOR and Mead looks up. It's after midnight on a Tuesday night and everyone else in the dorm is asleep. Or so Mead thought. Glancing back over his shoulder, he looks at his roommate, Forsbeck, who is nothing more than a series of lumps under a snoring blanket. It's probably one of his cohorts from down the hall. Rick or Dick or Joe or Bob, some monosyllabic person who has decided to take a late-night study break but cannot do it without the help of one of his codependent buddies.

Mead sits motionless and waits for whomever it is to leave. A pair of feet is visible along the crack under the door, or at least their shadow is. A minute goes past and then two. The visitor doesn't knock again but neither does he leave. Mead decides to ignore the feet and goes back to work. Picks up where he left off reading about the theory of Riemann surfaces that contains powerful results and deep insights into the behavior of complex functions, yoking function theory to algebra and topology, two key growth areas of twentieth-century math. There are hardly enough hours in the day anymore, what with Mead trying to write a paper of his own on the Riemann Hypothesis for his senior thesis. But the feet outside his door keep pulling his attention away from complex planes. When another five minutes go by, and the feet are still there, Mead puts down his book and pulls open the door, prepared to explain to whoever is standing on the other side of it that his roommate is asleep and does not wish to be woken. Mead has no idea if this is true or not, but then neither does he care because it is enough that Mead does not want his roommate to wake up.

On the other side of the door, however, he does not find Bob or Rob or Joe or Dick, but Herman Weinstein.

HERMAN DOES NOT LIVE ON THIS FLOOR. His room is two stories up and all the way over on the other end of the building. Mead sometimes goes for days — even a week — without running into him. But that does not mean that he does not see him, that he is not fully aware of the guy's presence here on campus. Mead has been aware of Herman since day one of freshman year. But this year — senior year — they seem to be crisscrossing each other's paths almost constantly. It sometimes feels to Mead as if Herman is stalking him. Which is a crazy thing for him to think because they live in the same dorm and are taking the same Mon-Wed-Fri class. Of course their paths would cross. And Herman has never given Mead more than a cursory glance. He barely seems to register him on his personal radar. There's just something about the guy, something Mead cannot quite put his finger on, that makes him think all this crossing of paths is more than mere coincidence.

"I was beginning to think you really weren't in there," Herman says.

"I'm studying. Or was."

"Thank you, I'd love to," he says and steps past Mead into the room.

Herman invited Mead up to his dorm room last quarter, an invitation Mead never took him up on because he didn't perceive it as sincere. And because of this math professor of theirs: Dr. Kustrup. As a matter of fact, Mead had forgotten all about that invitation until now.

Herman plops down on his bed and picks up the book Mead was just reading. "Bernhard Riemann, eh? A mathematician's mathematician. Don't you ever read for pleasure?"

Mead tries to grab the book from his hand but Herman holds it out of arm's reach. "What do you think you're doing? You're going to wake up my roommate."

"Forsbeck the Bear? No way. He doesn't sleep, he hibernates."

And as if on cue, Forsbeck rolls over, groans, and starts snoring again.

"See?" Herman says and stretches out on Mead's bed, making himself at home.

Mead looks back at the open door, hoping that Herman will take the hint and leave. It isn't as if they are friends or anything. Quite the opposite, in fact. At least as far as Mead is concerned. When Herman doesn't take the hint, Mead says, "Why are you here, Weinstein?"

"I couldn't sleep and thought to myself, who else do I know who might be awake at this ungodly hour of the night, and you came to mind."

"Yeah, well, I was just going to shut off my light when you knocked."

Herman reaches up and turns on Mead's radio. Strains of Bach's Goldberg variations fill the room. Forsbeck groans but doesn't wake up.

"I love Bach," Herman says. "His compositions are flawless. If one could turn mathematical equations into music, they'd sound just like Bach, don't you agree?"

As a matter of fact, Mead *has* had that thought, but never in a million years would he have presumed that anyone else on the planet would have made the same observation. Least of all Herman. "I've never really thought about it," he says.

Herman places his hands behind his head and closes his eyes. Oh Christ. What if he falls asleep? Mead looks at the rug on the floor between his bed and Forsbeck's. It's one of those oval braided rugs, the kind one always sees on the floor in front of an open hearth, or at the feet of some grandmother in a children's fairy tale. His Aunt Jewel gave it to him right before he left for college. It probably wouldn't be too bad to sleep on. Which is what Mead is figuring he's going to have to do if Herman doesn't get his butt out of Mead's bed real soon. This is so like Herman, to barge in and take over without even asking. Mead reaches for his book—so he can finish reading the chapter he started before he was so rudely interrupted—and glances down at Herman. He actually looks like a nice enough person when his face is in repose, when he isn't smirking at some thought or somebody. When he's awake, however, Herman gives Mead the feeling that he is looking down at the world, that he thinks he is better than everybody else because his father is filthy rich and his family vacations in Europe. What must it be like to be handed all this—a top-notch education at a top-notch university—and never have done anything to earn it other than being born into the right family? Mead can't imagine that it means very much to Herman. Perhaps that is why the bad attitude. Perhaps if being here meant as much to him as it does to Mead, the guy wouldn't go around acting like such a jerk all the time.

Herman opens his eyes and Mead pulls back, startled. "I thought you were asleep," he says.

"Really? You weren't going to kiss me?"

"What? No, I was just reaching for my book."

Herman shuts off the radio and hops out of Mead's bed. When he reaches the door, he turns back and says, "Thanks for the company. I'll see you around." And then he closes it.

Mead stares at the crack under the door. Herman stands there for another good minute before he finally leaves.

THE CLASS THEY ARE TAKING TOGETHER is called Function Theory. Mead usually arrives early, seeing as how his previous class is in the same building, but today he makes a point of arriving late because he doesn't want Herman to try to sit with him. Not after last night. So he hides out in the men's room, inside one of the stalls, to kill time. A moment later the professor who teaches the class, the aforementioned Dr. Kustrup, enters the bathroom. He brushes his teeth at the sink, runs a comb through his hair, and splashes cologne on his cheeks as if he were preparing for a date instead of a lecture. He is also the chairman of the math department. Newly elected. Mead would never have voted for the man, if he had had a say, that is. He would never have signed up for this class, either, if he could have avoided it. Not after the experience Mead had in the last class he took with Dr. Kustrup. But the subject matter of the course made it too important for Mead to boycott—in light of the thesis he has to write—and he can always go to Dr. Alexander after class to decode any nonsense in the day's lecture. Perhaps Dr. Kustrup is taking extra care to look the part of his new role. Mr. Important-on-Campus. Mr. Top-of-the-Heap. But it will take more than toothpaste and a splash of cologne to cover up the mathematical stench coming from his mouth.

Mead waits until the professor has left then slips down the hall and into the classroom just as the lecture begins. He never even looks around to see if Herman is present. Mead doesn't have to because before class is over Dr. Kustrup will undoubtedly call on "Mr. Weinstein" to answer some question or other. He always does. Without fail. Being as how Herman is the twinkle in the chairman's eye. His star pupil. At the end of class, Mead is the first one out the door.

But somehow, despite all his dodging and avoiding, Mead runs into Herman anyway. In the library when his guard is down, his mind focused on the critical line, the line on which all non-trivial zeros of the zeta function are said to lie—at least those that have been calculated. But is it true for all zeta zeros? The Riemann Hypothesis says yes but no mathematician—in the 130 years since this theory was written—has been able to either prove or disprove it.

Something flutters down through the air like a leaf and lands on Mead's open textbook, obscuring some of the absolute and relative values of the error term. It's a concert ticket. Mead looks up and sees Herman standing over him, holding an identical ticket in his hand. "Bach," he says. "Front-row orchestra seats. This Friday."

"I can't go," Mead says.

"It's just two hours. You can study when you get back."

"This is an eighty-dollar ticket and I don't have eighty dollars."

Herman pulls out a chair and sits down across from Mead, leans over the table, and says, "It's on me. Or rather, it's on Dr. Kustrup, who invited me to join him and his wife for an evening on the town. Me and a date, that is. Only I'm not seeing anyone seriously right now so I thought, who do I know who would really enjoy this?"

Not seeing anyone? But Mead was under the distinct impression that Herman was dating Cynthia Broussard and that he has been doing so since freshman year. What happened? Did they break up? Not that it makes any difference. Not anymore. It was a long time ago when Mead asked her out. Water under the bridge and all that. The idea of attending a concert with Dr. Stuckup Kustrup bothers him far more. But then hasn't Mead told himself that he is over that betrayal too? Oh, what the hell. It's Bach and it's free. Mead stares at the ticket. The great harpsicordist Gustav Leonhardt will be conducting. Mead would cut off his right arm to see that man conduct a live concert. "Two hours?" he says.

"I'll have you home before your carriage turns back into a pumpkin."

DR. STUCKUP KUSTRUP'S WIFE is a plump woman. Rubenesque. If it were a cold night and the heat got cut off, she is the one with whom a person would most want to curl up. The professor opens the passenger door and offers his elbow, which she takes with her right hand, using the other hand to keep the hem of her dress from dragging on the ground. He may be a prick but he also appears to be a gentleman.

Mead follows the Kustrups and Herman up the steps and into the concert hall. He has walked past this building a dozen times but never actually been inside of it. And the thing is, no photograph could ever do justice to the sheer magnitude of the space. The high-domed ceilings and massive chandeliers make Mead feel small and insignificant. A mere mortal among giants. The way he felt in church as a child. And when the music fills the air, it is as if God himself has entered the concert hall. Forget all those sermons the ministers used to go on at length about week after week, trying to hammer the word of God into Mead's head and make it stick. If there is a God, this is how he communicates.

Through music. And if there is a vehicle through which God speaks best, it is Johann Sebastian Bach. The only distraction is Dr. Kustrup, or rather his cologne. The same stuff he slapped on his neck before class. The smell reminds Mead of the inside of a barn in winter. It makes his eyes water and his nose itch but even that cannot take away from the pleasure of Bach.

During the intermission, Dr. Kustrup buys three glasses of wine: one for himself, one for his wife, and one for Herman. Even though Herman is only twenty. Mead orders a glass of seltzer with a twist of lime.

"I'm so glad you could join us this evening, Mr. Fegley," Dr. Kustrup says. "How are you enjoying the concert so far?"

"The company pales in comparison," Mead says.

The professor laughs. "You haven't changed, Mr. Fegley. You're still every bit the high-minded youth I first met nearly three years ago." He turns away to talk to Herman.

"So you're the infamous Theodore Mead Fegley," Mrs. Kustrup says. "Herman tells me you're quite the genius."

"Herman has talked to you about me?"

"Oh, yes. He talks about all the people who impress him and he's met quite a few of those through his father. Herman idolizes brilliant men but doesn't quite see himself as one of them. As an intellectual. I disagree, I think Herman is quite brilliant, don't you?"

Mead looks over at Herman, who is laughing at something Dr. Kustrup has just said as if it were funny. But the professor is one of the dullest and most self-serving men Mead has ever been unfortunate enough to meet. An opinion that is apparently not shared by Herman. Or maybe it is. It's impossible to say for sure. That must be why the professor gives Herman such high marks on all his papers. The idiot doesn't even know he is being snowed.

"He's gifted," Mead says. "I'll give you that."

As they leave the concert hall, Dr. Kustrup invites "the boys" back to his house for coffee. Mead throws Herman a dirty look. The deal was two hours. The concert and nothing more. Herman smiles and says, "I'm afraid I can't this evening, Dr. Kustrup. I have a paper due on Monday that I haven't even started. You know how it goes." And so the professor drops them off at the dorm.

"Thank you," Mead says to Herman when they reach the second floor of the dorm, where Mead's room is. "For everything. I enjoyed it."

"You can't beat Bach," Herman says.

"No, you can't," Mead says and heads down the hall. When he reaches the door to his room, he glances back and notices that Herman is still standing there on the landing. He looks striking in a suit, like a model posing for an ad for a luxury car or an expensive bottle of champagne. Moneyed but vacuous. He appears to be lost in thought, gazing at somebody or something that isn't there. Then he snaps out of it, looks up, and sees Mead looking back. "Good night," he says and continues on up the stairs.

Mead changes out of his suit, returning it to the back of his closet where it will remain until graduation day, now just a few months off, and settles down to read more about critical lines and relative error. Since it is Friday, Forsbeck will be out until the wee hours of the morning, off indulging in some all-night pizza party with his many and sundry friends. And Mead is finding it hard to stay focused on the pages of his book. He misses the seesawing sound of Forsbeck's snoring, which helps to drown out the other noises in the dorm. The thudding bass of someone's stereo. The opening and closing of doors. The giggle of a female in heat. Every time footfalls come down the hall, Mead braces for the sound of someone knocking on his door. Not just someone, but Herman. Mead's new best friend. All of a sudden. Out of the blue. For reasons unknown. But each time the feet walk right on by.

He looks up from his book and glances out the window for the hundredth time. Maybe he should have accepted the professor's invitation. After all, he had been enjoying himself. Perhaps they would have sat around the professor's fireplace and discussed music. Shared their views on Leonhardt's interpretation of the variations. Mead would have enjoyed that too. They could have listened to a studio recording of the same piece (which Dr. Kustrup must surely own) and compared it to the performance they just heard, an experience that could never be had back in High Grove, Illinois, where all that anyone ever listens to on the radio are weather reports or the market-share values of pork bellies, soybeans, and corn.

Mead glances out the window for the hundred-and-first time and sees Herman walking away from the dorm. He has changed out of his Giorgio Armani suit into a pair of blue jeans, his hands stuffed deep into his pockets. He walks fast, as if he is cold or in a hurry, pulls open the door of the student center, and disappears inside. Mead does his best to return his attention to his textbook, looking up from time to time to see when Herman comes back, only he never does. At midnight, the lights in the student center are shut off and the door is locked. At two o'clock, Mead closes his book, turns out the light, and crawls into bed.

The next morning, when Mead is coming back from the cafeteria—having eaten his breakfast before most of his peers arose—he runs into Herman in the stairwell. Heading out. He looks well rested and is wearing another suit. "Morning," he says as he passes by Mead at a trot and keeps going. And Mead decides that Herman must have slipped back into the building while he was deep into reading about real and imaginary axes of the value plane.

MEAD HAS NEVER BEFORE BEEN on the fourth floor of his dorm and for some reason it surprises him how much it resembles his own floor with the same gray carpeting, same brown doors, and same scuffed-up, off-white walls. Some of these doors are open, some closed. Music floats out of one of the open doors: the whining guitar of an angst-ridden rock star. It's a tune Mead recognizes—the recognition a by-product of living in the dorms—but he could never put a name to it. A boy emerges from one of the other rooms. He smiles at Mead as he passes by him on his way down the hall to the bathroom. A boy Mead has never seen before. Or maybe he has. Maybe Mead has passed the guy on the stairs a hundred times and just doesn't remember.

Mead continues down the hall of brown doors until he finds number 48. It happens to be one of the closed doors, meaning that Herman may or may not be inside. Mead raises his hand to knock and then hesitates. What if Herman is out and his roommate is in? Mead has no idea what he would say to the guy. What reason he would give for his unexpected appearance. He looks down at the CD in his hand. A two-disc set of Bach's orchestral suites conducted by Nikolaus Harnoncourt. He bought it yesterday even though he doesn't own a CD player because he figured that Herman probably does own one and because he thought the guy might enjoy listening to this recording with him. It seemed like a good idea at the time but now Mead just feels stupid.

He turns to leave as the boy who passed him on the way to the bathroom passes him again on the way back to his room. "Try knocking again. He usually studies with his headphones on," the guy says, then disappears behind a closed door.

Whether he is referring to Herman or to his roommate, Mead has no way to know, but he knocks anyway, softly, as if he doesn't mean it, and someone says, "Come in."

Mead opens the door, sees Cynthia Broussard sitting on the bed, and blushes. So apparently she and Herman are still dating. Cynthia looks good. Great actually, as if she just stepped out of the pages of *Vogue* magazine. A far cry from the pretty but plain girl Mead met freshman year. Having a rich boyfriend apparently agrees with her. "Sorry," he says. "I must have the wrong room," and starts to back out. But before he can close the door, Herman gets up off the other bed—the one against the opposite wall—and grabs the knob.

"Mr. Fegley," he says. "What a pleasant surprise."

"You're busy," Mead says. "I'll come back another time."

"Don't be silly. Cynthia doesn't mind, do you, sweetheart? I mean, it's not as if we were in here having sex or something." And Cynthia blushes, as if she is embarrassed to have been caught *not* having sex.

"Where are my manners," Herman says. "Cynthia, this is Mead Fegley."

"I know," Cynthia says. "How have you been, Mead?"

"So you two know each other," Herman says. "Should I be jealous?"

"We were friends," Cynthia says. "Freshman year."

"I should go," Mead says and starts to back out of the room again.

"What's that you've got there, Fegley?" Herman says. "A CD?" And he snatches the set out of Mead's hand before Mead can leave. "Ah, a German recording of our dear friend Bach. Did you know that the overture suite originally found its place at the beginning of an opera? An invention of the French, its slow introduction of royal gesture was intended to symbolize the appearance of the sovereign. These particular suites were created during Bach's last stay in Köthen before commencing his cantorate at the Leipzig Thomas church."

"Impressive," Cynthia says, her eyes glistening as if Herman has just read her a love sonnet by Shakespeare.

"Really, I should go," Mead says and tries to take the CD back but Herman dodges his hand, removes the silvery disc from its case, and pops it into his player. As the music swells, filling the drab dorm room with all the richness of the ages, Herman gestures for Mead to sit down on the unoccupied bed—the one on which he was just sitting—and plunks himself down next to Cynthia. Tucking his stocking feet up under his thighs, yoga-style, Herman closes his eyes and appears to absorb the music through every pore of his body. Cynthia closes her eyes, too, and rests her head on his shoulder.

Mead sits on the unoccupied bed as if it were a straight-backed chair. Too embarrassed to look at the lovey-dovey couple, he chooses instead to gaze around the room. The walls are bare except for a calendar that boasts a black-and-white photograph of the Eiffel Tower. It hangs above a desk cluttered with textbooks, ledger pads, and a typewriter. The old-fashioned kind with circular keys that stick if not properly oiled. Only, knowing Herman, it probably isn't just any old typewriter but the one on which Hemingway wrote *For Whom the Bell Tolls.* Or the one Steinbeck used to create *The Grapes of Wrath.*

Sitting on the other desk in the room are an open bag of potato chips, a six-pack of Pepsi (with two cans missing), and a half-eaten package of Oreo cookies, but no books, pads, or pens that might suggest the presence of a roommate, which means that Herman bunks alone, another undeniable sign of the privileges afforded to the well-to-do. What Mead doesn't understand, however, is why Herman has chosen to reside in a dorm in the first place, when it is obvious—by the full-length suede jacket hanging on the back of his door and the closet overflowing with designer suits and shirts and shoes—that he could well afford to take an apartment off campus.

"Listen to that," Herman says. "The trumpet and bass-drum."

"Some people believe it wasn't part of the original suite," Mead says.

"Some people are idiots," Herman says, eyes still closed. "It's obviously been integrated into the orchestra movement as an activating moment."

If Herman were a girl, Mead would be in love right now for they appear to speak the same language, at least when it comes to music. What a surprise. Perhaps Mead has been too quick to judge. Perhaps he misread Herman when he first met the guy freshman year. Mead tucks his feet up under his thighs, in imitation of Herman, and closes his eyes. The first overture ends and the second one begins. The music washes over Mead and transports him to another time and place, to the court of the Duke of Celle where dancers swirl around him. At the end of the performance, an announcement will be made. Mead will be knighted by the duke for having deduced—by the changing pattern of the stars in the sky—that the earth is round. His discovery will be revered by all and his name will go down in history, far outlasting his short stay here on earth.

Mead opens his eyes and sees Herman looking at him. The guy does not get embarrassed and pull his eyes away as most people would but continues to stare until Mead gets uncomfortable and drops his eyes. The music ends and the room turns cold and hollow again. Cynthia opens her eyes and says, "Oh my god, that was the most beautiful thing I've ever heard." She slides her hand into Herman's and he squeezes it. With her other hand, she presses his cheek to her lips and kisses him. And the whole time Herman keeps looking at Mead.

"I should be going now," Mead says, and this time Herman does not object. Cynthia turns his face to her and kisses him full on the lips, as if Mead has already left. But when he tries to get up, he realizes that his legs have fallen asleep and he has to shake them out before he can walk, further delaying his departure. Mead then goes to retrieve his CD from the player, which happens to be on the shelf over Herman's bed, but when he reaches for it, he has to pull his arm back fast so Herman won't run into it as he lies back on the bed with Cynthia on top of him. "That's all right," Mead says. "You can give it back to me later." And realizes that he is in no particular rush to get it back since he himself has nothing on which to play it.

On Monday, Mead skips his between-classes hideout in the men's room, goes directly to his Function Theory class, and takes his usual seat in the front row. Herman comes in a few minutes later, sees him sitting there, and waves. Mead smiles and waves back, expecting Herman to sit down next to him. But he doesn't. He sits three rows back and all the way over on the other side of the room, and for some reason this bothers Mead. Because he thought things were different now. He thought they were friends. Embarrassed, Mead tucks his chin to his chest, opens his textbook, and stares at the printed pages, feigning an interest in the equations written there. Pretending he doesn't care that nothing has changed while at the same time he's feeling angry at himself that he does care. At the very least, he expected Herman to give him back his CD. Unless he thinks it was a gift, which it most certainly was not. Mead paid for it and Mead should be able to keep it even if he doesn't have any way to play it on his own.

By the end of class, however, Mead has decided to give Herman another chance. Instead of bolting out of his chair and down the hall—as he normally would—Mead sits tight and pretends to review his class notes. But again Herman walks past him without saying a word. Goes up to the professor and asks him a question in a voice too soft for Mead to hear. Dr. Kustrup answers him then turns away to erase his class notes from the blackboard. Herman leaves while the professor is still erasing and still he does not say anything to Mead. When Dr. Kustrup turns back around and sees that Mead is still sitting there, he says, "May I help you with something, Mr. Fegley?"

"No, thank you," Mead says, angrily scoops up his books, and heads out of the classroom and then out of the building. In his haste, however, he does not look where he is going and bumps into some student crossing campus from another direction, a student drinking a cup of coffee. The hot liquid swooshes up out of the cup and splashes all over Mead's notebook and left sleeve. Instead of apologizing, the guy says, "Hey, watch where you're going, buddy," and stomps off with a scowl on his face. Hoping to salvage his notes, Mead turns around, runs back into the building, and down the hall to the men's room. It reeks of Dr. Kustrup's cologne. Mead runs cold water over the sleeve of his shirt and then reaches for a paper towel to dry off his notes. Only the dispenser is empty. "Shit," he says and ducks into one of the stalls to get some toilet paper. And that's when he sees them: two pairs of shoes facing each other in the next stall. And as he is looking, one of the pairs of shoes lifts up into the air and disappears.

Mead mops up the pages of his notebook, throws the soiled tissue into the toilet bowl, flushes, and then gets the hell out of there as fast as he can. By the end of the day, he has convinced himself that he did not see what he thought he saw. By the next day, however, he finds himself checking out everyone's shoes as he walks from class to class. Dozens upon dozens of people are wearing brown shoes just like the ones in that bathroom stall—people like Dr. Kustrup—but no one else smells of the same cologne.

Well past midnight, there is a knock on Mead's door. Forsbeck is asleep so he doesn't respond. Mead stares at the shadow of two feet in the crack of light under the door but makes no move to open it. When they don't go away, he knows who it is and debates whether or not to answer the door. Wonders how long Herman is willing to stand out there before he gives up and leaves. One minute. Ten. Twenty.

After just two minutes, Mead gets up and pulls open the door. "You're going to wake up my roommate."

"I bought you a present," Herman says and hands Mead a Marshall Field's bag.

He takes it and says, "Why?"

"Because I'm a nice guy, that's why," and pushes past Mead into the room, flopping down on his bed. "Go ahead, open it. I want to see the expression of delight on your face when you see what it is."

Mead opens the bag and lifts out a CD, the one he left in Herman's room last week. "This isn't a present, Weinstein, it's mine."

"Keep going," he says. "It gets better."

The other item in the bag is a cardboard box with a model number printed on the side of it. Mead pulls out the box and stares at it, blank-faced.

"Hmm," Herman says, "not exactly the expression I was hoping for." He gets up off the bed and takes the box out of Mead's hand, then starts rummaging through his desk drawers until he finds a pair of scissors. He cuts away the packing tape and says,

"It's small, but it works just as well as the one I have in my room. Plus, it's portable." He plugs various wires into various sockets then plugs the player into the wall and places the headset over Mead's ears. "It's the newest technological gizmo on the market: a portable CD player. You'll be the envy of all your friends." He then takes the CD out of Mead's hand, pops it into the player, and hits the PLAY button. Trumpets blare loudly into Mead's ears, startling him, then the violins start up. He looks over at Forsbeck, afraid the music might wake him, but his roommate is deaf to the orchestra playing at full volume in Mead's ears.

Herman keeps talking, his lips flapping up and down, but Mead cannot hear him. The guy is smiling, obviously pleased with himself. He pats Mead on the arm, waves goodbye, and shows himself out the door. Mead steps out into the hall and watches as Herman walks away. Glances down at the guy's shoes and sees a pair of olive green suede loafers. One-of-a-kind. And that's when Mead knows that he wasn't seeing things, that there *were* two pairs of shoes in that bathroom stall.

3

THE LIFE OF A RIVER

High Grove
Eight Years Before Graduation

MEAD PERCHES ON THE STEPS just outside the junior high school, like a bird ready to take flight at the first sign of danger, his eyes darting left and then right as he scans the grounds, as he mentally records the various activities of his fellow classmates. He sips through a straw the chocolate milk he keeps tucked inside his coat pocket and sneaks bites from the peanut-butter-and-jelly sandwich he has hidden up his sleeve. He always eats his lunch like this, on the sly while the other kids are preoccupied with playing, and not in the school cafeteria. He gave up on the cafeteria years ago when he got tired of finding caterpillars hidden in his macaroni-and-cheese and grasshoppers buried in his mashed potatoes. He prefers to spend his lunchtime in the boys' room behind the closed door of a stall accompanied by the whoopee cushion he purchased with his allowance at the five-and-dime. In case anyone should come looking for trouble. As a result of this predilection, he has a new nickname: Windy Teddy. But at least now his food pyramid no longer includes a subcategory for arthropods.

As the front door to the school squeaks open behind Mead, he tucks the milk carton back into his pocket, the sandwich up his sleeve, and sits with his arms crossed over his chest. As a precaution. But it's just Percy, Mead's cousin. The last time they attended the same school Mead was in second grade and his cousin was in fifth, back before Mead started skipping grades, before the label of "genius" got slapped on his forehead. Next year Percy will be across town in the high school, but for now they are once again roaming the same halls.

Percy places his hand on Mead's head and messes up his hair. "Hey, lazybones, get up off your sorry ass and join me on the ballfield. I'll pitch you a few easy ones."

"I'd love to," Mead says, "but I haven't lifted anything heavier than a pencil in five years and if I strain my wrist I won't be able to write and then I'll flunk all my tests and my mother will kill me and it'll all be your fault."

"Blah, blah, blah. Listen, you might be able to fool other people with your genius brand of double talk but I'm not other people, I'm your cousin. No one's gonna laugh at you. I promise. At least give it a try."

"Maybe tomorrow; there's something else I need to do today." And Mead holds up his spiral notebook and a twelve-inch ruler as proof.

"Come on. One lousy pitch, that's all I'm asking."

"Tomorrow," Mead says and again holds up his notebook and ruler.

"You always say that."

"I know, but today it's true."

"Okay, cousin, have it your way," Percy says and trots down the steps and across the asphalt playground toward the ballfield. When the other kids see him coming, they part like the Red Sea to let him pass and someone tosses Mead's cousin a baseball. As

Percy warms up his pitching arm, the boys fight over the batting order.

They couldn't be more different, Mead and his cousin. Like night and day. Brains versus brawn. Intellectual geek versus sports hero. But it won't always be like this. Or at least this is what Mead tells himself, that his cousin's stature as most popular kid will be short-lived, his moment in the spotlight extinguishing with the end of grade school, his days of glory forever moored in the past. Mead tells himself that his own best days still lie ahead, that his god-given skill set will grow in popularity when he sheds the skin of childhood and emerges anew as a grownup, that one day he will be as beseeched by his peers as Percy is today. Only Mead's popularity will stay with him all the way through the end of his life. He just has to be patient, to hold out for a few more years. Mead cannot wait to get out of grade school, go off to college, and start his life for real. It can't happen soon enough. But it can happen sooner than usual if he continues to excel at school, if he continues to skip grades. Mead doesn't have time to waste on sports. He has more important things to do, like working on his science report. And so he gobbles down the rest of his sandwich, slurps up the last of his chocolate milk, and heads out across the schoolyard with his notebook and ruler tucked under his arm.

Percy is standing center stage in a circle of mud that is High Grove Junior High's best imitation of a pitcher's mound. His sleeves are rolled up and a Cardinals baseball cap is pulled down low over his eyes as he coils his long, lanky body into a tight spring and then tosses off his signature pitch: a curveball that sails over home plate so fast that the kid at bat cannot send it back. Someone yells, "Strike!" and the defeated hitter hands the bat off to the next kid in line, who makes several warm-up swings before stepping to the plate, before Percy sends another ball speeding through the air so fast that Mead cannot keep his eyes on it. The baseball smacks into the catcher's mitt with enough force to knock the poor guy on his ass. Several kids clap their hands and chant, "Feg-lee! Feg-lee! Feg-lee!" as the next victim steps up to the plate.

One kid in the crowd sees Mead, nudges his buddy, and calls out, "Hey, do you still wet your bed, Ted?" The buddy laughs and Mead takes his cue to exit, ducks his head, and starts walking away. Then the buddy says, "You gotta be really smart to make an A+ fart." And they both laugh. Mead walks a little faster.

"Hey," Percy says, steps off the pitcher's mound, and walks toward the two boys who are taunting Mead. "You two got something you want to say to my cousin?" And every kid on the ballfield turns to see what all the fuss is about. Every last kid there turns and looks at Mead, who tucks his chin to his chest and walks even faster. He wishes his cousin wouldn't do that, wouldn't draw attention to Mead's humiliation. "You got something to say to him," Percy says, "you're gonna have to run it by me first."

"We were just kidding around," the kid who started it says.

"Apologize," Percy says.

"Sorry," the buddy says.

"Not to me, to him," Percy says and points at Mead.

"Sorry," the first kid calls out to Mead's retreating back.

"Yeah, sorry," his buddy says but with very little feeling behind it.

Mead almost breaks into a run.

"Hey, cousin," Percy yells. "Come on. Take a swing at bat. Just pretend the ball is one of these guy's heads and knock it out of the park."

Mead keeps going.

"You'll feel a lot better afterwards."

And keeps going.

"Okay, well, maybe tomorrow then," Percy calls out, then turns and heads back to the pitcher's mound. All eyes follow him and Mead sighs with relief.

The life of a river. That is the name Mr. Belknap has given this science project. An eight-week study of a six-foot-by-six-foot plot of land that includes some section of the creek that runs along the base of the hill behind the school. Every Wednesday morning the seventh-grade science teacher escorts his class across the asphalt school grounds, past the ballfield, and down the hill to draw diagrams and make notes on how their section of the creek has changed. But Mead did not find the allotted thirty minutes of class time enough to record all the changes he saw today so—with his ruler in one hand and his spiral notebook in the other—he is taking it upon himself to return to the creek and finish up what he started in class.

Mead is halfway down the hill before he sees them and stops. Four boys in his grade, the kind of boys who would rather use their hands to make rude noises than ask questions in class. High Grove Junior High's latest crop of juvenile delinquents. And they are not here for the same reason that Mead is. They are standing at the bottom of the hill with their backs turned to Mead, holding their dicks and peeing into the creek. And the one on the far end is peeing into Mead's six-foot-by-six-foot science project. Deciding that maybe now is not the best time to take those measurements after all, Mead turns to leave and steps on a twig, snapping it. The tallest one looks around. Freddy is his name. Freddy Waseleski, the kid who holds the record for most-missed-days-from-school in all of High Grove. He has probably been held back as many times as Mead has been promoted. "Hey, weirdo," he says. "What're you looking at?"

"Nothing," Mead says. "I was just going to take some measurements." And he holds up his twelve-inch ruler as proof.

"Measurements of what?" Freddy says and his dimwit friends all laugh.

"Hey, I know who you are," says the one who just peed into Mead's plot as he puts himself away, as they all put themselves away and zip up. "You're that freak kid from the elementary school. The genius."

"How old are you, freak?" another one of the boys says. "Eight?"

"No, I'm ten."

"Give me your ruler, freak," Freddy says. "I got something I wanna measure with it." And more laughter ensues, the kind that usually precedes the flushing of someone's head down the toilet. So Mead does as he is told, walks the rest of the way down the hill, and hands his ruler to Freddy. The tall boy snatches it out of his hand and says, "Drop them."

"Drop what?" Mead asks.

"Your pants, freak, so we can see your dick. You saw ours, so now we get to see yours. Drop your pants or I'll drop them for you."

Mead glances back over his shoulder. The kids on the ballfield are chanting "Feg-LEE, Feg-LEE." Percy must be on the mound waiting for the next kid to step up to the plate. Perhaps he is looking around for his cousin right now, checking to make sure he is all right, but Mead is nowhere to be found. Percy probably assumes that he went back inside, that he's hiding out in the boys' room, and returns his attention to the business at hand. Winds up and sends another curveball whizzing over the plate.

Freddy pokes Mead with the ruler. "Hey, freak. I said drop them. Now!"

Hands shaking, Mead reaches for his zipper. "I wasn't watching you."

"Faster."

Mead's pants drop to his ankles. His whole body trembles as he tugs down his Carter's and the boys start to laugh, making their all-too-expected comments about the diminutive size of his preadolescent genitals. Mead closes his eyes and waits for them to get their fill of fun and leave, only they don't leave. Freddy pokes him in the stomach with the ruler and says, "Now hand over your report."

Mead opens his eyes. "What?"

Freddy pokes him again. "I thought you were a genius, freak. You know what I'm talking about, your science report. Hand it over. I always wanted to get an A in science. My old man'll be so proud."

"No," Mead says and hugs the spiral notebook to his chest.

Freddy looks at his friends. "No? Did he just say no?"

"He couldn't have," one of them says. "He's too smart to say that."

Freddy pokes Mead again. Harder. "Hand it over, freak, or you'll be sorry."

"No. I've put a lot of hard work into this project. Half my final grade will be based on it. You can't have it."

He moves fast, so fast that Mead does not have time to react. In one swift motion, Freddy knocks Mead down, flips him over, and pins him to the ground. With his knee digging into Mead's back, Freddy says, "You ready to hand it over now?"

"No."

"All right then, have it your way, freak." And while the other boys hold Mead's arms and legs to the ground, Freddy takes the ruler and slides it into the crack of Mead's butt. A cold dread starts at the base of Mead's skull and races down his spine. His heart thuds against the ground. Freddy isn't just a juvenile delinquent; he is downright crazy. "I'll give you one more chance, freak," he says. "Hand over your report or I'll measure just how far I can shove this ruler up your ass."

Unable to speak, Mead nods his head.

"Is that a yes, freak?"

He nods again and manages to squeak out a sound that resembles a yes.

Freddy grabs the notebook and, knee still buried in the middle of Mead's back, rips it in half. Then rips it again and again and again, every tear going straight through Mead's heart, pieces of paper fluttering down through the air like feathers off a maimed bird. When Freddy is done, he tosses the carcass of the notebook into the creek, lifts his knee off Mead's back, and says, "If you breathe a word of this to anyone, I'll come back and finish what I started, do we understand each other?"

Mead nods again but otherwise does not move, even when the boys climb back up the hill. Not until their voices have receded into the distance does he dare lift his face out of the dirt and sit up. The front of his shirt is soaked with urine. Still shaking, he pulls it off over his head and dunks it in the creek. Splashes water on his chest. Then wrings out his shirt, puts it back on, and steps into his pants. Only then does he retrieve from the ground all the bits and pieces of his notebook. The pieces Freddy threw into the creek are ruined beyond repair.

Mead climbs back up the hill and sees Percy still standing on the mound. His cousin pitches a fastball in over the plate. The batter swings, misses, and the catcher yells out, "Strike!" Then the bell rings, signaling the end of recess, and everyone starts heading back toward the school, laughing and talking. Percy glances around the schoolyard until his eyes land on his cousin. Mead waves as if to say that everything is fine, that he will be along in a minute. The last thing he wants is for his cousin to see Freddy's handiwork. Mead is humiliated enough as it is, he does not need his cousin to add to his misery with some misplaced act of heroism. And it works. Percy nods back, then trots off in the direction of the school. Not until he has disappeared inside does Mead start to make his own way back.

THE FOLLOWING WEDNESDAY, the last week of the project, Mead re-sketches his six-foot-by-six-foot plot of land then, from the bits and pieces of still-legible notes, tries to re-create his report. But the project he hands in is not even worth grading. Mr. Belknap grades it anyway and gives Mead the first C of his life. "Is everything all right at home?" the teacher asks and Mead nods.

But four weeks later, when his mother gets a look at his report card, everything is not all right.

"What happened?" she asks Mead.

"Nothing," he says.

"Do you see this?" she says and holds the report card not six inches from his face. "C. That means average. You are not average, Teddy, you're an exceptionally bright boy. Is this your idea of a joke? Or maybe you're feeling rebellious, is that it? Maybe you've decided it doesn't matter how you do in school. Maybe you think slacking off in your studies is okay. Maybe this is all a big joke to you. But it isn't okay and it's not a joke, Teddy, it matters more than you can even imagine."

"I don't care," Mead says. Which is a lie. He does care. He hates that C even more than his mother does. She should know this. She should know him. Why doesn't she ask him if anything is wrong? Like his teacher. Not that he would tell her if she did ask. He would be too embarrassed. But still, she could at least ask. And so he says what he says to get back at her. To piss her off because he is mad. And it works.

"All right," she says. "Fine. You want to know what average is going to get you in this life? I'll show you." And she stomps to the front hall closet and comes back with his overcoat. "Put this on; we're going for a ride."

At first Mead thinks she is going to drive him over to the junior high so Principal Jeavons can give him a lecture, so the man can talk to Mead about grade point averages and SAT scores and all the other things universities care about so much. Which suits Mead just fine. He would love to get his hands on some college guides, to take a peek inside, to get a preview of his much-anticipated future, but he doubts Principal Jeavons has any of those lying around. That's high school territory, after all. Mead wonders what it would take to get his mother to drag him into *that* principal's office.

But she drives in neither the direction of the junior high nor the high school. Instead she gets on the state highway and heads for St. Louis. And Mead's hopes begin to rise again. Maybe she is bypassing both schools and taking him directly to St. Louis University. Maybe she will take him to the library. A university library. A real library. Because the one in High Grove is a joke. Cookbooks, farming manuals, and hunting magazines. That is about the extent of it. Mead would give his right arm to walk among the texts of great scholars. It'd be like dying and going to heaven. He can hardly wait.

Only she doesn't go there either. An hour and a half later she pulls up in front of Wessman's Funeral Parlor and says, "We're here. Get out."

A funeral parlor? She drove an hour and a half to take Mead to a funeral parlor? Geez, if she wanted him to attend a funeral, they could have just stayed in High Grove. They might have had to wait a day or two for somebody to die, but she could have made her point just as well there and saved on gas too. Whatever that point might be. Dead people don't scare Mead. There was an open casket at his grandfather's funeral a few years ago.

The old man looked exactly the same lying in that casket as he had two days earlier lying in his bed, only with more makeup. "Pull up your grades or you'll be burying dead people for the rest of your life like your father." That's all she has to say. But no, Mead's mother has to go and make a big production out of it. Drive home her point. So fine, let's just do this thing and go back home.

"Sit down and I'll be right back," she says then disappears inside Mr. Wessman's office. Once every month or so, Mead's father has to come down here to pick up the body of some High Grove resident who spent his or her final days in the St. Louis Hospital, or in one of the city's many nursing homes, and bring it back home to be buried. So unless Mead's mother is planning to stick a corpse in the front seat between the two of them for a ride home, Mead doesn't know what she hopes to prove with this whole charade.

"Okay," she says as she emerges from the office a moment later, "let's go." And she gets onto an oversize elevator not unlike the one at Fegley Brothers, only fancier, with inlaid wood panels and brass fixtures. The doors close and the elevator lurches into motion, heading south. Only then does it dawn on Mead that he is maybe not as prepared for whatever his mother has in mind as he first thought. "Just remember," she says, "that I'm doing this for your own good."

The elevator shudders to a stop and the doors open. The first thought Mead has is that someone should turn up the thermostat. The second thought he has is that someone should open a window because it stinks down here. Like a chemistry lab. Like his uncle Martin after the man has spent a couple of hours in the basement of Fegley Brothers, only a whole lot stronger. All such thoughts go flying out of Mead's head, however, when he sees what lies before him. Dead bodies. At least thirty of them are laying on stainless steel gurneys, naked as jaybirds. Men and women alike. Lifeless as fallen trees. Some with sutures in their necks, others with stitches in an arm or a leg. All of them wearing toe tags. And not a single one of these bodies is under a white sheet.

Mead's stomach heaves and he throws up on the floor. He turns and runs back into the elevator, frantically pushing on the CLOSE button until the doors start to respond. But his mother sticks her hand between the doors and they reopen. Then she steps onto the elevator and hands Mead a Wet-Nap to clean up his face. He gets a whiff of rubbing alcohol and almost heaves again, turns away from her, presses his hot cheek against the cool brass plate, and presses the CLOSE button several more times. The door responds and the elevator begins to rise.

His mother grabs his face, turns it toward her, and wipes his chin with the Wet-Nap as if he were two years old. "Hold still," she says as she swipes at his cheeks, then releases his face and tucks the damp tissue back inside her purse. "And that," she says, after snapping closed her handbag, "is what average will get you."

THE NEXT MORNING MEAD WAKES UP feeling hotter than a furnace. He splashes cold water on his face and dresses for school anyway. At the breakfast table he can barely get down his eggs and toast. "Are you feeling all right?" his mother asks and tries to touch his forehead but Mead pushes away her hand, still mad about yesterday. "I'm fine," he says, scoops up his schoolbooks, and hurries out the door before she can touch him again. The November air is cold and feels good on his face, but Mead has walked barely two blocks when he is overcome by a wave of dizziness.

A horn honks and he looks up. His Aunt Jewel rolls down

the window of her car and says, "Teddy, you'll catch your death walking to school in this weather. Hop in."

Normally he would say no and keep going, but today he makes an exception, opens the back door and crawls inside. Percy is sitting in the passenger seat up front. He turns around and says, "You look horrible, cousin, like you're gonna puke or something."

"Percy," Aunt Jewel says, "please don't talk like that. It's crude." Then she glances at Mead in the rearview mirror and says, "You do look awfully pale."

"I'm fine," Mead says and tries to stop shivering in his aunt's overheated car.

She pulls up in front of the junior high and Percy starts to get out.

"Aren't you forgetting something?" she says and Percy goes, "Oh, right," and pulls his woolen hat on over his head.

"I mean a kiss," she says and points to her cheek. Percy glances back over his shoulder at Mead. "Oh, right," he says again, kisses her, and bolts from the car.

Mead cannot help but feel jealous. He wonders what it would be like if he and his cousin were to switch mothers for a month. What it would be like to have his Aunt Jewel fuss over him the way she fusses over Percy, who obviously does not know how good he has got it. A month, that's all it would take to knock some sense into his cousin's head, to let him know how lucky he is. Maybe then he wouldn't jump out of the car quite so fast.

Mead scoots across the backseat to get out when his aunt says, "Wait a second there, young man," then reaches over the seat back and presses her cool palm to his hot forehead. "Why, you're burning up, Teddy. You can't go to school."

"I'm fine."

"You are not fine, you're sick as a dog. I can't believe your mother let you leave the house in this condition. You stay right where you are, I'm taking you home."

And just like that, the energy goes out of him. Mead could not get out of the car if he wanted to but he no longer even wants to. As his aunt pulls back out onto the road, Mead lies down and closes his eyes. The heat overcomes him and he falls asleep and dreams that he is down by the creek again with Freddy and his evil cohorts. "Drop your pants or else," Freddy says but just then Mead's Aunt Jewel appears at the top of the hill and yells, "Get away from my son, you no-good thugs, or I'll call the police." And off they run.

Mead wakes up when his Aunt Jewel wraps her arms around him. "Come on, you," she says and lifts him out of the backseat, which is an amazing feat when you consider the fact that his aunt is barely five-foot-two and cannot weigh much more than he does. Too weak to object, Mead wraps his arms around her shoulders and lets her carry him to the house.

"What happened?" Mead's mother says when she pulls open the front door.

"You have one very sick little boy on your hands," Aunt Jewel says and carries Mead to his bedroom.

"He said he was fine when he left here fifteen minutes ago," his mother says.

Jewel sets Mead down on his bed. Takes off his coat. His shoes. "You can't always take them at their word, Alayne. Especially boys. Percy never knows when he's sick until I tell him." Mead lies back and his aunt pulls the bedsheets up over him. "Let him sleep for a couple hours and then feed him some chicken soup."

"I know how to take care of my own son, Jewel," Mead's mother says, an edge creeping into her voice. "I've been doing it for ten years."

"I know, Alayne. I'm sorry, I didn't mean to imply—"

"Thank you for bringing him home. You can go now."

Aunt Jewel leaves and Mead falls asleep. When he wakes up, he sees it crouching next to his bed for the first time: the six-legged creature. Startled, he sits bolt upright and gasps. "Are you feeling better?" it says and, thinking that he is hallucinating, Mead rubs his eyes and looks again. This time he sees his mother. "Well, are you?" she says.

Mead nods. "I think maybe my temperature has gone down."

"No, I mean do you feel better now that you've embarrassed me. That was the point of all this, wasn't it? To get back at me for yesterday?"

"No."

"I'm sorry that you threw up, Teddy, I really am. I just had to make sure that you understand the importance of doing well in school. You and I aren't like your father and his whole side of the family. We're cut from a different cloth. I want you to have the educational opportunities I never had. To fulfill your true potential. I only did it for you."

"Fine. Got it." Mead says, closes his eyes, and rolls away. "Do you think maybe I could have some soup now?"

The straight-backed chair scrapes across the floor as she gets up to leave. But she doesn't come back with soup; she comes back with two aspirin, a cup of herbal tea, and his schoolbooks. Placing them on his bedside table, she says, "I spoke with Mr. Belknap just now. He's willing to change your C to an A if you'll do a project for extra credit."

"Fine," Mead says, pops the two aspirin into his mouth, and washes them down with the lukewarm tea. Just so long as it has nothing to do with that creek.

Mr. belknap gives mead a list of projects from which to choose and tells him that, if he would like, he can also submit it for inclusion in the county science fair.

"Are prizes awarded?" Mead asks.

"Yes, indeed," Mr. Belknap says. "First prize earns a blue ribbon and one hundred dollars. Second prize—"

"I don't care about second prize," Mead says. "I plan to place first."

And so he picks the project he figures will give him the best shot at winning the blue ribbon: running a mouse through a maze. The mouse part is easy. Mead just goes to the pet section of Woolworth's—where eleven of them are running around inside a glass aquarium bedded with sawdust—and observes his prospective subjects for a few minutes before choosing the most active and inquisitive one of the bunch: a white mouse with a single gray spot the size of a dime on its hind end. He also buys a wire cage, a running wheel, a bag of sawdust, and a water bottle. The maze part is harder. Because he has to build one. And because he has no skills when it comes to anything involving power tools. Like his mother said, Mead is not like his father and that whole Fegley side of the family. He is not good with his hands. And so he goes to someone who is.

"You want me to do what?" Percy says.

"I'll give you half my prize money when I win."

"And what if you don't win?"

"Don't worry, I will."

And so Mead starts going over to his cousin's house every day after school. The house his father and Uncle Martin grew up in. The house his grandfather Henry Charles built with his own two hands. There's a shed on the property where Uncle Martin stores some of the overflow inventory from the store (i.e., the older stuff that didn't sell) until Goodwill or the Salvation Army can come by with a truck to pick it up. The place where it all started: Henry Charles's workshop. The shed where the man built his first chest of drawers for the president of the local bank and, several years later, his first casket for the same customer. And the rest is history, or at least Fegley history.

Percy clears a bunch of cardboard boxes off the workbench. Christmas ornaments and old baby toys and toddler clothes that Mead's Aunt Jewel does not have the heart to throw out. Or, in his cousin's words: junk. Buried underneath all this junk is a band saw that requires some maintenance before it can be used. But Uncle Martin is happy to help out, crawling under the old saw with a wrench in one hand and an oil can in the other as if it were an old car in need of a tune-up. Then he takes the boys to the lumberyard, going over Mead's blueprint for the maze with the owner, the two of them knocking heads like a couple of old geezers. Percy rolls his eyes and sighs a lot but Mead kind of enjoys it. Kind of enjoys having his uncle take an interest in what he is doing.

"All right, Dad," Percy says when they get back to the shed. "You can leave now. Teddy asked *me* to help him, not you." And he nearly pushes his father out the door. "You have no idea," he says to Mead after Martin is gone, "what it's like having that man for a father. He's always sticking his nose into everything I do. I can hardly breathe around here without him getting involved."

"Excuse me," Mead says. "You have met my mother, haven't you?"

"Oh. Right. So maybe you do know."

And then they begin in earnest. Percy dons a pair of goggles and sends the first piece of wood through the band saw. Shavings and sparks fly through the air. Mead measures and Percy cuts. And, piece by piece, the maze begins to come together.

MEAD IS SITTING IN HIS BEDROOM, drawing up the chart he will use to track the progress of his experiment, when his mother bursts in and plunks down on his desk four packages of Kraft

American Cheese Slices, individually wrapped. "Does this belong to you?" she asks, all accusatory-like, as if she just found a stash of pot in his underwear drawer.

"Yes."

"And what's wrong with the food I buy you?"

"It's not for me; it's for my science experiment."

"What experiment?"

"The one Mr. Belknap assigned me for extra credit." And he holds up the wire cage containing the mouse.

His mother studies the small rodent as she might a long-lost orange found in the back of the refrigerator with a full beard of white-and-blue mold sprouting on its skin. "And what exactly do you plan to do with this mouse?"

"Win first prize in the county science fair," Mead says.

His mother picks up the packages of Kraft American Cheese Slices. "All right. But that filthy rodent goes the day after the fair, got it?" She marches out of his room.

THE MAZE TAKES EIGHT AFTERNOONS to build. Eight afternoons spent hanging out with his cousin Percy. Aunt Jewel pops in and out of the shed with cookies and lemonade but the rest of the time it's just the two of them. They don't talk much, except to compare notes on the progress of the maze. Percy seems to be enjoying himself as much as Mead is—maybe more—even though he has next to nothing to gain from it. No grade. No ribbon. No mother to get off his back. Which Mead finds somewhat puzzling. So on the sixth afternoon, he asks, "Why are you doing this?"

"Dovetail joints? Because they hold better than glue. I know it's taking a bit longer but it'll be worth it in the end. Trust me."

"No, I mean why are you helping me?"

Percy gives Mead a why-are-you-even-asking-me-that-question look and says, "Because you asked me to, cousin."

"I know, but would you jump in front of a train if I asked?"

Percy stops sanding and looks at Mead. "How fast is the train going?"

"All right, never mind. I'm sorry I asked."

Percy goes back to sanding then says, "Do you ever think about the future?"

"All the time."

"Me, too. What do you see?"

"World peace."

Percy gives Mead his stop-being-such-a-smart-aleck look.

"Okay," Mead says. "Maybe not world peace. I'd be satisfied to just graduate from high school in one piece and get on with my real life."

"Me too," Percy says.

"Really? But you have it so good. You've got tons of friends. A great mom."

"Well sure, things are great now but I'm talking about the future. Does it ever scare you? The thought of life after high school?"

"No. Quite the opposite. I can't wait."

"It's just that when I look at my dad—at his life—it just seems so, I don't know, lonely. There's no one standing on the sidelines cheering him on."

"You'll just have to learn to cheer yourself on."

"I suppose," Percy says, picks up two notched pieces of wood, and slides them together. His dovetail joint is perfect. Setting it aside, he reaches for another piece of wood and starts cutting more notches. "That's why," he says.

"Excuse me?" Mead says.

"You asked me why I'm helping you and I'm telling you, okay?"

They don't talk for the rest of the afternoon, except to compare notes on the progress of the maze.

* * *

WHEN THE MAZE IS DONE it looks like a whatchamacallit from the pages of a Dr. Seuss book. Three separate mazes, all starting at the same point, loop around, cross over, and dip under one another, ending at three different locations. The shortest route, accessed through a hinged door marked **A**, offers three wrong turns, a bridge, and two tunnels to reach the end where a single one-inch square of American cheese will be waiting. A second door, marked **B**, leads to a maze twice as long as **A** and features twice as many wrong turns, bridges, and tunnels. When successfully completed, the same one-inch reward will be at the end. Following this logic, the third door, marked **C**, leads to the longest and most difficult maze of them all, and offers the same reward.

"So what exactly do you hope to prove?" Percy asks.

"My hypothesis," Mead says, "is that mouse, like man, wants to do the least amount of work to gain the largest amount of reward, his life choices based primarily on monetary gain. Only in a mouse's world, money equals cheese."

"Sounds kind of cynical, if you want to ask me."

"I didn't ask."

MEAD BEGINS WITH AN EXPERIMENTAL RUN, the baseline against which he will gauge all future runs. He places the mouse in the starting box, opens door **A**, and starts his stopwatch. The furry critter feels its way along the freshly glued plywood walls, noting every nook and cranny with its whiskers. It peeks around each corner it encounters, exploring all the options, including the dead ends. It crawls through a tunnel and up into the red tube that arches over maze **B**, sniffing high and low. In just thirty seconds, the subject completes the first three-quarters of the maze, then it suddenly turns around and heads back toward the start.

"What're you doing, Mr. Cheese?" Percy yells at the mouse. "You almost had it. Turn back around, you're going the wrong way."

"Maybe he can't smell the reward," Aunt Jewel says. "You should've used real cheese, Teddy, not that processed stuff. Something with a strong scent, like Roquefort."

"Mr. Cheese?" Mead says. "Where did that come from?"

"The little guy needed a name," Percy says and shrugs, "so I gave him one."

Mr. Cheese gets tired of the maze and decides to try and get out. Stretching his body up the wall as far as it'll go, he scratches his front feet against the smooth surface of the plywood, hoping for traction, and comes upon a little drop of hardened glue. He grabs hold of it and hoists himself up off the floor, but not high enough to scale the walls of his prison. As one minute passes into two, and two into three, Mr. Cheese continues to scratch and claw at various parts of the wall, making no attempt whatsoever to complete the maze.

"Looks like you got yourself a defective mouse there, cousin," Percy says. "If I was you, I'd exchange him for a better model."

"He's a perfectly fine mouse," Jewel says. "He'll figure it out. Do you know how long it took me to get you potty-trained?"

"Mom! Geez, could you think of anything more embarrassing to say?"

Jewel ruffles Percy's hair with her hand and he pulls away. And Mead feels that all too familiar pang of jealousy for what his cousin takes for granted.

Mr. Cheese sits down and starts grooming his face.

Percy stands up. "I'm gonna go pitch a few balls with Dad. Let me know if Mr. Cheese ever figures it out."

Jewel gets up too. "Would you like anything to eat while you wait, Teddy? Some cookies or something?"

"No, thanks, Aunt Jewel. I'm fine."

But she's back five minutes later with a plate of brownies and a glass of milk.

"How's he doing?"

"Not so well," Mead says and picks up a brownie. "I shouldn't have fed the subject this morning. He's too complacent. I'll have to note that in my observations and alter my controls for a better result." He takes a sip of milk.

Ten minutes later, Mr. Cheese completes the maze and finds the cheese. Aunt Jewel claps her hands and cheers. Mead clicks the stopwatch and writes in his notebook: "Maze **A**: First run completed in 29 min. 37 sec. Remarks: Subject has no sense of why it is here or what it is supposed to be doing. Without incentive, it has no sense of urgency and so takes its time exploring whatever crosses its path. Having now discovered the cheese, however, I anticipate improved performance in all future runs."

Mr. Cheese finishes his reward and sniffs around in search of more food. Mead scoops the subject up in his hand, sets out a second piece of cheese, places the subject back in the starting box, and starts the stopwatch.

By the end of week one, Mead has run Mr. Cheese through all three mazes several times and established a "reference point" against which he will compare all future runs. Now it is time to start the real experiment. Now it's time to see how the subject will react when presented with a choice. Instead of opening just one door, Mead will open two and the subject will have to decide through which maze it wishes to run. As soon as the subject makes its choice, the selected door will be closed, committing the subject to its decision. A cause-and-effect relationship. Mead has also decided, as one of the controls of his experiment, that Mr. Cheese will conduct only six runs per day. Six runs equal six pieces of cheese. It will be left up to the subject to decide how hard it wants to work for its six pieces of cheese per day.

"Seems kind of cruel, if you ask me," Percy says from his ringside seat, having regained an interest in Mr. Cheese once the mouse started clocking in each run under thirty seconds.

"I didn't ask," Mead says and sets the subject in his starting box for his first run of the day.

MR. CHEESE SCAMPERS AROUND inside the kitchen sink, his toes clicking against the stainless steel basin, sounding like rain against a windowpane, while Mead sits on the floor and cleans out his cage. Wearing a pair of his mother's rubber gloves, Mead sticks his hand through its open door, pulls out last Sunday's *St. Louis Post-Dispatch*—which has been chewed up and shaped into a nest—and dumps it into the trash can under the sink. He then pulls out the bottom tray, scrapes off all the mouse droppings, and slides it back into place. Mead is still sitting on the floor, ripping up yesterday's newspaper and stuffing it into the clean cage, when his father enters the kitchen.

"I had a pet when I was your age," he says. "A rabbit by the name of Peter. You know, for Peter Rabbit." He takes a glass out of the cupboard, holds it under the cold-water tap, and fills it. Residual drops of water drip off the faucet into the sink and Mr. Cheese saunters over to check one out, then laps it up. "He's a cute little fella."

"He's not a pet, Dad, he's the subject of my science experiment."

His father looks over at him. "I know what your mother said, Teddy, about you having to get rid of him after you complete your experiment, but that may not be necessary, not after she sees how well you're taking care of him."

Mead stands and places the clean cage on the counter. "Mice can live up to two years in captivity, did you know that?" He takes off the gloves and picks up Mr. Cheese, who immediately starts crawling up his arm. It tickles. When the mouse reaches his elbow, Mead lifts him by the tail and puts him back in his hand. But Mr. Cheese immediately starts up his arm again, crawling all the way to Mead's shoulder this time. Once there, the mouse stands up on his hind legs and appears to whisper a secret into Mead's ear. Mead giggles because the mouse's whiskers tickle, picks up Mr. Cheese by the tail, and sets him back in his cage. "Besides, a scientist isn't supposed to become attached to his subject. It's not professional."

His father drinks his water and sets the empty glass in the sink. "I'm afraid it's too late for that," he says and leaves the kitchen.

So far Mr. Cheese has performed pretty much as expected, consistently choosing the shorter of whichever two routes he is offered, proving the mouse to be a smart subject, his actions motivated by reward. By now he knows the mazes so well that he doesn't even hesitate before choosing door **A** over door **B**, or door **B** over door **C**. He has got it down pat. So it's time to change things up, to further challenge the subject. Mead will accomplish this by varying the size of the reward at the end of each maze. Now, the longer the run, the larger the reward will be. With the promise of a larger payoff, Mead hopes to entice Mr. Cheese to change his behavior, to opt for the longer maze over the shorter one. To work a little harder in hopes of acquiring a bigger reward. To make different life choices based on a different outcome.

The call comes in over supper. "I'm on my way," Mead's dad says to the county coroner and jots down an address. Mead's mother wraps up the uneaten portion of his meal, so he can finish it in the car on the way, while Mead's father calls Martin. "There's a crime scene involved," he says into the receiver, "so it could take a while. Why don't you meet me over there. The address is 221 Rosebush Lane. Sheila Waseleski."

"Waseleski?" Mead says when his father hangs up the phone. "There's a kid in my grade by the name of Waseleski."

"What happened?" Mead's mother asks.

"Gunshot wound to the head," Mead's dad says. "They suspect the husband. Seems he has a history of violent behavior."

It cannot be the same family. There must be two Waseleskis in town. But the next day at school everyone is talking about it. How Freddy's father killed his mother over an undercooked hamburger. And Freddy is nowhere in sight.

The memorial service is set for Saturday and Mead's mother insists that Mead go.

"No," he says.

"He's a classmate of yours. It wouldn't look right if you didn't."

"We've only been classmates for six months and next year I'll either skip another grade or he'll be held back again."

"You're going. End of discussion."

The funeral chapel is an annex off the furniture store where mourners can socialize, view the deceased, or pray, depending on which of three rooms they are standing in. Mead stands next to the coat rack, ducking behind it every time one of his classmates enters, snubbing them before they have a chance to snub him.

Freddy does not show up until the two-hour service is nearly over, looking almost unrecognizable in a suit that was probably purchased at Sears just this morning. His hair has been cut and combed, his sneakers replaced by black shoes. He is accompanied by two girls, both younger than himself, who Mead takes to be Freddy's sisters, and a female adult who obviously is not his mother because she is the one lying in the next room pumped full of formaldehyde.

A hush goes through the chapel as word spreads that "the children" have arrived. Necks crane this way and that to get a look at their faces. Freddy appears to try and stare a hole in the floor, presumably so he can fall through it. He repeatedly shrugs the hand of the female caretaker off his shoulder but eventually he is coaxed into the viewing room to say goodbye to his mother.

"At least when Freddy's father shot Freddy's mother, he was thoughtful enough to shoot her in the side of the head," Mead's uncle said at dinner last night. Okay, so maybe those weren't his exact words, his point being that it was a lot easier to camouflage the entry and exit wounds the way it happened. For the sake of the children. So that their last memory of their mother's face would be a pleasant one. Or at least as pleasant as these things get.

When Freddy steps up to the casket and looks down into the face of his thirty-one-year-old mother, does he see it? Does he see the yellow bruise on her left cheek? It's all Uncle Martin could talk about this morning: How he was afraid that it might still be visible through the makeup and powder he so painstakingly applied to her face and neck. The almost-healed bruise was from a prior altercation Mr. Waseleski had with Mrs. Waseleski. Uncle Martin placed the time of contact at two weeks prior to her death. But even if Freddy doesn't see it, he must know it's there. He probably witnessed the actual punch.

Freddy stands over his mother for a long time, looking down at her face, then turns to the female caretaker and says, "Who put red lipstick on her? My mom never wore red lipstick. She thought it made her look like a whore. She only wore pink. Who put this lipstick on her? Who's trying to make my mom look like a whore?"

"Freddy, please," the female caretaker says and places her hand on his shoulder. "It's all right. It was an honest mistake."

He shakes her hand off. "No, it ain't okay. It's insulting. I want somebody to wipe it off her mouth. Right now."

"Freddy, please. I think it's time for us to go."

"No! I'm not leaving till they fix my mom."

"Freddy—"

"If somebody don't wipe it off her right now, I'm going to." And with that, he grabs a box of Kleenex, pulls free a fistful of tissues and begins to rub at his mother's mouth. Only then does he discover that it has been stitched closed with sutures. He drops the wad of tissues and reels backward, knocking over a wreath of lilies and then falling on top of it. Mead's dad abandons his post at the door and rushes into the viewing room. He tries to help Freddy to his feet but the fourteen-year-old boy has the strength of ten men and shoves him away. Undeterred, Mead's dad tries again and this time Freddy allows the kindly funeral director to lift him to his feet, then falls into his arms and starts crying, bawling his eyes out.

It is hard for Mead to believe this is the same boy who threatened to shove a ruler up his ass just last month. He does not want to feel sorry for Freddy Waseleski. Why did his mother make him come to this funeral? Mead turns and bolts out of the chapel, swiping away tears as he runs home.

A WEEK BEFORE TURNING IN his extra credit project, Mead sits down to compile his observations and draws up a chart to illustrate his findings in a simple and visual way. Aunt Jewel supplies him with a large sheet of poster board and several colored markers to make the chart and his father buys him an easel on which to display it. On the day of his class presentation, Uncle Martin loads the maze into the back of the hearse, because it is too big and cumbersome to fit inside anything else, and gives Mead a lift to school.

Mead emerges from the passenger side of the hearse with a cloth draped over Mr. Cheese's cage and looks up to see several of his open-mouthed classmates staring back. Among the many gapers is Freddy Waseleski, back after a one-week absence to recover from the loss of his mother. Mr. Belknap helps Uncle Martin carry the maze into the school, Mead follows behind them with his chart under one arm and the cage in the other, and Percy takes up the rear carrying the easel. Since Mead does not have science until third period, he leaves Mr. Cheese in Mr. Belknap's care and goes off to his other classes. But he finds it hard to concentrate on what his teachers are saying. He keeps thinking about his presentation. And about Mr. Cheese. He hopes that none of the other kids are bothering him. That Mr. Cheese won't be too nervous and distracted to perform. Not that it is necessary. Mead's presentation does not rely upon it. All his results are in. He just thinks it will be more interesting if the students can watch Mr. Cheese do his thing. Plus, he wants to give the mouse his moment in the spotlight. It seems only fair.

But his fears go unwarranted. As soon as Mr. Cheese touches down in the maze, he's off and running. The presentation is a hit. Such a hit that Mr. Belknap has Mead repeat his presentation for the other seventh-grade science class, the one with Freddy Waseleski in it.

Freddy stands over the maze with the other students and watches as Mr. Cheese goes through his paces. The whole time Mead expects the juvenile delinquent to reach in, grab the mouse by the neck, and strangle him. But he doesn't; he just looks.

THE NEXT DAY MEAD GOES TO CLEAN OUT Mr. Cheese's cage and sees some mysterious pellets in the bottom of it. After pulling out the soiled newspaper, he tosses the pellets in the trash but remains concerned. It isn't until the following day that Mr. Cheese begins to show signs that something is not right.

"I think Mr. Cheese has been poisoned," Mead says to his mother. "He needs to go to the vet."

"Poisoned? By whom?"

"This kid in school."

"What kid?"

"Does it matter? I can't win first prize if I show up without a mouse," Mead says, knowing that this isn't true. He only says it because he believes his mother cares more about his winning that prize than she does about saving the life of some filthy rodent.

And it works. She takes him. Mr. Cheese runs in circles around the examining table because his left side has already become paralyzed. "The poison has been in his system too long," the vet says. "All I can do is put the little guy out of his misery." Afterward, the veterinarian asks Mead if he would like to take the mouse home.

"No," his mother answers for him. "That won't be necessary. It wasn't a pet."

"I'm sorry," his father says when Mead gets home. "He was a cute little fella."

"I want to know the name of this boy you suspect poisoned your mouse," his mother says. "I want to have a talk with his parents. He may have cost you a place in the county science fair. He should be punished."

"I don't care about the stupid science fair," Mead says, storms down the hall, and slams his door.

BUT HE DOES WIN FIRST PLACE and his mother immediately loses interest in revenge. Mead offers half his winnings to his cousin, as promised.

"Keep your money," Percy says. "I don't want it."

"A deal is a deal," Mead says. "Take it."

And so Percy does. He pockets the fifty bucks and says, "So who's the bastard who killed Mr. Cheese? I wanna wring his neck."

"I have no proof that he did it."

"It was that Waseleski kid, wasn't it?"

Mead says nothing.

"I knew it. I'm gonna kick that guy's butt."

"No!"

"Why not?"

"Because. He lost his mother."

"I didn't know you were such a softy, cousin. Okay, fine, I won't. If he ever does anything else to you, though, I'm gonna kick his butt for sure."

But it's a lie. Mead is not a softy; he's just scared to death of Freddy. And he knows that no matter how much his cousin may want to protect him, that when Mead needs him most, Percy won't be there.

ON SUNDAY, MEAD AND HIS PARENTS go to Uncle Martin's house for dinner. It's something they do pretty often so he doesn't think much about it, not until Aunt Jewel opens the front door dressed all in black. "Come on, you," she says, takes Mead by the hand, and leads him around to the backyard. Uncle Martin, Percy, and Lenny are all there, also dressed in black, standing over an open grave. It's a small grave, just big enough for the green Stride Rite box Percy lowers into it. Mead has no idea whether or not Mr. Cheese is actually inside the box. But it doesn't matter. Lenny throws a shovel of dirt over the box. "Would you like to say a few last words?" Aunt Jewel asks.

Mead shakes his head. He couldn't speak if he wanted to; he's too choked up.

"Then I will," Mead's mother says. "I'm sorry, Teddy. I didn't know."

But he has no idea what her apology is for. Not knowing about Freddy? Making her son go to Mrs. Waseleski's funeral? Letting the vet throw out Mr. Cheese? Or taking Mead to the basement of Wessman's Funeral Parlor? And does she really expect him to forgive her for all that with a simple I'm sorry? Because he can't; he just can't.

4

FRESHMAN DISORIENTATION

Chicago
Three Years Before Graduation

MEAD ORDERS THE HAM SALAD SANDWICH PLATE and the waitress places in front of him a pile of food large enough to feed a family of four for a week. Or at least that's the way it looks to Mead, whose stomach has shrunk to the size of a pea, shriveled by a mixture of anxiety and excitement. He can still feel Aunt Jewel's arms around him, hugging him goodbye as if he were leaving forever. Reluctant to let go. It was kind of embarrassing but at the same time it was kind of nice. Percy felt it too. That hug. Mead saw it in his cousin's eyes. It was something Mead had never seen there before: a look of jealousy. When it was his turn to say goodbye, Percy chucked Mead on the arm and said, "Don't drown in the ocean, cousin."

"Chicago is on a lake, not an ocean," Mead said.

"Still, it's a lot bigger than the pond you're used to swimming in."

"What pond? Snell's Quarry?"

"Just be careful," he said and ruffled Mead's hair.

Mead finally got it, that Percy was talking in metaphor. Uncle

Martin was more direct. "You're gonna find it harder to wrap those college professors around your little finger than your father. Don't worry, though; if you can't handle it, you can always come back here."

But going back is not an option. Not to Mead. He is not just leaving home to go to college; he is leaving behind his entire past. All those verbal taunts from his so-called peers. All the meddlesome needling from his mother. And, most important, Freddy Waseleski. Mead is going to start over with a clean slate. It's his turn now. For the first time in his life, he will be surrounded by his intellectual equals. No longer standing in the shadow of his popular cousin. Competing not on an athletic field but on the playing field of the mind. And to go along with this new life, he will take on a new name. He no longer wants to be known as Theodore or Ted. No longer wants his name to rhyme with either floor or dead. From here on out, he will be known simply as Mead.

His mother reaches across the table and stuffs a paper napkin into the collar of his shirt. Mead pulls it out and glances up at the waitress, who is placing sodas on the table for him and his parents and smiling. "Mom," he says. "Stop that."

"You're going to get mayonnaise on your new shirt, Teddy."

"I am not."

"Not if you use this napkin," she says and stuffs it back in his collar.

"Dad," Mead says. "Make her stop."

But the man is too busy reading his road map, committing to memory the exit ramp off the interstate that will take them to campus. And so Mead gives in. For the last time. Leaving the napkin in place, he picks up the ham sandwich, takes a bite, and a piece of lettuce falls out, bouncing off the napkin on its way to the floor.

He chews but cannot swallow. Glances out the window as an eighteen-wheeler heads out of the Truck Stop Cafe parking lot back onto the interstate, heading south. Mead almost drops his sandwich, rips off the napkin, and runs after the truck. It is a comforting thought: ditching his parents and heading back home. After all, Mead is only fifteen. Way too young to be going off to college. And yet here he sits, about two hours outside of Chicago, the first Fegley ever to be accepted into a university. At any age. A fact that his mother has repeated so many times—to the butcher, to the postman, to her bridge partners, to her hairdresser, to anyone who will listen—that Mead has lost count. What he has not lost count of is how much his college education is going to cost his father, because his mother keeps reminding him. As if she were the one out there breaking her back to pay the tuition plus room and board instead of his father.

But it is just a fleeting thought. Running back home. An irrational wave of fear. Complete foolishness. Because there is nothing for Mead to run back home to.

He washes down the sandwich with a slug of soda and belches.

"Teddy," his mother says. "Where are your manners?"

"Mead," he says. "I go by Mead now." He takes another bite.

CHICAGO SOUNDS TO MEAD LIKE DAWN, the traffic and the people and the horns as noisy as the birds in High Grove chirping in a new day. Only in Chicago it seems that dawn lasts all day. His father parks in front of the dorm and tucks the braided rug Aunt Jewel gave Mead as a going-away present under his arm. "A little something to make your dorm room feel more like home," she said as she handed it to him.

"Put that back in the trunk," his mother now says. "It's an embarrassment."

"No," Mead says, not having felt strongly one way or the other about the rug until his mother opened up her big yap. "I want it. The floor is probably hard and cold."

"So we'll buy you another throw rug. A tasteful one."

"But I like this one," Mead says.

"It belongs in a farmhouse, Teddy, not a college dorm."

"Dad," Mead says.

"It is a gift, Alayne," he says.

"Fine," she says. "Have it your way." And she stomps off.

MEAD'S ROOMMATE HAS ALREADY MOVED IN. Pete is his name. Pete Blankenship. He shakes Mead's hand and says, "How old are you anyway?"

"Sixteen next month."

"What are you, a genius or something?"

"Teddy got a 1600 on his SATs," Mead's mother answers for him as she unzips his green-and-blue plaid suitcase.

"Mead," Mead says. "I prefer to be called Mead."

"Cool," Pete says as Mead's mother transfers her son's underwear from his suitcase to the dresser. "So what room did you get assigned to for the big exam tomorrow?"

"Room 1214 in Epps Hall," Mead says, grabs his cotton briefs out of her hand and says, "Mother, I can do that."

"Hey, me, too," Pete says. "We can walk over there together."

She turns back to the suitcase and lifts out a shirt and a pair of pants. Laying them over the back of the chair, she says, "I think you should wear these tomorrow."

"I can pick out my own clothes, Mother," Mead says, takes them off the chair, and hangs them in the closet.

She looks at Pete and says, "My son may be smart, but he doesn't know the first thing about how to dress." Then she takes the shirt and pants back out of the closet and lays them over the back of the chair as Mead's father unfurls the rug on the floor.

"Hey, cool rug," Pete says.

"Thanks," Mead says. "My aunt gave it to me."

Mead's mother rolls her eyes. Yes, Mead is going to like college life; he is going to like it a lot.

HIS PARENTS TAKE HIM OUT TO DINNER. They will check into a hotel room afterward and start back to High Grove first thing tomorrow. It's an upscale restaurant filled with several sets of parents and their departing offspring, the air tense with a mixture of excitement, fear, and sadness. "Make sure you go to bed early," Mead's mother says loud enough for the people at the next table to hear. "You have a test to take in the morning."

"I know, Mother," Mead says. "You don't have to remind me."

"I packed earplugs for you in case your roommate snores."

The guy sitting at the next table, who looks like a potential classmate, glances over at Mead and smiles. Embarrassed, Mead says, "I'll be fine, Mother."

"Call and let us know how you did. After the test."

Mead rolls his eyeballs skyward to let the guy know that he knows that his mother is being annoying. That he is above such henpecking. "I won't find out for a day or two. Not until it's been graded."

"So call us then. It's important that you do well on this test, Teddy."

"Alayne," Mead's father says. "Don't worry. He'll be fine."

At the coat check, on the way out, the guy from the next table bumps into Mead accidentally on purpose and says, "Chicago University, am I right?"

"How did you know?"

"The test. Tomorrow. Tell your mother not to worry. Your

performance won't be reflected in your permanent record. It's just for placement."

"She knows. And she won't be happy unless I place out of all the freshman level courses."

"Ah. She's one of those mothers."

"There are others?" Mead says.

"You bet," the guy says and points his eyes at his own parents. "Good luck."

Moments later, Mead's parents drop him off in front of the dorm and hug him goodbye. As they drive away, it hits Mead that they are really leaving. That for the first time in his life he will truly be on his own. For a moment he is paralyzed with fear, unable to move forward or backward. Then he remembers that he has a test to study for, snaps out of it, and heads up to his room.

THIRTY HEADS ARE BOWED OVER THIRTY DESKS. Thirty pencils poised over thirty exams. Thirty brains firing off synapses like the Fourth of July. It is Mead's second day at college and it is starting off with a bang, with a six-hour comprehensive exam before a single class has even been taken. Now this is Mead's kind of school!

Chicago University wants to know how much Theodore Mead Fegley of High Grove, Illinois, already knows. It does not want to waste his time teaching him introductory physics if he already knows the basics. It does not want to bother him with calculus if he has already mastered it. Neither does it want to inflict upon him any repetition of a dozen or so other subjects if he already has the knowledge. The university wants to give him credit — literally, four credits per course — for all the knowledge he has brought with him, and let him proceed from there.

Mead has been sitting with Pete, along with twenty-eight of

his other freshman peers, ten minutes into the comprehensive exam, when the door to the classroom bursts open and this tall, lanky kid with a mop of black hair comes charging through it. The same guy Mead spoke to at the restaurant last night.

"Sorry I'm late," he says to the professor in attendance and, by way of his loud voice, to all thirty students in the classroom. "I overslept. I just got back from France and my internal clock is all screwed up. Please forgive me. The name is Weinstein. Herman Weinstein." And he thrusts his hand at the professor as if he were a salesman making a business call and not a student of higher education.

"That's quite all right, Mr. Weinstein," the professor says and, instead of shaking his hand, gives Herman a copy of the exam, then motions for him to take a seat. The tall, lanky boy strides past Mead, seemingly without seeing him, and leaves a scent of Paris and romance in his wake, something Mead did not notice in the restaurant. He has never before met a guy who wears cologne. The men in High Grove tend to smell like fresh-cut hay or cow manure or husks of corn or some combination of all three. Herman walks all the way to the back of the room before taking a seat, scraping the feet of his chair across the floor as he gets comfortable, then leans back with one leg crossed over the other as if he were here to enjoy a cup of cappuccino rather than take an exam. Mead finds the young man's presence distracting even after he settles down. He can smell his cologne from four desks away. He finds the boy's whole demeanor to be rather insulting, something else Mead did not pick up on last night. As if being here is more of an inconvenience than an honor. Well, it's an honor as far as Mead is concerned. To be here. In Chicago. On this campus. In this classroom. To be in the presence of so many like minds. It is a dream come true, as far as Mead is concerned. He would like to get up and change desks, to put as much distance as possible between himself and Mr. Paris France. But he doesn't because to do so would be disruptive to the other students. And that would be rude. And Mead is not a rude person. Instead, he shifts position so as to block the young man from his sight and goes back to work on his exam.

Five hours later he is done. With fifty minutes to spare, he goes back over the entire exam, double-checking any answers about which he was unsure or conflicted. But that only takes another twenty minutes. So, quietly as possible, Mead pushes back his chair and gets up, tiptoes to the front of the classroom, and hands his exam to the professor, who glances up in surprise, first looking at his watch, then at the exam, then at Mead. "Thank you, Theodore," he finally says. "You may go."

"Mead," Mead says. "I prefer to go by Mead."

"Okay, Mead. You may go. Good luck."

When he gets to the door, Mead glances back over his shoulder. It is important to him, for some reason, that Mr. Paris France see him leave early. And he does. Herman raises his hand as if making a toast at a dinner party and smiles. Well, it's not quite a smile; it's more of a smirk. Mead smirks back then ducks out of the room still unsure as to whether the guy recognized him from last night or not.

He heads back to his room to wait for Pete so they can go to dinner together and talk about the exam. They didn't get to talk much last night. While Mead was having dinner with his parents, Pete apparently met up with some other students and didn't get back to their room until pretty late. Mead suggested they review the periodic tables of the elements together—for the chemistry part of the exam—but Pete wasn't interested. "If I don't know that shit already, it's not going to do me much good to try and learn it now," he said, then fell into bed and off to sleep. Mead ended up studying alone.

When an hour goes by and Pete does not return from the exam, Mead starts to think that maybe he should have waited for him outside the classroom instead. But Mead isn't very good at this kind of thing, at having a friend. He doesn't know the ins and outs of how it all works. He just assumed that Pete would come back to their room but apparently he was wrong. He decides to wait some more, in case Pete got hung up on the way back. Mead would hate to go off to dinner and miss him. He doesn't want Pete to think he wouldn't wait for him. And so Mead stays in their room until half an hour before the cafeteria closes, until he has to leave or miss dinner altogether. He's sliding his tray along the buffet when he looks up and sees Pete sitting at one of the tables with half a dozen other students, talking and laughing.

Mead feels like a fool. A complete and utter fool. What made him think college was going to be any different from high school? Or junior high? Or elementary school? Doing his best to hide behind his tray, he heads toward an empty table—one preferably next to a window—when he hears his name. "Hey, Mead. Over here," Pete calls out and waves him over. Relieved, but also wary, Mead approaches the table with caution. In case it's a trick of some kind. "I was just telling my friends about you," Pete says. "About my genius of a roommate. Have a seat. Everyone, this is Mead. Mead, everyone."

He sits at the end of the table, next to this pretty girl with long, brown hair. She introduces herself as Cynthia Broussard from Virginia, then says, "Pete tells us you're only fifteen. Is that true?"

"I'll be sixteen next month."

"It must be hard always being younger than everyone else."

"It's not so bad," Mead says. "You get used to it."

"Hey, great button-down shirt," a boy at the other end of the table named Rick says. "I used to wear one just like it to church on Sunday."

"Yeah," another boy says. "You don't have to be so formal. You're in college now, you can wear whatever you want."

"His mother picked the shirt out for him," Pete says, "after unpacking his suitcase and telling him when to go to bed."

"Get out of here," Rick says. "Are you serious?"

"Dead serious," Pete says.

"Hey, you shave yet?" another boy asks.

Mead blushes. "I don't see how any of this—"

"No," Pete says. "Not unless there are razor blades hidden inside the first-aid kit I saw his mom tuck inside his sock drawer."

"Now I know you're kidding," Rick says.

"I am not," Pete says. "I swear."

Mead stands up. He has had enough. It *is* just like high school all over again. Or junior high. Or elementary school. "I have to go."

"No," Pete says. "Stay."

"No, really," Mead says. "I have something I have to do." And he picks up his tray and heads for the exit, having had nothing to eat.

"Hey, Mead," Pete says. "Don't go. I was only teasing. Come on. I'm sorry."

But he keeps going, sliding a baked potato into his napkin and then into his pocket as he exits the cafeteria. Sits alone in his dorm room and eats it. Mead tells himself that things will improve as soon as classes start. That it will be better this way, without the distraction of friends. After all, Mead's father is not footing the bill for tuition so his son can sit around and socialize. Mead has come here to get an education and an education he will get. Tomorrow he will go to the library and familiarize himself with the floor plan. He will seek out the quietest corner in which to study. Yes, this is all for the best.

By the time his roommate returns, Mead is under the bedcovers, facing the wall.

"Hey," Pete says. "I brought you something." And he places what smells like a cheeseburger on Mead's desk. "Listen, I'm sorry about earlier. I was just kidding around. Really. I didn't mean anything by it."

"Apology accepted," Mead says but does not turn around.

"Okay, well, a bunch of us are going to hang out in Rick's room for a while. He's got a TV. Feel free to join us if you'd like."

"No, thank you," Mead says.

"Okay, well, if you change your mind, his room is at the end of the hall."

And Pete leaves. Only then does Mead roll over and pick up the cheeseburger, checking carefully between the buns for any foreign objects before finally taking a bite. Even then he isn't sure that someone hasn't spit on it but he is too tired and too hungry to much care. He gobbles it down and then heads for the bathroom to brush his teeth for bed. He isn't alone. Someone is taking a shower. As Mead is flossing, the shower shuts off and a moment later he sees, reflected in the mirror, a girl stepping into his line of vision. A stark naked girl drying her hair with a pink towel. Mead drops his eyes to the sink, all embarrassed. He must have wandered into the wrong bathroom. Maybe he can slip out without her noticing. He was distracted. That must be it. He was upset about Pete and not paying attention. But wow, what a great mistake. The only other females Mead has ever seen naked were the ones in the basement of Wessman's Funeral Parlor. He lifts his eyes back up to the mirror. This girl looks a lot better than they did.

She looks up too, sees Mead staring at her, and screams, then covers her body. "Holy shit," she says, "you scared me. How the hell did you get in here?"

"With a 1600 on my SATs."

"You mean you're a student? Here? I mean, you look so young."

"Sorry. I must've wandered into the wrong bathroom."

Then she laughs. Not a mean laugh, just a laugh. "Didn't anybody tell you? All the bathrooms in this dorm are unisex. Welcome to college."

"YOU'VE PLACED OUT OF ALL the entry level courses," Dr. Kustrup says. He is Mead's faculty advisor. "Congratulations, you're a sophomore. Not bad for one week of college, not bad at all."

"Thank you, sir," Mead says and squirms in his chair. It's hot in the professor's office. Too hot. Mead wishes the man would open a window or something. Let in some fresh air. After all, it is sixty degrees outside, which would make it about thirty degrees cooler than this room. "So," Mead says, "what happens now?"

"Well, Theodore, let's start with your curriculum. I'm guessing you're interested in a math major, otherwise I wouldn't have been chosen to be your advisor."

Dr. Kustrup is wearing one of those tweed jackets with patches at the elbows as if he wants to make sure that he won't be mistaken for something other than what he is: a college professor. He strikes Mead as a man who wants to fit in, something at which Mead has never been much good. Perhaps he should ask the professor where he bought the jacket, then go out and buy one just like it for himself.

"Yes, sir, Dr. Kustrup," Mead says. "Math or possibly physics. I haven't yet decided which."

The professor leans forward on his desk, leans on his elbow

patches, and says, "I'm going to come clean with you, Theodore. I was not originally chosen to be your faculty advisor. I requested that you be assigned to me. You want to know why? Because you strike me as a young man with a lot of potential. But I want to be more to you than just an advisor, Theodore, I want to be your mentor."

"Mead, sir, I prefer to be called Mead."

"Have you thought at all about your future, Mr. Fegley, have you thought at all about where you'd like to be in five years? Ten? Twenty?"

"No, sir, I thought for now I'd just focus on where I ought to be next week."

Dr. Kustrup laughs. "You're not only smart, but funny too. I like that. Humor is a sign of great intelligence. But I can see already, Mr. Fegley, that you are going to benefit greatly from my guidance. I see this a lot in boys from rural backgrounds. A lack of foresight. No sense of possibility. Well, not to worry, son. You're in good hands now because I've thought about it for you. The Institute for Advanced Study in Princeton. That's where I'd like to see you end up, Mr. Fegley. Have you ever heard of it?"

"No, sir, I haven't."

Dr. Kustrup smiles as if he has just proved his own self-worth. "It's where all the truly brilliant minds go, Mr. Fegley, to learn from the best and the brightest, where geniuses are paid to exchange ideas, one generation mentoring the next. Albert Einstein himself was once a member of the faculty. Paid to think, Mr. Fegley. Can you imagine anything better? Before you walked into my office this morning, would you ever have imagined that such a place even exists?"

No. Never. Not in Mead's wildest dreams. He wants to hear more. He wants to know all about this oasis of knowledge. "Have you ever been there, Dr. Kustrup?"

"When I was a much younger man. Yes. When I had time to research and write and publish my own papers. But eventually other obligations got in the way. I married and started a family and had less time to devote to my beloved math. Such a luxury is reserved for the young and unattached, Mr. Fegley. You've got to strike while the iron is hot. So tell me, are you ready to strike?"

Heart racing, Mead perches on the edge of his chair and says, "What do I have to do to get in?"

HE'S STANDING OUTSIDE OF EPPS HALL as if waiting to meet someone. Mead recognizes him right off: Mr. Paris France, better known as Herman Weinstein. The guy glances up and looks directly at Mead, who nods as if to say hello, but Herman shows no sign of recognizing him back. He stares at Mead blank-faced. It's terribly unnerving. So Mead drops his eyes and decides to play along, to pretend as if they have never before met. Which they haven't. Not formally, that is. Who knows, maybe the guy truly does not remember Mead. After all, it was Herman who came waltzing into the exam late, making a public spectacle of himself, attracting all that attention, not Mead. There was that odd wave near the end of the exam when Mead was leaving but perhaps, in the world that Herman comes from, it is common to wave to people who will be forgotten a moment later. Maybe Herman is one of those socialite types who treats everyone he meets as if they are his best friend but in fact has no true friends at all. Mead trots down the front steps then glances back to see if Herman is still looking at him. But the guy is gone.

DR. KUSTRUP SIGNS MEAD UP FOR HIS COURSE in Theoretical Geometry. Eighteen students show up for the first day of class, twelve show up on the second, and by the end of two weeks, there are only seven students remaining. Even Mead, who has never met a math class he did not love, who went through four math tutors just last summer, is finding it difficult to keep up. The professor's lectures are, to say the least, confusing. But Mead cannot figure out if it is himself or the professor who is the problem. By the end of the third week, however, he is all but convinced that he does not have what it takes to understand the concepts of higher mathematics. That he is woefully in over his head. It was easier in High Grove. Easy to be the big fish in such a small academic pond. Mead remembers what Percy said to him right before he left. About drowning in the ocean. And now it seems to be coming true. And so Mead does what any drowning man would do: He thrashes about in the water hoping to find air.

MEAD IS HUNCHED OVER HIS GEOMETRY BOOK, deep in thought, when someone says, "Must be really interesting, should I leave you two alone?" He looks up and sees Cynthia Broussard standing over him, the girl who was sitting with Pete and his friends in the cafeteria that day. The girl who knows that Mead's mother picks out his clothes for him. That he does not yet shave. "Actually," Mead says, "I don't understand a word of what I'm reading. They may have to send me back to high school."

She laughs, then sets her lunch tray on the table and sits down across from him. "Don't worry, we all feel that way. The first year is supposed to be the hardest."

"Really?" Mead says and closes the book, leaving his finger tucked inside to mark the page. "This is a common occurrence?"

"You say that as if it's never happened to you before."

"It hasn't."

She laughs again. "I like you, Mead. You're different. Very open and honest. Very real. It's refreshing. Most the boys around here are only interested in one thing."

"Beer?"

She laughs again. "Well, that too, I guess."

Cynthia eats her salad and continues to talk. About her classes. About how she has not yet picked a major. And Mead listens. Then she glances at her watch and says she has to get to her next class, that she hopes to run into him again sometime. Then she stands up and leaves. Only then does Mead remove his finger from the pages of his geometry book. His concentration shot. His place lost. And the thing is, he doesn't care. For the first time in his life, he doesn't really care.

"DAMN IT ALL TO HELL, NOT AGAIN."

Mead looks up from his geometry book. He thought it might be better to study out of doors for a change, to get off campus and away from the cafeteria. Seven days. Seven days in a row he sat at the same table at the same time hoping to run into Cynthia again, but she never showed up. And now he has fallen even further behind in class. He thought maybe the fresh air would clear his head, that it might wake up some latent brain cells, but so far it isn't working out that way. He just keeps getting interrupted. First there was the homeless man looking for spare change, then it was the garbage truck, and now this: some old guy with bloodhound jowls and long, gray hair pulled back into a ponytail. Some half-senile senior riding around the city on his hundred-year-old rusting bicycle instead of the bus so he'll have enough money at the end of the month to pay his utility bill. Some crazy lunatic cursing at life.

"Excuse me," Mead says. "Is everything all right?"

The man looks up as if surprised to discover that he is not alone in the world. "No, everything is not all right," he says. "The chain on my bicycle fell off and now it's jammed in the gear and I can't get it out."

Mead gets up off the bench he has been sitting on for the past two hours and steps over to the bike. He watches the old guy tug at the chain a few times, then lays down his geometry book and says, "Here, let me give it a try."

"It's jammed in there too tight," the old man says. "It's hopeless." But he steps back anyway, his hands covered in black grease. Mead wraps his clean hands around the chain, yanks once, and it pops right out. He turns to the old guy and says, "You must've loosened it up."

The old man does not respond, just takes a handkerchief out of his pocket and offers it to Mead. "Here. Wipe off your hands."

"Thanks," Mead says and takes the handkerchief even though he has one of his own in his back pocket, so the old guy won't feel completely useless. And while he is wiping his hands clean, the half-senile senior points to Mead's geometry book, with all Mead's various and sundry notations scrawled in the margins, and says, "You're going about it all wrong."

"Excuse me?"

"You're taking Theoretical Geometry with Dr. Kustrup, am I right?"

"Yes. How did you know?"

"Because only Kustrup could turn simple logic into a complicated labyrinth. Allow me to lay out for you some of the basic principles of geometry, just enough to get you back on the right track." And the old man proceeds to pull Mead up out of the depths of the ocean, to give him the mathematical equivalent of CPR. Then, just as suddenly, he hops back on his bike and says, "I have to go. If I'm late, the wife worries and when she worries, I have to explain. And I hate to give long explanations."

"Wait," Mead says. "Who are you? Are you a teacher or something?"

"Yes, something like that," the old man says and pedals off

before Mead can ask him any more questions. He catches a glimpse of the license plate, though, hanging from the back of the seat. It's easy to remember because there are only three letters: PNT.

ANOTHER SEVEN DAYS COME AND GO. Mead eats lunch in the cafeteria every day but Cynthia never shows. He is beginning to think that she is avoiding him, that he said or did something wrong. But what? Mead barely said a word. Maybe that's it. Maybe he should have talked more. What he needs is another opportunity. One more chance to get it right.

He goes back to the park too. The following Saturday. Sits on the same bench hoping to run into the old guy again, but he never shows either. So Mead goes to the library. He looks through the CU faculty directory for a professor with the initials of PNT and, finding none either past or present, comes to the conclusion that the old man must have taught at another university. Way back when. Mead feels disappointed that the old professor did not come back to the park looking for him, that Cynthia never came back to the cafeteria, and so he does what he always does when confronted with the frustrations of everyday life: He throws himself back into his studies.

FOUR STUDENTS SHOW UP FOR THE FINAL EXAM. Mead gets the only A. But Dr. Kustrup is not the slightest bit concerned. He does not seem to get it that his students' failures are really his own. As a matter of fact, he seems quite pleased with himself.

"My job is to separate the men from the boys," he says to Mead as they sit together in his stuffy office. "I'm known around here as the gatekeeper to the math department. If a student cannot pass my course, then he just does not have what it takes to be a mathematician. Only the best get past me. Only the brightest and the best."

Mead might beg to differ but he doesn't say a word because he knows better. And because Dr. Kustrup has promised him a glorious future.

MEAD SEES HER CROSSING CAMPUS. Cynthia Broussard. He sees her and drops his eyes to the sidewalk in case she looks up. To avoid an uncomfortable conversation. An awkward moment. She has probably forgotten all about him by now, all about their lunch that day. A day Mead cannot stop thinking about.

"Hey," she says. "Mead, long time, no see. How're you doing?"

He looks up then into her big brown eyes. "I got an A," he says. "In geometry."

"Congratulations."

"Actually, I got A's in all my classes."

"See, I told you there was nothing to worry about."

"And I'm sixteen now, have been for six weeks. I've started shaving, too. Last month, in fact. Bought a razor and everything."

She laughs. "That's great, Mead. Sounds like things are working out for you."

And it gives him a burst of confidence. Her laugh. So he says, "How come I never see you in the cafeteria anymore?"

"Oh. I got a part-time job working in the administrative office."

Mead is relieved to hear this, to know that she has not been avoiding him after all. "I enjoyed it," he says. "That lunch."

She smiles. "Yeah, so did I."

"Maybe we could do it again sometime. Lunch."

"I'd like that," she says. "I'd like that a lot." Then glances at her watch. "Oh, shoot. I'm late. I'll see you around, Mead, okay?" And she rushes off.

He watches her go, her long brown hair bouncing around her shoulders as she hurries away. He has a date. He actually asked a girl out and she accepted. It only dawns on him later, when he is lying in bed unable to sleep, that he forgot to pick an exact day.

THOSE A'S CATAPULT MEAD right onto the Dean's List and get him an invitation to the big man's office. As Mead sits outside the dean's wood-paneled sanctuary, he cannot help but wish that his mother were here to witness the moment. To see all her hard work and dedication come to fruition. She would be tickled to death. And she would probably tell him to sit up straight and tuck in his shirt, so he does just that.

"He's ready to see you now," the secretary says. "You can go right in."

Dean Falconia is a tall, thin man with very straight posture and a quiet air of confidence about him that reminds Mead of his dad. He likes him right off.

"It's an honor to finally meet you," the dean says as he shakes Mead's hand and gestures for him to sit down. "It's rare for us to have a matriculating student as young as yourself. Even rarer for one to do so well in his first quarter."

"Thank you, sir."

"I just wanted to congratulate you, Theodore, to tell you face-to-face how proud and excited I am to have you here at Chicago University. Keep up the good work, son. You're off to a fine start."

"Mead, sir, I prefer to be called Mead."

"I understand that your father runs his own business."

"Yes, sir, he does, sir."

"That's hard work, running one's own business, and he has obviously passed that work ethic onto you. You're lucky to have been given such a good role model."

"I suppose, sir."

The dean stands up; their meeting is over. "If ever you need anything, Mead, or have any questions, I hope you won't hesitate to call on me."

"I won't, sir. Thank you, sir." And he shakes the dean's hand once more.

On the way out of the building, he sees him again. Herman Weinstein. The guy is leaning against the stoop, staring off into space, waiting for who knows what. They exchange a look but Mead does not nod. Not this time. He acts as if he does not recognize Herman and keeps going. At the bottom of the steps, though, Mead cannot resist turning back to see if Herman is looking at him. But the guy is gone.

Mead rides the train home for Christmas. He has been gone only a couple of months but it feels like years. He can hardly wait to tell his mother about Dr. Kustrup and the Dean's List and the Institute for Advanced Study. He will spring the good news on her over supper when his dad and Uncle Martin and Aunt Jewel and Percy are all over at the house, sitting around the table, eager to hear tales from the first Fegley ever to attend a university, everyone hanging on his every word. Mead will start with a brief description of each course, followed by a quick summary of what he learned. Build up the suspense. Make it clear how hard he has studied. Then he will hit them with the Dean's List. That's the part that will most impress his mother. What he will not mention is Cynthia. Because it is too soon. He will save that news for his next visit home, after they have been dating awhile. For now he wants his family to focus exclusively on his academic achievements. Only that is not how it happens.

"He did what?" Mead says.

"Packed his bag and took off," Mead's mother says. "Last week. There was no note or anything. He just disappeared—poof—

without a clue." She is stuffing a twenty-pound turkey as she talks, filling its ass with bread crumbs. "Your aunt and uncle are worried. They don't know what to think, where to look for him. They've just been worried sick."

So he did it. Percy actually did it. He packed his bags and ran off to join a minor league baseball team just the way he said he was going to. Mead thought his cousin was bluffing. After all, that was five years ago. A lifetime ago. They were just kids, dreaming out loud. Truth be told, Mead didn't think Percy had it in him to just up and leave without telling anyone. After all, his cousin has everything a person could possibly want right here in High Grove. Great parents, loads of friends, local fame. Isn't that enough? Why is Percy being so greedy? It's supposed to be Mead's turn now to take center stage and get all the glory. Mead's turn to be the most popular guy in town. He's waited a long time for this, through nine long years of torture from his fellow classmates. It isn't fair.

Poor Aunt Jewel, she must be freaking out. Mead should say something. He should speak up and tell his mother that he knows where Percy is. He should put his aunt and uncle out of their misery. But Mead gave Percy his word: He promised his cousin that he would not tell. And so he doesn't.

"I want you to be extra courteous this evening," his mother says. "Sensitive to what your aunt and uncle are going through."

"What? Like usually I'm not?"

The front doorbell rings. "That must be them now," his mother says, ignoring his sarcastic comment. "Answer the door for me, will you, Teddy?"

"Mead, Mom. I like to be called Mead now."

"Go," she says and waves him out of the kitchen with her oven mitt.

"Well, look at you," Aunt Jewel says when Mead opens the

door. "The big university boy all grown up. College must be agreeing with you. You look great, Teddy. Come here, dear, and give your old aunt a hug. Doesn't he look great, Martin?"

"Hmph," Mead's uncle says and brushes past them into the living room.

He almost says something right then and there, almost tells his aunt and uncle where Percy is, to put their troubled minds at ease. But a promise is a promise. Besides, if he were to tell, he wouldn't know if he was doing it for his aunt or uncle or for himself, as a way to get back at Percy for breaking their unwritten agreement, for trying to retain the title of "most popular boy in High Grove" beyond its natural expiration date. So Mead keeps his mouth shut. After all, he did not come home to talk about his cousin; he came home to talk about himself.

"I've been assigned to this faculty advisor," Mead says once everyone is seated around the table, "who believes that I have what it will take to be invited to study at this elite institute in Princeton where Einstein himself once taught."

"That's wonderful, dear," his Aunt Jewel says and pats his hand.

"But hardly a surprise," his mother says. "Tell us more about this institute, Teddy."

"He's run off with some harebrained idea of joining a ball club," Martin says. "I'll bet my life on it. I thought some sense had gotten knocked into that boy's head when they passed him over for the draft. Some busybody scout must've encouraged him to try and get signed on as a free agent. I've got half a mind to hop in the car, drive down to Houston, and drag that boy back home by the collar."

"I'd have to advise against that," Mead's dad says. "First off, you don't know that he's in Houston. And secondly, he'd just turn right around and go back. I think you should let this thing play itself out, Martin. Let Percy come back on his own. In his own time."

"Lynn's right," Mead's mother says. "I mean, what're the odds that he's actually good enough to get signed as a free agent anyway? Now, Teddy, tell us about that institute."

Martin slams down his fork. "And what makes you think that my son is not good enough, Alayne?"

"Calm down, Martin, I'm just being supportive. You just said yourself that you don't want him playing professional ball. So Teddy, as you were saying."

"I don't want him to not play because he isn't good enough," Martin says. "He is damn well good enough. I don't want him to play because he belongs here. In High Grove. Working alongside his old man."

Mead's mother shakes her head. "Well, now you're just not making sense."

"Oh, I'm making sense, all right, I'm making plenty of sense. It's a family tradition, Fegley Brothers. A way of life passed down for one generation to the next. But then I guess you wouldn't get it, would you?" And he glares at Mead.

"By the way," Mead says, pleased to have the floor again. "Does everyone here know that I completed my freshman year of college in one week?"

"I'm just saying," Mead's dad says, "give Percy some time. Playing on that level entails a lot of physical and mental stress. I'm not sure he's prepared for it, that Percy knows what'll be expected of him. He'll come home when he figures that out, when he realizes he's in over his head."

"And I made the Dean's List," Mead says. "It's really quite an honor."

Martin shoves back his chair and stands up. "In over his head? Have you ever seen my son pitch? He could never get in over his head."

Mead excuses himself from the supper table but no one notices, except maybe his mother. He goes to his room and closes the door. Next break he'll just stay in Chicago.

MEAD KNOCKS ON DR. KUSTRUP'S OFFICE DOOR. "Come in, come in," the professor says and waves him into the office. It isn't until after Mead has entered that he sees the professor already has a guest, none other than Herman Weinstein.

"I'm sorry," Mead says and starts to back out. "I didn't realize you were busy. I must be early. I'll just wait out here in the hall until you're done." But when he checks his watch, he sees that he has arrived right on time.

"You're not early at all, Mr. Fegley," Dr. Kustrup says. "Mr. Weinstein and I were just chatting about the skiing conditions in the Alps and lost track of time. Please, have a seat. This is great, actually; it's about time you two met. Mr. Weinstein here is my other protégé. I feel quite blessed to have the both of you under my tutelage at one time, quite blessed indeed. You two should get acquainted. You have a lot in common, you know, what with both of you breezing through your comprehensives and diving straight into your sophomore years. Well, Mr. Weinstein here needed a little brushing up on his calculus, but I've caught him up to speed and now he, too, is on the fast track to an early graduation. Please, Mr. Fegley, sit down."

Mead is surprised. He wouldn't have taken Mr. Weinstein for an exceptional student of academe. Cocky, yes. A little bit creepy, absolutely. But exceptional? No. The guy stands up and extends his hand. "Please," he says, "call me Herman. And you are?"

"Here to work out a course schedule for next quarter," Mead says and lets the guy's hand hang unattended in the air.

"Apparently I've overstayed my welcome," Herman says. Then, smooth as silk, as if it was what he intended all along, he pats Mead on the shoulder, then reaches across the professor's desk and shakes his hand instead. "I'll talk with you later, Frank. *Ciao.*" Then he turns back to Mead and says, "He's all yours, Mead. Take it away." And leaves. And Mead wonders how it is that Herman Weinstein knows that he does not like to be called Theodore.

"Mr. Fegley," Dr. Kustrup says after Herman has left. "Speaking to you as your faculty advisor, and as a friend, allow me to suggest that you might want to brush up on your social skills. It just so happens that Herman's father is someone who could be of considerable importance to you down the line. The dean of all things possible and impossible. That's what Herman likes to call him. In other words, the man has connections, very important connections. He could be quite influential in deciding whether or not you someday get an invitation to attend the Institute for Advanced Study in Princeton."

"Oh," Mead says, "that explains it."

"Explains what?"

Why the guy has such a cocky, better-than-thou attitude, that's what. But Mead keeps this observation to himself. "Thank you, sir, for the tip. About my social skills, I mean. And about Mr. Weinstein. I'll keep them both in mind."

MEAD LOOKS FOR HER IN THE CAFETERIA. While walking across campus. In the library. He even strolls through the administrative building a couple of times hoping that he will run into her in the hall. But Cynthia is nowhere to be found. Mead has almost convinced himself that she has dropped out of college—gone back home to Virginia—when he sees her exiting the student center. "Cynthia," he calls out and waves his hand over his head. She looks up and smiles and his confidence grows. "I've been looking all over for you," he says once he has caught up to her. "I forgot to pick a day. For our lunch. Last time we talked."

"That's so sweet," she says. "That you remember."

"Of course I remember. I haven't thought about anything else since. Well, you know, except about my coursework. So when do you want to do it?" Mead says and blushes because he knows what that might sound like and that is not what he means, not at all. "Lunch, I mean. When do you want to do lunch?"

She smiles again. "I'm sorry, I can't."

"Excuse me?"

"I'm afraid I might have given you the wrong impression before. I like you, Mead, I really do. You're smart and funny and sweet, but you're only sixteen. I mean, my little brother is sixteen. I'm flattered. Really, I am. But it just wouldn't work out. You and me. Dating. I'm sorry."

Mead feels dizzy. He thinks maybe he has heard wrong and yet he knows he has heard right. That he is being rejected. Again. Because of his age. Because he does not fit in. Does not conform to some preordained mold. Only this is worse. Worse than spitballs, worse than name-calling, worse than having his head flushed down the toilet.

Cynthia places her hand on his arm. "Don't worry, Mead, you're a nice guy, a really nice guy. In a few years the right girl will come along, you'll see." Then she leaves. But the touch of her hand lingers, burns a hole straight through Mead's heart.

HE STUDIES AT THE LIBRARY until it closes at midnight then heads back to the dorm. Mead hates Saturday night. It only serves to remind him of how much he does not fit in. Dr. Kustrup suggested he work on his social skills but Mead's problem has nothing to do with social skills. Not one goddamned thing. His problem is his age and no amount of effort on Mead's behalf will ever change the simple fact that he has always been too young to socialize with his academic peers.

Music greets him even before he opens the front door, escaping from a window on an upper floor as if a mental patient is crying out for help. He enters the dorm and the music gets louder, throbbing through his body as if someone is pounding on his head with a hammer. Mead reaches for the doorknob to his room feeling like a gambler at a slot machine. Will Pete be in there with his gaggle of rowdy friends? Or are they hanging out in Rick's room tonight? In which case Mead will be able to enjoy at least a modicum of peace and quiet. Mead crosses his fingers and opens the door. Jackpot, the room is empty.

He grabs his toiletries and heads down the hall to the bathroom. Someone is in the shower, could be male or female. He brushes his teeth and hopes it is female, hopes she did not hear him come in. If he is lucky, he will get a quick glimpse of her body before she notes his presence and covers herself up. That is all he is hoping for, a quick glimpse. That's all he needs. He can take it from there.

His mouth is full of mint-flavored paste when the shower shuts off and a girl steps around the corner, his luck still holding. She either does not know he is here or does not care as she takes her towel and proceeds to dry her hair. Mead stops brushing and watches her, or rather her reflection in the mirror. He wonders what Cynthia is doing right now, if she is spending her Saturday night with some age-appropriate date, making out in some dorm room with a twenty-year-old undergraduate with a mediocre grade point average and a questionable future.

"Lights out!" the resident advisor yells out in the hall. "All stereos off. Now!"

The dorm goes silent, quiet enough to hear the water running in the sink. To hear Mead's heart pounding against his chest as he continues to stare at the naked girl. One or the other causes her to lift her eyes and, when she does, she sees Mead looking back.

"Oops," she says. "I didn't realize anyone else was here, otherwise I'd have been more discreet." And she proceeds to cover herself with the towel. Mead drops his eyes, ashamed. A moment later she taps him on the shoulder and he looks up. "Your face," she says and points at the mirror, then leaves. Mead checks out his reflection and sees a swath of toothpaste extending all the way from his mouth to his left ear.

An envelope arrives in Mead's mailbox, postmarked Houston, Texas. He knows who sent it even before he opens the envelope and finds inside a snapshot of Percy wearing a minor league baseball uniform, a bat slung over his right shoulder, a smile plastered across his face. On the back of the snapshot he has scrawled, "Hey, cousin, we did it. We both got away. I'm a free agent! Yours, Percy."

Mead tucks the snapshot inside his *Concepts of Math* textbook and closes it.

So it turns out that Mead's father was wrong. It seems that this whole professional baseball thing is neither too physically nor too mentally challenging for Percy to handle after all. Well, one thing is for certain: Percy is not going to give up the helm without a fight. Mead is going to have to do more than simply graduate from college in order to outshine his cousin. Way more. Because even Mead knows that being a math major is nothing compared to being a major league ballplayer. Not in the eyes of the citizens of High Grove, Illinois. No way. Not that Percy is there yet. But the possibility grows stronger every day. Which means that Mead has got to stay on top of his own game. He has got to make sure that, come hell or high water, he will get into that exclusive institute in Princeton where Albert Einstein himself once taught.

"CAN I GIVE YOU ANOTHER REFILL on that, honey?" the waitress standing over Mead asks.

"Yes, thank you," he says and she refills his glass with milk.

Mead has been coming to this off-campus coffee shop for breakfast every day—ever since Cynthia blew him off—to cut back on the probability of running into her again. He fills up on pancakes and eggs and bacon and then skips lunch, going to the cafeteria only for dinner, showing up right before it closes, when the place is nearly deserted. The food is better here at the coffee shop anyway. And it doesn't cost much. He fed himself for two weeks on the money his mother sent him for a new shirt. This weekend he will call home and tell her he needs a new coat. That ought to get him through to the summer. The view is better too. Mead likes it when the waitress leans over the table to refill his glass, likes the scenery her low-cut blouse provides.

"You must be really smart," she says, standing over him now, looking at the books Mead has spread across the table. She smiles when she says this and Mead wonders if she is flirting with him, if all these books make Mead look older than his sixteen years. "Do you go to school around here?" she asks.

"I'm a matriculate of Chicago University."

"A what?"

Who is he fooling. Mead could never date a girl who doesn't speak the same language he speaks. He picks up his milk and drains the entire glass in one gulp, sets it back down on the table.

"My, my," the waitress says. "You are one thirsty young man." And she leans over to refill his glass once more.

"THERE HAVE BEEN SOME exciting developments taking shape in the math department," Dr. Kustrup says to Mead. "Changes of which you may not be aware since your head has been buried so deeply inside your books the past two quarters." And he says this as if it is a bad thing, as if Mead should be spending less time studying in the library and more time skiing in the Alps in Switzerland.

"I'm sorry, sir," Mead says, "but my father has poured a rather large portion of his life savings into my education and I'd like to see him get his money's worth."

Dr. Kustrup laughs. "Yes, I recently learned that you turned down a rather generous scholarship in favor of paying for your own college education."

"My father turned it down, sir, not me. It's his money, not mine."

"And why, may I ask, would he do such a thing?"

"I don't know, sir. Perhaps he felt the value of my education would be compromised if it were based upon a bribe."

"A scholarship can hardly be considered a bribe, Mr. Fegley. Quite to the contrary, in fact. Most people would consider it high compliment."

"My father is not most people, sir."

Dr. Kustrup laughs again. "And I see that you take after him. Well, that's a fine attitude, Mr. Fegley. Admirable even, but one that is a tad bit naïve. I'm not saying that your education isn't important—it most certainly is—I'm just saying that there are other things that are equally important."

"Such as?"

"Such as interaction with your colleagues. Do you realize,

Mr. Fegley, that I see less of you than I do of any other student under my watch?"

"I'm a self-starter, Dr. Kustrup. I don't need much supervision."

The professor gets up from behind his desk and walks over to his window that looks out over the quad below. As usual, it is stiflingly hot in his office. Mead wishes Dr. Kustrup would fling open the window, would let in some fresh air. But he seems to like it this way, all stuffy and enclosed. He sits on the radiator under the window, looks at Mead, and says, "I've recently taken on some new responsibilities, Mr. Fegley. I've been elected by my fellow colleagues to take over the helm next year. You're looking at the new chairman of the mathematics department."

Mead wonders how this happened. Dr. Kustrup must have skills that outshine his teaching ability. Organizational skills, perhaps. People skills. Why else would he have been chosen to chair the department? But, more important, Mead wonders how this will affect him, if it might improve his chances of getting into that institute in Princeton.

"Congratulations, sir," he says.

"Thank you, Mr. Fegley," Dr. Kustrup says. "There are a few downsides, however. Next year I won't have as much time to devote to my students. I'll only be able to teach two classes per quarter instead of my usual load of four, what with all my added responsibilities as chairman of the department."

"Of course," Mead says, still wondering what the downsides are.

"Additionally," Dr. Kustrup says. "I'll only have time to mentor one of you."

"Excuse me?" Mead says.

Dr. Kustrup steps back over to his desk. He sits down, leans forward on his elbow patches, and says, "I'm sorry, Mr. Fegley, but I had to make a choice and I've decided that it will be in everyone's best interest if I work exclusively with Mr. Weinstein next year. Don't take this personally. You have a lot of potential, Mr. Fegley, but you're younger, almost three years younger than Mr. Weinstein. You have a great future ahead of you but I feel that you will need more time to mature into the mathematician I know you can one day be. I think the smartest thing you could do right now is slow down. Go home for the summer. Relax. Take up a hobby. Diversify your interests. You'll get there, Mr. Fegley, don't worry. I just won't be the one helping you make it happen."

Mead hears it. He actually hears the saw cutting its way through the floor, sees its nose moving up and down, sees the curve of the line it is cutting around his chair. Any minute now the floor will give way and Mead will fall through it.

"Don't look so forlorn, Mr. Fegley. I'm not going to leave you high and dry. I've reassigned you to Professor Alexander. He's going to be your new faculty advisor. He's a brilliant mathematician. I'd introduce you to him right now only he's away on sabbatical working on some top-secret project. He's been working on it for decades, won't let anyone here at the university in on what it is. Anyway, as soon as you return in the fall, I'll make all the necessary introductions."

Mead stands up. "May I go now?"

"Don't leave angry, Mr. Fegley. You just wait and see. You'll do fine without me." He stands up too, and extends his hand across the desk. "It's been a pleasure."

Mead refuses to shake the hand of a traitor. He turns and storms out of the professor's office, leaving the man's hand hanging in midair.

HE IS STILL FUMING ABOUT DR. KUSTRUP when he sees Cynthia Broussard. She's walking across campus holding his hand. Her boyfriend's hand. The guy she chose over Mead. Cynthia does not see Mead but her boyfriend does. The guy looks right at him and then looks away. Then they disappear around the corner of Epps Hall. The two of them. Still holding hands. Cynthia Broussard and Herman Weinstein.

WITH ONE SWEEP OF HIS ARM, Mead knocks every book on his shelf to the floor. Damn him! Damn that sonofabitch Herman Weinstein! It isn't fair. It isn't fair that Herman should get Cynthia, that he should get Dr. Kustrup. What is the point? What is the point of studying hard and working your ass off if some lucky sonofabitch who just happens to be rich and good looking and three years older can just walk off with all the prizes? Isn't being a good person worth anything anymore? Doesn't hard work account for something? Has it gotten to the point where the only way to get ahead in this world is to spend your free time skiing in the Alps?

Mead glances at the floor and sees Percy in the form of a snapshot looking back. It must have fallen out of Mead's math book. His cousin is laughing. In the photograph. Mocking Mead. Telling him that he will never have what the Percys and Hermans of this world have: the adoration of everyone they meet. Mead picks up the photograph and rips it in half, then rips it again, and again, letting the pieces flutter to the floor.

5

97.6°F

High Grove
Six Days Before Graduation

A FIGHT IS TAKING PLACE IN THE HALL, two people arguing over who knows what. A broken stereo. Stolen weed. A girl. Mead folds his pillow over his ears to try and block out the noise but it doesn't help; their voices penetrate like a pounding drum. It's one of the things he hates most about living in the dorms: the noise of all those other people interrupting his thoughts. There's nothing he can do about it but get up and head to the library for some peace and quiet. Mead rolls over to grab his alarm clock, to see what time it is, and grabs air instead. Because he isn't in the dorm. He's at home.

Sitting up makes him feel dizzy. He has a boulder on his neck where he once had a head. But it's all coming back to him now. The Lodge last night. The beer. His uncle. Dry-mouthed and heavy-lidded, Mead drags himself out of bed and into the hall. The door to his parent's bedroom is closed but he can hear what they're saying nonetheless, loud and clear.

"What could you've been thinking, taking him to the Lodge, getting him drunk?"

"I didn't get him drunk, Alayne."

"You're encouraging him, is what you're doing. He needs to see the terrible mistake he's making. We need to get him back up to the university. He's throwing away his life, Lynn. Are you just going to sit back and let him do it?"

"He asked me to let him figure things out on his own so that's what I'm doing."

"No, what you're doing is watching your son flush his life down the toilet, that's what you're doing."

"Would it be so awful if he came back here, Alayne? If he worked in the store with me and his uncle? Would it really be the end of the world?"

"Yes!"

Mead goes into the bathroom, closes the door, and turns on the shower. To drown out their voices. Standing in front of the sink, he rummages through the medicine cabinet looking for something—anything—to put an end to his throbbing head and queasy stomach. Forsbeck used to wash down a handful of aspirin with a can of Coke before heading off to class after a night of rabble-rousing. He swore by it. But Mead's mother doesn't have any aspirin—she never gets headaches, she only gives them—so he grabs the next best thing: a package of Alka-Seltzer.

While the tablets effervesce, Mead grabs his stomach and tells it to hang in there for a couple more seconds. Tells himself that he isn't going to throw up again. The only other time his stomach felt this bad was when Dean Falconia called Mead into his office to tell him the good news. "A great development," was how he put it. "Exciting news." "An event." But Mead just felt sick to his stomach.

He steps under the spray of hot water and lets it pound against the back of his neck until he cannot feel it anymore. Only then does he unbutton his shirt—the one he wore to the Lodge last night and never took off—and let it drop, along with his sleep-pressed trousers and day-old underwear, to the bottom of the tub. By the time he steps back out of the shower and shuts off the water, the house has gone quiet. The argument is over. He wraps a towel around his waist and tiptoes back across the hall, leaving a trail of water droplets on the floor. The perfect foil. Because as soon as his mother sees them, she starts yelling again. At Mead, this time, for ruining her beautiful hardwood floor, for being so inconsiderate. And the yelling gets worse when she discovers his clothes in the tub. None of which bothers Mead. He'd rather she yell at him about clothes and water than about ruining his life. At least those are things about which she can do something. Not his life. There's nothing she can do about that and neither can he. Thanks to Herman. Except, of course, what he is doing. Like working in the store. Like trying to make things right with his uncle.

Mead dresses quickly, throws open the window, and crawls through it, landing in the middle of his mother's flowerbed. Something else about which she will be able to get mad and he will make right. He pulls on his shoes as he runs down the driveway, buttons his shirt as he hurries along the street. Only when the house is out of sight does he slow to a walk. He just needs to give her a few days to get used to the idea, to come to terms with the new reality. Next week things should begin to get better—after graduation has come and gone—because then there won't be anything to fight about anymore. It will be a done deal. Until then, Mead intends to put as much distance as possible between himself and the six-legged creature.

A SHINY BLACK CADILLAC SITS IN THE LOT behind Fegley Brothers, parked next to an equally shiny black hearse, both of which have been washed and polished by Lenny for today's big event: the funeral of Delia Winslow. Mead's father will be acting as head of ceremonies, leading the parade (i.e., funeral procession) through the streets of High Grove to the cemetery, located just on the outskirts of town. An event that takes place on an average of once a week, putting food on the Fegley table and clothes on the Fegley back. It's also what paid for Mead's college education. Dead bodies. And all the pomp and circumstance that goes into bidding them a proper adieu. And Mead doesn't want to have a thing to do with it. He decided a long time ago that he wants to be cremated. No casket. No flowers. No ride to the cemetery through the streets of town. He wants to go without the fuss. Put his ashes in an urn and stick him on a library shelf, that's what he'd like: for his dust to mingle with the dust of great books. A thought he has never shared with his father out of fear that it might upset him. And what would be the point? Because by that time the old man will be long gone.

Mead's dad steps out of the Cadillac dressed to the nines. Black suit, black tie, black shoes. The exact same outfit he was planning to wear to his son's graduation next week. How appropriate it would have been had Mead taken Herman up on his offer. Unbeknownst to his father, he would have been attending a funeral of morals, so to speak. But Mead didn't even consider Herman's offer. Not for a second. And for that reason he gets to live another day with his head held high.

"You crawled out the window?" his father says.

The man looks tired, as if he spent his whole morning being yelled at. He's probably wondering if maybe it wasn't in his best interest to stand in solidarity next to a boy who thinks the best way to deal with his overwrought mother is to climb out a bedroom window, even if that boy is his beloved son. "Sorry, Dad."

"The dean called again. He wants you to call him back."

This is not what Mead wants to hear. "Yeah, well, we don't always get what we want, now do we?"

His father stares at him. Mead can almost see the gears moving in his head, can see the words forming on his tongue. He wants to ask his son why he came home, why he won't talk to the dean. Why he's sitting here on the bench behind the store and not in the university library doing final edits on his senior paper. He wants to know so he will have something to say to his wife the next time she starts yelling at him. To defend his actions. To give him a reason to keep standing behind his son. But he doesn't ask. Instead he says, "The wake is scheduled to begin at ten. Do me a favor and run over to the A & P. We're low on everything: Kleenex, half-and-half, styrofoam cups. I made a list." And he hands it to Mead along with a company credit card. "And don't forget to buy something for yourself. For breakfast. You must be starved."

Mead thinks to say thank you to his father. For standing up to Mead's mother. For not prying. For trusting his son to do the right thing with his life. But before the words can find their way to his lips, his father turns and disappears inside the store.

A RED VAN COMES DOWN THE ALLEY next to Fegley Brothers. Mead waits for the van to pull into the parking lot and get out of his way so he can go to the A & P. It backs up to the rear door and a young man of about Mead's age hops out. "Flower delivery," he says, "for the Winslow funeral." And he hands Mead a clipboard with a contract attached to it.

"I'm not authorized to sign this. You'll have to ask my father. He's inside."

"Oh, all right." The young man starts toward the door, then turns back and says, "Hey, you're Teddy Fegley, aren't you?"

Mead looks at the young man again. He has no idea who he is or why he thinks he knows Mead. Neither does he care. So he turns and starts to walk off.

"Oh, come on. You must remember me. Simon McClod? Sixth grade? We were in the Audubon Society together. You were president and I was secretary."

Oh, great. Another former classmate. This town is just crawling with them. Yes, he remembers, all right. He remembers the teacher deciding it would be fun to form a little club and elect officers. Mead was immediately nominated for president and his nominating committee was terrific. Very supportive. They flushed the head of anyone who dared oppose their chosen man down the toilet. And on the day Mead stood at the front of the room and lead the class through a recitation of the Audubon pledge, they showered him with their undivided support by pelting him with spitballs and rubber bands.

"Sorry," Mead says. "You must have me confused with someone else."

"No, it's you, all right. The little genius. That's what we used to call you. So, wow, what're you doing here? Hey, have you invented anything yet? Something I might've heard of?"

"The VCR," Mead says. "I invented the VCR."

"Really?"

Mead contemplates walking off and leaving Mr. McClod to gather his eyeballs up off the ground and put them back in their sockets. You ask a ridiculous question, you get a ridiculous answer. But then he changes his mind, "I'm joking. The VCR's been on the market for about a decade. I'd have had to've been eight when I invented it."

But Simon remains skeptical. Mead can see it in his eyes. He still thinks it might be possible. Now he doesn't know which version of the story to believe: the one that's the truth or the one that will be more fun to tell all his friends down at the Lodge or the local pub or wherever it is the young Mr. McClod hangs out after work.

* * *

MEAD RIPS OPEN A PACKAGE OF SALTED PEANUTS and eats them as he makes his way up one aisle and down the next in search of the items on his father's list. His mother would have a conniption fit if she saw him right now. She hates it when people snack on food they have not yet bought. "It's low class," she has been known to say on more than one occasion, "like wearing red underwear under white pants." Mead pops several more peanuts into his mouth, licking the salt off his fingers as he makes a right turn and heads down the frozen food aisle. And that's when he sees her: a woman dressed in bedroom slippers and a bathrobe. She's reaching into the ice-cream freezer, the top half of her body gone, hidden among half-gallon containers of fudge swirl, mint chocolate chip, and cherry vanilla; the lower half is surrounded by a foggy mist where the cold freezer air has mixed with the warmer air of the store. A grocery clerk sees her, too, and gives her the kind of look people usually reserve for the homeless and mentally disabled. "May I help you, ma'am?" the clerk says, but she cannot hear him, either because her head is in the freezer or another world. It's hard to tell which. So he says it again, louder this time, as if perhaps she is deaf as well as crazy. When she still does not respond, the grocery clerk looks at Mead as if to say, *what am I supposed to do now?* And Mead answers back with a look that says, *you got me.*

When she finally dislodges herself from the freezer, she looks at the clerk, neither surprised to see him nor aware that she is doing anything unusual, and says, "Why is it that the flavor I want is always way in the back, can you tell me that?" And she places the hard-to-find half-gallon of peppermint stick ice cream in her shopping cart.

"I don't know, ma'am," the clerk says and closes the freezer door as if getting that door closed were the most important thing in the whole wide world.

"Aunt Jewel?" Mead says.

The grocery clerk and woman look up at the same time.

"Teddy," the woman in the bathrobe says. "What're you doing here in High Grove?"

"I got home a couple days ago, Aunt Jewel, didn't Uncle Martin tell you?"

She looks at the grocery clerk, as if he might know the answer, then says, "My nephew's a genius. He graduated from high school when he was fifteen. Valedictorian of his class. And now he's a college graduate at the age of only eighteen. Isn't that wonderful? We're all so very proud of him."

The clerk looks at them both, as if they are equally nuts then heads off down the aisle to guard other frozen foods from the hands of other mindless customers.

"Why aren't you dressed, Aunt Jewel?"

She glances down in horror, as if expecting to discover that she is stark naked and looks reassured to discover that she isn't, then smiles and says, "I just wanted to pick up some ice cream, Teddy; it hardly seemed worth getting all dolled up for."

Which sounds plausible enough, in its own crazy way, so Mead lets the subject drop. In addition to peppermint stick ice cream, there are six one-pound containers of iodized salt in his aunt's cart. "Are you planning on baking something?" he asks.

"What? Oh no, this salt's for your uncle."

Mead looks at her. Waits.

"For the backyard. To kill the poison ivy."

"Oh." He walks her to the checkout counter, offering to put her items on his father's credit card, in case it also did not cross her mind to bring along some money. Only it did cross her mind and she insists on paying for her items herself.

It never dawned on Mead before just how much his aunt reminds him of Dr. Alexander. She with her bedroom slippers, he with his long ponytail. Neither of them very much concerned about what anyone else thinks. Mead imagines the two of them meeting by chance on a street corner, Dr. Alexander offering to give Jewel a ride home on his bicycle so she won't get her pink slippers dirty, his aunt accepting, the two of them leaving a trail of gaping mouths and flapping tongues in their wake. Unaware and unconcerned. It must be wonderful to get to a point in your life where you don't care anymore. Where you are so confident about who you are that it doesn't matter what anyone else thinks. Mead can only hope that he gets there one day soon.

Since his aunt walked to the store, he offers to escort her home and carries her groceries under the false pretense that he was heading in her direction anyway. This she does not object to. As a matter of fact, she seems pleased as punch to have his company and asks him to tell her about college life in the big city.

"There really isn't much to tell, Aunt Jewel. I went to class and studied in the library, is all. I didn't get off campus very often. Except, you know, that one time I flew out east." He stops talking. Shit. Why did he bring that up? The last thing he wants to do is remind his aunt that he missed her son's funeral. But she doesn't seem to make the connection, doesn't seem to be really listening. Instead of getting upset, she says, "And how about girls? Have you met anyone special?"

A brunette pops into Mead's head. She is lying on his bed, sleeping. Mead wraps his arm around her and falls asleep too. When he wakes up, she's gone.

"No, Aunt Jewel," he says. "No one special."

When they reach his aunt's house, she takes her groceries from him. "Thanks for walking me home, Teddy. I enjoyed the company." She walks up the driveway and lets herself in through the side door, waving goodbye before she disappears inside. Mead waits until the door shuts behind her then heads back over to the store.

* * *

THE PARKING LOT BEHIND FEGLEY BROTHERS is now filled with cars, the wake having already begun. Shit. Mead didn't realize how long it had taken him to walk his aunt home. He enters the chapel through the back door. The main room is filled with mourners who have gathered to socialize before paying their last respects to the dearly departed. The place is pretty crowded. Delia had a lot of friends, enough to keep Mead's father occupied as Mead hurriedly sets out the Kleenex boxes, then rips open a package of foam cups. He is arranging them in towers on the refreshment table when he is suddenly struck by a terrible thirst. It's those peanuts. He should have bought something to drink too, while he was at the store but he wasn't thinking about himself at the time; he was too busy worrying about his aunt. He picks up one of the foam cups and fills it with half-and-half.

"That's for the coffee," some woman says. "Not for drinking."

Like Mead doesn't already know this. Why do people do that? Why do they go around stating the obvious all the time? So what if he wants to drink his half-and-half by the cupful. Is it a federal crime? So what if his aunt wants to wear her bedroom slippers to the grocery store. Is she breaking any laws? No. No laws broken. No federal crime. No end of the world.

"It just so happens," Mead says, "that I drank a whole pot of black coffee for breakfast this morning, now I'm drinking the cream that goes in it, and later on I'll be helping myself to a large bowl of sugar."

The woman stares at him as if he were nuts. It is a very satisfying look. Perhaps now she has learned her lesson. Maybe next time she will think twice before walking up to some stranger and offering her unbidden advice.

"I know who you are," she says. "You're Alayne Fegley's son. The genius."

Oh shit. A classmate and now a friend of his mother's. Both in one morning. Could this town be any smaller?

"You wrote some kind of paper, didn't you? Gave a big presentation in front of a bunch of important people. Your mother can't stop talking about it. How proud she is of you. How much smarter you are than all the other bridge players' sons." The woman laughs as if she has just told a joke, then grasps hold of Mead's wrist. "Do you mind?" she says. "I've never touched a genius before."

Mead wants to yank his hand free, to flee the room. What does she think he is, a circus sideshow freak? Step right up, folks. For one dollar you can see a two-headed woman, a human baby with a tail, and a mathematical genius. He knocks back the entire cup of half-and-half in one gulp and says, "Yeah, well, we pretty much feel like regular human beings. I mean, all except for our body temperature. Did you know that geniuses have an average body temperature that's a full degree cooler than that of the average man? That's right, 97.6°F. And it's this cooler body temperature that scientists are now linking to superior brainpower. Something to do with how our other vital organs function more efficiently, allowing more oxygen-filled blood to travel up to our brains. You can feel it, can't you? That I'm cooler than average?"

"I can," the woman says. "You know, I really can."

Mead's uncle is glaring at him from across the room. The man may not know what Mead is up to but he's pretty damn sure it falls under the category of "no good." Sliding his wrist free, Mead says, "Excuse me, but I've got to go."

"Why aren't you wearing a suit?" Uncle Martin says.

"A suit? Why would I be wearing a suit?"

"Didn't your father tell you this morning? All our pallbearers are required to wear suits." Martin glances at his watch. "My brother may be willing to put up with your childish crap, but I'm not. You've got thirty minutes to go home, get changed, and get back here before we head out to the cemetery."

Yeah, right. Like Mead is going to go home and risk being cornered by the six-legged creature. No way. No how.

MEAD FLIPS A SWITCH and the circuit breaker thumps. That's how much voltage is running through the wires that power the twenty-three klieg lights attached to the ceiling of the selection room. Enough to light a stage on Broadway. Enough to light two stages. All for the benefit of show. Each one directed at a different casket. The most expensive models are kept up front, the ones meant to catch your eye as you first walk through the door. The farther into the room you go, the cheaper they get, with the cheapest model sitting all the way in the back corner next to the fire exit. One step up from a pine box. It is the rare customer who makes it all the way to the back of the room, who dares to bury his dearly departed in the economy casket.

Mead is not up here to look at caskets, however. He is more interested in the wardrobe department. After-Life Men's Wear is located on the third floor of Fegley Brothers in a walk-in closet off the selection room. That's not its official name. That's just what Mead called it when he was little. Clothes for the man who doesn't own anything suitable in which to be buried, or has shrunk so much in the last six months of life that his own clothes no longer fit.

Mead pulls a suit off the rack and holds it up to his chest. The jacket is too broad in the shoulder but it would probably fit Percy just right. He wouldn't like it, though. If Percy could have had his say, he would have been buried in his baseball uniform, but he didn't. Was it an open casket ceremony or closed? Questions like this Mead has not felt permitted to ask. Because he wasn't there. It depends on whether or not his cousin's face made contact with the windshield. Whether or not he was wearing a seat belt. Did he think about that as his car swerved off the road? Did he throw his hands up in front of his face to save his father from having to do a lot of arduous reconstruction? Or did he deliberately let it splinter the glass?

Monday afternoon. That's when it happened. Around one o'clock. Percy must have arrived at the dorm around noon, just in time for lunch. It would have been nearly empty. The dorm. Did he realize that it was spring break? But of course, he must have. He also would have known that Mead stays on campus during these breaks. Aunt Jewel would have told him. Or Uncle Martin. Somebody. How long did he wait before giving up? And what was so pressing that he had to come to Chicago anyway? Why couldn't he have waited two more months for Mead to come home? What was so goddamned urgent?

Pulling on the tailored black jacket, Mead suddenly remembers what distinguishes an After-Life suit from a regular suit: the zipper down the back. Which makes it easier to dress a man with stiff arms. Shit. What is he going to do now? He doesn't have time to run home and change anymore. It's this or nothing. So he pulls on the jacket and hurries back down to the chapel.

Mead makes his way through the reception area, nodding politely to mourners, all the while keeping his back to the wall. Most of them have left already, returned to their cars for the ride out to the cemetery. Mead slips into the viewing room and waits for the other pallbearers, stands next to a wreath of lilies nearly as tall as he is. Delia is no more than an arm's length away, lying in her open casket, but Mead refuses to look. Not after what he saw back at her house. He'll just wait until his father comes and closes the lid before he gets any closer, thank you very much.

But his father is not the one who comes through the door first. Samuel Winslow is: the son of the deceased. Shit. Last time Mead spoke to the man, he was handing the undertaker's son a cold drink so he wouldn't pass out. He nods at Mead as he makes his way toward the casket. Mead tries to slip out of the room, to give the man a little privacy, but before he can escape, Samuel says, "She looks so calm and peaceful, don't you think?"

"I wouldn't know, I haven't looked."

Samuel frowns. "Well then, you have to. My mother would be mortified if she thought someone was going to remember her as you last saw her."

Maybe she would be, if she were alive; but she isn't, she's dead. Mead glances toward the reception area. Where the hell is his father? What is taking him so long? Why doesn't he get this show on the road?

"Please," Samuel says. "For me."

Shit and double shit. Looking at Delia is the last thing in the world Mead wants to do right now but he doesn't seem to have much choice. He'll just glance at her real fast. Quick and painless like a flu shot. Mead steps over to the casket and peeks down. And is shocked. Because this woman does not look the slightest bit like the one Mead and his dad picked up at the Winslow house yesterday; she looks a million times better. Dead, she still looks dead, but she no longer looks repugnant.

"Wow. My Uncle Martin did an incredible job."

"Yes, he did," Samuel says and smiles. "My mother hasn't looked this great in years. She'd be pleased."

"Teddy!"

Mead turns at the sound of his name. His uncle is standing in the doorway with a frown on his face. But what else is new. He motions for Mead to come over. "She looks great, Uncle Martin," Mead says as he crosses the room. "You did an amazing job. Really, you're a genius."

"A genius? You're calling me a genius?"

"I mean it as a compliment, Uncle Martin."

He crosses his arms over his chest. "This is all a big joke to you, isn't it?"

"What? No, why do you say that?"

Martin spins Mead around, grabs the back of his jacket, and says, "What the hell is this? What are you, a fucking comedian?"

The jacket. Mead forgot all about the stupid jacket, forgot to keep his back to the wall. He looks over at Samuel, who is looking back. Shit. Mead would give anything to switch places with Delia right now.

"Is there a problem here?" It's Mead's father. Five minutes too late.

"Look at what your son's wearing, Lynn. He's making a mockery of this dear woman's funeral."

"I am not," Mead says and yanks himself free of his uncle's grip. Stands up straight. But he doesn't sound convincing, even to himself.

"Here," Samuel says and steps forward to offer Mead the jacket off his own back. "Why don't you wear mine."

"That's very kind of you, Samuel," Mead's father says, "but not necessary."

"Please," he says. "I insist. I'll be fine in just a vest."

And so, under the gaze of his uncle and his father and the son of the deceased, Mead takes off the After-Life jacket and puts on Samuel's.

"See?" Samuel says. "It fits perfectly. I knew it would."

* * *

Funeral processions are notorious for moving slowly, but this one just might be the slowest on record. Or so it feels that way to Mead, sitting in the passenger seat next to his father. Several times he looks over to try and gauge the man's mood but his father's face remains as impassive as ever. His eyes glued to the street. The only hint of how he might truly feel revealed through the white knuckles on his hands as they grip the steering wheel at two-and-ten.

"I'm sorry," Mead says. "I didn't mean to be disrespectful. Really."

Nothing.

The hearse passes under a stone arch and through a wrought-iron gate before beginning its uphill ascent along a paved road that bisects the cemetery. To the left and to the right are row upon row of headstones that face south like sunbathers on a beach trying to catch the best rays of light. Somewhere among them lies Mead's cousin, doing the eternal sleep. Being here makes it real to Mead for the first time: the fact that Percy is dead and not just out of town or otherwise engaged.

"Where is he?" Mead asks.

His father nods off to the right. "Lying next to your grandfather."

"I thought you were saving that spot for yourself."

Nothing. Mead decides to try another approach.

"Guess who I saw in the A & P this morning? Aunt Jewel. She was wearing bedroom slippers and a bathrobe."

"That's not funny, Teddy."

"It wasn't meant to be."

His father looks over. Finally.

"She bought a half-gallon of ice cream and six cartons of salt.

She said she hadn't seen any reason to get dressed up for the occasion."

"You're being serious."

"I walked her home; that's why I was late getting back. I'm worried about her."

"Did you tell your uncle?"

Mead looks over at his father. "Please. What do you think I am, crazy?"

THE MINISTER DRONES ON AND ON about Delia Winslow—about what a great wife she was, about how devoted to family and church she was—but it is obvious that he did not really know her because not once does he mention her cherry pies. Mead stands as still as a soldier at attention and tries not to notice that his uncle is glaring at him from across the open grave, his eyes shooting poison darts that rarely miss. Afterward Mead hands the jacket back to Samuel. "I'm sorry," he says, "for having put you out in this way." But Samuel shrugs off the apology and says, "You remind me of myself at your age. So full of life. So distant from death. It was my pleasure."

The good feeling does not last. As soon as Samuel Winslow ducks into his car and drives off, Martin hands Mead a shovel and says, "I think it's time you learn what it is your father and I do around here. From the ground up."

Mead stares down into the hole in which Delia's casket now rests. "You want me to shovel dirt?"

"Maybe a few aching muscles will teach you a little respect."

And he walks off. Just like that. Mead glances around for his savior: his father. Surely he won't allow Uncle Martin to stick his son with a gravedigger's job. But he has already left, slipped into the hearse and out of sight while Mead wasn't looking.

"Shit," Mead says.

Lenny hands him a pair of leather gloves. "Here, wear these. It'll help."

MEAD IS READY TO QUIT AFTER TEN MINUTES. After twenty, he's exhausted. Lenny, on the other hand, has the strength of ten men. And yet he is twice as old as Mead. So Mead picks up his shovel and gives it another try. Sweat rolls down his forehead and into his eyes, stinging them. His shirt is sticking to his back. It's enough to drive a person mad. Mead sets down his shovel, takes off his shirt, and mops his brow with it. If only his mother could see him now; she'd be horrified. On the strength of that thought, he keeps digging.

"Want some sunscreen?" Lenny says.

Mead shakes his head. "I'm fine." And he keeps digging, but can barely lift his arms. Each shovelful of dirt feels as if it is going to be his last.

Someone is walking through the cemetery, over on the far side. Mead looks up, hoping that it is his father come back to rescue him, but it isn't. Where the hell is the man anyway? Okay, fine. So maybe his father thought it would be a good idea for Mead to do this for a while. A little manual labor to teach him to be more respectful. Blah, blah, blah. But enough is enough. Mead has been out here for almost an hour now in the hot, blazing sun. His father should know better. After all, Mead was excused from gym class for nine years in a row.

He's closer now, the cemetery walker. He seems to be heading this way. Mead stops digging and shades his eyes for a better look. That walk. He recognizes that walk. It belongs to only one person that Mead knows and that person is Herman Weinstein. He's here. Holy shit. He's here in High Grove. It's not that Mead hasn't been expecting him; he just didn't expect him quite so soon. But that's not true either. He'd wanted Herman to follow him. That was the plan: to lure the guy away from his lair. Only now that he is here, Mead realizes that he doesn't have any idea what to do next. "Lenny," Mead says. "Do you have a gun in your truck?"

"It ain't worth killing yourself over, Teddy. Pace yourself and you'll be fine."

"What? No, you don't understand. That person over there, walking this way, he's dangerous. You know, crazy, like a dog with rabies."

Lenny stops shoveling and looks up. "Where? I don't see no one."

"Over there," Mead says and points. "Right over there."

Lenny walks over to his pickup truck and reaches into the back. Mead thinks he's reaching for the shotgun but instead he lifts out a cold can of Coke and hands it to Mead. "Here. I think it's time you took a break."

"Are you trying to tell me you don't see him?"

"What I see is a very exhausted and confused young man."

Lenny is staring at Mead the way the grocery clerk was looking at Aunt Jewel. "I'm not crazy, Lenny. He's there. Look." But when Mead looks again, Herman is gone.

Lenny and Mead toss their shovels into the back of his truck. Job done. And Mead is still breathing, a miracle in and of itself. He hurts, though. His arms, his back, his legs. Hell, there isn't one square inch of his body that doesn't hurt.

"Your uncle and I are going huntin' tomorrow. You should join us."

"Yeah, right," Mead says. "Me out in the woods with my uncle and a loaded gun. Great idea, Lenny."

"Seems to me your uncle is the one ought to be afraid." And he looks out across the cemetery in the direction Mead thought he just saw Herman, as if Mead is the crazy one. Which he is not. He saw Herman. He knows he did. Lenny opens the driver's side door and says, "I'm gonna stop by my house before heading back to the store, get cleaned up and check in on my dad. He ain't been feeling too good lately. Would you like me to drop you off at your house?"

"No, not particularly. You have met my mother, haven't you?"

"I'll drop you at the store then," Lenny says. But their exit from the cemetery is blocked by a blue Dodge coupe that is trying to come in while they are trying to get out. The driver honks her horn several times. "Why don't she just go around me?" Lenny says. "She's got plenty of room." He waves her through and she pulls up alongside the truck, rolls down her window. A pretty blonde in dark sunglasses. Peering over the top of them, she says, "Have you got a Theodore Fegley in that truck? I was over at the furniture store looking for him and his father said he was over here."

Lenny looks at Mead and raises his eyebrows. "Seems that the young lady is looking for you."

She lifts the dark shades up off her eyes. "Hey, Theodore," Hayley Sammons calls to him through the open car window. "Don't tell me you forget about our date. We were supposed to go swimming, remember? Out at Snell's Quarry?"

Hayley peels down to a two-piece bathing suit that makes her look like a model straight out of the pages of a Sears Roebuck catalog: pretty, perky, and shapely, but not too shapely. Not *Penthouse* shapely. Not sleazy. She looks like a nice, Midwestern girl with a nice, normal body. Dropping her clothes in a heap, she walks out onto a low ledge of rock and dives in. Just like that. Without even first testing the water with her toe. She swims out several yards before popping back up to the surface.

Mead crawls into the backseat of the Dodge to put on a pair of swimming trunks that Hayley just happened to have in a duffel bag in the trunk of her car. She claims they belong to her brother, but Mead suspects a boyfriend. Or ex-boyfriend.

In the midst of changing his clothes, someone screams. Mead covers himself with his hands and peers out the window expecting to see the horrified face of one of his mother's friends staring back. Or another one of his ex-classmates. Instead he sees a body falling through the air, cannonball-style. It hits the lake and sends a geyser of water skyward. Back in the 1800s, Snell's Quarry was mined for limestone; in the early 1900s, it was abandoned; and sometime around the middle of that century the residents of Grove County turned it into a popular swimming hole. Rocky Beach. Limestone Lake. It goes by many names and has many personalities.

Mead pulls on the swimming trunks and gets out of the car just in time to see another boy jump from the highest point of rock. Dead Man's Leap. That's what it's called. The story goes that a quarryman leapt from that ledge to his death the day he learned they'd be closing the place down. Back before it was filled with water. Now it's looked upon as a rite of passage: boys as young as eight jumping off that rock in the belief that when they hit the water they will be men.

Mead sits on a low ledge of rock and dangles his feet in the lake. The water is cool and feels good after shoveling all that dirt under a hot summer sun. He takes a moment to check out the other swimmers in the lake, in case one of them is Herman. But none is. Then he turns around and checks out the sunbathers, but none of them is Herman either. Maybe Lenny is right. Maybe he was seeing things. That has to be it. Hard labor and hot sun will do that to a person, make him delusional. This is exactly what he needs. To sit and relax. To dangle his feet in cool water and watch a pretty girl swim back and forth across the lake. Like Forsbeck always says, "Nothing rejuvenates a man like a woman." He was referring to the women who fold out of men's magazines, but Mead is pretty sure it applies to this situation too.

"Aren't you coming in?" Hayley asks.

Mead shakes his head. She pulls herself up out of the lake and sits next to him on the rock, then leans forward to wring out her hair. Like the girls in the unisex bathroom back at the dorm. "So what was it like going off to college so young," she asks, "going off to a big city all alone at the age of fifteen? Were you scared?"

"No."

"Liar. You must've been scared. At least a little."

"I never really thought about it."

Another scream pierces the air as a boy, knees tucked up to his chin, drops from the cliff and hits the water in an explosion.

"When I was twelve," Hayley says, "my father took me to the west coast. I'd never even been outside of High Grove before. But he had, hundreds of times. He's a train conductor and travels all over the United States. He used to tell us stories about all the places he'd been, all the people he'd met. He'd bring back avocados from California, red rocks from Colorado, and coconuts from Florida. He made the world beyond High Grove seem so exciting and full of adventure, so when he asked me to come along with him that summer, I jumped at the opportunity. It was to be our little secret: the two of us sneaking off to California together. I wasn't supposed to tell my mother because then she'd want to come along and my father wanted it to be just us two. So we made up a story. We told her we were going to visit my father's relatives in Kansas because we knew how much she disliked my aunt, and it worked. She stayed home with my brother and I got my father all to myself.

"It was great. I still remember sitting by the train window and watching the world go by. I was amazed at how big it was. Our country. How varied. There were mountains and canyons and forests and rivers where the water ran so fast you'd drown trying to cross them. Or so my father said. It was beyond anything I could've ever imagined. Then we got to California and I saw the ocean. It was huge. As big as the sky. I never wanted to go home. But of course, I had to. And it was pure torture because even after I got home I wasn't allowed to tell anyone about where we'd been, about all those wonderful experiences I'd had. I had to keep them all to myself because otherwise my mother would've found out and been really mad."

Mead looks over at Hayley. Her hands are tucked under her legs, her chin raised up to the sky, a smile on her face so broad you would swear she was looking at her beloved Pacific Ocean right now.

"Did she ever find out?" Mead asks.

Hayley lowers her chin and stares at her feet, her toes drawing circles under the water. "Three summers. My father took me to the west coast three summers in a row. Then, on the fourth, he told me he was gonna take my brother Eric instead. Oh, was I mad. I was so furious that I went and told my mother all about it. No way was I going to let my little brother go to California without me, even if it meant dragging my mother along. But you know what? She already knew. She'd known all along. All that time I thought my father was lying to my mother, when in fact he was lying to me."

She looks up at the sky again. Smiles. Then looks over at Mead and says, "What about you, Theodore? Has anyone ever lied to you?"

"Yes," he says and pushes off into the water.

* * *

SITTING TOGETHER ON THE FAR SIDE of the quarry, Mead and Hayley look back across the water toward the parking area. Hayley says, "I've never been very good at math. I guess that would make me stupid in your book."

Meads shakes his head. "Mathematical thinking is deeply unnatural. It makes things complex where they would at first appear simple. Take, for example, this rock we're sitting on. Describe it to me."

"This rock? I don't know. It's big. And hard."

"Exactly. Now if you give me a ledger pad and a pen, I can probably get back to you with a mathematical description of it in about a week."

"So what you're telling me is that *math* is stupid, not me."

"Not stupid, no. It seems impractical when applied to something as simple as a rock but when that same principle is applied to a complex idea—like the theory of relativity—the beauty of mathematical thinking becomes clear. The complex becomes simple."

A boy jumps off the cliff and screams. Hayley and Mead look up as he falls through the air. When he hits the water, Hayley grabs Mead's hand and says, "Come on, Theodore, let's go jump off a cliff."

He pulls his hand free. "No way. I'm not going up there. Someone got killed once jumping off that ledge."

"That was before the quarry got filled with water, Theodore." She grabs his hand. "Come on. Let's not think about it, let's just do it."

A PREADOLESCENT BOY, who apparently has not a single working brain cell in his entire head, steps off the cliff. His body drops out of sight, his feet disappearing first, followed quickly by legs, torso, arms, and head, the quarry swallowing him up whole. He screams as he falls through the air and hits the water with a loud splash.

"You're looking a little pink there, Theodore," Hayley says and touches her index finger to his right shoulder, leaving behind a white mark. "Did you think to put on any sunscreen?"

"I'm fine, Mother," he says.

"Sorry," Hayley says. "I was just commenting."

"Hey," some kid behind them yells. "Stop holding up the line and jump already."

"Why don't you go next," Hayley says to Mead.

"No," he says. "Ladies first."

She gives him a look that suggests that she suspects he is trying to get out of this altogether, but she steps ahead of him anyway. "There's really nothing to it, Theodore," she says as she stands silhouetted against the blue sky, her body a perfect figure eight. Mead squints and she looks naked. He could squint at her all day and maybe work up a mathematical equation to define her body. The sines and cosines of lust. An algebraic equation that sums up the seductive qualities of the female body. The complex made simple. But he really should not be thinking about Mr. and Mrs. Sammons's daughter in this way. He needs instead to start thinking about what to do next, now that Herman is in High Grove. If, indeed, he actually is.

Hayley bends her knees and jumps. Screams all the way down.

"It's your turn," the boy behind Mead says. Some teenager with pimply skin, red hair, and a sunburn that looks as if it's going to keep him up all night.

"I know," Mead says and steps to the edge. Hayley bobs to the surface below and looks up. "Come on, Theodore," she says. "Jump. It's fun."

The quarry looks different from up here. Bigger. Rockier. Mead imagines that he is standing exactly where that quarryman was standing eighty years ago. Looking down. Thinking about all those years he spent chipping away at this rock to feed his family. All the holes he drilled to make casings for sticks of dynamite. All the stone he hauled off one chunk at a time. Each year the quarry got deeper, wider. Twenty years he worked here, maybe thirty. Thirty years digging his own grave. So really, Mead got off easy because he only wasted three years of his life. Less, really, because he didn't even learn about the Riemann Hypothesis until his second year of college. And he didn't become entwined with Herman until this year. All those long hours of hard work undone by one person. Like the fellow who closed down the quarry.

"Hey, buddy, are you gonna jump or what?"

Mead looks down at the smooth surface of the water but all he sees are hard jagged points of limestone. He begins to tremble. It starts in his knees and works its way up his body. A cloud passes in front of the sun and the air turns cold. Mead tries to step back from the ledge but can't. He's frozen. Is this how the quarryman felt? Afraid to go forward, unable to go back? Frozen in time? Someone touches Mead's shoulder. He turns to see who it is and his heart leaps up into his throat. Because it's Herman.

"You shouldn't do that," Mead says. "Sneak up on people like that."

"We have unfinished business, Fegley. You walked out on our deal."

"We didn't have any deal, Weinstein."

"Of course we did, Fegley. Don't be coy. You're too smart to be coy."

"I'm not smart, I'm an idiot. Otherwise I wouldn't have let you trick me."

"Trick you? I'm hurt, Fegley. I thought we were friends."

"No. We were never friends, because friends don't screw each other."

"Some friends do," Herman says. "And they enjoy it too."

"Go away," Mead says and tries to shrug off Herman's hand.

"Not until you agree to come back."

"No," Mead says. "Never."

"In that case, Fegley, you leave me no choice." And Herman grabs Mead with both hands and pushes him off the cliff.

Mead opens his eyes and sees several faces looking down at him. Is he lying in a morgue? He checks out the faces in search of his Uncle Martin. He doesn't want anyone else to embalm him because Mead knows that before his uncle injects formaldehyde into any body, he always performs the two tests of death. The first involves a saucer of water, placed on the chest of the deceased to detect the shiver of a beating heart or a working set of lungs; the second, a rubber band wrapped around a finger, white means go, red means stop. But Mead does not see his uncle; all he sees is the pimply-faced kid with red hair. And Hayley.

"Theodore," she says, "are you okay?"

Mead sits up, surprised to find that he is still at the top of the cliff in one piece and not at the bottom in several. "Where's Herman?"

"Who?" Hayley asks.

"The guy who tried to push me off the cliff just now." Mead turns to the pimply-faced kid. "You saw him, right? Tall guy? Dark hair?" The pimply kid shakes his head. "But you must have. You were standing right here the whole time."

The pimply kid looks at Hayley and shrugs.

"No one tried to push you, Theodore. You fainted."

"But he was here. I saw him."

Hayley takes hold of Mead's hand. "Come on, Theodore. Let's go back to the car. I think you've had enough sun."

He shakes her off. "I don't have sunstroke, Hayley, I saw him."

She sets her hands on her hips, like his mother. "Look at yourself, Theodore. You're red as a cooked lobster."

And the thing is, he is red. Bright red. Shit. It's going to keep him up all night.

Hayley digs a pair of jeans and a baseball jersey out of that duffel bag in the trunk of her car and pulls them on over her bathing suit, but they don't fit. They're too big. She has to fold over the waistband and roll up the cuffs. "You stay put and I'll be right back," she says and disappears into the five-and-dime, leaving her car to idle in its parking space with Mead in it. Heat is radiating off his arms. He has grown three shades redder in the short amount of time it took to drive back into town. You could fry an egg on his chest. No kidding. This is what happens when you spend twelve years hidden in the stacks of the library followed by three hours in the midday summer sun. Mead redirects the air-conditioning vents and holds his arms in front of them to get the full benefit.

Hayley comes back with a brown paper bag, out of which she takes a jar of Noxzema, a bottle of aloe vera gel, and a six-pack of chilled soda. Mead picks up the six-pack and presses it against his chest.

"You look worse," Hayley says.

"Thanks."

Squeezing a blob of green goo into her palm, Hayley slathers it all up and down Mead's arms and legs. It feels good, cool to the touch. Then she rubs it over his chest, the way his mother once massaged his chest with VapoRub when he had bronchitis.

"Is Herman the one who lied to you?" she asks.

Mead doesn't answer, just concentrates on her cool hands.

"Turn around so I can do your back."

He turns around and thinks about another girl he liked and then lost. The one he met after Cynthia. Herman's fault again.

"Do you want to tell me about it?"

"No."

"Okay. Well, that just about does it." Hayley removes her hand from Mead's back and closes the lid on the aloe vera bottle. "Give the gel a chance to sink in, then put on some Noxzema. And drink plenty of fluids." She reaches into the duffel bag and pulls out a red T-shirt. "Here, put this on so you won't stick to the seat."

Mead pulls on the cotton tee over his head. It's a couple of sizes too big for him. Little brother, my foot. No one drives around with a duffel bag full of her brother's clothes in the trunk of her car. And they certainly don't fit her. There's no doubt in Mead's head: Hayley has got a boyfriend. Or an ex-boyfriend.

"I didn't graduate," Mead says. "Commencement ceremonies are set to take place in six days. I just left."

"Why?"

"I'd rather not say."

"Okay." Hayley opens one of the cans of soda and takes a sip, then sits back to stare out the front windshield. Is she afraid her boyfriend is going to walk by, see the two of them sitting in her car, and get angry? Mead would rather not get punched in the face. He already knows what it feels like to be on the fist end of that deal and it isn't very good. Unless, of course, he's her ex-boyfriend.

"I'm being blackmailed," Mead says.

Hayley turns around. "By Herman?"

"I thought I saw him in the cemetery this morning, only now I'm not so sure."

"Have you told the police?"

"No, I haven't told the police and I'm not going to. It'd be pointless. Herman functions beyond the long arm of the law."

"My god, Theodore, what happened?"

"He lied to me, Hayley, that's what happened. He lied." And for all Mead knows, she's lying to him right now. About her little brother. About these clothes.

She sits back and gazes out the window. "What does he look like?"

"Herman? A rich boy from Princeton."

"Well then, he ought to stick out like a sore thumb around here."

Mead looks over at Hayley, scanning the streets of High Grove for a rich boy from Princeton, and allows himself a smile.

6

SUFFERING OLD FOOLS

Chicago
Two Years Before Graduation

It's been raining for the past twenty-four hours straight. Puddles everywhere. But at least for the moment, it isn't coming down hard. Which is a good thing because Mead does not have an umbrella. He finds them cumbersome and more trouble than they're worth. After all, it's just water. So he pulls the hood of his rain slicker over his head, tucks his books under his arm, and starts off across campus.

Contrary to Dr. Kustrup's advice—and partially because of it—Mead decided to stay in Chicago for the summer. And when he found out that his new faculty advisor would be returning from his sabbatical to teach during the summer quarter, it sealed the deal. That's where he is headed right now, to meet with this Dr. Andrew Alexander. Only this time Mead did his homework first: He looked up the professor in *Who's Who in America*. It seems that the mysterious Dr. Alexander also matriculated at a young age—sixteen to be exact—right here at Chicago University. He had his doctorate in mathematics by the time he was twenty-three and then headed out east to spend a year at the Institute for Advanced Study before taking a string of teaching jobs at a series of universities—including King's College in Cambridge, England—before finally ending up back here at CU. Mead wasn't quite so upset after reading that, especially after he looked up Dr. Kustrup in the same volume. It seems that he didn't start college until he was nineteen. And it wasn't Chicago University he attended but some lesser school in the Midwest. And he didn't get his doctorate until he was twenty-eight. And, oh yeah, he lied. He never attended the Institute for Advanced Study in Princeton. There isn't one mention of it in his bio at all. And all those papers he claims to have published? Apparently he lied about those, too. Or maybe they just weren't important enough to get a mention in *Who's Who.*

Mead comes to a crosswalk and has to wait, along with two other students, for the light to change. As they're waiting, a man comes pedaling up the street on a bicycle, a green Schwinn that looks as if it were purchased at a yard sale. The man riding the bike has a cap pulled down low over his eyes so it's hard to make out his age. He's also wearing a lightweight zipper jacket, khaki trousers, and loafers. One of the students says, "Look at that old fool, will you?"

"You know who that is, don't you?" his buddy says. "I see him around all the time. He's a professor here on campus. Rides that bicycle all year round. Rain, snow, sleet. Doesn't matter."

At that moment a car speeds through the intersection, trying to beat the yellow light, and hits a puddle, sending a geyser of water up over the bicycle and its rider. The professor raises his fist and shakes it at the car. If he curses, Mead does not hear it.

The first student laughs. "Like I said, old fool."

Mead glances down at his own feet, which are clad in loafers similar to those on the professor. He wonders what the student would say if he noticed. Something derogatory, no doubt. And perhaps he'd be right, seeing as how Mead's feet are soaking wet, water having already seeped in through the hand-stitched seams. Perhaps Mead is just a young fool. Or maybe a person only notices these things when a friend points them out.

But the student does not notice Mead. The light changes and he crosses the street with his buddy. They turn and head off to the right, Mead goes to the left and heads for the quad.

Yesterday he picked up the class schedule and read through all the course offerings in the math department. One class in particular caught his eye: Introduction to Analytical Mathematics. The class is being taught by the widely traveled Dr. Alexander. Mead figures that if the man is going to be advising him, then he should take at least one of his classes to decide whether or not the professor has anything worthwhile to say. If he still has all his marbles. Because the other thing Mead read about Dr. Andrew Alexander in *Who's Who in America* is that he was born in 1910. Which makes the man all of seventy-seven years old. Which makes him four years older than Mead's grandfather Henry Charles was when he died.

Mead exits the quad and heads up the walkway toward Epps Hall, where the math department is housed. Chained to the bicycle rack in front of the building is the green Schwinn that just passed him back at the intersection. Apparently the old fool on the bicycle is a professor in the mathematics department. How odd that Mead never before noticed the bike. He tries to calculate what the odds are that the old fool is his new faculty advisor. Mead didn't get a look at his face, nor could he see his hair, stuffed as it was up under the cap, so he didn't get a reading on the man's age. It's a three-speed bicycle with a bell on the handlebar, a wire basket on the back, and a blue license plate that reads: PNT.

His heart suddenly beating faster, Mead trots up the stairs to the second floor. Could it be that Mead's new faculty advisor is the old man he met in the park? But that would be too good to be true. And the initials, they're all wrong. But what if it is? What if the old fool on the bicycle and the old guy in the park and Dr. Andrew Alexander are all the same person? Mead stops just short of his new faculty advisor's office. A familiar voice is coming from inside of it: Dr. Kustrup's voice. The door is nearly closed so the chairman cannot see him but Mead can hear plenty.

"I need you to consider my offer seriously, Andrew," he says. "It's selfish of you to continue teaching at your age. There's a whole new generation of mathematicians out there and it's only fair that one of them be given a shot at working here, only I don't have the budget to add another salaried staff member so I need you to do the honorable thing and step down. I mean, you're seventy-seven, for god's sake. It's time, Andrew, it's time."

"Have you received any complaints about my teaching?"

"No, but that's not the point."

"It may not be your point, Frank, but it's mine. I'm not changing my answer."

"You're being unreasonable, Andrew."

"This meeting is over." A chair scrapes across the floor. "I'm expecting a student at any moment so I'll have to ask you to leave."

Mead leaps away from the door just as Dr. Kustrup throws it open and charges through it. The man's face is beet red. He's so mad that he doesn't even see Mead as he storms past him and disappears around the corner at the end of the hall. And Mead is so mad that he almost goes after the guy to give him a piece of his mind. Not only did Dr. Kustrup dump Mead but he handed him off to the very professor he is now trying to get rid of! Well, screw him. The man couldn't talk his way out of a 4 x 4 matrix if he wanted to. Mead is not going to let Dr. Stuckup Kustrup get the better of him. He is simply going to graduate from this university — with top honors — without him. Hell, he's going to graduate in spite of him. And he is going to do it with the old fool on the bicycle.

Mead hesitates before entering the professor's office. Perhaps he should give the old man a few minutes to cool down, to regain his composure. He's bound to be even more pissed off at Dr. Kustrup than Mead presently is. Only he isn't. Instead of sitting behind his desk stewing about the unpleasant encounter, the professor is standing at his blackboard writing out a series of mathematical expressions, the piece of chalk in his hand clicking against the slate like a bird singing in a new day. "Dr. Alexander?"

He turns around. And it's him all right, the old guy with bloodhound jowls and long gray hair pulled back into a ponytail. Mead smiles and the professor smiles back. He remembers too.

"Mr. Fegley, I presume?"

"Mead, sir, I prefer to be called Mead."

"Come in, come in," he says and waves him into his office. "Tell me, Mead, do you know what a harmonic series is?"

"Yes, sir. It's the addition of terms continuing indefinitely."

"And if it's divergent?"

"The total has no limit."

"And if it's convergent?"

"It creeps closer and closer to a finite sum but never quite reaches it."

"Excellent," Dr. Alexander says. "Excellent." He turns back to his chalkboard. The professor's pant legs are soaking wet and he is standing in stocking feet. A pair of loafers sits on the radiator under his window.

"Dr. Alexander? I'm sorry but I couldn't help but overhear part of your conversation with Dr. Kustrup."

"Oh, that. Don't worry about that, Mead, I'm not going anywhere. That man has been trying to get rid of me for years. Put the old geezer out to pasture, so to speak." He stops writing and turns around. "Old is just a state of mind, Mead. I don't feel any different today than I did when I was your age, so why should I retire? So I can go home and stare at the walls? Watch too much TV? Drive the wife crazy? Or maybe he wants me to open up a bookshop like that physics professor they bribed into retirement a few years back. But I'm not interested in shelving books, Mead. I need to keep my mind engaged and challenged." He turns back to the board. "Besides, I have tenure. Kustrup can't do a damned thing but squawk."

Mead sets his books down on the professor's desk, next to his wet cap. "I'd like to sign up for one of the courses you're teaching this quarter. Introduction to Analytical Mathematics."

"I think that sounds like a fine idea, Mead."

"Sir. The license plate on your bicycle outside reads PNT. I'm just curious. What does that stand for?"

"Prime Number Theorem. Tell me, are you familiar with it?"

"No, sir, I'm not."

"Not to worry, Mead, you'll learn all about it in my class." And he goes back to writing on the board.

"Uh, sir? Shouldn't we sit down and figure out the rest of my schedule?"

"Sign up for whatever you'd like, Mead. After you complete my course, then we'll discuss what you should do next."

"Uh, all right, sir. Then I guess I'll be going."

"One other thing, Mead."

"Yes?"

The professor turns around one last time. "Stop calling me *sir*. It makes me sound too important."

* * *

A POSTCARD ARRIVES in Mead's mailbox postmarked St. Louis. On the front is a photograph of Busch Stadium. A short message is scrawled across the back. "I can't believe I'm being paid to play baseball! I've been promoted to Class A status and will be going on a whirlwind tour of the United States care of the St. Louis Cardinals. Not a bad gig for a kid from little old HG. Life is great! Love, Percy."

Shit. No matter how hard Mead works, Percy somehow always comes out on top. And with next to no effort. Life on a silver platter and all that crap. Mead should send his cousin a picture postcard of the campus library. On the back he could write, "Studied here until midnight on Saturday night. It was awesome!! The books are incredible. University life is great! Love, Mead." Only he figures his cousin wouldn't get it, so instead he drops Percy's postcard into his sock drawer, scoops up his textbooks, and heads over to Epps Hall.

DR. ALEXANDER BEGINS HIS LECTURE on the first day of class talking about Western Europe in the years following the Napoleonic Wars, about a section of Germany being ruled by the king of England. A few of Mead's classmates exchange looks of confusion. Others check their class schedules to make sure they're in the right classroom, to make sure they have not inadvertently wandered into a Western Civilization class by accident. The rest roll their eyes and smile knowingly because they got warned ahead of time to expect odd behavior from the old professor. Dr. Alexander sees them all reacting and smiles back.

"This is the world," he says, "into which Georg Friedrich Bernhard Riemann was born. In the village of Breselenz, a flat, dull countryside of farm, heath, marsh, and thin woodland. An undeveloped region where, in the early nineteenth century, one was either a craftsman, a domestic servant, or a peasant. Or a minister. Which is what Bernhard's father was: a country parson who struggled to feed and clothe his six children, only one of whom lived a normal life span. And it wasn't Bernhard."

The kid sitting in front of Mead squirms in his seat and glances at his watch. Mead imagines him heading over to the administrative building at the end of the hour to drop the class and wonders if he should follow, wonders if the old professor has begun to lose his marbles. Or maybe the unair-conditioned classroom is causing him to have a mental meltdown. After all, this is supposed to be a math class.

"Needless to say," Dr. Alexander continues, "there were few opportunities in such a place for young men like Bernhard so he was sent to live with his grandmother in Hanover, eighty miles away. But the young Bernhard was homesick the whole time, a poor scholar interested in only one thing: mathematics. It was understood, however, that he would follow his father into the ministry so he entered the University of Göttingen as a student of theology."

Mead sits up a little straighter in his chair. He is starting to like where this rather unconventional lecture is headed. Already he likes this Bernhard Riemann. He sounds like Mead's kind of guy. Perhaps Dr. Alexander is not so addle-minded after all.

"The school was at a low point when the young Bernhard arrived in 1846, in the middle of a political upheaval. It did have one major attraction, however: It was home to Carl Friedrich Gauss, the man who discovered the Prime Number Theorem. The greatest mathematician of his age, Gauss was sixty-nine and did little teaching by that time, but he gave a lecture on linear algebra that our young hero attended. Afterwards, Bernhard confessed to his father that his true love was mathematics and thirteen years later, in 1859, Bernhard published a paper that mathematicians have been trying to prove or disprove ever since: the Riemann Hypothesis."

The rest of the lecture is spent discussing the Riemann Hypothesis in purely mathematical terms. Including its genesis, the Prime Number Theorem. Many of the terms Dr. Alexander uses are unfamiliar to Mead. But this does not discourage him. It heightens his desire to know more. And he leaves Dr. Alexander's class having been bitten by the same math bug that once bit Bernhard.

A SECOND POSTCARD ARRIVES, this one postmarked Cleveland, Ohio. On the front is a photograph of that city's baseball stadium. Another short message is scrawled across the back. "I got to pitch in both the fifth and the sixth innings. My fastball clocked a respectable 92 mph and no runs were scored while I was on the mound. Not bad for a day's work, not bad at all. Hope things are going as well for you. As always, Percy."

Mead drops the postcard into his sock drawer and heads off to class.

DR. ALEXANDER'S TEN-WEEK COURSE ENDS, leaving Mead hungry for more. As the other students race out of the room, in a hurry to begin their four weeks of freedom before the fall quarter gets under way, Mead lags behind. Approaching the professor as the man erases the chalkboard, Mead says, "So when do you think would be a good time for me to meet with you to discuss what I should do next?"

Dr. Alexander does not answer, just keeps erasing. So Mead asks again. Louder this time. "Excuse me, professor? You said we could meet after I finished this course to discuss my curriculum. That you'd advise me."

Still nothing. What is wrong with the man, is he deaf? He never seemed to have trouble hearing any of the students' questions in class but then no one ever asked that many because the professor was always so precise in his explanations.

"Dr. Alexander?" Mead yells. "When should I come by your office?"

The professor turns around. "Tell me, Mead, how would you apply the basic prime-finding process to all real numbers up to 701,000?"

"That's easy," Mead says in a quieter voice. "With a pen, a pad of paper, and a list of the primes up to 829."

"That is correct," Dr. Alexander says and sets down the eraser. "Meet me in my office next Monday at two and we'll discuss the young Mead Fegley's future."

THE PROFESSOR'S DOOR IS OPEN but his chair is empty. Mead checks his watch to see if perhaps he has arrived early but he hasn't, he is right on time. Well, Dr. Alexander has to be around here somewhere. Mead saw his bicycle locked to the rack outside so he can't have wandered far. Maybe he's in the men's room. Or up in Dr. Kustrup's office turning down another request to retire. Uncomfortable with entering an empty office—with seeming propriety—Mead strolls down the hall to get a drink of water from the fountain, then glances at his watch again. Perhaps this is the wrong day. Maybe Mead is supposed to meet with the professor tomorrow. But even as he thinks this, he knows it isn't true. This isn't Mead's fault; it's Dr. Alexander's. He probably forgot all about their meeting, seeing as how the man does not appear to be very fond of his advisory-type responsibilities. Maybe that's why Dr. Kustrup assigned Mead to him: to put one more thorn in the old professor's side, to try and annoy him into retirement.

The phone on Dr. Alexander's desk rings, startling Mead. It chimes four times before an answering machine picks up. "I'm not here right now," the professor's voice says, "which means I'm elsewhere. Leave a message if you must, or better yet, send a fax." A loud dial tone is followed by a click as the machine shuts itself off.

Mead is beginning to wonder if he should do the same. Send a fax. "I showed up at two and you weren't here," he could write. "So tell me, which paper do you think more strongly influenced Bernhard Riemann, Chebyshev's First Result or Chebyshev's Second Result? And why?"

Mead glances at his watch a third time. It's now ten after the hour. He'll give the professor five more minutes and then he is leaving. The man may be a brilliant teacher but he sucks as a faculty advisor. Besides, Mead has better things to do with his time than stand around waiting for some head-in-the-clouds aging mathematician, who may or may not show up because he has little interest in being an advisor and even less interest in whether or not Theodore Mead Fegley of High Grove, Illinois, becomes a mathematician, to make an appearance. But then what? Mead will have no choice but to go back to Dr. Kustrup and ask for another advisor and Mead would rather switch majors than ask Dr. Stuckup Kustrup for any more help ever, and so he continues to wait.

Someone inside of Dr. Alexander's office coughs. Mead peers in through the open door but the chair behind the professor's desk is still empty. Maybe Mead just imagined it. The cough. But then he hears it again. "Professor?" he says. "Is that you?"

The old man's head pokes up over the far side of his desk. A pale white crown sprouting a frazzled outgrowth of gray hair. "Mead. It's about time you got here."

"What are you doing down on the floor? Are you all right?" Mead asks. "Do you need help getting up?" But when he steps around the desk, he sees that the professor is sitting cross-legged on a yoga mat, a pair of headphones wrapped around his neck. A portable tape player is sitting on the floor next to him.

"I'm fine, Mead, but I was beginning to get worried about you. You're late, you know."

"No, I'm not. I've been here for twelve minutes, standing outside your office. What is that, a relaxation tape?"

"I guess you could call it that, or you could call it inspirational. I listen to it whenever I get in a rut trying to solve a problem. When I need to push my thinking in another direction. It's Brahms. Are you a fan of Brahms, Mead?"

"He's okay, but I prefer Bach."

"Ah, Bach. He would've made a great mathematician."

"Why do you say that?"

"Because he had an intuitive mind. All great men have intuitive minds." Dr. Alexander rolls up his mat and stashes it behind the door, then gestures for Mead to take a seat in his guest chair. "Next time, Mead," he says, "knock."

ANOTHER POSTCARD ARRIVES. From Detroit, Michigan, this time. With yet another photograph of yet another baseball stadium. "The weather is great," Percy has scrawled across the back. "The fans are great. I pitched two more no-hit innings today but my shoulder is beginning to show some wear and tear. Thank god the season is almost over. My arm could use a rest. I could use a rest. Love, Percy."

The guy seems to be showing his first signs of stress. Mead tries not to get too excited about it though. Next season the golden boy will probably come back stronger than ever. Like always. Mead drops this postcard into his sock drawer, along with all the others, picks up his book bag, and heads over to Dr. Alexander's office.

ADDICTED. THAT IS THE ONLY WORD Mead can think of to describe what he is feeling. Stoned on math. Every time he discovers another theory or argument or conjecture related to the Riemann Hypothesis, he gets a head rush. Lately he has been forgetting to eat, forgetting to sleep, and he has been losing all track of time. Days merge into weeks merge into months. He has even missed a few classes. He showed up for philosophy only to find the classroom empty, the door locked. That's how he discovered that it was Friday, not Tuesday. So he came back to the dorm to study. It's quiet here during the day when everyone else is off to class, quieter even than the library. Plus, it never closes.

The phone rings but Mead ignores it. The caller is probably trying to contact his new roommate. Pete's replacement. Some vulgar boy by the name of Dave. The first time they met, the guy made a really original observation about how young Mead looks, then proceeded to brag about how many chicks he banged over the summer. They haven't spoken since, except to say "Hey" when their paths inadvertently cross.

The phone continues to ring, to the point of annoyance, so Mead finally picks up the receiver and says, "He's not here."

"Teddy?" his father says. "Is that you?"

"Oh. Hi, Dad. I thought the call was for my roommate. What's up?"

"I just got back from the railroad station. Did you miss your train?"

"What train? What're you talking about?"

"Do you even know what day it is?"

"Of course I do; it's Thursday."

"And?"

"And what?"

"Should I be worried about you, Teddy?"

"No, I'm fine. Why?"

"It's Christmas Eve, that's why."

Addicted. That's the word, all right. High as a kite on math.

* * *

Dr. alexander is tapping his chalk against the blackboard, deep in thought, relating a message in Morse code. "The field of Number Theory," he says to Mead, "arose out of the sheer complexity of Riemann's zeta function. It studies the statistical properties of the spacings between non-trivial zeros of the zeta function. That is, all zeros which sit on the critical line." He studies the board some more and the matrices he has written on it along with their characteristic polynomials. He taps his chalk. "It is theorized," he says, "that if one cannot discover exactly what is going to happen, that perhaps one can discover what on average is most likely to happen. It is more a physicist's approach to problem-solving than a mathematician's—less precise, but an area of study worth investigating because in Bernhard Riemann's time there was no distinction between math and physics. He would have used both disciplines in his work." The professor writes out an equation then hands the chalk to Mead. "I want you to generate some zeta zeros using this—it's called the Riemann-Siegel formula—so you can familiarize yourself with his thought process."

It takes several minutes, and a good chunk of board, for Mead to calculate his first zeta zero, but he does it successfully.

"Do another one," Dr. Alexander says.

And so Mead fills another chunk of board.

"And another."

Mead calculates a third zeta zero along the bottom edge of the board, a fourth along the top edge.

"You can use the eraser, you know," Dr. Alexander says.

And so Mead does and fills the board again. And again. And again.

"It is theoretically possible," Dr. Alexander says, "that the Riemann Hypothesis will one day be disproved by this very process, by discovering a zeta zero that does not sit on the critical line. That's all it would take, you know. One zero. But attempting to find that zero, by the process you are now undertaking, will take more than your lifetime and mine put together."

Mead stops writing and turns around. "There must be a faster way to calculate them than this," he says, "than doing each one by hand."

"As a matter of fact, there is. Tell me, Mead, are you free this evening?"

DR. ALEXANDER GIVES MEAD DIRECTIONS to his home, puts him on a bus, and then, despite the below-freezing temperature, pedals off on his bicycle. Ten minutes later, Mead arrives at the address he wrote down. The professor's green Schwinn is leaning against the side of a small Tudor house, a rusty old Volkswagen diesel Rabbit is sitting in the driveway, and a fresh layer of snow coats the front yard. Mead follows the professor's footprints to the front door and knocks. A stout woman with a broad smile answers. "It's so nice to finally meet one of my husband's students," she says, takes Mead by the arm, and leads him into the house. "You must be very special. My husband never brings his work home with him. You're the first." She then pats Mead on the hand and offers him a cup of hot chocolate, as if he were nine, and Mead accepts. A potbelly stove sits in the middle of the living room, which is pungent with the smell of cats, three of which are sleeping on a chaise longue upholstered in their fur. Mead's mother would be horrified. A pigsty, she'd call the place. A house unfit for living, let alone entertaining. But Mead isn't here to socialize.

"It's this way," Dr. Alexander says and motions for Mead to follow him down a set of stairs to the basement.

The smell of cat is even stronger down here where a litter box sits next to the furnace. The rest of the basement is crammed full of old furniture, like the second floor of Fegley Brothers, like the shed behind Uncle Martin's house. "The wife's hobby," Dr. Alexander says, dismissing the furniture with a wave of his hand as he leads Mead past an armoire and a chiffonier to the far end of the subterranean room where, sitting on top of a workbench, is a contraption that looks vaguely like the inside of a watch, only much bigger and more complicated. Like something out of a mid-century science fiction movie.

"This is it," the professor says. "This is my zeta function machine."

On the wall above the machine are several mechanical drawings. The paper they have been drawn on is yellow with age, the transparent tape holding the paper in place edged in brown and bubbled in spots as if the drawings have hung here for years.

"This looks a lot like the mechanical computing device Alan Turing set out to build back in the 1930s," Mead says.

"I see you've done your homework, Mead. But this isn't simply like it, it *is* it."

Mead stares at Dr. Alexander, thinking the old man is trying to pull a fast one on him. A pop-quiz kind of thing. "It can't be," Mead says. "Alan Turing never finished it. He abandoned the project when World War II broke out."

Dr. Alexander sits down at his workbench. "Did I ever tell you where I was in the spring of 1938?"

"No, but I read your entry in *Who's Who in America*. You were at King's College in Cambridge that year."

"That's exactly right. Listening to a lecture given by Alan Turing. The man was convinced that the Riemann Hypothesis was false and had set out on a mission to find a zeta zero off the critical line. This machine was going to speed up his computing time exponentially. I was twenty-eight at the time and completely drawn in by the man's charisma and enthusiasm. Spent two months of my life in the engineering department at King's College cutting gear wheels for the Turing machine. When I later learned that he had abandoned the project, I decided to build one myself."

"Your secret project," Mead says and Dr. Alexander raises his eyebrows. "Dr. Kustrup happened to mention that you were on sabbatical last year working on a secret project." He runs his index finger over a gear wheel. "Does it work?"

The professor scratches his head. "I'm still working out a few kinks."

"But there are electronic computers now, you know," Mead says. "And they are said to work much faster."

"I know," Dr. Alexander says. "It'll be a race to the finish."

It isn't until Mead finds another postcard in his mailbox that he realizes six months have passed since the last one arrived. Not since last August. He'd forgotten all about them, quite honestly, and all about Percy. The photograph on this postcard, however, is not of a baseball stadium. It is a photograph of the Fegley Furniture Store taken several decades ago, shortly after Mead's grandfather, Henry Charles Fegley, first opened the place. That's him standing by the front door with his two young sons, Lynn and Martin. They are both wearing knickers — Mead's dad and uncle — and squinting against the bright sun. Mead knows the postcard well, Fegley Brothers has been printing them up and giving them away as promotional pieces for decades. Mead flips the card over. "Looks like this is the team I'll be playing with from now on," Percy has written. "Missed you over Christmas. Try and make it home this summer!!! Love, Percy."

Mead calls home immediately. "What happened?" he asks his mother.

"They didn't re-sign him," she says. "It had something to do with his being a free agent. Apparently they picked some lesser player over Percy because the boy was an officially sponsored player. Or at least that's the way it was explained to me. No one talks about it. It's kind of a sensitive subject."

"So how is he handling it? Being back home, I mean."

"He mopes around a lot but he'll be fine. You should give him a call."

Mead knows that he should but, the thing is, he's glad his cousin failed. Finally. He feels bad for Percy—he really does—but at the same time he doesn't. And he's afraid it might come across on the phone. That he's glad. And so he doesn't call.

MEAD DOES NOT GO HOME over the summer either. It isn't a conscious decision. He actually considers the option of taking a break, going home, and relaxing for a few months. Especially when he realizes that he has not been home in nearly two years. How did that happen? How did so much time go by so fast? Here he is, ready to commence on his third—and final—year of undergraduate study, his eighteenth birthday just around the corner, and yet it feels as if he just left home last month. As scary as that is to think about, at least Mead knows he has put the time to good use. He has studied hard, finding his true vocation in life and focusing on it to the exclusion of all else. Perhaps he should go home and visit with his cousin; let his mother show him off to all her friends. It has an appealing ring to it. But when Mead next thinks about it, summer has come and gone and the dorms start filling up with students once more.

A CHEESEBURGER LANDS ON MEAD'S DESK with a thump, startling him. He looks up from his ruled legal pad and sees Forsbeck standing over him. "I brought you something to eat," he says. "You haven't been away from that desk all day. Did someone forget to tell you it's Sunday? The day of rest?"

"I'm not religious," Mead says.

"Forget religion, you need to kick back and relax, man, or you're going to burn yourself out."

"I'm fine," Mead says. "Thanks for the burger."

Forsbeck sits down on Mead's bed. Shit. The guy wants to talk, to be friends. It happens every fall: new school year, new roommate. This time Mead has been stuck with a guy by the name of Charles Forsbeck, a transfer student from another university who is so far proving to be no different from Mead's other roommates: a young man pumped up on testosterone who seems more interested in using his newfound freedom to explore the workings of a brassiere than the shelves of the library, who somehow manages to find the time to attend and pass all of his classes despite a weekend habit of beer-drinking, pot-smoking, and girl-chasing.

Mead had a choice. He could have elected to take an apartment off campus. His father would have footed the bill. No problem. Only Mead had nobody with whom he wanted to rent this apartment. And he wasn't about to get a place all on his own. He has no time—let alone any interest—in cooking and cleaning up after himself. As a matter of fact, if the campus cafeteria were not located between Epps Hall and the dorm, Mead might very well have succumbed to starvation months ago.

"What's that you're working on anyway?" Forsbeck asks.

"It's called the Riemann-Siegel formula. I'm computing nontrivial zeta zeros."

"And how many more do you have to do?"

"It's hard to say, somewhere between one and one million. Until I find a zero that isn't sitting on the critical line."

Forsbeck makes a snorting noise through his nose. Half-laugh, half-derision. Or so Mead imagines. Then flops back on his bed. "You math majors are all the same," he says. "You're all nuts. My last roommate, he was a math major too. Used to study all the time. Around the clock. Then one night, toward the end of the year, he just burned out. Decided to spend the weekend partying for a change. Man, I've never seen anyone put away more beer than that little dude. He was about your size. Average height. Thin build. How much do you weigh, anyway? I'm guessing around one forty."

"Does your story have a point?" Mead says.

"What? Yeah, it sure does. That little math major drank himself straight into a coma. I couldn't wake him up for nothing. And I tried. Twice. Once in the morning before I headed off to class and again that evening. The paramedics couldn't wake him either."

Shit. So maybe Forsbeck isn't quite as boorish and insensitive as Mead first thought. At least now he knows why the guy might have wanted to transfer schools. "I'm not going to burn out, Forsbeck, okay? You have my word."

Forsbeck gets up off the bed and slaps Mead on the back. "Do me a favor, Fegley. If you should decide to flip, please do it in somebody else's room."

He comes out of the men's room in Epps Hall and walks past Mead, nodding at him the way one might nod to a stranger on the sidewalk or to someone one knows by sight but not name, then drops out of sight around the corner. Herman Weinstein. Shit.

Mead hasn't thought about the guy in ages. Forgot all about him, in fact. He hasn't even seen Herman since Dr. Stuckup Kustrup gave Mead the old heave-ho well over a year ago. And he realizes that any anger he might have felt toward the guy when the professor-turned-chairman first picked him over Mead is gone. He doesn't care anymore. He has Dr. Alexander now. And the Riemann Hypothesis. He has everything he could possibly need. He's happy. Mead almost turns around and goes after Herman. To thank him. "If it weren't for you," he'd say, "I might never have taken Dr. Alexander's class, might never have discovered Bernhard Riemann. Thank you for taking Dr. Kustrup away from me. Thank you very much." Instead, Mead trots up to the second floor to find Dr. Alexander's door open, his chair empty. Mead stands in the doorway and studies the man's chalkboard. "I see you have drawn a graph of the function J(x)," Mead says, "and filled it with a series of dots and dashes that resemble a sort of a staircase."

"Yes, I have," the professor's voice answers.

Mead steps inside and around the desk. Dr. Alexander is sitting cross-legged on his yoga mat on the floor, an amazing feat for a man his age. He pats the floor next to him and Mead sits down, crosses his legs, and says, "Why? What're we doing?"

"You tell me," the professor says.

Mead studies the chalkboard again. "You're preparing to turn the Golden Key."

"That is correct, Mead. It is the first equation in Riemann's 1859 paper. And what does it make possible?"

"It bridges the gap between counting and measuring. It gives us an expression of the zeta function in terms of calculus, which is $\pi(x)$."

"The central result in Riemann's paper. A powerful result."

A minute or two goes by in silence as the two men stare at the chalkboard.

"And what're we doing now?" Mead asks.

"Waiting for the final result to come to us."

"We could be waiting a long time."

Dr. Alexander puts his finger to his lips. "Don't talk, Mead, think."

HE PULLS OUT HIS RULED LEGAL PAD and computes a few zeta zeros while sitting on the hardwood bench outside the dean's office. One thousand, four hundred, and seventy-nine. That's how many zeros Mead has calculated so far. The chances of his disproving the Riemann Hypothesis in this manner—generating them one-by-one, in longhand—are nil. Mead knows that but he keeps doing it anyway because he wants it to become as natural as breathing. To train his mind to think the way Bernhard Riemann thought in hopes of having a spontaneous insight. Of making a mental leap to the next step. Dr. Alexander has his yoga; Mead has his zeros. But neither of their methods seems to be getting them anywhere. Perhaps they are going about it all wrong. They must be. What Mead needs to do is shake things up. Stop being so linear in his thought process. He knows that too, he just doesn't know how. So he picks up his ledger pad, generates another zeta zero, and waits for inspiration to come.

The door to Dean Falconia's office opens and Herman Weinstein steps through it. Mead doesn't lay eyes on the guy for over a year and now runs into him twice in one week. Or maybe he's just been studying too hard to take notice. Herman nods and says, "Congratulations, Fegley."

"For what?" Mead says, surprised that Herman remembers him, that he would care to remember the name of his roadkill.

"I'll let the dean tell you. I don't want to steal his thunder." Then he leans in real close. Close enough for Mead to smell his cologne. It's the same shit he was wearing the first time Mead met him. "I owe you an apology," Herman says. "I've always felt bad about the whole Kustrup thing, about his choosing me over you, but it seems you've done all right on your own."

Mead takes it back. He doesn't feel like thanking the guy. Apology, my foot. Herman doesn't feel the slightest bit bad about that. He thinks he's lording something over on Mead. He thinks Mead is still pissed off at Dr. Kustrup for dumping him. He apparently thinks he got the better end of that deal, which he most certainly did not, but it ticks Mead off that the guy thinks he did. And so he says, "I'm not on my own, I've got Dr. Alexander."

"Oh. Right. The old guy. I took his class on the Riemann Zeta Function last quarter. Interesting stuff. But I found the professor to be a bit too flaky for my taste, always sitting on the floor of his office and meditating. That's not my style."

"Dean Falconia is ready to see you, Theodore," the dean's secretary says. "You can go in now."

Thankful for the rescue, Mead says, "If you'll excuse me," and gets up off the bench. But Herman doesn't step out of the way so Mead has to go around him.

"Hey," Herman says. "We should get together some evening and hang out. I'm living in your dorm this year. On the fourth floor. Room 48. Drop up some time and say hi." Then he walks off without waiting for a response.

Yeah, right, like Mead wants to hang out with *that* guy.

DEAN FALCONIA SHAKES MEAD'S HAND and then motions for him to sit down. He tells Mead how impressed he is with his academic accomplishments, especially for such a young scholar, and Mead thanks him. It is a conversation they have had many times. Then the dean says, "I am also proud to tell you, Mead, that you have been elected to become a member of Phi Beta Kappa."

"I have? By whom?"

"By the chairman of the math department."

"Stuckup Kustrup? I mean, Dr. Kustrup?"

"As I'm sure you are aware, membership is extended only to the most elite scholars of higher education. It's quite an honor. Congratulations."

This must be why Herman congratulated Mead. He knows. But how did he find out?

"The guy who was in here before me," Mead says. "Did Dr. Kustrup elect him too?"

"Herman Weinstein? Yes. I'm lucky to have two such promising and talented young mathematicians studying here at once. Very lucky indeed."

Talented? Herman is talented at math? It's one thing to hear Dr. Stuckup Kustrup make this claim, another entirely to hear it from the dean.

"There is one additional reason I called you in here, Mead," the dean says and leans forward over his desk, a gesture that implies that what he is about to say is of grave importance. "It has come to my attention that you and Dr. Alexander have been spending a lot of time working on the Riemann Hypothesis. As I'm sure you are aware, Mead, it is a subject of great interest in the field of mathematics, one with which we here at the university would like to be actively involved. You understand, of course, that the person who proves or disproves the Riemann Hypothesis will achieve great fame, as will the institution where it happens. It is for this reason, Mead, that I would like to extend to you the following offer. Starting next quarter, I would like you to fill your curriculum exclusively with classes related to the Riemann Hypothesis and submit a paper on your findings at the end of the spring quarter. As your senior thesis."

"But I haven't yet made any findings, Dean Falconia."

"Don't worry, Mead, you don't have to prove or disprove the hypothesis, I just want you to work on it. Have we got a deal?"

Shit.

7

SCRUPLES AND PRINCIPALS

High Grove
Five Days Before Graduation

HUNGER WILL MAKE A PERSON do the damnedest things, like go home for supper when one knows good and well that one should stay as far away from the six-legged creature as possible. But there you have it, instinct winning out over reason. Mead peers through the windowpane in the back door. His mother is wearing an apron over a tailor-fit dress. She must be entertaining company. Good. That ought to keep her out of his hair. Mead just hopes it's somebody he doesn't know. That way he won't feel obligated to participate in the conversation. He can just eat and split.

She picks up a basket of rolls and heads into the dining room. As soon as the door swings closed behind her, Mead slips into the kitchen and down the hall to the bathroom. Pulling the borrowed T-shirt off over his head, he stares at his reflection in the mirror. Shit. He's now three shades redder than he was sitting in Hayley's car. Mead steps out of the swimming trunks. Double shit. His ass looks like a goddamned snowcap on a mountaintop. Glistening white. He turns on the shower, making it as cold as he possibly can, then steps under the spray and lets the water beat down on his face. And shivers. Not because the water is cold, but because of what happened to him up there on that cliff. Nothing like that has ever happened to him before. Mead does not have hallucinations. He is the most rational person he has ever met. But that must be what he had — a hallucination — because nobody else saw Herman. It must be the sun. Mead just got too much sun. He grabs the faucet and tries to make the water even colder.

Fifteen minutes later, he enters the dining room and watches his plan to eat and split flush right down the toilet because sitting at the table with his parents is none other than his junior high school principal, Mr. Jeavons. Could this day get any worse?

Mr. Jeavons stands up and extends his hand. "Teddy," he says, "it's so good to see you. You're looking well. All grown up."

Which just goes to show how obtuse the man is, because Mead does not look well. He looks burnt to a crisp. But instead of pointing this out, Mead shakes the man's hand and makes up a lie of his own. "Thanks, Principal Jeavons," he says. "You don't look so bad yourself." Mead doesn't have anything against the man. It just makes him nervous that his old principal is here in his living room. A place that, as far as Mead knows, he has never before been.

"Please," he says, "we're all adults here, Teddy. You can call me Sandy."

"Well, in that case," Mead says, "you can call me Mead."

The principal glances over at Mead's mother, as if to ask if that's okay. The poor bastard. He probably wishes he were at home right now, sitting down to supper with his own family. If, in fact, he has one. Mead wouldn't know. He has never thought of the principal as a regular person, a person with a life that extends beyond the four brick walls of the school. Even now it's hard to imagine. Principal Jeavons leaving his pants on the bedroom floor. Mrs. Jeavons yelling at him for always expecting her to pick them up. Mead prefers to picture the man seated in front of the television, a TV dinner on his lap, watching an educational show on the Discovery channel and taking notes. The ringing phone must have come as a surprise. And even more surprising was the voice at the other end: Mrs. Fegley's voice. Did she say it was an emergency? Drop everything and come right away? And what does she think is going to happen now that he is here? Mead is too old for detention. Has she told Mr. Jeavons what she wants him to say? Did she write the man a script? Or is he supposed to try and wing this one on his own?

"So I guess my mother told you," Mead says, "that I have dropped out of college. I mean that is why you're here, isn't it? To try and convince the young genius to go back? To pursue his life's calling? In which case I'd like to save you the trouble and tell you up front that this little meeting of the minds, or whatever it is, is a waste of time. Both yours and mine. I'm not going back so save your breath." Then he pulls out his chair, takes a seat, and helps himself to a generous portion of his mother's beef stew.

Head down, he imagines the conversation taking place between Principal Jeavons—sorry, *Sandy*—and his mother right now. A shouting match of the eyes. To drown it out, Mead makes as much noise as he can with his knife and fork. He slurps his Coke and belches. Anything to cut through the suffocating onslaught of silence.

"Teddy, er, Mead," the principal says, "your mother and I were talking before you came in. About the science fair you entered in seventh grade. I was remembering that elaborate maze you built, the one through which you ran your pet mouse. What was his name, Mr. Cheddar?"

"Cheese," Mead says. "His name was Mr. Cheese."

"Right. Mr. Cheese. He was such a big hit that Mr. Belknap now incorporates a mouse-and-maze section into his curriculum every year."

Mead chews fast, eager to finish his supper and get the hell out of here before his mother, by way of the principal, gets under his sunburned skin and starts irritating him all over again.

"It was such an honor having you as a pupil in my school, Teddy," the principal says, sounding as if he rehearsed the line in front of his mirror before heading across town. "You have no idea what a thrill it is for a small-town principal such as myself to cross paths with such a brilliant and promising young man as yourself. It was a once-in-a-lifetime experience."

Mead chews faster.

"Whatever setback has fallen upon you, I'm sure it isn't insurmountable. It's the one thing you didn't learn in my school: how to handle a setback and move on. The situation just never presented itself."

And faster.

"I suppose it's harder now than it would've been had it happened to you at an earlier age, if you'd already developed the skill to rebound. But it's not too late, Mead, it's never too late. If you'd like someone to talk to, someone to help you through this, I'd like to be that person."

Mead slams down his fork. "All right," he says, "I've heard quite enough. I'm leaving now." And he stands up.

His mother stands up too, and grabs his sunburned arm. Mead cringes in pain.

"Teddy, please, if you won't talk to me or your father, at least talk to Principal Jeavons. Let someone help you."

"You don't get it, do you? I don't want his help or your help or anyone else's help. That's what got me into this mess in the first place. Too much help."

"What mess, Teddy? Tell me."

He pulls free of her grip. "I don't want to be me anymore. I'm tired of being a genius. I quit."

"You can't quit, Teddy, that's who you are."

"No, it isn't. It's what you turned me into. I just want to be normal, another overlooked face in the crowd."

"You don't mean that, Teddy."

"You know what your problem is, Mother? You're a lousy listener. You have no idea who I am or what I want because you're too busy telling me what *you* want. Always dispensing unwanted advice. Well, I've got some advice for you: Leave me alone." And he stomps down the hall to his bedroom and slams the door.

FLOORBOARDS CREAK, WAKING MEAD UP. He rolls over and the six-legged creature is sitting there in the dark, staring at him. "Go away," he says.

"Look at you," it answers. "You're pathetic." But its voice has changed. It no longer belongs to his mother. It's deeper. Male. The creature leans forward, causing a shaft of moonlight to fall across its face. A bearded face. Mead sits up in bed and rubs his eyes. He must be dreaming, or maybe he is suffering from sunstroke, because sitting there in the straight-backed chair next to his bed is none other than Georg Friedrich Bernhard Riemann.

"Have you read my dissertation on complex function theory?" he asks.

"Yes," Mead answers, his heart suddenly racing. "Several times. It's brilliant."

"Sure. You say that now. Everyone says that now. But it received very little attention back when I first wrote it. Gauss was the only one who got excited about it. A brilliant man, Gauss. You do know who he is, don't you?"

"Carl Friedrich Gauss. Of course. He's only the greatest mathematician to have ever lived. I mean, aside from you, sir."

"The man was a fool."

Mead sits up straighter. "A fool? How can you say that? Why, he discovered the Prime Number Theorem, not to mention the Method of Least Squares."

"Neither of which he published, leaving other men to take the credit."

"What's your point?" Mead says, suddenly feeling defensive.

"I think you know what my point is, Mead."

"No, I don't. It's not the same, not even close. Gauss didn't care whether or not he got published, he didn't care about getting credit. All he cared about was the work."

"And what do you care about, Mead?"

Bernhard Riemann is starting to get on Mead's nerves, annoying him as much as his mother. Is there no limit to the reach of that woman's influence? The junior high principal, that's one thing, but how she managed to dredge a man up from the grave and convince him to hassle her son is beyond comprehension. "Go away," Mead says, and rolls over so his back is to the nineteenth-century mathematician. How dare he come in here with all his holier-than-thou crap. As if he knows the first thing about the way life is nowadays. It's a different time. A new century. Everything is much more cutthroat now. The man doesn't know shit. He publishes an outrageous theory and then leaves it to his fellow mathematicians to test its veracity. Talk about your big ego. Bernhard Riemann has been laughing at them all for a hundred and thirty years, watching an endless procession of men squirm as they attempt to prove or disprove his theory. Except that Mead almost has. Or at least thinks he has. Maybe that's why the dead man is here. Not to hassle Mead but to tell him that he is on the right path. That he has all but solved the greatest unsolved mathematical problem of the twentieth century. To congratulate him. After all, who would know better than the man himself? It would make all the difference in the world, just to know, to get confirmation directly from the source. To hell with the dean and Dr. Kustrup and especially to hell with Herman. Mead doesn't need to get published. The only person from whom he really needs to get recognition is the man who wrote the theorem in the first place: Bernhard Riemann.

With chills running up and down his spine, Mead rolls back over to face the great mathematician. To ask Bernhard Riemann if he is on the right track. To get the validation he so desperately needs. But it's too late; the man is gone.

HEADLIGHTS SWEEP ACROSS THE FRONT LAWN as a pickup truck turns the corner and pulls to a stop at the curb. The passenger door swings open and Mead crawls in next to Lenny. "What happened to you?" he says and offers Mead a cup of take-out coffee. "Looks like someone stuck you under the broiler and then headed off to bed."

"It was something like that," Mead says and pushes the cup away, unable to bear the heat of it. Unable to bear his clothes that feel like sandpaper against his skin.

From his perch behind the steering wheel, Uncle Martin glances past Lenny at his nephew, then puts the truck into gear and pulls away from the curb. Third-degree burns from head to toe and Mead barely gets a nod of recognition.

The streets of High Grove are deserted in the predawn hours, streetlamps twinkling like stars through the branches of the trees. But already the air is warm, a precursor to a hot day. The mere thought of the sun makes Mead wince with pain. At least he'll be sitting in the shade all day.

They exit High Grove and head north on the state road. Houses and trees drop away like a curtain to expose the surrounding landscape. Flat as a pancake. Mead cannot see it but he can feel it. The openness. The lights more distant now. Stars no bigger than pin-dots in the black sky. It's one of the few things he missed about High Grove when he was in Chicago: the stars. Sometimes, walking back to the dorm after dark, he would look up at the pattern of lit windows on the skyscrapers and pretend they were stars. He even fashioned a name for the constellation glowing from the Sears Tower. *Nachlass.* A German word used to connote unpublished papers found among a scholar's personal effects after his death. Like the ones now lying under glass in the Göttingen Library that had been found in Bernhard Riemann's home. Like the ones in the green-and-blue plaid suitcase shoved under Mead's bed. *Nachlass.*

A pair of green eyes looms up from the middle of the road and Martin brakes hard. Mead has to brace his arms against the dashboard to keep from sailing through the front windshield and it sends a jolt of pain through his entire crisped body. God forbid his uncle should drive a truck with working seat belts, his son barely three months in the ground after passing through a windshield to his own untimely death. If this truck ever had any belts, they've been decades lost beneath the seat cushions along with who knows how many other things Mead would rather not touch with his bare fingers. Lenny grabs the dashboard too, while trying to hold on to two cups of coffee. One of the lids pops off and the contents of the cup spill all over the front of Mead's slacks.

"Shit," Mead says, thankful that the coffee isn't piping hot. "Jesus, Uncle Martin, why didn't you just run over it? Then we could've just skipped the hunt, called it a day, and gone back home."

The engine goes dead and the headlights shut off. Martin turns in his seat and really looks at Mead for the first time all morning. "Hunting is not about killing," he says. "So if that's the reason you came along, you best open that door and get out."

Mead thinks about it. He thinks about opening the passenger door, getting out, and walking back to town in the pitch dark in his coffee-stained pants. He thinks about crawling back into bed and burying his head under the sheets. Then he thinks about the six-legged creature, breathing down his neck all day.

"Death is the goal of the hunt," Mead says, "not the hunter. I know, Uncle Martin. I haven't forgotten."

They remain in the dark. The three of them inside the truck like sitting ducks in the middle of the road. Mead almost wishes an eighteen-wheeler would come barreling around the corner and run the lot of them over. Put them out of their communal misery. But there's no speeding truck, just the sound of a songbird singing in a new day. It's a happy song, like a movement in an opera that presages a change for the better. A hint that something good is about to happen onstage, the tides about to turn, the worst behind us. Hope on the horizon and all that crap. Only this isn't an opera, it's real life.

Uncle Martin restarts the truck, which drowns out the songbird. He turns on the headlights and proceeds up the road.

TWELVE. THAT'S HOW OLD MEAD WAS the fall his uncle got it in his head to turn his nephew into a man by teaching him how to hunt. The year he went out and bought the young genius a shotgun for his birthday.

"A hunt is not a fight." And so began Uncle Martin's lecture on the philosophy of hunting, one that he would repeat over and over again like a sermon in church. "It assumes an inequality. A predator and his prey. One having a distinct advantage over the other. But it isn't a slaughter either. A hunt also assumes the prey has one distinct advantage over his opponent and that is his instinct, the very aspect of the hunt that draws man to it. A chance to return to his atavistic roots, to throw off all the stresses of his modern-day life. To banish reason in favor of instinct. To act instead of think." And like so many of the sermons in church, it bore little significance to Mead's young life.

"The best hunters learn from their prey," Martin said, "by mimicking them. To successfully hunt a rabbit, you will first have to learn how to think like one. To be quiet. To make no assumptions. And to look everywhere always. These are the three dictums of hunting."

And as if enduring the lecture wasn't bad enough, putting it into play was even worse. Boring beyond belief. Sitting in one spot for hours upon hours with no end in sight and yet remaining alert the whole time. Trying not to let his mind wander. Trying not to become so distracted by his thoughts that he could no longer see what was directly in front of him. But the young Mead failed. Over and over again. Got lost in his own thoughts until he was startled back into his surroundings when his uncle's shotgun went off. The only reason Mead even put on the bright orange vest, the double-twill pants, and the steel-toed boots was to see the look of horror on his mother's face. Her genius son suddenly transformed into a country hick. It was the best part of his uncle's present, that look on her face. Worth every chigger bite, bee sting, and poison ivy rash Mead had to endure as a result of tromping through cornfields after his uncle just so they could sit under a copse of trees for hours on end and wait.

That, plus the time he got to spend with his cousin.

MARTIN TURNS OFF THE STATE ROAD onto a rutted lane that runs between two cornfields that are chock full of rabbits multiplying faster than the corn can grow. The farmer who owns this land is more than happy to have as many as possible of them taken off his hands. Martin follows the lane to the end and parks under an oak tree. Then gets out of the truck, hops up onto the flatbed, and unlocks a metal box. After pulling on a neon-orange hunting vest, he tosses one at Mead. "God knows if you even need to wear it, looking as red as you do," he says, then lifts out a Remington 870 Special Field. A twenty-gauge single-shot. "You do remember how to load one of these, don't you?"

Mead takes the shotgun from his uncle and breaks it open with a flick of his wrist. He used to love doing that in front of his mother: breaking the shotgun open and then snapping it shut again in the middle of her kitchen. Like John Wayne. Like a wild-west hero. Just so he could hear her say, "Get that damned thing out of here before you kill somebody." Which wasn't going to happen because it wasn't loaded. Shot shells were like gold and Uncle Martin was the gold keeper, parceling out nuggets of it on a need-only basis. As he does now. Martin hands Mead a No. 6 shot shell loaded with 280 pellets, only three of which are necessary to kill a rabbit. Death might not be the goal of the hunter, but the odds weigh pretty heavily against any other outcome.

PERCY WAS FIFTEEN THAT FALL, when he tapped Mead on the shoulder and gestured with his hand for his cousin to follow him. Mead glanced across the cornfield to where his uncle and Lenny had hunkered down with their rifles and coolers: two bright spots of orange in a sea of dying cornstalks. Proof that rabbits are color-blind. Mead made a mental note of it, thinking that perhaps he would pursue the idea further in his next science project, then stood up and followed his cousin.

Percy lead him through a copse of trees to a neighboring field, set down his shotgun, and started doing push-ups. Mead glanced around to make sure his uncle and Lenny were completely out of sight, then set down his own shotgun and dug an algebra book out of his backpack as his cousin flipped over and started doing sit-ups.

"I have ten hats that cost $47.50 for all of them," Mead said. "How much will I have to sell each hat for to make a profit of a dollar on each?"

"I don't know," Percy answered as he pulled his elbows to his knees and then laid back down again. "How much?"

"Set it up in an algebraic expression letting *y* represent the answer and then solve for *y*."

Percy got up and started running in place, lifting his knees as high as they would go with each step. "I gotta tell you, cousin, I don't really give a damn how much you charge for your goddamned hats, I don't even wear one."

Mead closed the book. "Fine. Fail algebra. It doesn't make any difference to me. But you might wish you'd paid more attention in class when all those numbers in the ledger book don't add up anymore and you start losing money."

Percy stopped running. "Are you referring to the furniture store?"

"Maybe."

"That store ain't my problem, cousin. I've got other plans." Placing his right hand on his hip, Percy leaned over and touched his left hand to his right foot.

"I know," Mead said.

"What do you mean, you know. What do you know?"

"I've seen you. Through the window in the library. On the baseball field."

Percy stood up straight. "Since when did you start watching sports?"

"I wasn't watching sports, I was watching you."

"You were watching me? Really?" Percy smiled. "Do you love me, Teddy? Huh? Do you?" And he reached for Mead's cheek, trying to pinch it.

"Stop it," Mead said and pushed his cousin's hand away.

Percy glanced past Mead into the trees, making sure the coast was clear, then sat down next to him and said, "A scout came by the school the other day. He thinks I'm good enough to play professionally. You know, after I graduate high school. I'm gonna be a pitcher for the St. Louis Cardinals, cousin. Whadaya think of that?" And he made a fist to show off the muscle in his right bicep. "This arm is my ticket out of here."

"Does Uncle Martin know?"

"Please," Percy said. "He'd have my ass if he knew."

"But he's a big baseball fan, isn't he?"

"Sure, he loves watching other people play it, but not his son. He's got other plans for his son, plans that I am not the least bit interested in. I don't want to spend the rest of my life burying dead people. But then look who I'm talking to."

"What's that supposed to mean?"

"Spare me the act, cousin. You don't want to be an undertaker so bad that you're willing to spend every waking hour of your life studying your ass off to get out of it. Your father doesn't have any choice but to send you to college. Genius. Damned straight you're a genius, that was the most ingenious move in the world. I only wish I'd thought of it first."

"That's not why I study, Percy. I do it because I enjoy it."

"Yeah, right," he said, and stared out across the cornfield.

"But it's true."

"Well, if you love it so much then you can do it for both of us."

"You want me to do your homework for you? But that's cheating; it's wrong."

"It ain't wrong unless someone finds out about it and no one is gonna find out because neither you nor me are gonna tell anyone."

"I," Mead says. "Neither you nor I are going to tell anyone."

"Great. Then we've got us a deal."

MARTIN LEADS THE WAY, Lenny follows behind him, and Mead takes up the rear. The day is getting brighter by the second, the trees now standing in silhouette against an azure sky as the three men hike along the perimeter of the field. They walk for maybe ten, fifteen minutes before Martin finds a spot that suits him and hunkers down with his shotgun and cooler. Lenny steps past him, eyes set on another spot about twenty yards farther down, and Mead starts to follow. But Lenny raises his hand to stop him and nods at Martin. Mead shakes his head. Lenny gives him a stern look and Mead gives in.

He sits down on a rock maybe ten feet from his uncle. Far enough away to be out of swinging range but close enough to talk, should his uncle be so inclined. Should he decide that he wants to offer up an apology for how he has been acting toward Mead ever since he got home. If Mead could turn back time, he would do it. And next time around he'd turn down the airline ticket Herman offered him. He'd spend his one-week spring break on campus and stay in his dorm room the entire time. That way he would be there when Percy dropped by unexpectedly. And that way he wouldn't have had to come home one week before graduation. He could have given his presentation in Epps Hall and then he could have sat down and prepared his valedictory address for graduation day. But he can't. He cannot turn back time.

A brown rabbit hops out into the field maybe thirty yards away, well within shooting range. Uncle Martin lifts his gun into position, tucking the butt into his shoulder and sighting the animal down the barrel. *Look with your gun and shoot where you look.* Mead plugs his ears and braces for the shotgun blast.

PERCY SQUEEZED OFF THE TRIGGER and the loud report stunned the air, sending a flock of grackles flying up out of a tree. A cloud of black smoke rose from the end of the muzzle and drifted into Mead's eyes. He closed them and waved his hand through the air to clear it. When he opened them again, his cousin was holding the dead rabbit upside down by its hind legs. He strung it up to a tree and slit its throat.

"I'm not going to do your homework," Mead said. "It's wrong."

Percy inserted his knife into the back of the rabbit's neck and twisted off its head. Holding it in the palm of his hand, he said, "How much would it freak your mother out to learn that her precious little brainy-boy shot and killed a rabbit all on his own?"

Mead knew what Percy was trying to do. And it was tempting—boy, was it ever tempting—but it wasn't right. "That would be lying."

"Strictly speaking, yes. But there're many shades of lies, cousin, ranging all the way from black to white. You do my homework for me and this rabbit is yours."

Mead pictured his mother's face as he walked through the back door with a dead rabbit in a plastic baggie. Blood all over his hands. "It's wrong."

"I don't see it that way, cousin. I see it as one hand washing the other. That's the way it works in life. Family members are supposed to stick by one another. So what're you gonna do, are you gonna stick by me?"

Five. That's how many rabbits Mead supposedly killed and gutted that fall before his mother took his shotgun away and sent him to the library as penance.

* * *

MARTIN LOWERS HIS SHOTGUN and looks over at Mead, nods toward the rabbit. Hands shaking, Mead lifts his gun into position. This time he is going to do it. To pull the trigger himself. If he kills the rabbit, it'll make up for the five lies he told that fall. Wipe the slate clean. Clear his conscience. Right a wrong. The little brown rabbit lifts its head and sniffs the air, then looks directly at Mead. But it can't see him because he's in the shade and it can't smell him because he's downwind. The poor critter doesn't have a clue. All Mead has to do is squeeze off the trigger and that rabbit is his. It'll never even know what hit it. But Mead can't do it. Because when he looks at that rabbit he sees himself sitting in the university library, reading a book. If only he had glanced up every once in a while. Paid more attention to his surroundings. Then maybe he would be sitting in his dorm room right now and not here in this stupid field.

Mead lowers the gun. "I'm sorry, Uncle Martin. I knew."

"You knew? You knew what?"

"That Percy was going to run off. And that A he got in math freshman year in high school? That was mine. I did his homework for him. I should've told. When you and Aunt Jewel were freaking out that Christmas, I should've told you. And I should never have agreed to do his homework, but I did and I'm sorry."

Martin turns away from Mead, lifts the gun to his shoulder, and squeezes off the trigger. The rabbit does a backward flip through the air and lands on its side. Martin stands up and walks out into the field to retrieve his prey, the shotgun blast still ringing in Mead's ears. That must be it. That must be why he does not hear his uncle say anything back.

MARTIN AND LENNY DROP MEAD OFF at the house so he can change out of his coffee-stained pants before going to the store.

But instead of heading inside, Mead stands on the curb until his uncle's truck drops out of sight, then walks over to the local department store. He's searching through a rack of khaki trousers that look virtually identical to all the pairs of pants already hanging in his closet when he decides that he needs to make a change in his life. Beginning with his pants. He steps over to a table stacked with blue jeans, selects a pair, and ducks into the fitting room. Mead has never before owned a pair of blue jeans. His mother would never buy any for him. Only farmers and rednecks wear jeans, that's what she always said when he asked.

It hurts like hell pulling them on over his lobster-colored legs but the physical pain serves as a welcome distraction from all his other troubles. They fit more snugly than trousers, giving shape to parts of Mead's anatomy that heretofore had always remained hidden beneath loose folds of double-worsted gabardine. Mead checks out his backside. It looks sort of like a James Dean ass, the sort of ass with which girls fall in love. Girls like Hayley Sammons, for example.

Mead leaves them on and steps out of the dressing room. And almost runs smack-dab into Mr. Colgan. Shit. First his mother invites his junior high school principal over for supper and now this. His high school principal. In the men's department of Melnick's Department Store, checking out button-down shirts. It has to be a conspiracy, his mother working in concert with God or something. Mead turns to go in the opposite direction, to make a quick getaway, and trips over a display of sunglasses, almost knocking it down. Grabbing the first pair he touches, he slides them on over his prescription glasses and sidles along a wall of suits, feigning an interest in double-breasted tweed jackets as he makes his way toward the checkout counter. But there's a line. And a chatty girl working the register. Mead glances over his shoulder, looking for Mr. Colgan, but the man is nowhere in sight. He probably ducked into the fitting room or strolled off to another department. "Hurry up," Mead mumbles under his breath at the checkout girl, "before he reappears." Finally, it's his turn. Mead rips the price tag off his jeans and hands it to her along with the sunglasses.

"Teddy?" she says. "Teddy Fegley? Is that you?"

Oh shit, here we go again. Must be another classmate. "No," he says, "I get that a lot but I'm not him. I'm from out of town."

For a second it looks as if she is going to buy it, then her expression changes and she leans forward over the counter. "What's the capital of South Dakota?"

"Pierre."

"I knew it. I knew it was you. I'm Donna, Donna Eubanks. We were in the same class in second grade. With Mrs. Salter. You sat in the front row. That's the one state capital I could never get to stick in my head. Pierre. So wow, what're you doing now? What're you doing here?"

"I'm part of a traveling exhibit," Mead says. "Me and Stephen Hawking are doing a whirlwind tour of the states. And after that, we're off to Paris."

Donna looks confused. "Who's Stephen Hawking?"

"One of the most brilliant minds of the twentieth century," Mr. Colgan says.

Shit, so much for escaping sight unseen. Mead should've just stolen the pants.

"Mr. Colgan, sir, what a pleasant and unexpected surprise."

"Likewise," the principal says. "I was just reading about you in the local newspaper. Congratulations on your recent graduation. And on the presentation. Very impressive. But then I always knew you would amount to something. So where're you off to next?"

"Paris," Donna says. "He's going to Paris with that Stephen guy."

"And then I'm taking some time off," Mead says. "I thought I'd come back here for a while, take a break from school, you know, to gain some life experience."

Mr. Colgan's eyebrows shoot up into his hairline like two cockroaches running from the light of day. "Time off? Life isn't a vacation, Theodore. One doesn't take time off to experience it."

"I know, sir, I didn't mean it like that." Mead hands his father's credit card to Donna. "If you don't mind, I'm kind of in a hurry here." She takes it and rings up his purchase but not fast enough. It's as if he is back in high school, sitting in the principal's office, talking over all his options for college, back when he believed that it would lead him to a better life. Back when he believed every word that came out of Principal Colgan's mouth about the opportunities that awaited him there. But they were just more lies. Because now he knows that those opportunities come at a price. One he is not willing to pay.

"I gotta go," Mead says and bolts for the exit.

"Teddy," Donna says. "Wait. You forgot your card."

MEAD RINGS THE FRONT DOORBELL AND WAITS. He should have brought along the swimming trunks as an explanation for his unexpected appearance. He could have said he dropped by to return them, but that would have required stopping by his house first.

As he waits he hears a terrible racket coming from the garage, like someone is playing a warped vinyl album on a cheapo turntable at the wrong speed. It reminds Mead of the music his dormmates were fond of listening to on Saturday night when they got stoned. He couldn't blame them, really. It would have been intolerable to listen to in any other state of mind.

He rings the bell again, and is about to give up, when the door opens. Mrs. Sammons pulls a wad of cotton out of each ear and says, "Theodore. I'm sorry. I didn't hear the door chime." Then, on taking in his burnt skin, "My lord in heaven, what happened to you? You look awful."

"Is Hayley around?"

"I'm afraid not. She never stays in the house when her brother is practicing. Don't you think you should go to the hospital or something?"

"I'm fine, Mrs. Sammons. Just tell her I dropped by."

Mead walks back to the street and turns to leave, then changes his mind and turns back. Standing at the end of the Sammonses' driveway, he peers into the garage, where a set of drums sits next to a lawnmower, a ladder, and a couple of garbage cans. A pudgy teenage boy is perched behind the drums, whacking away at them as if he were beating up on his little brother. A second teenager is standing a few feet in front of him, strumming an electric guitar and screaming into a microphone. Mead waits, his red arms hanging at his sides radiating heat, until the song ends.

"Well," the guitar player says, "whadaya think?"

"Which one of you is Hayley's brother, Eric?" Mead asks.

"I am. Who wants to know?"

Mead studies Eric's frame. "What's your shirt size?"

"None of your business, creep."

"I'll bet you're a medium, just like me."

"Listen, if you don't leave right now I'm gonna call the cops, got it, pervert?"

"No problem," Mead says. "I'm leaving."

But fifteen minutes later he's back. He stands at the end of the driveway until Eric finishes his song. "What do you want now, pervert?"

"Your band appears to be missing a bass player," Mead says.

"Yeah? So?"

"So I thought I'd offer my services."

Eric looks at his drummer and then back at Mead, who is holding in his arms an instrument that is as tall as he is. "That's not a bass guitar, you idiot, it's a cello."

"Same difference," Mead says and draws a bow across the strings of his cello so Eric and his sidekick can hear what it sounds like. "I played for three years in the high school band. I'm pretty good. And I read music too."

As they lock heads to discuss the matter, Mead glances up at the house and sees Mrs. Sammons looking back through the kitchen window. She waves and he waves back. Hayley has got to come home sooner or later and when she does Mead will be here waiting for her. He hopes she comes home with her boyfriend because Mead would like to meet him. Oh, yeah. She has one all right. Mead is sure of it now. Because the clothes in that duffel bag, they no more fit her brother than they do Mead. Oh yeah, she's got a boyfriend, all right.

"Okay," Eric says. "You're in."

An hour later Eric decides to call it a day. And all Mead has to show for his effort is a throbbing headache to go along with his throbbing arms and legs. No Hayley. No boyfriend. Nothing.

"We'll meet back here tomorrow at ten," Eric says. "Nelson'll need your help loading his drums into the van."

Mead looks at the pudgy boy. "Why? Is he going somewhere?"

"Yes," Eric says. "Grange Hall. We've got a gig there tomorrow at noon."

"Excuse me?"

"A gig. A live performance."

A horn honks but Mead doesn't look up, he just shoves the sunglasses up the bridge of his nose and keeps pushing his cello along the sidewalk toward home. It's probably another classmate, another mini-reunion in the making, and Mead has had more than his fair share of those lately. If he keeps walking, maybe whoever it is will give up and drive away. Only they don't. They honk again. And only then does it dawn on Mead that it may actually be someone he wants to see—like Hayley—so he lifts his eyes. But it isn't Hayley; it's Dr. Alexander. Driving a black Buick sedan circa 1940.

Mead steps over to the car as the professor rolls down the window.

"Dr. Alexander, what're you doing here in High Grove? In this car?"

"It's a rental," he says. "Isn't she a beauty?"

Mead peers inside the sedan. The professor appears to be driving with one leg in a cast. Which seems a virtual impossibility. And yet here he is. "Since when do they rent out fifty-year-old cars?"

"Chaos," Dr. Alexander says. "If it looks like chaos, you need to step back, Mead, and keep stepping back until a pattern emerges."

"What are you talking about?"

"The Riemann Hypothesis. I've been meditating on that stack of zeros you left in my office. The answer isn't there, Mead. I've decided that number theory is a trail with a dead end. You were right to walk away, to blow off the dean. We have to go in another direction. Change our thinking altogether."

"That's not why I left."

"It isn't? Then why did you leave?"

Mead glances up to make sure no horse-drawn carriages or gas streetlights have sprung up on the street. Reassured that he is still planted solidly in the present, he looks back at Dr. Alexander and says, "When you were over there in England, at King's

College in Cambridge, did you ever dream of solving the Riemann Hypothesis?"

"Every night. Why?"

"How far would you have gone to pull it off?"

"You've been down in my basement, Mead. I think you already know the answer to that question."

"And how far is too far?"

"Get in the car, Mead. We'll talk about it on the way back to Chicago."

"No, I can't go back. My father is expecting me at the store."

"Then I'll give you a lift."

"No. Go away. Go back to Chicago," Mead says and walks away from the car as fast as he can pushing an oversized musical instrument. But Dr. Alexander won't leave him alone. The man follows close on Mead's heels in the black sedan, tooting the horn several times. Mead reaches the corner and the black sedan pulls up beside him. Shit, why won't the professor leave him be? Mead turns around to confront the professor one last time. "I said go away!" he yells. But it isn't Dr. Alexander who is pursuing him; it's his aunt and uncle in their brand-new Lincoln Continental. Jewel rolls down her window and sticks out her head. "Teddy, you're red as a tomato. Are you all right? We've been honking at you for five minutes. Get in and we'll drive you home. Your mother is worried sick about you and, frankly, so am I. We're on the way over there for supper right now. Come on now, get in."

"Aunt Jewel, did you see an antique car drive by here just now? A 1940 Buick? An old guy would've been driving it. A guy with long gray hair."

Jewel places her hand on Mead's forehead. "You're burning up, Teddy."

"I'm fine, Aunt Jewel. You must have seen it. He drove right up this street."

Uncle Martin gets out and walks around the car. "This won't fit in the backseat," he says and takes the cello out of Mead's hands. "I'll have to put it in the trunk."

Mead does not ask his uncle if he saw the antique sedan, he just gets in the car and feels his forehead. And the thing is, his aunt is right; he is burning up.

JEWEL STEPS FROM THE CAR wearing a simple blue dress and pumps. No bathrobe. No slippers. The only hint of the crazy woman Mead saw in the A & P yesterday is in her eyes, which point skyward as she walks across the lawn toward the front door, oblivious to the trail of words spilling from Uncle Martin's mouth, focused on some distant spot in the universe. The expression on her face reminds Mead of a conversation he once had with her when he was in first grade. Jewel was snapping beans in the kitchen, watching through the back window as Uncle Martin pitched balls to their then-nine-year-old son, Percy. "When I was your age," she said, "I used to dream about becoming a ballerina." Mead pictured her twirling across a stage, wearing an apron instead of a tutu, with a spatula in one hand and an eggbeater in the other. "Then I hit puberty," she continued, "and started busting out in all the wrong places. My hips were too wide, my thighs too thick. So I knew I had to come up with a new dream." Mead expected her to say something like housewife or mother. Instead she said, "I dreamed about becoming an aviatrix and flying around the world. Like Amelia Earhart."

Mead's mother opens the front door, surprised to find her son among the arriving guests. She looks at Mead and says, "You got another phone call. From Dr. Alexander. He wants you to call him back." Mead's father steps up behind her and says to Uncle Martin, "You're thirty minutes late. I was beginning to get worried."

"The delay is my fault," Aunt Jewel says. "I couldn't decide what to wear. I've been such a recluse lately. I haven't been out of the house in weeks."

"Yes, you have," Mead says. "I saw you in the A & P yesterday. Buying ice cream." Jewel seems nonplused by this information and looks to Martin as if he might be able to clear up the confusion, a look similar to the one she gave the store clerk. But he just glares at Mead and says, "If my wife says she hasn't been out of the house, then she hasn't been out of the house."

"But I saw her," Mead says. "At the A & P. I walked her home."

Martin looks at Mead's dad. "Your son is a liar, did you know that? He admitted as much to me in the woods this morning."

Everyone turns to stare at Mead, waiting for an explanation. But he has none to offer. Okay, so he lied about Percy. He pretended he didn't know where he was when he actually did. But he'd made a promise. Shit, if Mead had known his uncle was going to use his heartfelt confession against him, he would never have come clean. But fine. Whatever. No good deed goes unpunished. This time, however, Mead *is* telling the truth. And it's driving him nuts that no one will believe him. Not that his track record has been good as of late. Not that anyone in this room has any reason whatsoever to believe him. Not even his father. Mr. Switzerland. Mr. Neutrality. Fine. If they want to believe he made up that whole story about seeing Jewel in the A & P, fine. They can believe what they want; he can't stop them. But he did see her. He really did. But then again he also believes that he just saw Dr. Alexander in a 1940 Buick.

"Oh. Right," Jewel says. "I remember now. Teddy's right. I did run to the store to get ice cream. It just slipped my mind is all." And she squeezes his wrist in an affectionate way. But Mead gets the distinct impression that now *she* is lying.

* * *

HIS MOTHER PULLS HIM ASIDE and hands him a scrap of paper with Dr. Alexander's home phone number on it. "He sounded worried. Call him. He's a friend of yours, is he not?"

"I'm not lying about Jewel."

Since Mead won't take the scrap of paper, his mother tucks it into his shirt pocket. "If you don't want to talk to me or your old principal, fine, but at least talk to your professor."

"I'm worried about her. I think you should be too."

"Tonight. I want you to call him tonight."

THE ROAST SAT IN THE OVEN SO LONG that the meat falls right off the bone. "Just the way I like it," Martin says as Mead's mother piles one and then two and then three slices onto his plate. "Say when," she says but he doesn't utter a word as she adds two more slices. You'd think the guy hadn't eaten in weeks. But he wolfed down his dinner at the Lodge the other night, and snarfed up the sandwich Mead bought him for lunch, so the guy is hardly starving. "Why don't you work on that for starters," Mead's mother says and moves on to Jewel. "Just one for me," she says and waves the roast away, then stares at the slice on her plate as if it were a two-pound steak, cutting it up into tiny pieces and moving them around. Mead never sees her actually put any of it in her mouth.

"So how have you been doing?" Mead's mother asks Jewel. "I feel just awful because I've been meaning to drop by for a visit but something just always comes up."

Oh, but she's got plenty of time now. That is the point she is oh-so-subtly trying to make, is it not? Now that she doesn't have a graduation ceremony to attend. All the time in the world. Why doesn't she just come right out and say it?

"Oh, I'm fine," Jewel says. "Just taking one day at a time."

"She's been gardening," Martin says. "We've got enough cucumbers and carrots and green beans in our backyard to feed the whole county."

"And tomatoes," Jewel says. "Lots of big, red, plump tomatoes. They've always been Percy's favorite, you know. When he was little, he used to eat 'em like apples. Sweet as candy, he'd say. I don't know what I'm going to do with them all now, what with his being gone and all. I guess I'll have to can them."

"Isn't it a little early in the year for tomatoes?" Mead says, and his uncle throws him a dirty look but his parents don't see it; they're too busy staring at Jewel, waiting for her to start crying or something. But she doesn't, instead she pushes back her chair and says, "If you'll excuse me, I'm going to visit the little girls' room." Martin stands too, as if he intends to escort her, but she shoos away his hand and goes by herself. Since he's up anyway, Martin offers to refresh everyone's drink and disappears into the kitchen. As soon as the door swings shut behind him, Mead's mother leans across the table and says, "She seems perfectly fine to me."

"What're you saying, Mother, that I made it up?"

"No, but perhaps you're mistaken. Jewel never has had any sartorial sense. You probably mistook her frock for a nightgown."

"Yeah, right. And her fuzzy slippers were really high heels."

"All right, you two," Mead's dad says. "That's enough. I agree with your mother. She seems fine. Now let's just drop it."

"Why're you taking her side, Dad? Why don't you believe me? I don't think she's okay. I think she needs help."

"I'm not taking anyone's side, Teddy."

"Yes, you are."

The kitchen door opens and Martin backs through it balancing four whiskey glasses in his two hands. Mead glares at his father and folds his arms over his chest, feeling betrayed by the one ally he thought he had in this house. He's getting ready to throw down his napkin and make his all-too-common retreat to the sanctuary of his room when Jewel returns from the bathroom, a pair of swimming trunks dangling from her right hand, a red T-shirt from the left. "I found these in your bathroom," she says, "hanging on the shower rod. How did they get here?"

"I left them there," Mead says and blushes as if his aunt were holding up a pair of his boxer shorts. "Sorry."

Jewel looks over at Martin. "These are Percy's. They belong to our son."

"No," Mead says. "I borrowed them from a friend."

"What friend?" his mother asks, as if shocked to learn that he might actually have one.

"But they look just like Percy's," Jewel says.

Martin takes the swimming trunks from her and dangles them accusingly in front of Mead's face. "Where did you get these?"

"I just told you," he says. "A friend."

"What friend?" Martin says.

"What difference does it make what friend?"

"Just tell him, Teddy," Mead's dad says. And to everyone else in the room it probably sounds as if he is asking the question all cool and calm-like, but Mead can hear the undercurrent in his voice. An undercurrent of fed-uped-ness.

"They belong to Hayley's brother, Eric. Okay?"

Martin tries to give the swimming trunks back to Mead but Aunt Jewel snatches them out of his hand. "Let go," he says softly and has to peel away her fingers one at a time. "They aren't Percy's. Please let go."

Soon after this, they leave.

As the front door clicks shut, Mead turns to his mother and says, "Yeah, right. I mistook her crappy dress for a bathrobe. Aunt Jewel is obviously fine. Perfectly fine." He pulls back the curtain and watches his aunt and uncle amble to the car, Jewel's face turned once more toward the night sky, her dream finally come true. She's probably been flying around for months now. Ever since the accident. Taking in the sights as she passes over the mountain ranges of Asia, the jungles of South America, and the vast stretches of ocean in between. Flying above it all. Making her way slowly around the world like her hero, Amelia Earhart. But she isn't flying solo; Percy is up there with her. "I've always wanted to go to China," he says, "and walk along the Great Wall. I want to visit all Seven Wonders of the World. Then you can fly home, Mother, but not one minute sooner. We still have so much more to see together before you go home."

MEAD WAITS UNTIL AFTER HIS PARENTS have gone to bed, until all the lights in the house have been turned off, then waits a little longer. Then he crawls out of bed and down the hall and, with a flashlight pointed at the telephone, dials the number on the scrap of paper his mother gave him. He doesn't want to talk to the professor; he just wants to confirm that the man is there. Up in Chicago and not down here in High Grove. Heat stroke. That is the only plausible explanation, the only one that makes any sense.

The phone rings three times and then the professor's voice comes over the line. "Hello?" he says, but Mead does not answer. Neither does he hang up. "Mead? Is that you?" Dr. Alexander says. "Are you all right?"

"Why does everyone keep asking me that question?"

"Because we're worried about you. You've been under an immense amount of pressure. It's a lot to ask of an eighteen-year-old boy to speak before a crowd of seasoned mathematicians. I told the dean that much but he wouldn't listen."

"I trusted the wrong person."

"I was only looking out for your best interest, Mead."

"No, I'm not talking about you. Someone else."

"Who?"

"Dr. Alexander, did you ever own a 1940 Buick sedan?"

He laughs. "A long time ago, Mead, why do you ask?"

"I'm going to take your advice."

"And what advice is that?"

"To step back. I have to step back until I see a pattern in the chaos."

"When did I say that?"

"Good night, Dr. Alexander," Mead says and hangs up.

8

FLYING NONSTOP

Chicago
Three Months Before Graduation

MEAD BOARDS THE CITY BUS and rides through the park, over the interstate, and into one of the outlying neighborhoods to his coffee shop. He takes a seat in a booth by the window and orders three buttermilk pancakes with two sunnyside-up eggs, two sausage links, and a glass of milk. Then he takes out a copy of *American Mathematical Monthly*, folds it open to an article on the Riemann Hypothesis, and begins to read.

Mead has not had one good night's sleep since his meeting with Dean Falconia at the beginning of the year, when the man assigned to him the task of writing his own paper on the Riemann Hypothesis as his senior thesis. The first thing Mead did upon leaving the dean's office was go to Dr. Alexander's office. But he wasn't there so Mead headed over to his house. And they have spent nearly every waking hour since—collectively and separately—reading through old copies of *American Mathematical Monthly* and *Mathematical Intelligencer* that were archived in a dozen musty cardboard boxes in the professor's basement in search of all the articles related in any way, shape, or manner to the Riemann Hypothesis.

The waitress comes over and gives Mead a third refill on his milk. "Can I get you anything else, sweetie?"

"Yes. A roast beef sandwich."

"I'm sorry, we don't serve sandwiches before noon."

"That's okay," Mead says. "I don't plan to eat it before noon." He plans to take it back to the dorm for dinner since the cafeteria will be closed all week, what with everyone but Mead away on spring break.

The waitress checks out the magazine he is reading, then looks at the napkin upon which he has calculated a couple more zeta zeros (by now he does it without thinking), then smiles and says, "I'll see what I can do for you."

He is just finishing an article on the characteristic polynomials of matrices and the spacings between non-trivial zeros of the zeta function when Herman Weinstein slides into the booth across from him and slaps an airline ticket on the table. Mead is so startled that he chokes on his pancake and has to wash it down with a slug of milk. "How in the hell did you find me here?"

Herman shrugs. "I followed you." He pats the ticket. "Open it."

Mead does not have any interest in looking at Herman's ticket. He could really care less where the guy is going during the break. Italy. Switzerland. Greece. Or with whom. Although it would hardly be a stretch of the imagination to guess that Cynthia will be joining him. What girl could possibly turn down a week spent sunbathing on the sandy beaches of south France? Not that any of that matters to Mead. Just so long as Herman is as far away from here as possible. That way Mead won't have to worry that the guy is going to drop by for a chat in the middle of the night. That Herman will invite him out to the symphony one night only to snub him in class the next day and then act as if he doesn't exist for an entire month only to pop up in a crosstown coffee shop and offer him an airline ticket. Mead would prefer not to waste any more of his valuable time wondering whether they are supposed to be friends this week or not, so he pushes the ticket back toward Herman, opens another math periodical, and says, "No, thank you."

The waitress comes over and asks Herman if he would like to order breakfast. He declines her offer, claiming he does not have time to eat, and orders two cups of coffee instead: one for himself and one for the limousine driver parked at the curb outside, then slips the waitress an extra couple dollars to carry it out to him. God forbid Herman Weinstein should ride a city bus. At least he won't be staying long and Mead will soon be able to go back to doing what it was he was doing before he was so rudely interrupted.

Herman empties two creamers into his cup of coffee and adds three spoonfuls of sugar. "Aren't you even the slightest bit curious?" he asks.

"I'm curious about a lot of things, Weinstein, like whether or not there is life on other planets and if we'd recognize it if we saw it. Like how a bird that migrates over a thousand miles every winter ends up nesting in the same tree every summer. Like how incredible it would be to come back a hundred years from now—a thousand years from now—and see what shape the planet is in. But where you are going over spring break? No, I'm not curious about that at all."

Herman leans across the table. "Do I detect a note of jealousy, Fegley?"

"Don't flatter yourself, Weinstein. It's not very becoming."

He picks up the ticket. "Okay then, I'll open it." And he makes a grand show of removing the ticket from its sleeve, studying the contents. "Well, looky here, will you? It's a round-trip ticket to Newark, New Jersey."

"New Jersey? Sounds like you got gypped, Weinstein."

"Yeah, you're right. Here, why don't you go in my place." And again he offers the ticket to Mead. "Besides, your name's already on it."

Mead puts down his fork and looks out the window. The limousine driver has gotten out of his vehicle to smoke a cigarette and drink the cup of coffee Herman bought him. "Are you kidnapping me, Weinstein?"

"Ever heard of Bell Labs, Fegley? They've got this supercomputer there: the Cray X-MP. Fastest number cruncher made to date. Their researchers are being encouraged to run projects on it, to familiarize themselves with the algorithms appropriate to its architecture. And I thought, you know, it might be just the thing for someone studying the statistical properties of the zeta zeros, for someone who needs to compute huge quantities of numbers in a short period of time. You know, someone like you." And he sits back with this smug expression on his face.

He's good. So good that it makes Mead nervous. Hair is standing up on the back of his neck. Warning him. A sense of danger in the air as palpable as humidity on a hot summer's day. And yet he is tempted. More than tempted. He's excited. Thrilled beyond belief that such an opportunity has fallen into his lap. This could be exactly what Mead has been looking for. The new findings he needs to write his paper for the dean. There's nothing particularly original about the idea of gathering statistical information on the zeta zeros—several mathematicians have done so already—but none have generated the sheer quantity of zeros that a supercomputer could. Hundreds of thousands. Millions. Even hundreds of millions! A quantity far in excess of any computation made to date. Mead will not be able to definitively prove the Riemann Hypothesis this way but there is always the possibility that he will discover a single zeta zero that does *not* sit on the critical line, therefore definitively *dis*proving the hypothesis. And even if that does not happen, the sheer quantity of zeros generated will alone offer up a substantial preponderance of evidence in favor of the hypothesis being true. Mead has done all the groundwork. He's got the Riemann-Siegel formula imbedded in the back of his skull; all he needs to do is teach it to a supercomputer. So really, he has no choice. He has to go. If he were to let an opportunity such as this pass him by, why, it would be equivalent to admitting defeat. Mathematical suicide.

He takes the ticket and checks the departure time. "This flight leaves," Mead glances at his watch, "in two hours and forty minutes."

"So I guess you better hurry up and finish those pancakes."

Mead hands the ticket back to Herman. "I can't do it. I can't go. There's no time to tell Dr. Alexander. I'd want him to come with me. And besides, I haven't packed. My clothes are all back at the dorm. It's just not possible. Forget it."

"I already thought of that." Herman taps on the plate glass window. The limousine driver opens up the trunk and lifts out Mead's green-and-blue plaid suitcase.

IT IS AS IF MEAD HAS FALLEN into one of his mother's dreams as he steps out of the limousine that picked him and Herman up at the airport, onto the doorstep of a castle. Well, it's not actually a castle, it was just built to resemble one. All stone and turrets and arching doorways. It does not strike Mead as a place where a family lives. It's too big. Too formidable. A feeling that only strengthens when Mead passes through the front door into the vestibule. His Uncle Martin would love this place. He could embalm bodies in the study and roll them into the living room to await burial. It's that cold.

A butler offers to take Mead's jacket as if this were nineteenth-century England and not twentieth-century Princeton. Mead waves him away and says, "That's all right, I won't be staying long."

"Don't be ridiculous," Herman says, and takes off Mead's jacket for him. "It's late afternoon already. We won't be going to the lab until tomorrow. Come, I'll introduce you to my lovely mother." And he hands the jacket to the butler, then grasps Mead by the shoulder and guides him into the adjoining room.

But his mother isn't lovely, not in any literal sense of the word. Herman must have gotten his good looks from his father. Mrs. Weinstein is more what you would call a handsome woman, her appearance more that of a portrait than a person. It's the way she is dressed, all draped in cloth and bejeweled. And the way she is holding her body, all upright and shoulders back. And the way she is made up, all powder and hairspray. You'd have thought she was expecting the King of England and not just some friend of Herman's from school. But the thing is she does kind of look like a female version of Herman. She has the same cocky set of her jaw and the same eyes that seem to look through you more than at you. Mead distrusts her on sight.

"How very nice it is to meet you," she says and extends her hand to Mead, who is not sure whether he is supposed to kiss it or shake it. He opts for the latter. Then she does the same thing to Herman—extends her hand—and he kisses it. Which just strikes Mead as wrong on so many levels.

"Hermie's told us so much about you," Mrs. Weinstein says. "Please, have a seat. Would you like something to drink? Tea or coffee?"

"Coke," Mead says. "A Coke would be fine, thanks." And he sits in the chair nearest the front door. He feels better knowing there is an exit nearby.

As the butler strolls off to the kitchen to fill Mead's order, Mrs. Weinstein settles onto a red velvet couch under an oil painting of herself seated in front of two men in tuxedos, one flanking each side of her. It must have been commissioned a couple of decades ago because the Mrs. Weinstein on the wall is much younger than the one on the couch. With only one chin and all of her own hair. But the same rope of pearls hangs around each neck; the same sausage legs are stuffed into identical sequined pumps. Even as a young woman, Mrs. Weinstein would have been prettier as a boy than a girl.

"Hermie tells us that your father is a successful businessman," Mrs. Weinstein says. "That he owns a chain of furniture stores across Illinois."

Mead looks over at "Hermie." Since he has never spoken about his father with "Hermie," he is wondering what exactly the guy knows and how he found out. Herman either didn't get the whole story — from whomever he got it — or he has altered the facts by choice. "Not exactly," Mead says. "The other two stores are owned and run by my father's cousins. And they're all within the same county. And, really, there isn't that much money to be made in furniture; the big bucks come from the funeral side of the business."

"Your father's an undertaker?" Mrs. Weinstein says and raises her eyebrows.

What is taking that butler so long? They probably don't have any Coke in the house. Too provincial. The poor butler, or someone on the kitchen staff, probably had to run out and buy some. Shit. Mead should have just asked for a glass of milk.

"Well, there's no shame in that," Mrs. Weinstein says, making it sound as if, indeed, there is. "No shame at all."

MEAD IS GIVEN A ROOM that overlooks a garden complete with gazebo and koi pond. The windows open inward, like doors, and reach all the way from the floor to the ten-foot ceiling. He is standing by the open window, thinking about how one might fashion a ladder out of brocade curtains to escape, when Herman comes in and flops down on the four-poster bed draped in damask cloth. Enough to qualify this room as a boudoir.

"I was trying to make you look good, Fegley," he says. "My mother didn't need to hear all the gory details."

"And what exactly does your father do, Weinstein, to make enough money to support this place?" Mead says. "Where does it all come from?"

"Glass bottles."

"Excuse me?"

"My mother's father made a killing in glass bottles. He sold them to every juice and baby food maker this side of the Mississippi. My father had nothing to do with it."

"So that's what you'll do after college? Sell glass bottles?"

"Oh, the Weinsteins don't make bottles anymore, Mead, we just sit on the board of directors and make money. You know, so we can spend our time pursuing more lofty enterprises. Like my father. He's a Friend of the Institute for Advanced Study here in Princeton. He gives them a shitload of money and in return he gets to attend fireside chats and dine with intellectuals. It brings prestige to our family, so we can feel smart by association."

"So how come you ended up in Chicago? Why didn't you just go to Princeton University?"

"Because I wanted to get as far away from all this as I possibly could."

Mead studies Herman and tries to decide whether or not the guy is being serious. Decides that he isn't and concocts his own personal history for Herman. That he was indeed accepted into Princeton. That he spent his freshman year there cutting classes, getting drunk, and jumping out second-story windows until the school was left with no other option but to expel him, at which point his rich grandfather—the bottle king—bought Herman his way into Chicago University. Mead has to think this, otherwise he might have to feel some compassion for Herman, might have to see how someone with an ounce of humanity in his blood might want to escape all this.

Someone knocks. Mead looks up and sees a young man standing in the bedroom doorway. A frail, pasty-complexioned teenaged kid who looks as if he knows firsthand what it's like to get his head flushed down the toilet. "Hi, Herman," he says. "Mom told me you were here." He looks at Mead and smiles. "Hi, I'm Neil. Herman's little brother. I just got home from my piano lesson." He offers his hand to Mead to shake. He has a surprisingly confident and firm grip for such a slight boy, but not too firm. He looks like the kid in class with all the right answers, the one the teacher calls on in a pinch, the kid Mead would have wanted to be his partner in science class. Mead likes him right off.

Neil turns toward Herman. He seems to be waiting for his brother to get up off the bed and greet him with either a hug or a handshake. But Herman doesn't get up. He just looks at Neil and says, "So how's the young Mozart doing these days?"

"I'm fine. You know, considering." He turns back to Mead. "I have a busy schedule: two hours of piano practice every afternoon and six on Saturday and Sunday. I barely have time to get my homework done. It can be a bit stressful sometimes."

"Oh, don't listen to him," Herman says and rolls clear to the other side of the bed—away from Neil—to get up. "He's just showing off. My kid brother loves playing the piano, been doing it since he was three. He's got the gift, you know? Juilliard has been chomping at the bit to get their hands on him for years but my parents are making them wait. They want little Neil here to complete his high school education before going to the big city. Or at least that's the story they give because it makes them come off as protective parents. But what they're really doing is trying to create an atmosphere of demand for the little guy. It's very smart. Very savvy, wouldn't you agree?"

"I'm not that little anymore," Neil says. "I've grown two inches in the past six months alone. I'm almost as tall as you now, see?" And he runs around the bed to stand next to his big brother, places his hand on top of his head and brings it across until it touches Herman in the middle of his forehead. "I've just a couple more inches to go to catch up."

His hand is still touching Herman's forehead when Mrs. Weinstein appears in the doorway. "Mr. Weinstein just got home," she says, "so dinner will be served in a few minutes. Neil, why don't you go get washed up."

He drops his hand and rolls his eyes, like a typical teenager. "Okay, Mom," he says, appearing reluctant to leave the presence of his big brother, looking as if he still wants that hug. "See you downstairs," he says to Herman and heads out of the room. As he passes Mrs. Weinstein, she places her hand on his head and ruffles his hair. A very unportraitlike thing to do. It surprises Mead. She didn't show Herman any of that same affection. After she leaves, Mead turns to Herman and says, "I had no idea you have a brother."

"You say that as if it were an impossibility."

"It's just that you always struck me as an only child."

"What're you trying to say, Fegley, that you think I'm self-centered? Would a self-centered person have flown his classmate all the way out east just so he could sit in the same room as some computer for a few days?"

"You don't look like brothers."

"Which leads you to believe what? That my mother slept around?"

"What? No. I wasn't thinking that at all," Mead says and

blushes. He doesn't really need to know the ins and outs of the Weinsteins' personal life. Why does Herman do that? Why does he have to turn every conversation into a confrontation of some sort?

A bell tinkles, putting their conversation to a thankful end.

"Dinner is served," Herman says and motions to the open door. "Shall we?"

THE TABLE IS LARGE ENOUGH to accommodate Mead's entire high school graduation class. Mr. Weinstein sits at the head of it and motions for Mead to come sit next to him. The dean of all things possible and impossible, that's how Dr. Kustrup described him to Mead. The way he said Herman described the man to him. But the Institute has no dean. The phrase is merely metaphoric, one that conjures up the image of a smart man. A discerning man. An intimidating man. But Mr. Weinstein is anything but intimidating, at least in appearance. He's a slight man on the short side whose smile reminds Mead of a puppy. He seems genuinely pleased to meet him, kind of the way Neil comes across. Full of blind trust. He also happens to be one of the two men flanking Mrs. Weinstein in that living room portrait. The less handsome one. An average-looking guy who bears absolutely no resemblance whatsoever to Herman. If Mead were to run into Mr. Weinstein on the street, he would never guess the man came from money. Which he doesn't, of course; he's just married to it. All of which leaves Mead wondering who the other man in the painting is.

"I've heard great things about you," Mr. Weinstein says as a maid in a black dress and white apron sets down a bowl of soup in front of Mead. And he says it really loud, as if Mead were sitting all the way at the other end of the table and not at his elbow. As if he is more used to addressing crowds than individuals. Or perhaps he's a tad bit deaf. "It's rare for Herman to gush about a classmate, or even mention one for that matter. He never talks about his friends at all and, quite frankly, I'm surprised to discover that he has one." And he says it all serious-like.

Either Mr. Weinstein has the driest sense of humor of anyone Mead has ever met or the man is just plain mean. Mead chooses to go with the former explanation and waits for Herman's father to start laughing. To explain that he's just kidding. Only he doesn't.

Uncomfortable with the awkward silence that has descended upon the table, Mead directs his attention to the mantel above the fireplace on the far side of the room. There appears to be a fireplace in almost every room of the house, including the room in which Mead is to spend the night, and upon each mantel are displays of framed photographs as well as various trophies and awards, a preponderance of which feature Neil. Mead just assumed, when he saw the mantel full of piano trophies in his room, that he had been put up in Neil's bedroom for the night, but now it is starting to dawn on him that he may have jumped to the wrong conclusion and he wonders if Mr. Weinstein's less-than-complimentary comment about Herman just now might in some way be connected to the dearth of awards and trophies associated with his elder son.

Mead lowers his eyes from the mantel to Neil, who is seated directly across from him at Mr. Weinstein's other elbow. A definite similarity exists in body shape and maybe even a little in the face. It would not take a huge leap of the imagination to believe them father and son. Herman, on the other hand, is an anomaly. The prettiest one of the whole lot. A chromosomal fluke. What every pair of average-looking parents secretly hopes for: a beautiful progeny. It is becoming clear to Mead, however, that beauty does not hold much esteem in the Weinstein household.

Or perhaps it is Herman's very beauty that is at the heart of Mr. Weinstein's hostility.

"I understand that you and Herman have been doing some statistical work on the spacings between the zeros of the zeta function," Mr. Weinstein says, finally breaking the silence. "The Riemann Hypothesis. It's a mathematician's wet dream. The greatest unsolved puzzle of our time. I'm sure I don't need to tell you that the man who finally does solve it will go down in the history books."

Mead shifts his gaze to Herman, who is seated on the other side of Neil. Why, Mead almost blurts out loud, is your father under the impression that you and I are working together? Did you tell him that? But he holds his tongue because sitting right above Herman, on the mantel, staring at Mead, is a photograph of Neil shaking Leonard Bernstein's hand.

Herman doesn't know Mead is looking at him. He's too busy staring down into his soup. It's the first time Mead has ever seen him *not* look someone straight in the eyes. The first time he has seen the guy even approach a state of obeisance. "My father," Herman says, "spends his days surrounded by geniuses. Scientists, mathematicians, historians. All of them sitting around, thinking, pondering, waiting for something great to happen. It's a vocational hazard, bringing those expectations home with him at night."

"Hermie," Mrs. Weinstein says. "We have a guest. Please don't start."

"Start what, Mother?" Herman says and looks up at her all innocent-like. "I didn't start anything, you did. And as far as I know, you never stopped."

"That's enough," Mr. Weinstein says.

Mrs. Weinstein signals the maid to clear off the table. Herman slouches in his chair. Neil starts plucking at his eyebrows. The

Weinsteins make the Fegleys look blithely happy in comparison. In the silence that follows, broken only by the sound of dishes being cleared, Mead writes out a mathematical expression on his napkin. Only he doesn't realize what he is doing, not until Mr. Weinstein says, "That's the Riemann-Siegel formula, isn't it?"

Mead looks up. "Excuse me?" Then looks down again and sees what he has written. All over a linen napkin. Shit. He looks across the table at Mrs. Weinstein, expecting to see a look of horror on her face akin to the look on his mother's face the day he brought home that C on his science project. But she doesn't look horrified at all. If anything, she looks amused. "I'm sorry," he says. "I didn't realize what I was doing. It's a reflex."

"That's quite all right, Mead," she says. "It's just a napkin, we've plenty more in the buffet." And Mead decides that perhaps he was a bit too quick in his assessment of the formidable woman.

"That's right, Fegley," Herman says. "Around here we tolerate odd quirks in behavior. The odder the better. It's a sign of genius, you know. Oddity. Like my little brother over here. The young Mozart. Plucking the hairs out of his head as if he were preparing himself to be roasted for dinner."

Mr. Weinstein slams his fist down on the table, causing the water in his crystal stemware to splash out onto the tablecloth. "That's enough, I said. If you cannot be civil, Herman, then I am going to have to ask you to leave the table."

Mead waits for Herman to stand up, say something like, "I thought you'd never ask," and stalk off, but he doesn't. Instead he turns to face Neil and says, "Sorry, little brother. That was a low blow. Hey, I love you, you know that, don't you?"

Neil nods but does not look up from his lap, his fingers now tucked under his thighs where they won't do any more damage.

"Of course you know it," Herman says. "See, Dad? Everything's cool." Then he looks toward the kitchen door and yells, "All right, Selma, the coast is clear. You can bring in the next course now." No one else says a word. A moment later the kitchen door swings open and Selma backs through it carrying a tray.

After dinner, up in the boudoir, Herman sits on the window ledge and lets his legs dangle out over the courtyard. He is smoking a cigarette—something else Mead has never before seen him do—when he says, "I'm sorry you had to see that, Fegley. I'm sure my parents seem like nice people to you—too nice to have a sonofabitch son like me—but appearances can sometimes be deceiving."

"They didn't seem all that nice," Mead says, and Herman turns to look at him as if to gauge whose side he might be on. But Mead is only on one side: his own. "Are you working on the Riemann Hypothesis with Dr. Kustrup?"

"What?"

"Your father seems to be under the impression that you are working on the theorem, and since I'm choosing to give you the benefit of the doubt in assuming that you didn't tell him we were working on it together, I can only conclude that you've been working on it with Dr. Kustrup."

"I appreciate the vote of confidence, Fegley, I really do, but no, I haven't been working on it with Dr. Kustrup."

"So why did he say that? Why does he think you're working on it?"

Herman turns back to face the courtyard, draws deeply on his cigarette. "I don't know. My father came up with that one on his own. He would love to die important, to have his name immortalized in the indexes of encyclopedias and history books. But since he himself has been unable to accomplish anything truly great, it has now fallen on the shoulders of his two sons to do it for him."

"But you aren't working on it. You should've set him straight."

Herman is hunched forward on the sill like a gargoyle perched high up on a church steeple looking down on the people below. From a distance he might look menacing, but up close you can't miss the wry grin on his face. "My father has big dreams, Fegley. He believes he can make anything happen just by wishing it so. Who am I to dissuade him from such lofty notions?"

And suddenly Mead knows—or at least he thinks he knows—why Herman didn't set his father straight. He sits down on the bed and says, "When I was in seventh grade, I got a C on a science report. I won't go into all the gory details as to how that came about, just suffice it to say that my mother was none too pleased and decided to let me know exactly how she felt about my lackluster performance by taking me to meet the ghosts of my future should I decide to continue down said path. Should you ever be curious to check out the basement of a city morgue, let me forewarn you that, contrary to popular belief, there is no comfort in numbers."

Herman turns to look at Mead, then back out the window. "Your mother sounds like a real bitch."

"Your father sounds like a real sonofabitch."

Herman laughs. "He started me on piano lessons when I was five. I'd been practicing every day for three years when one day the old man comes home and his ears perk up and he's like, 'Shit, that's the most beautiful thing I've ever heard.' You should've seen his face. I'd never seen him smile like that before. Man, was he proud."

"You weren't playing, were you?" Mead says.

Herman inhales deeply on the cigarette. "Blindsided by a three-year-old. Can you believe it? He'd picked it all up by ear. Shit, I didn't even know the little guy was listening."

And so Mead lets the subject of the Riemann Hypothesis and who may or may not have been working on it pass.

* * *

It takes Mead forever to fall asleep. And when he finally does, it doesn't stick. He wakes up two hours later with his mind racing, all hopped up on math, computing zeta zeros in his head using the Riemann-Siegel formula. He can hardly wait to meet this computer. He wonders what it looks like. How big it is. How fast it will work. But most of all, he wonders how on earth he is going to communicate with it, if there will be an interpreter, someone fluent in zeros and ones to translate for him. One week. The airline ticket Herman purchased for Mead has a return date of one week from today. Already Mead is anxious about the time and about the fact that there isn't enough of it.

He throws back the covers, crawls out of bed, and paces about the room. It has begun to bother him again that Herman did not set his father straight on the Riemann Hypothesis. Did Mr. Weinstein really jump to the conclusion on his own that Herman and Mead are working together? Or did Herman lead his father to that conclusion? Mead would like to believe the former, would like to be able to take Herman at his word. But he cannot dismiss the notion that Herman might be snowing him. Trust in his fellow man does not come to Mead naturally; he has had a good many years of personal experience to build up a convincing argument to the contrary. Especially when it comes to his peers. And so he decides that the only way to clear his mind of doubt, the only way to be certain that Herman is being honest with him, is to seek out Mr. Weinstein and set the record straight himself.

Mead paces over to the window and looks out and, as the gods would have it, sees standing below him in the courtyard none other than Mr. Weinstein, smoking a cigarette and pacing back and forth himself. Unable to refuse such an opportunity, Mead quickly steps into a pair of trousers, exits the bedroom, and makes his way along the hall. Hurrying down the stairs, he does his best not to make any noise. The last thing Mead wants to do is alert Herman to his intention. He feels the need to get to Mr. Weinstein and tell him the truth before Herman figures out what is going on, before the guy has a chance to make Mead feel guilty for not taking him at his word.

At the bottom of the stairs, however, Mead stops up short. He hears talking and thinks that perhaps Herman has already gotten to Mr. Weinstein. That perhaps he, too, was having trouble falling and staying asleep because of what may or may not have been said but obviously got misinterpreted. Perhaps he is clearing up the situation right now, making things right with Mr. Weinstein. Then Mead hears laughter—canned laughter—and realizes that the talking is not coming from the courtyard but from a television set. He rounds the bottom of the banister, peers into the study, and sees the backs of two heads. Hears a giggle and recognizes it as belonging to Neil. Recognizes the mop of black hair on the second television viewer as Herman. And for some reason it makes Mead mad that Herman is down here watching TV with the little brother he is supposed to hate when he is supposed to be clearing up an important matter that could adversely affect his budding friendship with yours truly.

Mead turns and marches off in the direction of the courtyard, more determined than ever to clear things up with Mr. Weinstein, to keep Herman from getting even one ounce of credit for something he has not earned.

The door to the courtyard is open. Mead steps through it and finds Mr. Weinstein sitting on the stone bench next to the koi pond, still smoking. He thinks how different the man is from his own father, who goes to bed every night at ten. Who never sits at the head of even his own table. Who has never once made Mead feel guilty that he chose college and mathematics over undertaking and furniture. Who seems not the least bit interested in seeking greatness of any kind. Whose very livelihood has undoubtedly destroyed any possible notion of immortality. And he wonders which is harder: to have a bitch as a mother or a sonofabitch as a father?

Mr. Weinstein looks up. "Mead," he says. "I see that we suffer from the same affliction: insomnia."

"Oh, I don't suffer from insomnia, sir. I have a clear conscience."

"And what do you mean by that, Mead? Are you implying that I don't?"

"What? No, sir." Mr. Weinstein is twisting around Mead's words, making it sound as if he means something he does not. But this shouldn't surprise Mead. Herman does the same thing. Mead can see now that the apple has not fallen too far from the tree. "I didn't mean it that way, sir. I just meant—"

Mr. Weinstein laughs. An affected laugh. Just like Herman. "Relax, Mead, I'm just teasing. So tell me, what rouses a young man such as yourself—one with a crystal-clear conscience—out of sleep in the middle of the night?"

"I'm glad you asked me that, sir, because the thing is, I wanted to talk to you about something that was said at the dinner table tonight, an impression that somehow got made that is incorrect. I don't want to point any fingers. I don't want to overstep my boundaries and make assumptions for which I have no proof. Let's just suffice it to say that you seem to be under the misconception that—"

"You talk just like him, you know."

"Excuse me, sir?"

"Einstein. He also had this rambling, roundabout manner of speaking. Never quite getting to the point. It happens a lot with geniuses because their minds work faster than their tongues. I met him once, you know. Einstein. Has Herman ever told you that story?"

"No, sir. I'm sure it's quite interesting, sir, but I came out here to—"

"I was eight and had my own paper route. I used to carry the newspapers in this little red wagon of mine. So I'm out doing my rounds one morning when I pass this crazy old man with wild white hair who's talking to himself, having a conversation with someone who isn't there. Anyway, when he sees my wagon full of papers, he picks one up, hands me a dime, and keeps going. And the whole time he just keeps talking to this person who isn't there. Well, I was too afraid to say anything but now I'm worried because I know that when I get to the end of my route I won't have a newspaper for Mrs. Bechtel. Only she doesn't get mad; she laughs and says, 'Don't you know who that was? Why that was Mr. Albert Einstein. Hold on to that dime, son, it's been touched by the hand of greatness. It may hold special powers.'" Mr. Weinstein looks at Mead. "You know where that dime is now?" he asks, but before Mead can respond, he answers the question himself. "I had it framed and gave it to my son."

My son, he says. Singular case. As if he has only one. Mead does not ask Mr. Weinstein which son he is referring to because he's pretty sure he already knows. The answer as obvious as all those awards and trophies and photographs sitting on all the fireplace mantels.

"But I'm sorry, Mead," Mr. Weinstein says, "I interrupted you. You said you came out here to tell me something, to clear up some matter from supper. Please go ahead. I'm all ears."

Mead stands up. "It was nothing, sir. I just wanted to thank you for having me to your house. Thank you," he says and ducks back into the house. As Mead passes by the study on the way back to his room, he notices that the TV has been turned off, the room now empty. He wonders if Herman overheard any of the conversation Mead had with his father. If he stood in the shadows and said to himself, "See, Fegley, I told you my dad was a prick, do you believe me now?"

A SEAT BELT FEELS WOEFULLY INSUFFICIENT when you are hurtling along at speeds topping one hundred miles an hour. With the top down. Which is how fast Herman is driving as he weaves his silver Mercedes-Benz sports coupe in and out and around all the other cars on the highway. As if they were cones on an obstacle course. Where are the police? This is what Mead would like to know as Herman brings them within inches of their lives on at least four separate occasions. And the odd thing is, the expression on his face is set and grim, his knuckles white as he grips the steering wheel. He does not seem to be enjoying this any more than Mead is. And yet he keeps the gas pedal pressed flat to the floor, hurtling himself at full speed into the future.

"You really ought to slow down," Mead says.

"What?" Herman yells over the rushing wind.

"I saw you," Mead yells back. "Last night. Watching TV with your brother."

"You should have joined us."

"I didn't want to intrude."

"We were just watching TV, Fegley, not having sex."

"Why do you do that?"

"Do what? Have sex?"

No, Mead says to himself, why do you turn every serious conversation I try to have with you into a joke? Why do you insist on keeping me at arm's length? Why are you such a nice guy one moment and a total prick the next? But Mead realizes that he already knows why. He met him last night.

A loud siren pierces the air, causing Mead to turn around in his seat. A patrol car is following close behind them, its overhead lights flashing. Mead is filled with a sense of righteousness and relief, glad that Herman is being pulled over. After all, the guy was going at least forty miles an hour over the speed limit. He might have gotten into an accident and killed them both. He should be punished. And, heaven knows, the guy can well afford to pay the ticket.

"Shit," Herman says as he pulls to a stop on the shoulder of the highway. "Let me do all the talking, Fegley, okay?"

No problem. Mead intends to sit here and enjoy the show.

The police officer emerges from his car. He appears to be in his mid-thirties, in the prime of his life. He probably has a wife and two kids at home. A law-abiding man. The heart and soul of this great country of ours. He walks up to Herman's side of the car and says, "You two boys enjoying yourselves?"

"Good morning, Officer Keats," Herman says, reading the man's name off his lapel. "First off, I want to apologize for my reckless driving. You see, my friend here is visiting from out of state. He has an important meeting to attend and I'm afraid I overslept. As a result, he is now running late and, as his host, I feel personally responsible. I was just trying to make up for lost time."

"That's quite noble of you," the officer says. "May I see your driver's license and registration, please?"

"Of course," Herman says and proceeds to pull out his wallet. "I'd really like to make this up to you, Officer. To apologize for my lapse in good judgment. It is highly out of character for me to be so reckless. I want to personally thank you for doing your job and pulling me over to give me this warning. And I promise, sir, that I have learned my lesson, that I will abide by all traffic laws from now on." And he hands to the officer his license and registration and two hundred-dollar bills. Mead can hardly believe his eyes. Shit. Herman is probably going to go to jail for this. For bribing a police officer. And Mead will have no option but to go with him. Double shit. He can see it all now. His one phone call home to tell his parents that he is sitting in some jail somewhere in New Jersey, his begging them to wire him bail money so he can get to Bell Labs. Promising to explain it all to them later. The minutes and hours ticking away. Shit and double shit. At this rate Mead may never lay eyes on that supercomputer at all!

Only that isn't what happens. The officer looks at Herman's driver's license and registration, then hands them back to him. "Everything seems to be in order here," he says, the two hundred dollars having magically disappeared. "You boys drive carefully now and have a good day."

"Thank you, Officer Keats," Herman says. "We sure will." Then he starts up his Mercedes-Benz sports coupe and pulls back onto the highway.

Mead doesn't know what to say so he says nothing. He is horrified. Not only did Herman break the law once, but twice! And got away with it! This isn't right, this isn't right at all. Mead doesn't care how big of a prick the guy's father is; it doesn't give him the right to break the law.

"What's wrong, Fegley?" Herman says. "Why the long face?"

"You know damn well what's wrong, Weinstein. What you did back there was criminal. Just because you got away with it doesn't make it right."

"You sound ungrateful, Fegley. I was only trying to help because I know how eager you are to get to Bell Labs. But if you want me to turn around and take you back, I'll do it. Right now. Just say the word and we can catch the next flight to Chicago. It's up to you." And as he is talking, he pulls the car back over into the slow lane and signals as if to get off at the next exit.

He's grandstanding, of course. Acting like a spoiled brat. Punishing Mead for calling him out on his imbecilic behavior. "Very amusing, Weinstein. You've made your point."

"What point? I'm serious. The last thing I want to do is offend your sense of right and wrong. I think we should go back. I really do." And he exits off the highway.

He isn't serious. He can't be. What would be the point of flying Mead all the way out here only to turn around and take him right back? It doesn't make sense. Even for someone as rich as Herman. Mead gets the feeling, however, that he isn't bluffing. That, if Mead were to indeed ask, Herman would take him directly back to the airport. No questions asked. Which Mead finds baffling. Utterly confounding. But then very little about Herman makes sense to Mead.

"So what's it going to be, Fegley? Do you want to blow off this opportunity? Stick to your high moral ground? It's totally up to you. Just tell me what to do. Your wish is my command."

But Mead doesn't want to go back. He can't go back empty-handed. He has to get to that computer, otherwise he won't have a paper to present to the dean.

"So? Speak up now, Fegley, or forever hold your peace."

Shit. Why is Herman being such a prick? Mead isn't the one who just broke the law. Twice. Herman is. How dare he try to bring Mead down to his level. There is nothing immoral about what Mead is doing, nothing at all. He's not breaking any laws. This wasn't even his idea; it was Herman's! Mead crosses his arms over his chest. He should have set the record straight with Mr. Weinstein last night when he had the chance. Came up with it on his own. Bullshit! There is no doubt in Mead's mind that Herman told his father that they were working on the Riemann Hypothesis together. Not one ounce. Mead is so mad at himself right now he could spit.

"Come on, Fegley. Show me what you're made of. Yes? No? It's your call."

"Fuck you," Mead says.

Herman cups his hand over his ear. "Excuse me?"

"I said shut up and get back on the highway."

Herman circles the car around and accelerates back onto the interstate. "I would have done it, you know," he says. "I would have taken you back. I want you to remember that. I really would have."

"I said shut the fuck up."

MEAD RECOGNIZES HIM RIGHT AWAY. The other man in the portrait, the more handsome one standing behind Mrs. Weinstein. The name on his desk reads GERALD WEINSTEIN but Herman just calls him Jerry. As in Uncle Jerry.

Uncle Jerry throws his arms around Herman and gives him a bear hug, the kind of hug one athlete bestows upon another after a goal is scored or a basket is made. A hug that is more congratulatory than nurturing. Herman does his best to return the gesture but looks uncomfortable at best. Uncle Jerry then shakes Mead's hand—a vigorous up-and-down shake—and says, "Good morning, good morning, you're here bright and early." He glances at his watch. "It isn't even nine yet. I like that. You must be a good influence on our Herman. I've rarely known him to be up before noon." And he laughs, as if he has just told a joke. At least he isn't as mean as the other Mr. Weinstein.

Uncle Jerry is a president here at Bell Labs. Not *the* president, but one of many presidents who oversee various divisions. A tall, slender man who does not look like Herman exactly but has a manner about him that reminds Mead of Herman. The way he cocks his head, just slightly to the right, so that even when he is looking directly at you he does not quite make eye contact. "So you're the young genius who's going to give our Cray X-MP a run for her money," Jerry says. "Herman tells me that you only have a few days, so why don't we get you downstairs and get you started." And he leads them back down the hall toward the elevator.

Uncle Jerry takes them down to the basement, better known here at Bell Labs as the Lower Level, and introduces Mead to Earl Bellisfield, the tech guy. Then Jerry vigorously shakes Mead's hand again, wishes him luck, and says, "It was a pleasure meeting you, Mead. At first, I was quite disappointed when Herman told me he was standing me up, that he didn't want to go skiing with his dear old uncle over spring break as usual. I thought he must have met a girl and fallen in love. Then he told me what the real reason was and, I have to say, I couldn't be more pleased." Jerry steps back into the elevator. "Stop by my office at the end of the day. I'd like to take you both out to dinner this evening." Then the doors close.

Mead turns to Herman. "And what exactly did you tell him?"

"What do you think?"

"I honestly don't know what to think."

"Relax, Fegley. I just told him that I wanted to do a favor for a friend."

EARL BELLISFIELD IS A NERVOUS CHARACTER whose shirt won't stay tucked in and he doesn't care. "She's right in here," he says and opens a set of double doors into a room that is literally filled with computer. Wall-to-wall. Floor-to-ceiling. Mead has never seen anything like it. He wishes Dr. Alexander were here to see it with him. If he was, surely he would take that outmoded mechanical computing device he has languishing in his basement and set it out on the curb for the garbage man. Mead's fingers are tingling, as are his toes. He is short of breath. Light-headed. Afraid that if he does not sit down right now he is going to faint. That's how excited he is. How amazed he is to be standing here. In this room. In front of this gigantic supercomputer. It's the same way Dr. Alexander must have felt as he sat in that lecture hall at King's College fifty-odd years ago and listened to Alan Turing talk about his vision of a mechanical computing machine.

"Here," Earl says and offers Mead a sweatshirt. "You might want to put this on. We have to keep it cool in here for the Cray X-MP. She gets temperamental when she gets overheated." But Mead waves it away. "I'm used to the cold," he says. "My father is an undertaker."

So Earl gets right down to business. He sits Mead in front of the keyboard and proceeds to teach him the language of the computer. It's like trying to learn Russian. In one day. Mead stares at a stream of letters and symbols that have no meaning to him whatsoever. It is frustrating, repetitive, demanding, and boring all at once. And Mead loves it.

Herman taps him on the shoulder and offers him a sandwich. "Not now," Mead says. "I'm busy. I'll eat later."

"It is later," Herman says. "It's almost five."

"Five o'clock?" Mead cannot believe it. He just sat down. Almost a whole day went by just like that. "This is taking too long, Earl," he says. "I only have a limited amount of time. Can't I just tell you what I want the computer to do and have you type it in for me?"

"Sure," Earl says and gets up out of his chair. "But it'll have to wait till tomorrow. I've gotta take off. The wife doesn't like it when I get home late. It's just about now that the kids start driving her nuts. I'll be back in the morning, though. First thing. I'll key it in for you then."

"Yeah, come on, Fegley," Herman says. "Screw the sandwich.

I say we call it a day. There's this great steakhouse in town. Best T-bones north of the Mason-Dixon line. It'll be Uncle Jerry's treat. You can relax and start fresh in the morning."

"You go," Mead says. "I'm staying."

"Don't be crazy, Fegley. You've been going at this for eight hours straight."

"And I'll go at it for eight more if that's what it takes."

Mead turns back to the keyboard and types in more code. He refuses to look up. At either Earl or Herman. If they want to leave, fine, but he's staying. They will have to have him bodily removed because he won't go voluntarily. He's got only five days left and over a million zeros to compute.

"Two hours, Fegley," Herman says. "Give my uncle two hours of your time and I promise, I'll fix it so you can stay the whole night. Twenty-four hours a day all week. But you've got to give me something to work with. Please."

It almost sounds as if he's begging. But that is not why Mead gives in. He gives in because he needs the twenty-four-hour days. And because he trusts that Herman will get him back within the promised two-hour limit, the way he did after the concert with Dr. Kustrup. "Okay," Mead says. "But just tonight."

UNCLE JERRY ISN'T ALONE. Sitting at the table with him is a young woman. A pretty young thing who pops up out of her chair when she sees Herman, throws her arms around his neck, and plants a big old kiss on his lips. He must have one every place he goes. A different girlfriend in each city. Princeton, Chicago, Paris, Zurich. This one is prettier than Cynthia in Chicago. Or at least she works harder at it, with streaked hair, lots of eye shadow, and a plunging neckline. Mead wonders where Herman met her—if they went to high school together or met at a fund-raiser—but not enough to actually ask. He might mention it to Cynthia, though, next time he runs into her on campus. You know, that he met Herman's other girlfriend. Just so she has all the facts.

"Herman," the pretty young thing says. "You look sexier than ever. I guess Chicago agrees with you. Or somebody in Chicago." And she winks at Mead. As if he might tell her. Later. After they've all had a few too many drinks. Shit. Why did Mead agree to do this?

"And you, Michelle," Herman says, "look as luscious as ever." And he kisses her back. On the neck. One arm curled possessively around her tiny waist. Then he turns to Mead and says, "Excuse me, where are my manners? Fegley, I'd like you to meet Michelle, my Uncle Jerry's lovely wife. Number four, I believe she is. Or is it number five?" He directs this question at his uncle, who rises to his feet, shakes Mead's hand, and says, "I'm so glad you could join us for supper, Mead. Please, have a seat. Relax. Order whatever you want. Enjoy yourself."

But the next two hours are about as relaxing as sitting in a dry forest next to a boy playing with matches. Uncle Jerry fills the evening with one anecdotal story after another, all of them centered around skiing in the Alps with Herman. Apparently it's something they have been doing together for years. Ever since Herman strapped on his first pair of skis, according to Uncle Jerry. Or, as Herman tells it, "That was when Uncle Jerry was married to Suzanne, wife number two." Uncle Jerry also talks about a skiing trip where Herman broke his leg. Or, as Herman puts it, "The winter Uncle Jerry divorced Elaine; she was wife number three." The verbal sparring wears Mead out and, by the time they leave the restaurant, his head is pounding. He could care less about going back to Bell Labs, he just wants to crawl into bed—any bed—and sleep. But Herman holds true to his word and two sleeping bags materialize as if by magic from the trunk of his car. Herman rolls them out on the floor in front of the Cray X-MP and says, "I prefer to sleep on the right." Then he crawls into one of the bags, pulls out a copy of *Vanity Fair*, and starts to read.

Mead looks at Herman, lying in the sleeping bag, head bent over the glossy magazine, and realizes that his presence at dinner tonight was not, in fact, a prerequisite for getting permission to spend the night at Bell Labs. That those sleeping bags were already in the trunk of Herman's car, the agreement already made. That Herman's sole purpose for inviting Mead to supper tonight was for moral support. That his relationship with his uncle appears to be only marginally better than the one with his father. That Herman was, indeed, begging.

"Thanks for dragging me out to dinner tonight," Mead says.

Herman glances up. And Mead can tell, from the look in his eyes, that Herman knows that Mead knows why he was there. "No problem, you crazy fuck," Herman says. "Now get back to work."

By the time Earl Bellisfield returns the next morning, Mead doesn't need him anymore. Somewhere in the twilight hours of dawn, he began communicating fluently with the supercomputer, then taught the Cray X-MP a thing or two of his own. And one of the things he taught her was the Riemann-Siegel formula. Right away, the Cray X-MP started spitting out results, computing one zeta zero after the other. "Look at this," Mead says to Earl and shows him a stack of printouts. "Just look at it. She can compute a thousand zeros in the time it takes me to generate just one." Mead shivers and Earl hands him a sweater. Mead waves it away. "No, thank you. I'm not cold, Earl; I'm in awe."

Herman disappears for long periods of time to god knows where. But when he returns, he brings food. Hot food. Upon which Mead descends as if he has not eaten in days. And for all he knows, he hasn't. Because Mead has lost all track of time. He has no idea what day it is. Whether it is morning or night. Day 2 or Day 4. And he doesn't ask because he doesn't want to know. He just wants to generate as many zeros as possible in whatever amount of time he has left before he has to leave.

As the Cray X-MP computes, Mead looks over her printouts. All he has to find is one zero off the critical line. That's all. Just one will be enough to disprove the Riemann Hypothesis. The 130-year-old question answered. But as more and more zeta zeros spit out, each one of them calculated to the eighth decimal point, evidence starts to stack up, quite literally, in favor of the hypothesis being true. It isn't definitive proof. It is merely statistics. But it is enough to assure Mead that he will not be wasting the next god-knows-how-many-years of his life trying to definitively prove the theorem. The only question left is how. What leap of the imagination did Bernhard Riemann make that the rest of mathematical mankind is missing? Some basic step in logic is being overlooked. Mead needs to take his thinking to another level. Possibly in another direction. But which one? If only he could figure that out.

He awakes with a jolt, thinking he has heard a crash. Heart racing, Mead crawls out of his sleeping bag and over to the Cray X-MP, to make sure nothing has gone wrong. That she has not collapsed from exhaustion. But the supercomputer is fine, humming along as she calculates more and more zeta zeros. He glances at his wristwatch. It's 2:02. But whether it is the middle of the afternoon or the middle of the night Mead has no idea. Herman is asleep on the floor beside him. And Earl is nowhere in sight. So it must be nighttime. Mead crawls back into his bag and tries to fall back asleep but remains uneasy as if something terrible has happened.

He sits bolt upright. His parents. Shit. Mead forgot all about his parents. About the fact that he is twelve hundred miles away from where they think he is, on the floor in the basement of some office building next to a virtual stranger. He decides he better call them to let them know. He helps himself to the phone on Earl's desk, feeling bad even as he dials. He hates to wake his dad up in the middle of the night but reasons that the man will be happy when he realizes it is his son on the other end of the line and not the coroner. Only it doesn't ring. The phone is busy, the coroner having beat Mead to the punch. He sets down the receiver and waits a minute, waits for his dad to get off the line. He'll keep it brief. "I know you have to run out, Dad, just wanted to call and say hi. You'll never guess where I am." But the phone is still busy. Maybe his dad is calling Uncle Martin, to fill him in on the details. A meet-me-over-at-the-store-in-one-hour kind of thing. So Mead waits another minute then dials again. But the line is still tied up. Shit.

"Hey, Fegley," Herman says, having woken up too. "Who're you calling?"

Mead sets down the receiver. "Nobody," he says and suddenly feels silly. Like a kid away at camp for the first time. Missing his parents. Worrying about nothing. He crawls back into his sleeping bag but cannot fall back to sleep. Opens his eyes and sees Herman, propped up on one elbow, chin in hand, staring down at him. Herman smiles and Mead says, "What?"

"Nothing. I just like looking at you."

Mead sits up in his bag, feeling all self-conscious, and says, "So tell me, Weinstein, what's the story with that portrait in the front hall of your house?"

"Ah. You must be referring to the painting of the two Mr. Weinsteins with my dear mother."

"Jerry isn't just your uncle, is he? He's also your biological father."

"That's exactly right, Fegley."

"And based on what I saw at dinner the other night, I'm guessing that Jerry cheated on your mother with another woman, causing her to divorce him. It's odd, though, that she ended up marrying his brother."

"They were never married, Fegley; my mother and uncle were lovers. You have to understand, my mother is a very rich woman. She can pretty much do whatever the hell she pleases and get away with it. She only slept with Jerry because she believed her husband to be sterile and wanted an heir. It was merely an act of convenience. A means to an end." Herman looks over at Mead and smiles. "I'm a bastard, Fegley. How do you like that?"

"And your brother, Neil?"

"Oh, he's the real thing. A product of the mister and missus made possible through the miracle of modern science and a petri dish."

"That explains it then."

"Explains what, Fegley?"

"All those trophies on the mantelpiece."

Herman sits up in his bag and hugs his knees to his chest. "I was twelve when I learned the truth about my conception. It was Jerry who told me. On one of our many skiing trips. It just about blew my mind. But it explained a lot of things. Like why my father would rush Neil to the hospital if his temperature passed ninety-nine but would accuse me of faking it when mine rose to a-hundred-and-three. Why he always made room in his schedule to take Neil to his piano lessons but could never find the time to make it to a single one of my parent-teacher nights. I kind of lost it there for a while, after I found out. I started skipping school and drinking, and one day I thought it might be funny to lock my little brother in the garage with the doors closed and all four of my parents' cars running at once. After that my father did rush me to the hospital. You know, to a mental institution. Left me there for almost a year. I used to take it personally, my father's hate. Not anymore, though, not since the therapist at the institute explained to me that every time my father looks at me, he sees the two of them in his bed together. His wife and his brother. That he doesn't hate me, he hates them." Herman looks up at Mead. "That ostentatious display of trophies on the mantelpieces, it has nothing to do with me, Fegley, so I don't take it personally. That's just my father's way of getting back at my mother for hanging that portrait in the front hall."

But Mead isn't buying it, this whole act that Herman is putting on. Therapist or no therapist, he does not believe that anyone could experience that kind of open hostility over an extended period of time and not be affected by it. No way.

"So where are your trophies?" Mead asks.

Herman smiles. "You're making the assumption that I have trophies, Fegley. That's very kind of you."

"No, it isn't. You're smart. You got into Chicago University. And you do not strike me as the type to sit back and allow himself to be so easily dismissed."

"All good observations, Fegley, but you missed one detail."

"And what's that?"

But before Herman can answer, the door from the hall flies open and Earl walks through it carrying a can of Pepsi. Mead glances at his watch. It is now 2:34. "Shit," he says, "is it the middle of the afternoon?"

"Yep. The sun is shining and everything," Earl says. "You should take a break. Go outside and catch a few rays."

Herman crawls out of his bag. "Yeah, come on, Fegley. Take a ride with me back to the house. You can take a nice hot shower instead of washing up in the bathroom down the hall like some homeless person. You don't need to be here; the computer's doing all the work. Maybe I'll even show you my trophies."

Mead considers Herman's offer: a hot shower and a soft bed sound pretty good right about now. Plus, he never did set things straight with Mr. Weinstein. He never told the guy that he's working on the Riemann Hypothesis alone. Only now Mead feels that in doing so he would only be adding to the long list of demerits Mr. Weinstein has compiled against his bastard son. And so he says, "No, thank you. I prefer to stay here."

"What's wrong, Fegley? You don't look so good; is it something I said?"

Don't push it, Mead thinks to himself, or I might change my mind.

"Fine," Herman says. "I'll go alone. I'll just have to show you all my trophies another time."

THE CRAY X-MP HAS CRANKED OUT nearly a billion-and-a-half zeros, and counting, when Herman returns with Mead's green-and-blue plaid suitcase in one hand and his book bag in the other. "I hate to be the bearer of bad news, Fegley," he says, "but your time is up. We've got a plane to catch in four hours."

"Change the ticket," Mead says and reaches for a fresh batch of printouts. "I need more time."

Herman laughs, a sound that grates on Mead's nerves because it usually means he is being laughed at. "What's so funny, Weinstein?"

"I've already changed the ticket, Fegley. Twice. It's the third of April. The spring quarter's been in session for a week now."

Mead doesn't react, certain that Herman is yanking his chain.

Again. Like that whole bullshit story the guy told about his father and his uncle and his mother. About being a bastard. The more Mead has thought about it, the more convinced he has become that Herman made it up. That he has been playing Mead, using that whole poor-little-rich-kid bit to keep him from telling Mr. Weinstein the truth. By making Mead feel sorry for him. Well, Mead is not biting. Not this time.

Herman grabs the morning paper out of Earl's hand and points to the date on the masthead. "Here. Look at this. Do you believe me now?"

And there it is in black and white: Sunday, April 3. Mead cannot believe it. He grabs his book bag out of Herman's hand and starts stuffing it with printouts. He cannot believe that he has missed a full week of classes. Shit. What if something came up in one of the lectures that might have given Mead a new insight into the Riemann Hypothesis and he missed it? Mead would never forgive himself. His book bag quickly fills up and so he starts stuffing the printouts into his suitcase, removing a sweater, two pairs of pants, and several button-down shirts to make more room.

A limousine is idling in front of the building when Mead emerges like a mole from underground. He squints against the bright sunshine and crawls into the backseat, feeling grateful to Herman once again—and more confused than ever. Shit. How is he supposed to know whether or not the guy is telling him the truth? He doesn't even know what day it is. Mead fears that he may have become so jaded by past experience that he has simply lost all ability to trust. He is so certain that everyone is out to get him that he pushes his peers away before even getting to know them. Shit. If Mead keeps this up, he could very well go through life without making a single friend. And so he resolves to be less paranoid and more trusting. Starting now. He turns to Herman and says, "What is it?"

"What is what?"

"The observation about you that I missed."

Herman turns away from Mead and looks out the window at the rush of passing scenery. After a long pause, he says, "You're a smart guy, Fegley. Figure it out."

A SECOND LIMOUSINE DRIVER picks them up at the airport and takes them back to campus. When he pulls to a stop at the light, Mead leaps out with his book bag.

"Hey," Herman says. "Where're you going, Fegley?"

"I'm walking back to the dorm from here. I need the fresh air. I'll see you later." And he hurries up the sidewalk, leaving his suitcase behind. He half expects Herman to get out and come after him, but he doesn't. The light turns green and the limousine pulls away with Herman still inside.

His green Schwinn is locked to the bike rack in front of Epps Hall. Mead walks past it and up the stairs to the second floor, so excited that he has to restrain himself from running. Dr. Alexander's office door is open but his chair is empty. Mead knocks and says, "I don't have an appointment, but I thought I'd stop by and drop these off. I just got back from New Jersey. That's where I've been for the past two weeks. At Bell Labs. Using this supercomputer of theirs. This is just a small sampling of my results, of the billion-and-a-half zeta zeros she computed for me to the eighth decimal point. I thought you might like to take a look at them." And he pulls from his book bag a sampling of printouts and sets them on the professor's desk.

Nothing.

"I'll just leave them right here," Mead says, "in your in-box. By the way, they all sit on the critical line, every last one of them. I just thought you'd like to know." Then he backs out of the office, making as much noise as possible so the professor will think he has left. But he doesn't leave; he stands in the hall and waits. A minute passes, then two. Mead is beginning to think that perhaps Dr. Alexander really isn't in; he is about to turn around and leave for real when a hand pops up over the edge of the desk and feels around for the stack of printouts, then pulls them out of sight.

FORSBECK IS SITTING AT HIS DESK. Reading. On a Sunday afternoon. A rare sight indeed. Perhaps a little of Mead's good study habits are beginning to rub off on the guy. Mead drops his book bag on the bed and looks around for his suitcase. It's nowhere in sight. Shit. Herman must be mad at him and is holding it as ransom. Now Mead will have to go up to his room and apologize for bolting from the limousine. It was rude but Mead couldn't bear to sit still for even one more second. He had to share the fruits of his labor with Dr. Alexander right then and there, and he didn't think Herman would understand. Didn't want the guy to feel insulted by Mead's desire to share news of his exciting adventure with someone else. Didn't want to hurt his new friend. And yet by doing what he did, he realizes that he has made matters worse. Shit. Mead isn't very good at this friendship thing, no good at all. But then again, he hasn't had much practice.

Forsbeck turns around in his chair. "Hey, Fegley, where have you been? Everyone around here has been freaked out about your absence."

"I missed you too, Forsbeck."

The guy doesn't look so good. His eyes are all rimmed in red like maybe he drank too much beer and smoked too much dope last night. "That Weinstein guy on four has your suitcase," he says. "He also has something to tell you."

Shit, he is mad. Mead drops down on his bed, suddenly exhausted. As bad as he is at friendship, he's even worse when it comes to apologizing, having had no practice at it whatsoever. He'll go up tomorrow. He's too excited to do it right now. He'd probably just blow it anyway. Not show enough remorse or something.

"You better go up there," Forsbeck says. "I told him what happened while you were gone missing. I'd tell you too but he said he'd rather do it."

Mead looks at his roommate again. On second thought, the guy doesn't appear to be hungover; he appears to be upset. "What's wrong, Forsbeck? Did something happen?"

He looks away. "He's your friend. Better it comes from him."

And suddenly Mead is convinced that something bad has happened. To one of his parents. Or both. Shit. He never called back. He was going to call them back but then he forgot. Shit and double shit. A cold dread races up his spine. That crash that woke him up in the middle of the afternoon. It was something. He knew it. Mead can't breathe, can't swallow, can't think. But somehow he makes it out of his room and up to the fourth floor where Herman is sitting on the edge of his bed looking as if someone just kicked him in the groin.

"I'm sorry," Mead says. "I shouldn't have taken off like that. I apologize." He doesn't know why he says this. Maybe because he thinks it will change whatever it is Herman has planned to say next. That if he apologizes for one wrong that it might make right the other thing. The thing that is making Herman look at Mead with sorrow in his eyes. Mead actually hopes that this is a prank, some stupid let's-pull-one-over-on-the-smart-kid bit that Herman thought up to get back at him for bolting from the limousine.

Herman stands. "No, I'm sorry. Jesus, am I sorry. Your cousin. Apparently he came by to visit you while we were out east."

Percy? Percy came by the dorm? Another shiver of cold dread

races up Mead's spine. Shit, he was right. Something bad *has* happened to his parents, so bad that his cousin came by to deliver the news in person. Double shit.

"There was an accident," Herman says. "A car accident."

Mead's knees turn to water. He reaches for the spare bed, the one on which his suitcase is resting, and sits down. He is going to throw up, in a second he is going to hawk up the entire contents of his stomach.

"He was on his way back home when it happened," Herman says. "His car swerved off the road and hit a tree. He was killed on impact."

Mead looks up, not certain he has heard right. "My cousin? My cousin is dead?" Herman nods and Mead is overcome with relief. His parents are fine. They aren't dead. But that relief is immediately replaced by guilt. Percy is dead. He came by to visit Mead, found out he wasn't here, turned around to head home, and hit a tree. Mead stands up. "I have to go. I have to catch the next train to Alton. I have to get home for my cousin's funeral." He grabs his suitcase and hauls it off the bed, forgetting that it is stuffed full of paper, forgetting how heavy it is. The suitcase drops to the floor with a loud thud. Mead sets it upright and then tries to drag it toward the door but Herman blocks his path. "Get out of my way, Weinstein. I have to go."

"It's too late," Herman says. "The funeral was four days ago."

Too late? It's too late? First he missed his cousin and now he has missed his funeral? "When?" Mead says. "When did this accident happen?"

"Last Monday. In the afternoon. Around one o'clock."

One o'clock. Which means it was two o'clock on the east coast. Exactly when Mead heard the crashing noise that woke him up. But he couldn't have heard. He was over a thousand miles away. That must be why the phone was busy when Mead tried to call home, why the line was tied up for so long. It was the coroner calling, all right, to tell Mead's father that his nephew was dead. Or maybe his father was trying to get in touch with Mead at the dorm. Only he wasn't there. Shit. Shit. Shit.

"I'm sorry," Herman says. "I'm so sorry." And he hugs Mead.

But this is all Herman's fault, isn't it? If he hadn't kidnapped Mead and taken him out east, then Mead could have been here when Percy dropped by to visit. And if he had been here, then Percy would have been here too. In the dorms. At one o'clock in the afternoon. And not out on some road getting killed.

Mead pushes Herman away, grabs his suitcase, and drags it out the door and down the hall. He half expects Herman to come after him and stop him. But he doesn't. The guy just stands in his doorway and watches as Mead drags his suitcase down the stairs. *Thump, thump, thump, thump, thump, thump.*

9

COUNTERCLOCKWISE

High Grove
Four Days Before Graduation

"YOU BETTER HURRY UP AND GET DRESSED," Mead's dad says. "I'm leaving in ten minutes."

Mead looks up from his plate of scrambled eggs. "I am dressed."

His father stares at his T-shirt and blue jeans. "You need to put on a tailored shirt and a proper pair of pants. I can't have you out on the showroom floor looking like that."

"Like what?"

"Like you just fell off the back of a hay truck," his mother says.

"Like a customer," his dad says, "instead of a salesperson."

Mead scoops up the rest of the eggs. Talking with his mouth full, he says, "Sorry, I can't make it today, Dad. I have a gig."

"A gig?" his mother says.

"Yes. I'm playing in a rock band and we have a gig over at Grange Hall."

His mother places her palm to his forehead and Mead pushes it away. "I'm serious, Mom. I joined a rock band yesterday."

He can see it in both of their faces: disappointment. But Mead was being honest the other night when Principal Jeavons came over for supper, when he told them he just wants to be normal. Another overlooked face in the crowd. Someone no one could possibly be jealous or envious of. And no one could possibly be jealous or envious of a cello player in a half-assed garage band.

"I see," his father says, looking all let down and everything as he picks up the car keys. He's laying it on thick this morning, his disillusionment in his son.

"You see what?" Mead says. Shit, he liked it better when he couldn't read his father's moods, when the old man's face was a blank slate. When did this happen? When did Mead acquire the ability to read faces? He would rather his mother scream at him than look one moment longer at his father's long face.

"It's just that I thought you'd be spending more time at the store," his dad says.

"I will be. This just came up."

Mead's mother looks pleased. Her husband and son are fighting. A split in the seam of their male bond has begun to show; a fissure in her husband's all-too-compliant acceptance of their son's return home has begun to open. Her look says: I may once again have a shot at getting things to go my way.

"All right," his father says, but he doesn't look all right.

"I'll come by the store later," Mead says. "After the gig. I promise."

His father doesn't respond, just opens the back door and leaves.

MEAD HELPS NELSON, a pudgy boy whose eyes have become dulled by the consumption of too many refined sugars, unload his drums from the back of an old VW bus, circa 1968. They carry each piece, one by one, up onto the stage, making several trips past the folding tables and metal chairs that have been set up to accommodate today's event: some kid's sixteenth birthday party. Blue and yellow paper streamers have been draped around the room in an attempt to add a touch of festivity to the otherwise austere ambience of the meeting hall. Helium balloons hover in clumps above the middle of each table as if afraid to venture out on their own. The whole place has an air of forced gaiety. And it depresses the hell out of Mead.

Similar preparations are taking place in Chicago. A stage is being built. The grassy lawns of the quad are being cut short to create a carpet for the rows upon rows of folding chairs the university is setting up for its own annual party: the graduation of another class of students. In just four days. The last of the final exams have now been taken, most of the underclassmen gone home. Only the near-graduates remain, wandering the campus like stunned survivors, surprised that it is suddenly all over, finding sentiment in the arch of a doorway or the mustiness of an old classroom that they are seeing and smelling for the last time. Taking a moment to reflect before launching into the next phase of their lives.

Forsbeck is probably sound asleep, recovering from a late night of partying. Has anyone stripped down Mead's bed? Or is it as he left it: sheets tucked neatly under the mattress, pillow fluffed, blanket pressed smooth. Waiting for his return. And what about Herman? The poor guy probably hasn't slept a wink in days. Pacing up and down the halls all night, eyes rimmed in red, trying to figure out his next move. Wondering where he went wrong. Wondering when Mead is going to knuckle under and come back. Holding tight to his belief that he knows what makes Mead tick, that he knows Mead better than Mead knows himself, that his plan can still come to fruition. But Mead isn't going back. Because to do so would be admitting to something he is not yet ready to admit to. No, Mead is going to stay right where he is for as long as he has to. Until he is proved wrong. Until Herman comes to him. Which he will. And when he does, Mead will be waiting. And watching. Because that's what the best hunters do: They watch their prey. They study them until they have begun to think like them. And then they make their move.

"So how exactly did we get this gig?" Mead asks Eric as he switches on his guitar and strums a few discordant notes, the feedback from the amplifier giving off a resounding vote of no-confidence.

"Through Nelson. He works for Roger Frohlich over at the Burger Haven."

"If you need a job," Nelson says. "I can put in a good word for you."

"But you don't even know me," Mead says.

Nelson shrugs. "So?"

"Roger's cousin, Beth, is getting married next month," Eric says. "If he likes what he hears here today, he's gonna hire us to play at her wedding too."

"Grange Hall today, Madison Square Garden tomorrow," Mead says.

"Nah," Nelson says. "The reception's gonna be over at the Lodge."

Eric and the oil leaks (a name Eric came up with just last night) manage to mangle and make almost indecipherable a whole medley of rock classics, but none of the guests seem to much mind, mainly because no one is listening. There must be close to fifty sixteen-year-olds in the Hall, all of them talking at once, none of them paying the slightest bit of attention to the three young men onstage. Mead feels utterly invisible. He may very well have found his calling.

A buffet has been set up along the west wall and when the Oil Leaks take a break, after forty-five minutes or so, Mead heads straight for it, his pay for this gig consisting of twenty dollars and all he can eat. The servers are wearing red-and-yellow jerseys and red-and-yellow caps with the letters BH stitched onto them. Mead has his choice of a double cheeseburger or fish fillet sandwich, french fries or cole slaw, and either a Pepsi, Coke, or Snapple iced tea. He asks for a can of Coke but instead of handing one to him, the server says, "What the fuck are you doing here?" Mead's ears are ringing from standing in front of the amplifier, so at first he thinks he has heard wrong, then looks more carefully at the guy and sees Freddy Waseleski looking back.

It's hard to say which one of them looks more ridiculous: the High Grove High School valedictorian dressed like a no-frills rock star or the high school dropout dressed like a fast-food vendor. Freddy has a smirk on his face, the same one he wore down by the creek the day Mead stood before him in nothing but his birthday suit, a look that still has the power to send a shiver up Mead's spine.

"What happened to you, freak? Didja flunk outta college or something?"

"No," Mead says. "I left voluntarily. For ethical reasons."

Freddy scrunches up his face. "Well, you still talk like a fucking freak. So this is what you do now? Play some stupid violin in a rock band?"

"Cello," Mead says. "And yes, my life has amounted to nothing. That should make you happy. I mean, that is what you always hoped would happen to me, isn't it, Freddy? That I would fail? That I'd end up a nobody like you?"

"Whadaya mean, nobody? You're in a fucking rock band, freak. I'd kill to be in a fucking rock band."

"You're kidding me, right?"

A cloud rolls in over Freddy's face. "You're still the same snot-nosed kid. The boy with everything who don't even know how good he's got it. So what's the real reason you came home, freak? Has someone else threatened to shove a ruler up your ass?"

Mead lunges across the buffet table, sending Coke and Pepsi cans flying everywhere, grabs Freddy by the collar, and lifts him clear off his feet. "You're a prick, Freddy. A nobody, loser prick who I was once foolish enough to feel sorry for. Well, not anymore. Gum under my heel. That's all you'll ever be, Freddy, gum under my heel."

Freddy's eyes are bugging out of his face. He looks the way Mead felt down by the creek. Terrified. The look frightens Mead and so he lowers Freddy to the ground and lets him go. Shit. Why the hell did he go and do that? To Freddy Waseleski of all people. Mead shakes out his hand, still sore from punching Forsbeck in the face a few days ago, and wraps it around an ice-cold can of Coke before walking off.

MEAD HELPS NELSON LOAD THE LAST OF THE DRUMS back onto the VW van. Eric slides the door shut, shoves a ten-dollar bill into Mead's hand, and says, "Here's your cut. Now take your cello and get lost, you're out of the band."

"Out?" Mead says. "But I'm the only person in this band who actually knows how to play an instrument."

Eric turns to address Nelson. "Your boss Roger says we can forget about playing at his cousin's wedding next month."

"How come?" Nelson says.

"Because our bass player here punched one of his employees in the face."

"I did not punch Freddy in his face," Mead says. "I just grabbed him."

"That's not what Roger says."

"Well, Roger is wrong."

"I saw the guy's face, Fegley. It was all splotchy and puffed out."

"That's not from being hit, Eric, that's from subsisting on a diet of french fries and sugary colas."

Eric shakes his head. "What is it with you Fegleys? You all walk around this town acting like you're better than the rest of us."

"As if," Mead says, "as if you're better than the rest of us."

Eric looks at Mead as if he were dirt. "You're a prick, Fegley, just like that dead cousin of yours." He turns to walk away.

Mead grabs him by the sleeve. "What did you say? You take that back."

"Why, are you gonna hit me if I don't?"

"Yes."

But Eric doesn't take it back and Mead doesn't hit him. Because for all he knows Eric did think Percy is a prick, the same way Freddy thinks Mead is a freak. Instead he says, "You still owe me the other half of my pay."

"That's all you're getting, Fegley. Ten bucks. I'm keeping the rest as compensation for the fact that you cost us our next paying job with your hot temper."

"I don't have a temper," Mead says and realizes that he still has Eric's shirt balled up in his fist. He lets go of it and steps back. "And I didn't cost you your next job; you lost it because you can't carry a tune. I don't care what excuse Roger Frohlich gave you; the truth of the matter is you suck as a musician."

Mead picks up his cello and turns to go. Freddy Waseleski is loading trays of cold french fries and uneaten fish fillet sandwiches into the back of the Burger Haven van. He glares at Mead with hate in his eyes. The poor bastard, he didn't think Mead had it in him to fight back, to stand up for himself. And quite frankly, neither did Mead.

* * *

"STAY OUT OF THE LIVING ROOM." That is what Mead's mother says as he comes through the back door. Not "the dean called again and you have to call him back." Not "what the hell is wrong with you, you should be graduating, you're ruining your life." She's all dressed up. Pearl necklace around her neck, apron around her waist. Guests must be imminent. But it is too early for supper and too late for lunch. She scurries from refrigerator to stove to sink, trimming the crust off bread, piercing olives with toothpicks, spreading cream cheese over crackers. Which can mean only one thing: her bridge group is coming over. Well, his mother has nothing to worry about. Mead is no more interested in socializing with them than with Freddy Waseleski. The windbags of High Grove, that's what Mead's grandfather Henry Charles used to call them. The poor fellow spent the last six months of his life on a rollaway bed in the living room behind a folding screen, one organ after another withering and dying. But his hearing was just as sharp as ever and he used to have to lie there and listen to Mead's mother and her seven lady friends talk about everything from who was sleeping with the butcher to how much so-and-so spent on her daughter's wedding to what Mrs. Next-Door-Neighbor had done to her eyelids while on vacation in Florida. Afterward Mead's mother would feed him leftovers. Scallops wrapped in bacon, caviar on crackers, cheese melted over ham—none of which were allowed on his restricted diet and all of which probably contributed to his swift decline. Not that she'd admit it. She swore she was trying to make the man's last days on earth more enjoyable, but Mead is convinced she just wanted to get the stinky old guy out of her living room and into his grave as quickly as possible.

Mead picks up a triangle of toast with something green and lumpy on it and pops it into his mouth. Something about the fact that his mother wants him to leave makes him want to stay. "Your friends used to love it when you forced me to play bridge with them. What do you say I sit in for a hand or two today, for old times' sake?" he says and reaches for a second triangle.

His mother slaps his hand. "Those are for my guests. If you're hungry, help yourself to some of last night's leftovers in the fridge. But eat in your room. You aren't supposed to be here, you're supposed to be in Chicago, you're supposed to be graduating in four days."

"I'll take that as a *no*," Mead says and opens the refrigerator to get a soda but changes his mind when the front doorbell rings. "I'll get it," he says, closes the door, and starts toward the living room.

His mother steps in front of him. "I told you to stay out of the living room. I do not want to spend my afternoon explaining your presence when I don't understand it myself. Either go to your room or down to the store. Or have you already lost interest in it?"

"No, Mother, I have not lost interest in it. I told you this morning; I had a gig. Remember? It might be nice if you were to take an interest, to ask me how it went."

She crosses her arms over her chest, all war-like. "How did it go?"

"I got fired."

"Good." She takes off her apron, checks her reflection in the toaster, and says, "When I come back in here, I want you to be gone." Then she disappears through the swinging door.

MEAD IS MORE TIRED THAN HE THOUGHT and decides to lie down before heading over to the store. Just for a moment. But when he next opens his eyes, it's four o'clock, the day nearly gone. Shit. Now he's going to have to look at his father's long face all evening, a reminder of what a disappointment he has been to the old man since he got home. Here, but at the same time, not here. At least not at the store. It seems kind of silly to head over there at this late hour, but Mead decides to go anyway. If for no other reason than to appease the man who welcomed him home, maybe not with open arms, but at least without asking any questions.

He steps across the hall to splash water on his face and brush his teeth. The living room is quiet; the bridge ladies have gone home. He listens for the sound of his mother washing dishes in the kitchen but hears nothing. Perhaps she is out front saying her goodbyes. Now would be a good time to slip out of the house unnoticed.

Mead walks back into his room and stops up short. His green-and-blue plaid suitcase is lying open on the bed like a gutted animal, his zeta zero statistics strewn all over the mattress like entrails. And hunched over the whole mess is the six-legged creature. "Hey," Mead says, "what're you doing? Those are my personal papers." Stepping past the creature, he scoops up an armload of printouts and stuffs them back into the suitcase. But they won't fit; they keep spilling back out onto the mattress. "Hey," Mead says. "Give me that." And rips a page of zeta zeros calculated to the eighth decimal point from the creature's hand. A hairy hand. Too hairy to be his mother's. Which can mean only one thing: Bernhard Riemann is back.

"Mr. Riemann, sir. I'm sorry, sir. I thought you were someone else."

Bernhard Riemann peers at Mead over the top of his wire-rimmed spectacles and says, in a heavy German accent, "I see that you got hold of my formula for computing zeta zeros. Have you been to the Göttingen Library?"

"No, sir. I've never been overseas. I got it out of a book in the library on campus. In Chicago. It's called the Riemann-Siegel formula, in honor of the guy who discovered it among your *Nachlass.* A Mr. Carl Siegel."

"They named my formula after someone else simply because he found it?"

"Yes, sir. I'm curious, sir, why you didn't include it in your published paper?"

"It wasn't necessary to the work, Mead. I merely used it to compute a few zeros, to satisfy myself that the hypothesis was right. It's very time consuming, all that long computation. I found it to be a waste of time. You, on the other hand, have computed over a billion of them. Tell me, young man, how did you do it?"

"With a supercomputer, sir."

"A what?"

"An electronic machine that computes numbers at the speed of light."

"I see. And may I ask why you bothered?"

"Why, to try and prove your hypothesis, sir."

"And did you?"

"Yes. No. I mean, I computed nearly a billion-and-a-half zeros and every last one of them sits on the critical line. I'd say the evidence weighs heavily in favor of your hypothesis being true."

"But you aren't sure."

"I'm pretty sure, sir, but no, not a hundred percent sure."

"What a waste of time."

"Excuse me?"

"You're going about it all wrong, Mead."

"Excuse me for saying so, sir, but mathematicians have been trying to prove or disprove your hypothesis for over a hundred years and this right here in my suitcase is the closest anyone has ever gotten."

"Idiots. The lot of them. Writing papers. Awarding one another with useless honors. It's pointless. A total waste of time and talent." Bernhard Riemann gets up out of the straight-backed chair and walks over to the window, the light outside throwing him into silhouette. "A function is not a mere set of points on a line, Mead. It is an object. A unified whole. Until you modern-day mathematicians stop thinking in terms of formal computation and start using your heads intuitively, you're never going to prove or disprove a thing. That is what you want, Mead, isn't it? To prove my hypothesis?"

"Yes, sir. The man who successfully does so will be world famous."

"And is that what you're looking for, Mead? Fame?"

"No, sir. You're twisting my words around, sir. I fell in love with the challenge. I set out to solve the greatest unsolved puzzle. But then things got out of hand. Other people got involved. People in search of fame and money and opportunity." Mead tries to look Bernhard Riemann in the eye but can't because the man's face is in shadow. "You must've dealt with similar situations in your own time, sir. Have you any advice to share with me?"

"Stop being logical, Mead, and rely more on your intuition."

"That's it? That's all you've got? How is that supposed to help me?"

Someone behind Mead places a hand on his shoulder, causing him to jump. He spins around and sees his mother. Shit. How long has she been standing there?

"Teddy, who were you talking to just now?"

"No one," he says. "Go away. I'm busy."

"I've never seen you like this before, Teddy. Talking to walls. Seeing people who don't exist. I'm really starting to get worried."

"I said go away!" Mead turns back to face the window. To finish his conversation with Mr. Riemann. To ask him to better explain what he means. But the man is gone.

MEAD FINALLY MAKES IT THROUGH the front door of Fegley Brothers at four thirty. The place is quiet, just a few customers strolling about the showroom floor. He heads straight for the back office—to find his father—but he isn't there. And neither is Uncle Martin. As a matter of fact, there isn't a single soul around other than those few customers. Not even Lenny. Mead opens the back door and checks the parking lot. The white hearse is gone, which means his father is out picking up a body. Which means his uncle is down in the basement getting ready for its arrival. Which explains everything except Lenny's absence.

Someone knocks on the office door.

"Excuse me," a man says to Mead, "but could you please help us? My wife and I have a few questions we'd like to ask about one of your sofas."

"Uh, I don't actually work here," Mead says. "But if you can hold on a moment, I'll find someone who does." And he ducks past them and upstairs to the second floor, hoping to find Lenny there. But the salesman is nowhere in sight. So Mead heads up to the third floor. It is highly unusual for Lenny to just up and vanish like this. If Uncle Martin were to find out, he'd throw a fit. Probably fire the guy on the spot. Could Lenny have stepped out for a cup of coffee? No. But that doesn't make sense. He'd never take off while Mead's father was out doing a body removal. He'd wait until he got back and then go. Shit. Where is he?

Mead runs back down to the main floor. "Just one more minute," he says to the waiting couple as he passes through the showroom into the chapel next door, hoping to find someone. Anyone. And he does. He finds Lenny sitting in one of the pews, his head bowed as if in prayer. "I hate to disturb you," Mead says, "but there's a couple in the showroom who need some assistance." Lenny doesn't respond. Jesus, what is he doing? Sleeping? Uncle Martin is going to fire his ass for sure if he finds out about this. "Lenny, for god's sake, wake up. We've got customers. Come on." Mead grabs the man's shoulder and gives it a good shake.

But when Lenny turns around, Mead realizes that it isn't him at all: It's Herman.

"Hey, Fegley, it's about time you showed up. I've been sitting in here all day waiting for you. Where the hell have you been?"

Mead feels dizzy. Confused. First Bernhard Riemann and now this. Mead doesn't know what to believe anymore, what is real and what's just in his head. "How did you get in here?" he asks. "What have you done to Lenny?"

"Now Fegley, is that any way to greet a friend? Come on. Sit down. Let's talk. I'm willing to let your betrayal pass, you know why? Because I know you didn't mean it. And I know in my heart of hearts that you'll make good on our arrangement."

"My betrayal? You betrayed me, Weinstein. You gave me an ultimatum."

"I don't like that word. Ultimatum. It sounds so . . . final."

"Go away," Mead says. "You aren't even real; I've just conjured you up."

"Oh, but I am real, Fegley, as real as it gets. It's time for you to get your head out of your books and deal with it. This is life, Fegley. Just deal with it."

"I said go away!" Mead lunges at Herman, his arms passing straight through his body. "See? I told you, you aren't real. Get out of my head, Weinstein. Get out of my life. Why won't you just go away?"

A horn honks twice. His father's signal. He's back with the body. Mead turns to leave the chapel then turns back. Just to make sure. Herman isn't there.

MEAD PASSES BACK THROUGH THE SHOWROOM but the couple is gone. Shit. He just cost his father a sale. Unless he conjured them up too.

Mead pulls open the back door just as his father is getting out of the hearse. The man looks up and says, "So glad you could finally join us today, Teddy."

"Sorry, Dad. I meant to get here earlier."

"That's two days in a row, Teddy, that you meant to come by the store."

"Yeah, well, I'm here now."

His father opens the rear door of the hearse. "Maybe you should think about calling back the dean, Teddy. Maybe you can still work something out with him."

"What? I can't do that, Dad. I told you."

"Well, you're gonna have to do something, Teddy, because this isn't working out. For either of us. This isn't the place for you." And he slides out the gurney, the body on it hidden beneath a white sheet.

"I'll do better, Dad."

His father shakes his head. "It's not a matter of doing better, Teddy. You need to find something you're passionate about, something that's important to you, because this obviously isn't."

Mead grabs the end of the gurney, holding it tight so his father can't walk away. "That's not true, Dad. This is important to me. It is. I'll prove it to you." The freight elevator opens and Uncle Martin steps out. Shit. The last thing Mead needs right now is more crap from his uncle. "Let me prove it to you, Dad."

Uncle Martin looks at Mead and then at his father, and Mead gets the distinct impression that the two of them have been talking. Making decisions about him behind his back. Writing him off. His uncle he can understand, but not his father. Mead never thought his father would write him off like this. And it hurts.

"So how's our Mr. Fullington doing?" Uncle Martin asks, ignoring Mead.

"Been dead for about an hour now," Mead's father says.

"Arthritic knees. Pretty dehydrated. You might have a bit of trouble finding a good artery."

Martin takes the gurney from Mead's father and pushes it toward the waiting elevator. "Tell Lenny not to worry. I can take it from here."

"He's not here," Mead says, trying to shoehorn his way back into the conversation. "That's what I was going to tell you, Dad. That I've been looking all over for him." Mead feels horrible saying this, knowing that he is getting Lenny in trouble just to get himself out of trouble. But he has to prove to his father that he cares, that the family business is important to him. "There were customers in the store. I tried to help. I tried to find him, but he wasn't anywhere to be found."

His father and uncle exchange a look.

"What? What did I do wrong now?"

"We know he isn't here, Teddy," his father says.

"Oh. All right. Well. Just so you know. I mean I wasn't trying to get him in trouble or anything. I was just trying to help."

"Jesus, Teddy," Martin says. "Don't you know who Mr. Fullington is?"

Mead looks at the lumpy sheet on the gurney. "Should I?"

His uncle shakes his head and pushes the gurney onto the elevator.

"Who is he?" Mead asks and looks to his father for a helping hand, but the man doesn't have one to offer.

"Mr. Fullington is Lenny's dad," Martin says.

What? Shit. Oh shit. Mr. Fullington is Lenny's dad? Lenny's last name is Fullington? Then Mead remembers, after he and Lenny finished up with Delia's grave, he remembers Lenny saying something about his dad being ill, about his needing some medication. But Mead had no idea the man was so ill. Double and triple shit.

The elevator door begins to close. Mead grabs hold of it and squeezes on next to his uncle and Mr. Fullington.

"What're you doing?" Martin says.

"Going downstairs."

Mead's father lifts his eyes off the ground where they have been hiding in shame and looks at his son.

"I want to do this," Mead says to him.

His father grabs the door as it begins to close again. "Teddy, it's all right. Get off the elevator."

"No," Mead says. "This is important to me."

He knows what his father is thinking: that he is being ridiculous. That he is grandstanding. That he doesn't really want to do this. Maybe that's all true, but it doesn't matter because he's doing it anyway. And no one is going to stop him.

"Okay," his father says, and lets go of the door.

10

PARENTS' WEEKEND

Chicago
Six Weeks Before Graduation

THERE'S A TRADE SHOW IN CHICAGO THIS WEEK. Well, there's probably a trade show in Chicago every week, but this one Mead knows about because his father attends it every year. It's sponsored by the National Association of Funeral Homes. A hundred thousand square feet of booths selling everything from formaldehyde to suits to forceps to caskets. Plus seminars on flower displays, the best techniques for preparing an autopsied body for the open casket, and the relaxation response for stressed-out funeral directors.

Mead has never attended one of these trade shows. He's usually too busy with classes and studying and life in general. His father usually just stops by the dorms on the evening of his last day and takes him out to dinner, someplace that offers an early-bird special. Not because the man is cheap but because he wants to get on the road as soon as possible for the six-hour drive back to High Grove.

This year, however, Mead's mother decided to come along.

MEAD GLANCES OUT THE WINDOW. He's not expecting his parents for another ten minutes but sometimes his father shows up early.

Not late, like most people, but early. A man whose life revolves around other's people schedules, who thinks nothing of getting up in the middle of the night to remove a body from the home of the deceased. A man who has spent many a birthday at memorial services, several wedding anniversaries presiding over graveside funerals, and a fair share of national holidays consoling the bereaved.

Mead digs through his dresser drawer for a tie. If it were just his father coming he wouldn't bother. But he knows his mother and she is going to want to go to someplace nice. Someplace where the men are required to wear a tie. But the only tie he owns has been sitting in the back of his sock drawer for almost three years now. The last time he wore it was to his high school graduation. It was a present from his mother, a gift for the gifted. He spent an entire hour in the bathroom trying to get the knot just right, then his mother took one look at it, sighed, and retied it herself. No son of hers was going to stand before a gymnasium full of parents and give the valedictory address looking as if he had just stepped off the back of a hay truck even if half the men in the room actually had just stepped off hay trucks.

The navy blue tie in question is covered in white sock lint, which Mead attempts to remove with a piece of scotch tape but a few stubborn specks cling as if for life and he has to pinch them off between his thumb and forefinger, like aphids from a rose bush. The tie is creased too, in several places, so Mead takes it down the hall to the bathroom. He tries to smooth out the wrinkles by wetting his palm under the hot water faucet and then pressing it down over the creases. But this doesn't work. It just makes things worse. Now he has a wrinkled tie with dark, wet splotches all over it.

Mead puts it on anyway, consulting the bathroom mirror to make sure it at least hangs straight. It's the first thing his mother will notice: his tie. She reads ties the way a fortune-teller reads a crystal ball. As if one's destiny can be seen in it. And he knows exactly what she'll see when she spots his: a small-town boy who still has bits of straw stuck in his hair.

A toilet flushes and one of the stall doors behind Mead opens. Herman steps out wearing a silk bathrobe. It's open in the front so Mead can see what he's wearing underneath it. Which isn't much, just a pair of jockey shorts. It's a common enough sight around here. Boys in jockey shorts. Or no shorts at all for that matter. Ducking in and out of the shower. Not Mead, though, he prefers to keep his private parts private, a result of always being three to four years younger than his classmates. He not only wears boxers but he wears them straight into the shower, removing them just long enough to clean his crotch before wrapping a towel around his waist and dashing back to his room.

Herman steps up to the sink next to Mead to wash his hands and nods at the tie. "What's the big occasion?"

"My parents are in town. They're taking me out to lunch."

Herman shuts off the water and reaches for a paper towel. He studies Mead in the mirror, shakes his head, and says, "Come with me."

"I can't. They're going to be here any minute. What're you doing in here anyway? Your room isn't even on this floor." And he looks at the open robe again, at Herman's hairless chest, at his white jockey shorts, and wonders where the guy left the rest of his clothes.

Herman grabs Mead's tie and pulls on it, choking him. "This is a disgrace," he says. "I've got a hundred better ones hanging in my closet. You can have your pick."

Mead yanks the tie out of his hand, loosens the collar. "No, thanks. Besides, they're probably here already."

Herman shrugs. "Okay, it's your funeral," he says, as if he knows Mead's mother well, as if he knows what she will say, and heads out of the bathroom.

Mead looks in the mirror and watches him go. Relieved. The way he always feels when Herman leaves. Even after the trip out east. Which was by far and away the nicest thing anyone has ever done for Mead. And yet he still finds himself feeling wary whenever Herman is around. On guard. Against what he is not quite sure. There was that incident in the men's room with the two pairs of shoes. But Mead has no proof that it was Herman. Or Dr. Kustrup. And then there was that time in the basement of Bell Labs when Herman was looking at Mead all weird and stuff. But then people have been looking at Mead like that his whole life. What he has got to do is stop assuming that the world is out to get him. He's been trying to work on it, trying to improve his social skills the way Dr. Kustrup suggested instead of hiding in the stacks of the library all the time; he just hasn't yet found the right opportunity.

Mead turns his attention back to his reflection, to his tie. He sees his mother take one look at him and shake her head, much as Herman just did. Only she won't shrug and walk away, she'll make stabs at him all through lunch. Tell him that he needs to get a haircut, to tuck in his shirt, to hike up his pants so the cuffs won't drag on the ground. That he should sit up straight, chew with his mouth closed, and get his elbows off the table. All things of which Mead is guilty, it's true. He does let his shirt hang out and his cuffs drag, he does slouch at the table and talk with food in his mouth, but he only does these things when his mother is around, to bug her.

Mead pulls off the tie, tosses it into the trash, and steps out into the hall just as Herman is starting up the stairs. He looks back when Mead pokes his head out the door.

"You got anything up there that'll match this shirt?"

Herman smiles. "Go to your room. I'll be right back."

SHE'S SITTING ON FORSBECK'S BED, the unmade bed. She probably assumes that it belongs to her son but Mead made his bed this morning. He makes it every morning, something he started doing as soon as he moved out of his mother's house. It grosses him out, the fact that his mother is sitting on his roommate's soiled bedsheets, home to dust mites, mildew, sweat, and millions of microscopic Forsbecks that met with certain death last night thanks to the *Penthouse* magazine that Mead's roommate "reads" every night before drifting off to sleep. It grosses him out but at the same time it pleases him.

"There you are," she says. "Your father and I were beginning to think you'd taken off again. Without notice. He's sitting downstairs in the car, keeping an eye out for your whereabouts."

Mead glances at his watch. It's a quarter to twelve. He had no idea he'd been in the bathroom that long. He wonders who let his mother in the building, how she found her way to his room. "I'm sorry, Mother. I've apologized for that like a million times. What else do you want me to do?"

She gets up off the bed, pulling herself to her full height that, even in heels, only brings the top of her head to Mead's chin. But what she lacks in stature, she makes up for in tone. "For starters, you could write your aunt and uncle a letter."

"I sent them a condolence card."

"A card? He's your cousin, Teddy. Or was. The closest thing you'll ever have to a brother. I think you can do better than a card."

It's all his fault, that's what she is really trying to say. That he wasn't where he was supposed to be and now his cousin is dead.

"Fine, I'll write a letter. I'll apologize for my existence. Will that make you happy?"

"I don't appreciate the sarcasm, Teddy."

"Was I being sarcastic? I didn't notice. I mean I've been kind of busy, Mother. I have a paper to write by the end of the year. For the dean. That's why I was out there. I was doing research, collecting important data. I was working, Mother, not goofing off. This paper is to take the place of my final exams and I have to hand in a comprehensive outline of it on Monday. That's in three days."

"This week. I want you to write that letter this week," his mother says, then grabs the collar of his shirt and adds, "Why aren't you wearing a tie?"

HERMAN APPEARS IN THE DOORWAY at that very moment, holding a Pierre Cardin tie, a navy blue and maroon number that probably cost as much as the dress suit Mead's mother is wearing. And she wears nice clothes. The woman does all her shopping at Marshall Field's right here in Chicago. Albeit mostly by mail. Herman has changed out of his bathrobe into a pair of pressed trousers and a shirt that he is still buttoning up when he hands Mead the tie and says, "You ran off in a hurry and left this in my room."

Mead's mother looks horrified, always at the ready to believe the worst about her son. As if Herman just handed him a pair of boxer shorts instead of a tie. Mead sighs and says, "He's kidding, Mother. It's a loan. He's loaning me one of his ties."

"Ah," Herman says, "so this must be the mother of the genius. Mead talks about you all the time, Mrs. Fegley. It's an honor to finally meet." And he takes her hand, as he took his own mother's hand, and kisses the back of it.

He's lying, of course. Mead has barely said a word about his mother to Herman. And the few words he has said have been anything but complimentary. But it's a lie that Mead appreciates, especially when he sees the effect it has on her.

"And who might you be?" she asks like a preteen girl with a sudden crush.

"Herman Weinstein, ma'am. The thoughtless soul who whisked your son off at a moment's notice without once entertaining the notion that his absence would cause such a stir or result in such a horrible and unspeakable outcome. May I extend to you my deepest condolences on your recent loss. I truly, truly am sorry." And the whole time he's talking, he's holding her manicured hand between his two manicured hands, as if cupping a baby bird. Even for Herman, he's laying it on pretty thick. So thick that Mead fears he might gag. But his mother doesn't seem to notice the affectation. Or perhaps she doesn't care. She laps up his attention like an alley cat that hasn't seen milk in a month and says, "Oh, so you must be Teddy's friend from out east. The one from Princeton. Herman, did you say?"

He looks at Mead and smiles. "So you've told them about me then."

Mead blushes for reasons he is not quite sure. He is either embarrassed for himself or for his mother or for them both, it's hard to say. "No. Yes. I mean I had to explain where I was when I disappeared. How I paid for the round-trip airfare. How I got access to the Cray X-MP."

"My father was very impressed with your son, Mrs. Fegley. And the man is not easily impressed, believe you me."

This is news to Mead. He had no idea he had impressed Mr. Weinstein. But which one? The one in Princeton, the one married to Mrs. Weinstein, the one with connections to the Institute for Advanced Study? Or the other one, the one who works at Bell Labs, Herman's biological father? Either way, Mead is pleased to learn that he—Theodore Mead Fegley of High Grove, Illinois—was able to impress such powerful and important men. Especially considering how little time he spent in their presence. Of course, they both knew why Mead was out there, that he spent two weeks in the basement of Bell Labs cranking out the largest number of zeta zeros known to man. Herman most certainly told them. And Earl would have backed up this claim. It's probably a good thing Mead didn't spend more time in their presence. If he had, they might have picked up on the fact that he doesn't much care for them personally. As father figures, they both suck. Big time. But Mead isn't looking for a father figure; he already has a perfectly good one. What he needs are influential men with important connections who can get him into that Institute in Princeton. And either Mr. Weinstein will fit that bill quite nicely.

Unless, of course, Herman is lying.

"I'd love it if you could join us for lunch," Mead's mother says. "As a way of our thanking you for your generosity toward our son."

"Herman can't join us," Mead says. "He has to go to class. This is a university, after all, Mother, not a country club."

"I'd love to," Herman says.

"Wonderful," Mead's mother says.

It feels strange sitting in the back of his father's Cadillac with Herman Weinstein seated next to him. Like two parallel planes intersecting. An impossibility in the world of mathematics. And yet here Mead sits, straddled between two separate worlds that were never intended to meet. It feels wrong, like something bad is going to happen. Like his mother is going to pull out a photo album and show Herman baby pictures of her son. Or tell him about the time Mead was four and ran around the backyard in nothing but his birthday suit. Embarrassing stuff. The kind of stuff you hope to leave behind when you pack your bags and move three hundred miles away from your parents. When you change your name from Teddy to Mead in hopes that you are finished with the past. Or maybe Herman will mention something about the scantily clad girls in the unisex bathrooms. Or the marijuana smoke that slips out from under closed doors on the weekend. Stuff Mead would prefer his parents not know about, stuff they wouldn't understand, stuff his mother would automatically assume he was taking part in.

But his fears are unwarranted. Herman is utterly charming. He listens attentively as Mead's mother tells him about her church group and about the bake sale they sponsor every June to raise money for the homeless. "Last year we raised nearly five thousand dollars," she says, making it sound like five million. "Thanks to my husband, Lynn, who donated the twenty-five hundred." And Mead realizes that he is witnessing something he has never seen before: his mother sucking up.

He sits up higher in his seat for a better view. Mead is quite impressed by Herman's performance because instead of coming back with a retort of one-upmanship, instead of mentioning that his mother sponsors a fund-raiser for AIDS that actually does pull in millions as opposed to thousands of dollars a year, instead he tells her how honorable her church work is, how he was brought up to view acts of charity—no matter how big or small—as more indicative of class than any amount of personal wealth.

It doesn't really matter what Herman says after that; Mead's mother is sold. At the restaurant she lets him select her appetizer (crab soufflé) and entrée (veal roulade) and even lets him order a bottle of wine for the table (something French with a 1957 vintage) even though she rarely drinks alcohol because it makes her skin flush. It's almost as if Mead and his father aren't there, as if Herman and Mead's mother are on a date.

Mead's father is a harder read. He doesn't seem so much impressed with Herman as tolerant. Like another day at the office, another afternoon spent listening to the family of the deceased talk about whatever it is they need to talk about. He's a man who has heard it all—and then some—and doesn't need to listen anymore. A man so talented at not listening that you think he is even when he isn't. Or maybe it's the other way around: that he continues to listen even though he has no godly reason on earth to do so. A true saint. Either way, it isn't until the check arrives—and the head waiter hands it to Herman—that Mead's father speaks up. "This is my treat," he says. "You're a guest of my family."

"Thank you, Mr. Fegley," Herman says, "but I really want to take this. It was such an honor to meet all of you, to meet Mead's family, that I'd really like to pay. To thank you for this opportunity."

"That's very nice," Mead's father says, "but it's not the way I do things." And he says it with an edge in his voice.

Mead's spoon is halfway to his mouth when his hand freezes. He glances past it at his mother, who looks equally surprised, who looks as if she'd like to hide under the table, who looks as if she is going to recriminate her husband as soon as they get back to their hotel room this evening, wagging her finger in his face and telling him how he embarrassed her in front of nobility. Or at least her perception of nobility.

But Herman is smooth as a pat of butter on a warm roll. He simply hands the bill over to Mead's father and says, "Thank you, sir. That's very generous of you."

* * *

Since tomorrow is Saturday—and Mead has been loaded up with fresh guilt about Percy's death being his fault—he accepts his mother's invitation to accompany her and his father to the last day of the trade show. Even though he can think of about a million things he would rather do. Including clipping his toenails. It hardly seems like a fair exchange—attending a trade show to make up for the loss of his cousin's life—but it is all Mead has to bring to the table at the moment. He would be attending it today too, if not for his afternoon class. Which he may not get to on time if his mother doesn't zip it and let her new best friend, Herman, exit the car. Mead fears she is going to invite him to the trade show too, but something holds her back. Perhaps some residual embarrassment about what her husband does for a living, as if burying people were any less glamorous than producing glass bottles for a fruit juice company.

"We'll swing by and pick you up at nine," Mead's father says before heading back to their hotel.

Since Mead is going to be losing a full day—a day he should be using to write that outline for the dean instead of attending a trade show—he skips dinner and goes directly from his Friday afternoon class to the library, where he throws himself into his work, not even bothering to look up from the table until the overhead lights flicker to signal closing time. Mead scoops up his papers and stuffs them into his blue-and-green plaid suitcase, then drags it over to the exit and waits for his turn in line. The students ahead of him hand their backpacks, one at a time, to the librarian so she can peek inside and make sure they aren't trying to smuggle out any reference books or microfiche discs. When it's his turn, Mead places his suitcase on the counter and unzips the top. But the librarian doesn't bother to rifle through his papers. She has seen both them and the suitcase before. Every night since Mead got back from New Jersey. Instead she says, "If you don't mind my asking, what is all of this for? It looks as if you're on a quest to solve the mystery of life."

"Not life," Mead says. "The Riemann Hypothesis."

"Well, it must be very important; why else would a nice-looking young man such as yourself devote so many of his Friday nights to solving it?"

Mead lifts his head and looks—really looks—at the librarian for the first time. She appears to be in her mid to late twenties. Not pretty, exactly, not in a glossy magazine sort of way, but pretty enough. With a clear complexion and large round eyes. He imagines her waking up every morning and greeting the new day with a smile, as if expecting it to be yet another amazing and wonderful adventure.

"At the end of this quarter I will be giving a presentation of my paper to my fellow students. If you would like to attend, I could probably arrange for that to happen."

"The end of the quarter," she says. "That's still several weeks off. Maybe one night you could take me out for a cup of coffee and give me the condensed version."

Drops of sweat break out across Mead's upper lip. Is the librarian flirting with him? Or is she just being nice? The way Cynthia was just being nice. "I think you should know," he says, "that I'm only eighteen."

She smiles. "Theodore... that is your name, isn't it? Theodore?"

"Mead," he says, figuring she must have gotten his name off his library card. "I prefer to go by my middle name, Mead."

"Okay, Mead. I'm only guessing here, but I get the feeling you're a lot more mature than your age suggests. I mean, I've seen a lot of eighteen- and nineteen- and even twenty-year-old students wandering around this campus, and not one of them seems to treat their time here at the university as seriously as you do. Am I right?"

It is as if she already knows him.

"Anyway," she says and zips his suitcase shut for him. "I'll be looking for that invitation to your lecture. I'd love to hear it."

MEAD LUGS HIS SUITCASE UP THE STEPS of the dorm one at a time. For some reason, it feels ten times heavier than it did this morning. Or even an hour ago. At the top of the stairs, he sets it down and sits on top of it as rock and roll music gallops down the hall and tramples over him like a herd of stampeding buffalo across an open field.

Every Friday night for the past three years it has been the same old thing: Mead sitting alone at the desk in his room while the rest of the boys and girls in his dorm pair off. A mating ritual that includes loud music, too much alcohol, and copious amounts of coffee the following morning. And to think that tonight he could have done something different. He could have taken the librarian up on her offer and taken her out for a cup of coffee. He could have talked to her about his trip out east and the wealth of statistical data he collected that all but proves the Riemann Hypothesis. Something in which she seems to be genuinely interested. But no, he had to make her feel foolish for even having brought it up. "I'm only eighteen." That's what he said, assuming that she would find him too young. Only it didn't faze her. Not one bit. She said he seemed mature. So why didn't he say something else? Why did he clam up? He blew it, plain and simple. And he didn't even have the sense to get her name.

A couple of boys stumble through the front door and up the stairs past Mead, smelling like vats of beer. The taller one, a blond in ripped jeans, trips over the corner of Mead's suitcase and falls to the floor. "Hey, buddy," he says, "either take that thing back to your room or move out." And his friend laughs as if this were funny.

Mead could always go back to the library. She might not have left yet. She might still be there turning off lights, putting books back in the stacks. Perhaps he can catch up with her in the parking lot, before she gets into her car and drives off. Yeah, right. He'll chase her down in a dark parking lot like a stalker or a deranged lunatic. Great idea.

Mead gets up and drags his suitcase down the hall toward his room, swinging wide around a couple leaning against the wall, making out. The door is shut. Odd for a Friday night. Forsbeck isn't usually so antisocial. Mead opens it and discovers why, sees Forsbeck's bare ass pumping up and down in the air, a female leg sticking up in the air on each side of it. And Miss Kitty ankle socks. She's wearing Miss Kitty socks like a grade school girl. Either because her feet are cold or because Forsbeck was in too much of a hurry to allow her to first take them off. Mead closes the door.

The lights in the hall flicker. "It's midnight," the resident advisor yells. "All stereos off." Then he walks down the hall, banging his fist against the closed doors. The entire floor turns silent as a monk's retreat as couples scurry into dark corners to hide like cockroaches from the light. When the resident advisor is satisfied that his demand has been met, he mounts the stairs to terrorize the inhabitants of the third floor.

Mead sits on his suitcase and waits for Forsbeck's "friend" to leave. Only she doesn't. A couple of stereos come back on. Not as many as before. Not as loud. Just loud enough to cover the grunting noises coming from various rooms. Just enough to give the loving couples—many of whom will not remember each others' names in the morning—time to finish their business.

Mead strolls down the hall and into the bathroom, dragging

his suitcase with him. Tucked into the side pocket is a travel kit his Aunt Jewel gave him before he left for college. As if he would be on the road for days instead of hours. He's never had a reason to use it before now. Mead pulls out the toothbrush and listens to the sound of rushing water coming from the showers. Someone is in there, someone Mead hopes is female. A moment later the shower shuts off and a girl steps out from behind the wall, a girl with a very large bruise on her left breast. When she sees Mead looking at her in the mirror, she covers herself with her towel, and that is when he notices the bruises on her arms. He looks at the girl again. Shit, he knows who she is. Cynthia Broussard. Herman's Cynthia. Mead had no idea she was living in his dorm, let alone on his floor. He turns around to face her. "Excuse me," he says. "I know this isn't any of my business, but are you all right?" Which is apparently not the right thing to say because she bursts into tears. Shit, what is Mead supposed to do now? "I'm sorry. This is really awkward," he says. "How about I turn around and you get dressed, okay? See? I'm turning around. I'm covering my eyes. And once you're dressed I'll walk you over to the health services office and you can tell the nurse what happened and she'll be able to give you some medical attention and whatever other kind of help you might need."

"No," she says. "No help. I'm fine. Please, Mead. No help."

He uncovers his eyes and turns back around. Cynthia has stepped into her robe and cinched it closed. "Who did this to you?" he says. "Herman? Did he hurt you?"

She shakes her head. "It was an accident. I fell. I was in a hurry and I tripped and fell. It was stupid. I'm fine. Really, I'm fine."

She's lying. It's obvious as hell that she is lying. She must be scared, that's what it has to be. She's afraid of Herman, of what he might do if she tells on him. "Okay, well, how about I take you to an emergency room off campus. You really should see a doctor and make sure you're okay."

"No. Thank you. Oh god, this is so embarrassing." And she laughs. But it isn't a real laugh. It's another lie. "Don't tell Herman you saw me like this. Please. He already thinks I'm such a klutz. Okay? No one can know."

"Okay," Mead says.

"Promise?"

"I promise."

"Okay," she says and smiles weakly, then gathers up her clothes and ducks out of the bathroom.

Back out in the hall, Mead parks his butt on his suitcase and waits for the resident advisor to swing through for a third and final time. Cynthia may have said not to tell Herman but she said nothing whatsoever about keeping it from the resident advisor. And yet when the RA does make his appearance, Mead hesitates. Because what does he know? Maybe it wasn't Herman; maybe it was somebody else. Or maybe Cynthia really did fall down. One thing he knows for sure: It won't do any good for him to report the incident if she is just going to lie about it. And so, in the end, he says nothing.

After the stereos all fall silent, Mead presses his ear against his door and hears a female giggle. It seems that Forsbeck's friend is planning to spend the night. Shit. Mead rolls his suitcase to the end of the hall and lugs it up two flights of stairs, then presses his ear against the door of room 48—to make sure the coast is clear—before he knocks. Herman answers wearing nothing but a pair of jockey shorts. He looks at Mead, then at his suitcase, smiles and says, "You running away, Fegley?"

"You have a scratch on your neck."

Herman reaches up and touches the scratch. Two parallel red lines above his right collar bone. "Dry cleaner," he says. "I forgot to remove their tag and the damned staple got me."

"That's a pretty deep scratch for a staple to make."

Herman frowns. "What're you trying to say, Fegley?"

But he promised. He promised Cynthia he wouldn't say anything to Herman. Innocent until proven guilty and all that stuff. "I would suggest that you never take your shirts back to that place again."

Herman smiles. "So what's with the suitcase?"

"Forsbeck has an overnight guest. Can I crash on your spare bed?"

MEAD HEARS A NOISE AND LOOKS UP. The librarian is shelving books, pushing one of those carts all libraries have down the aisle. She smiles at Mead and goes about her business as if everything is normal. Only it isn't, because she is naked. All the way naked. Not even any shoes on. Mead glances around to see if anyone else in the library has noticed, but no one has. So he gets up and starts to take off his shirt, so he can cover her up. But before he can get his shirt off, the shelves begin to tremble and books start to fall off them, start to tumble down on top of the naked librarian, burying her alive. Mead leaps into action and starts digging through the books, throwing them off to the left and the right, digging as fast as he can. But no matter how much he digs, he can't find the librarian.

MEAD WAKES WITH A START, his heart pounding in his chest. He sits up and looks over at Herman, who is sound asleep in the next bed, not a troubling thought in his head. It is inconceivable to Mead that anyone could inflict the kind of harm that was inflicted upon Cynthia and then sleep so soundly. Two weeks.

Mead spent the better part of two weeks with Herman at Bell Labs and never once saw even a hint of violence in his behavior. Even after his father made that derogatory statement about him at the dinner table, even after his other father flaunted his very young wife in his face. Mead pulls the sheets up to his chin and watches Herman sleep until he himself slips back into unconsciousness. He finds himself in the library again, the librarian shelving books. Naked. He walks over to her to check out her breasts. Which are perfect. Not a bruise in sight. He places his hands over them to cover them up. To protect them. To protect her. She smiles and says, "Thank you, Theodore."

TAP, TAP, TAP, TAP, TAP.

Mead opens his eyes and squints across the room at Herman, who is still sound asleep. So Mead rolls away, closes his eyes, and tries to fall back to sleep himself, to pick up his dream where it left off, with the librarian's breasts in his hands. He reaches down under the bedcovers and wraps his hand around Little Teddy, who isn't so little at the moment. He runs his finger over the tip and imagines he is rubbing it over one of her nipples.

Tap, tap, tap, tap, tap.

The bed behind Mead squeaks as Herman gets out of it. Apparently someone is knocking at his door. Then Mead remembers. His parents. They were going to stop by and pick him up at nine. He drops his dick and sits up in bed. "Shit, what time is it?" he says. "Is it after nine?"

Herman is standing over Mead, naked under an open robe. His little soldier at attention. Only it's not so little. You would think that having been born good looking and rich would have been enough, but no, Herman apparently lucked out in the endowment department, too. He closes the front of his robe over his tumid member but it remains all too obvious.

"Don't answer the door," Mead says.

"Why not?" Herman asks.

"Because. It might be my mother."

"Your mother? Why would your mother come knocking on my door?"

It's a good question, one for which Mead does not have a ready answer. He glances at his wristwatch. It's nine-fifteen. Plenty of time for her to have dropped by his room, found him missing, and started a manhunt. And since Herman was the individual responsible for the disappearance of her son the first time around, it only makes sense that she would start with him the second time around.

As Herman reaches for the doorknob, Mead leaps out of bed and grabs his wrist. "I said don't open the door."

Herman looks down and smiles. Mead follows his gaze and sees that his own dick is peeking out from between the folds of his boxer shorts. Mortified, he goes to put himself away, his hand still inside his shorts when Herman pulls open the door.

THE CHARLEMAGNE, referred to on the order form as Model No. 5163-2XB, is made out of redwood culled from the *Sequoia sempervirens* in California. The farming of sequoias is strictly regulated by the Federal Bureau of Conservation and Wildlife and, for that reason, only a couple hundred are cut down each year, making the Charlemagne a truly rare and special casket for the most discerning customer.

This is the spiel the salesman rattles off as Mead and his parents look on. The top-of-the-line casket has been polished to a shine and set upon a revolving pedestal. Like a new car at the automotive show, it is cordoned off with velvet rope. A pretty lady in a sparkly evening gown—and way too much makeup—stands next to the Charlemagne and smiles broadly as she opens the lid to show Mead and his parents the satin-lined interior, then runs her hand over the fabric in a suggestive way. The salesman then unhooks the rope and invites Mead and his folks inside for a closer look.

His father raps his knuckles against the side of the casket and asks the salesman what kind of a warranty comes with it. His mother runs her hand over the fabric, in much the same manner as the pretty lady, and declares it to be soft. Mead stands behind them both, looks at his wristwatch for something like the twentieth time in the past five minutes, and says, "My roommate had an overnight guest, that's why I was upstairs."

The pretty lady in the sparkly gown overhears Mead and raises her eyebrows. The salesman pretends he is deaf. Mead's mother turns around and says, "Not now, Teddy. This is neither the time nor place for such a discussion."

"You said the same thing in the car. And in the parking lot. You're making this into a bigger deal than it is by not letting me explain."

Mead's father asks how much the Charlemagne costs. The salesman hands him a glossy brochure and says that he can knock ten percent off the total price if an order of six or more caskets is placed at one time.

"Okay," Mead's mother says, "so explain to me why I didn't see any girl in the room when your roommate answered the door. I had a clear view of that boy's bed and there wasn't anything in it but a magazine."

"So she must've left sometime in the middle of the night or early this morning. But she was there last night, Mother. I saw her. Or at least I saw her socks."

"Her socks?"

"Yes, she was wearing Miss Kitty socks," Mead says, as if this detail alone should be proof enough that he is telling the truth.

"Then why was your suitcase in his room? If you were just up there for one night, to get away from your roommate as you claim, why pack a whole suitcase?"

"There aren't any clothes in it, Mother, my suitcase is full of papers."

"Papers? What papers?"

"Research papers for my senior thesis."

Mead's father orders two Charlemagnes, leaving his name and number and a deposit check for one thousand dollars with the salesman. The pretty lady re-hooks the velvet rope and Mead follows his parents to the next display.

THE REAL REASON MEAD'S MOTHER joined his father on his trip north to the big city this year was to meet Dean Falconia. Without Mead's knowledge, the dean cordially invited Mr. and Mrs. Lynn Fegley to join him for lunch in the dining room in Baylor Hall, the place where all well-to-do alumni with open pocketbooks and parents of matriculating students are invited to dine with the dean while in town. As a stopover between the art museum and the opera house.

"I don't understand why I have to go," Mead says. "I can see the dean on any day of the week."

"Because," his mother says, by which she means that he is still on probation for having killed his cousin, not to mention the additional personal indignities she has had to suffer as a result of Mead's sleeping arrangements. "Straighten your tie," she says, "and tuck in your shirt."

So Mead tucks in his shirt and follows his parents up the stone steps and through the arched doorway that leads into Baylor Hall. The black-and-white checkered floor of the dining hall reminds him of a giant chessboard, and Mead cannot help but feel like some kind of pawn, a thought that solidifies into fact when he sees who is sitting at the table with Dean Falconia.

"Mr. and Mrs. Fegley," the dean says. "I'm so glad you could both make it." The man is decked out in a pinstripe suit and ascot, as if he were British royalty and this was the Queen's palace. "I'd like you to meet Dr. Kustrup, the chairman of our mathematics department, the man who has been instrumental in bringing along your son."

Dr. Kustrup? Instrumental? Dean Falconia has got to be kidding. From whom is he getting his information?

Their table is draped in white linen and decorated with hand-painted china and crystal stemware. It looks better suited for a museum than a dining hall. Mead can tell his mother is impressed for something like the hundredth time this weekend. First Herman and now this. Dr. Kustrup pulls out her chair and she smiles at him as she sits down.

"I'm very excited about the work Mead's been doing," Dr. Kustrup says as he nibbles on his shrimp cocktail, red sauce dribbling onto his beard.

This comes as quite a surprise to Mead, who has not spoken more than two words to the professor all quarter. But somebody else apparently has.

"It is unheard of," Dr. Kustrup says, "for a mathematician as young as your son to have grasped, let alone mastered, theories of such complexity."

"Where's Dr. Alexander?" Mead asks. "Why isn't he here? If anyone around here is going to take credit for bringing me along, it should be Andrew Alexander."

Dr. Kustrup and Dean Falconia exchange a look, then the dean clears his throat and says, "I'm afraid he couldn't make it, Mead."

"Couldn't make it or wasn't invited?"

"Teddy," his mother says. "If Dean Falconia says the man couldn't make it, then I'm sure he couldn't make it."

"It's quite all right, Mrs. Fegley," Dr. Kustrup says. "I understand how Mead feels. He and Dr. Alexander have spent many an afternoon working together. His loyalty is to be commended. But the dean and I have big plans for your son. With our help, he will be able to take his work to the next level, to get exposed to the right people, people guaranteed to grant your son a fruitful future in the world of mathematics."

The dean goes on to explain that invitations are being sent out to all the big-name mathematicians, inviting them to attend Mead's presentation. That there is a great deal of interest in the work he is doing in the area of number theory. An auditorium has been booked, a cocktail hour arranged. "This is going to be," the dean says, "the most important event the university has sponsored all year."

Mead's mother is impressed. Dr. Kustrup is impressed. The dean is impressed. Even Mead's father looks impressed. And all those impressed faces are making Mead feel sick to his stomach. When did this happen? How did Mead's presentation of his senior thesis to a classroom of his peers turn into this overblown dog-and-pony show? And why didn't anybody tell him about it before now? Their expectations are too big even for this ballroom-size dining hall. Mead stares up at the high-domed ceiling, at a chandelier that looks as tall and wide as a Christmas tree, and wonders what the odds are that it will break free and come crashing to the floor in the next five minutes. And if it were to fall, would it even kill the right people? Because, really, Mead does not see any other way out of his predicament.

BUT THE CHANDELIER DOES NOT FALL. Lunch ends and Mead walks with his parents back to their car. Along the way, however, another kind of miracle happens when they stumble upon Dr. Alexander sitting under an oak tree eating a sandwich out of a brown paper bag. Couldn't make it my foot! He's wearing his usual uniform of a button-down shirt with an inked-stained pocket and khaki pants with heel-worn cuffs. Mead is so happy to see the man that he nearly gushes as he introduces the professor to his parents. "Mom. Dad. This is the man who introduced me to analytical mathematics, to Bernhard Riemann and his famous unproven hypothesis." Dr. Alexander has a bit of trouble untangling his seventy-eight-year-old legs and then getting himself into the upright position and, in the process, some of his hair comes loose from the rubber band holding it back and falls over his face. The professor tucks his hair behind his ear and extends a hand to Mead's mother. "You have a very bright and talented son, Mrs. Fegley. He reminds me of myself when I was his age. You must be very proud."

"Thank you," she says, but never lets go of her purse. Back at the car, Mead says, "The least you could have done was shake the man's hand."

"He looked dirty."

"He's not a leper, Mother, he's brilliant. Smarter than the dean and Dr. Kustrup and the whole rest of the mathematics department put together. But more importantly, he is my mentor and friend."

"I liked the other professor better," she says and gets into the car.

Mead sighs with relief when the taillights of his father's car drop out of sight.

By the time Mead walks back to the oak tree, Dr. Alexander is gone. As is his bike from in front of Epps Hall. Mead thinks about hopping the city bus and riding out to the professor's house to have a talk with him, to ask Dr. Alexander if he knew about the lunch at Baylor Hall, if he knows about this three-ring circus into which the dean and Dr. Kustrup have roped Mead. And whether or not he thinks it is a good idea. If perhaps he shares Mead's concern that it is too much too soon. In the end, though, he decides he does not have the time. Instead, he walks back to the dorm to get his suitcase and then heads over to the library. He's still got about three-and-a-half hours before closing. Time enough to get some work done, to finish mapping out that stupid outline for the dean. Visiting mathematicians. Shit. That's heady stuff. If Mead is going to do this, then he has to do it right. To make a good impression. What if he gets up on the stage in front of all those seasoned mathematicians and makes a fool out of himself? His reputation will be destroyed. His name will be mud. His future will be over before it has even had a chance to begin!

Mead trots up to the fourth floor and finds Herman sitting on his bed, fully clothed for a change, and reading a book—a thriller of some sort, not a textbook—and listening to a Bach concerto. The scratch on his neck is not visible, hidden as it is beneath the collar of his shirt. Might it really have been made by a staple?

"So how was your lunch in Baylor Hall?" Herman asks.

"How did you know about that?"

He sets down the book and swings his feet off the bed. "Your mother happened to mention it to me. Yesterday. At the restaurant."

Mentioned it to him? When? Mead didn't even know about the lunch until ten minutes before it happened. Why would she tell Herman about it and not her own son? Unless of course she was trying to impress him. Maybe she brought it up while Mead was in the bathroom?

He sits down on Herman's spare bed. "Can I tell you something?"

"Anything. What?"

"I'm having serious second thoughts."

"About?"

"My paper. This presentation I'm supposed to give. The whole thing is getting blown way out of proportion. The dean has invited professional mathematicians, the most brilliant minds in the field, people like Michael Berry and Hugh Montgomery, to come listen to me. Me! Shit, I'm going to look like a fool up there on that stage."

"You're kidding, right? Please tell me you're kidding."

"You told Dr. Kustrup, didn't you? You told Dr. Kustrup about our trip out east, about the Cray X-MP, and then he told the dean."

"Yes, I told him. I mean, he *is* my advisor."

"But don't you see? Now he's acting as if the whole thing was his idea. He's trying to take credit where none is due. It isn't fair, don't you see how that isn't fair?"

"Relax, Fegley, you're overreacting. Dr. Kustrup is the head of the department. He's allowed to brag about his students."

"No. He had his chance and blew it when he—" Mead cuts himself off.

"You're still pissed because he passed you over for me. I understand. That was a shitty thing for him to do. But hey, look, you did fine without him, right? Better even. So what do you care? Look at it this way: He needs you more than you need him."

"Maybe. But it's still wrong."

"I don't think you really give a damn about Dr. Kustrup; you're just nervous."

Mead gets up and paces. "But what if some mathematician sitting in the audience stands up in the middle of my presentation and says, 'You made a mistake, buddy, you forgot to extend the log function to complex numbers.' "

"Did you?" Herman asks.

"No!"

"So you got nothing to worry about. Jesus, Fegley, I wish I had your problem. You do realize, of course, that after you give this presentation, you'll be set. You'll be able to study wherever you want. Graduate schools and mathematical societies will be clamoring over one another to get at you. Hell, if it bothers you that much, I'll give the damned presentation for you."

Mead stops pacing. "No, you're right. This is the best thing that's ever happened to me. Thank you, Weinstein. Thanks a lot." And he picks up his suitcase and leaves.

THE OVERHEAD LIGHTS FLICKER. Four students are standing in line ahead of Mead. Each one in turn opens his book bag so the librarian can inspect its contents, then exits through the turnstile. When it's Mead's turn, he swings his suitcase up onto the counter and unzips it.

"You're good to go," the librarian says after a cursory glance.

He re-zips the suitcase. "I don't know your name."

"It's Shirley," she says. "Shirley Tanapat."

Lifting the suitcase down off the counter, Mead proceeds through the turnstile. Once on the other side of it, he stops and turns around. "I was wondering, Shirley Tanapat, if you might like to go out for a cup of coffee?"

11

THE COLOR OF RESURRECTION

High Grove
Still Four Days Before Graduation

THE DUNGEON. THE BASEMENT. The preparation room. By whatever name he chose to call it, the room below the store had stimulated Mead's imagination more than any other single thing or thought or place in his childhood. Because of what he knew took place down there. But mainly because he had never actually been down there. Rats and cobwebs and green slime oozing from the walls, that is what he pictured. Dead people rising up out of their caskets to stretch their legs, enjoy a cup of coffee, and read the local newspaper. Three or four of them sitting in a circle, sharing their obituaries with one another. Reminiscing, laughing, crying, and generally having a good time.

But one night Mead woke up and found himself lying in the dark. Alone. He'd been in first grade for all of one month and had already been tripped, given a dead bird, and had his lunch stolen. And he longed for a friend. Any friend. So he got out of bed, got dressed, and walked over to the store. In the dark. Rode down to the basement in the freight elevator feeling scared but determined, eager to share a cup of coffee and a laugh with the dead men. To pet a rat. To find out what green slime feels like. What he found instead was a room as cold and antiseptic as the science lab at school. No coffee. No rats. No green slime. The place was cleaner than his mother's kitchen counter. But all was not lost because lying on a stainless steel table in the middle of the room was a dead man. One man. A naked man under a clear plastic sheet.

Mead walked closer for a better look. The man's eyes and mouth were closed as if he were asleep. Mead folded back the sheet and shook his arm, hoping to wake him up. But the man was cold as a leftover chicken leg. Then Mead saw it. The incision in the side of his neck. The skin stitched together like a baseball. And Mead knew beyond a shadow of a doubt that the man was never going to wake up, that there would be no jovial retelling of stories past, that when a man dies he takes his stories with him.

Mr. fullington's eyes are wide open. He stares up at the ceiling, his mouth in rictus as if shocked to discover the condition into which he has gotten himself.

"Here, put these on," Uncle Martin says and tosses Mead a pair of latex gloves and a white smock, then proceeds to undress Mr. Fullington with a pair of scissors, dropping pieces of his striped pajamas into a metal trash can marked biohazard. He places an iron block under the dead man's head as if it were a pillow and hands Mead a sponge. "You wash and I'll flex," he says, lifts Mr. Fullington's left leg, and bends it repeatedly at the knee as if the dead man were a paraplegic and Uncle Martin his physical therapist. "It's to relieve rigor mortis," he says as explanation, "so the embalming fluid can get deep into the muscle tissue."

Mead does a lousy job washing Mr. Fullington. He cleans only what he can get at without having to actually touch the deceased with his hands and leaves the rest to his uncle. Like

Mr. Fullington's backside. And his genitals. Mead won't go near them. No way. He tries his best to not even look down there. Because it's none of his business. This is, after all, Lenny's dad and not some boy in the college dorm who thinks he is carrying a trophy between his legs.

Mead does a better job shaving Mr. Fullington's face with an electric razor. Actually, the whole thing gets easier as he goes along, once he gets past the initial shock. Once he has gotten used to the idea of handling a dead person. Mead just keeps thinking about Lenny. About his loss. About making Mr. Fullington look presentable for the funeral. About making it easier for Lenny and his family to accept his passing. Who did this for Percy? Who washed his body and flexed his legs? Surely it wasn't Uncle Martin. Which means it must have been Mead's father. Shit. Mead should've been here. He could have helped. He could have shaved his cousin's face. But if he had been around to attend the funeral, he would have been around to greet Percy when he came by the dorm to visit, and then his cousin wouldn't have needed anyone to wash his body and shave his face and flex his legs at all.

Martin picks up a long needle, threads it with a suture, and shoves it through Mr. Fullington's upper lip. "Oh shit," Mead says and flinches, feeling the pain that Mr. Fullington cannot.

"You doing all right over there, college boy?"

"Yes, I'm fine, Uncle Martin."

"You sure? Because you look about as pale as the deceased here."

It would help if Uncle Martin sounded as if he were the least bit sympathetic to Mead's predicament—to the fact that this is his first time—but he doesn't. He sounds mean and revengeful and condescending. "I said, I'm fine."

"All right then," his uncle says and threads the suture through

Mr. Fullington's lower lip. Mead bites down on his own lip and takes a deep breath, telling himself that he isn't going to throw up, reminding himself that Mr. Fullington can't feel a thing. That he is dead. But it doesn't help. The room grows dark and then everything goes black. Like the lights on a stage at the end of Act One.

"Uh, Uncle Martin? I can't see."

"My hands aren't that big, Teddy, you can see just fine."

"No, I mean I can't see. At all. The room is pitch black."

"What're you talking about, I've got every light in the place on."

"I know but I can't see, Uncle Martin. I can't see because I'm blind."

His uncle does not respond. He is probably waving his hand in front of Mead's face right now, trying to make him blink. Trying to catch him in another lie. But Mead isn't a liar, he's just a fool who befriended the wrong person. Not a genius, a fool.

"Put your head between your knees and take a deep breath," his uncle says.

"What?"

"I said, put your head between your knees!" Martin yells as if Mead has not only been struck blind but deaf, too.

He follows his uncle's instructions and inhales a mixture of ammonia and formaldehyde. Which doesn't help. It just makes his lungs burn. A chair scrapes across the floor, followed by the sound of footsteps. Shit. His uncle is leaving. Mead hopes he isn't going upstairs to tell Mead's father what has happened. That will just convince the man that he is right: Mead does not belong here. That he should call the dean and go back to Chicago. But he can't, he just can't.

A hand touches the back of Mead's neck. It feels cool on his sun-scorched skin. His uncle's hand. And Mead starts to cry. Just like that. Out of nowhere. For Mr. Fullington. For Percy. For his Uncle Martin and Aunt Jewel. For himself. For this whole fucked-up world where nothing turns out the way you think it's going to. He wishes his uncle would remove his hand, would walk back to his own side of the embalming table, would just get on with it. That Mead can handle. Getting on with it. But not this. Not the thought that someone feels sorry for him. That there is some reason in the world to feel sorry for him. Because there isn't. Mead can handle mad. Uncle Martin can be as mad at Mead as he likes. But not this. Mead does not want pity.

"Ancient Egyptians were the very first embalmers," his uncle says. "They took up the art back in 3000 BC. But then you probably already know that, being as how you're a college student and all."

Mead wipes his nose with the back of his hand. What the hell is his uncle talking about? Why is he giving Mead a history lesson? Now? Of course he knows about the Egyptians. Everybody knows about the frigging Egyptians. They teach you about them in grade school, for Christ's sake. But he wills his uncle to keep talking.

"Of course their first attempts were pretty rudimentary. Hardly what you'd call an art. All they did was wrap the deceased in resin-soaked linen. It didn't do much to preserve the body but it did a terrific job of preserving the body shape."

His uncle removes his hand from the back of Mead's neck, his hard-soled shoes slapping against tile as he walks back around to his side of the table. His chair scrapes across the floor. He's getting on with it. Good. This Mead can handle. Metal clinks against metal like silverware at the dinner table as his uncle lifts instruments off his tray and resumes his work.

"It wasn't until around 2600 BC that they began to remove what they considered to be the four primary internal organs: the lungs, the liver, the stomach, and the intestines. Not the heart, though. Early Egyptians didn't hold the heart in too much esteem."

Uncle Martin turns on the pressure gauge that will pump Mr. Fullington full of formaldehyde. It makes a rhythmic *ka-plunk, ka-plunk, ka-plunk, ka-plunk* sound that mimics the beat of Mead's heart.

"The primary organs were put into a canopic jar and buried alongside the body in the belief that the dead would need them when they woke up on the other side."

The shroud of darkness surrounding Mead begins to lift and he sees his uncle pick up Mr. Fullington's left arm and make an incision in his skin, just below the armpit. He sees him insert a syringe into an artery, sees him attach a tube that is hooked up to the five-gallon container of embalming fluid.

"After the Old Kingdom collapsed, around 2200 BC, the entire process from death to burial became much more elaborate, sometimes taking up to seventy days to complete. First the body would be washed in natron, a preserving salt found in great quantities on the flood plains of the Nile. Then it was coated in resin and the soft-tissue organs removed, all except for the heart. It remained in place not for sentimental reasons but because the Egyptians of that time believed it to be the seat of intelligence and will."

Uncle Martin makes a second incision on the inside of Mr. Fullington's upper thigh and inserts a second syringe, this time into a vein, and then attaches a tube. It immediately fills with dark red blood that rushes out of Mr. Fullington into a second five-gallon container that sits on the floor. Mead stares at the container and waits for the room to go black again.

"The body was then placed under heaps of powdered natron," Uncle Martin says, "to draw out moisture and prevent bacteria from decaying the flesh. It would often remain there for up to forty days."

But the room does not go black. Mead is okay. He is going to be okay.

"When the body was finally returned to the embalming table, the internal cavities were rinsed with spices and palm wine and stuffed with resin-soaked linen and sawdust. The flesh was rubbed with a lotion made of juniper oil, beeswax, spices, and natron, then painted with a molten resin to toughen the skin and make it waterproof. And the face was painted green. Egyptians thought it to be the color of resurrection. Green. You know, like spring."

"O flesh of the King," Mead says, "do not decay, do not rot, do not smell unpleasant."

Uncle Martin looks up.

"You taught me that. It's a prayer, right? What Anubis, the god of embalming, says to the dead as he dusts them with spices."

Uncle Martin continues to stare, long enough to make Mead uncomfortable. As if now *he* is going to start crying. But he doesn't. He catches himself, turns his attention back to Mr. Fullington, and says, "As man passes through death into immortality, it is imperative that his body remain whole so it can function again in the afterlife."

"Uh, we're still talking about the Egyptians, right?" Mead says. "I mean, you don't really believe that, do you?"

"In the afterlife? Why not?"

"Because. We know better now."

"We only know what we think we know."

Now it is Mead's turn to stare. "He's not coming back, Uncle Martin. You do know that, don't you?"

His uncle gets the most hurt expression on his face. As if he didn't know that. Shit. Mead should have kept his mouth shut.

Here they were getting along for the first time since he has been home—talking civil to each other and all—and Mead had to go and screw it up by saying something rational. As if there is anything rational about Percy's death. Or Mead's being here in this room. Or anything else that has happened in the past few weeks. It is as if the whole world has spun out of control into chaos.

Mead figures that any second now his uncle is going to either start crying or start yelling. But he does neither. Instead he pushes back his chair and stands up. Walks over to the wall cabinet and pulls down an old cardboard box that is sitting on top of it. He sets the box on the floor, folds back the flaps, and lifts out a mask. A papier-mâché mask made of newspaper and flour and brown paint. A crudely crafted dog's head. An art class project. A child's interpretation of the jackal-headed god, Anubis.

"He made this when he was in the third grade," Uncle Martin says. "His mother was so impressed. She thought he was gonna grow up and be a great sculptor. The next Michelangelo. But I knew better. I knew he was destined to be a great embalmer just like his old man." Martin rotates the mask in his hands, looking at it from all sides. "When I was a young man draining the lifeblood out of all those dead bodies, pumping them full of formaldehyde, I didn't believe. Those people were as pickled as gherkins in a glass jar. No way were they going to wake up on the other side and live again. No way, no how." Martin sets down the mask, picks up Mr. Fullington's hand, and begins to massage it, working the embalming fluid down into his fingertips. "Then one day that all changed. It was the middle of the night and I was all alone. I was feeling sorry for myself because it was New Year's Eve and everybody else was out whooping it up, having a good time, partying and all, and I was down here. Working on a body. And suddenly I knew."

"Knew what?" Mead says.

"That I wasn't alone. Because they came to me that night. The spirit of every person I'd ever embalmed. I was surrounded by them."

"Were they by any chance drinking coffee and reading obituaries?"

"What? No. I couldn't see them, Teddy, I felt them, though. They were here all right. No doubt about it." Martin sets down Mr. Fullington's hand and picks the jackal mask back up. Puts it in its box and sets the box up on the shelf.

"So," Mead says. "Is he here?"

"Who?"

"Percy. Is he here right now?"

His uncle sits quietly for a moment and then says, "No."

Mead and his uncle resurface an hour-and-a-half later. The store is closed, the showroom dark. But Mead's father is sitting in the back office, going over the day's receipts. He looks up when they walk in, his face expectant. "So how did it go?"

"Mr. Fullington looks as handsome as the day he got married," Martin says, and ducks into the bathroom. A moment later, the shower turns on. Mead's father looks at the closed door, then at Mead, and says, "No, I meant how did it go for you?"

Mead drops into the nearest chair. "Ancient Egyptians thought the heart to be the seat of intelligence and will. Not the brain, but the heart. What do you think, Dad?"

His father stares at him, as if searching for the right answer, then says, "I asked your mother to hold supper for us. You can shower at home."

Mead nods and gets up again. Reaches for the back door.

"Teddy?"

"I'm fine, Dad."

"I didn't mean what I said earlier," he says. "There will always be a place for you here. No matter what. You do know that, don't you?" But Mead hears him say, "The heart. I believe the seat of intelligence and will is housed solely in the heart."

Mead lugs his green-and-blue plaid suitcase out of the closet and drops it onto his bed, unzips the top, and lifts out a single sheet of zeta zeros. He has right here in front of him a billion-and-a-half reasons to believe the Riemann Hypothesis is true. But they are just statistics. A measurement of averages, not proof.

Statistically speaking, it should have been a breeze. Presenting this paper. Appeasing the dean. Graduating from college. Continuing on with his studies. But for one single aberration—one zero off the critical line, so to speak—that has proved Mead's entire theory on life false. Single-handedly, Herman has pulled the rug out from under Mead's feet. Cast his entire future into doubt. That one aberration—Herman Weinstein—has thrown Mead's once ordered and calculated world into utter chaos.

A chair scrapes across the floor behind Mead. The six-legged creature is back. Unsure of what form the monster will choose to take today, he turns around to face his avenger. The devil on his left shoulder, so to speak. No longer haunted by its presence but merely annoyed by it. Resigned to its ubiquity. It's a constant reminder of all the ways in which Mead has fallen short of expectation. He turns around and says, "Go away and leave me alone."

"Is that any way to talk to your hero?" Bernhard Riemann says.

"You aren't my hero. Not anymore. I've lost faith in the sanctity of math."

"All faith gets tested from time to time, Mead, but the true believer does not allow himself to be so easily dissuaded."

"I just meant it as a metaphor."

"And a good metaphor it is. Think about it, Mead. Think about what your life would be like if you had to change your belief system every time someone challenged it."

"Shut up. Shut up and leave me alone."

"You have to stand up for what you believe in, Mead, or else sooner or later you won't believe in anything at all. You'll be a lost soul."

"I thought you were a mathematician, not a frigging minister."

"I am a mathematician but my father was a minister and I learned a thing or two from him about faith. No one can take it away from you, Mead, except yourself."

"I said shut up. Leave me alone. Get out of my head. You aren't even real. You're a figment of my imagination. So just go away." Mead puts the page of zeta zeros back in the suitcase and zips it up. Heaves it off the bed and drags it toward the hall. But Bernhard Riemann gets up off the chair and steps in front of him, blocking his path.

"Where're you going with that, Mead?"

"None of your business. But I'll tell you anyway. I'm putting it out on the curb. Next to the garbage cans. So it can go where it belongs. In the incinerator. I mean, it's worthless, right? That's what you said. A big waste of time. A pile of useless statistics. A way to blow smoke up the dean's ass. Besides, if I burn it, I also get rid of the other problem that's been haunting me."

"Ah, you must be referring to Mr. Weinstein."

"Good guess. But then I shouldn't be surprised that you guessed right seeing as how you're both taking up unwanted space in my head."

"You sound bitter, Mead."

"And why shouldn't I be? Because of you, I no longer have a future in math."

"You're blaming this on me?"

"Yes."

"But I'm not the one who befriended the fellow, Mead. You are. You know, you really aren't a very good judge of character."

"Hey, I knew he was bad news from the moment I laid eyes on him. I didn't pursue his friendship; he pursued mine. Bribed it out of me is more like it. Okay, so I let my ambition get in the way of good judgment. I confess. I should've stuck with my gut. But then I wouldn't have had anything to show for all my hard work. No big presentation for the dean. No dog-and-pony show for the university. Don't get me wrong, I'm not blaming the dean. I willingly accepted Herman's bribe. Not for the dean, but for me. And the irony of the whole thing is, I still have nothing to show for all my hard work. Plus, I have this whole Herman fiasco on my hands. So it's just as you said: pointless."

"Not pointless, Mead. Misdirected maybe, but hardly pointless."

"All logic and no intuition. I know. I heard you the first time. I guess I should have taken more notes on those hunting excursions with my uncle. Maybe if I'd been more alert, if I hadn't been so caught up in myself, maybe I would've steered clear of Herman, would've realized that accepting a favor from him would come at a price. But no, I thought we were friends. That's how pathetic I am. A small town genius with an overblown ego and no life experience whatsoever when it comes to people."

"You're being awfully hard on yourself," Bernhard Riemann says, only without a German accent. Which means the six-legged creature has morphed again. Mead glances up to see what trick his mind is playing on him now. And there, standing before him, is none other than Henry Charles Fegley. His grandfather. But as a young man. The way he appears on the Fegley Brothers postcard.

"What're you gawking at, Teddy, did I forget to button myself up?" And he glances down at the crotch of his pants—circa 1930—to make sure he hasn't.

"Grampa Henry? What are *you* doing in my head?"

"Well, since everyone else is getting to speak his mind, I thought I might throw in a word or two of my own. If you think you're the only one who ever ran into bad news, Teddy, think again. I had some grand ideas when I was your age. My father was a carpenter from the old country—Germany—and taught me his trade. And I was good. The Leonardo da Vinci of dovetail joints. The president of the local bank filled his home with my handiwork. So one day I decided to approach him for a loan so I could start my own business. And unbeknownst to me, he made himself my partner. You see, I could saw and sand and finish but I couldn't read. It was all based on blind trust. It wasn't until my business exploded and he ran off with all the profits that I learned how naïve I had been. Oh, was I furious. I stopped building furniture altogether. I was not going to let that man benefit from my hard work. I'd rather starve than be taken for a fool even for one more day!"

"But you died a rich man," Mead says.

"Not rich, Teddy, but better off than most. Thanks to your grandmother. She's the one who taught me how to read. And I started all over again. Started with nothing because that banker had taken all my money. I built furniture in exchange for food. I built myself a reputation that reached as far as Alton, where I got another business loan. And this time I read every word of the contract before signing."

"Great. So what you're telling me is that my bad luck was inevitable. A Fegley curse. Unavoidable."

"It's only a curse, Teddy, if you allow it to be one."

"Lemons into lemonade. Got it," Mead says and sets down his

suitcase, shoves it back into the closet, and flops back on his bed, burying his face beneath his arms. He no longer feels like putting the suitcase out on the curb. At least not today. He hasn't the energy. He'll just throw it out another time. When there aren't so many people around hassling him.

"What's all this talk about a curse?" the six-legged creature asks.

Shit. Its voice has changed again. No longer low and male but high and female. Mead drops his arms and looks up at his mother, sitting in the straight-backed chair. Her arms crossed over her chest, all war-like. Mead wonders how long she has been sitting there. "How much did you hear?" he asks.

"Oh, I've been hearing plenty, Teddy. Dolores Fischer told me she ran into you at Delia Winslow's wake and that you told her some cock-and-bull story about how your lower-than-average body temperature makes you smarter than the rest of us."

Mead sits up, convinced that he is on the verge of losing his mind. That is, if he hasn't lost it already. "Oh, that," he says. "She touched me, Mom. Like a monkey in a zoo. She had it coming."

"I see. And Sandy McClod. She says you told her son, Simon, that you invented the VCR. Did he touch you like a zoo animal too?"

"I was kidding. I told him I was kidding, did he tell his mother that?"

"And apparently you and Stephen Hawking have a speaking engagement in Paris. Perhaps I'll fly over there to catch it since I missed the one you were scheduled to give in Chicago three days ago."

"You know Donna Eubanks's mother?"

"Eubanks? No. Mr. Colgan told me. Your high school principal. When he returned this to me." And she holds out the credit card Mead left at the department store. "He's worried about you, Teddy. We're all worried."

His mother has run out of accusations and resorts to staring. And it is a good stare, good enough to make the hairs stand up on the back of Mead's neck. But she's not done yet. She's just warming up, just getting to the good stuff. She uncrosses her arms and leans forward. "You punched Freddy Waseleski in the face?"

"I did not! That is an out-and-out lie! I merely grabbed his collar."

His mother shakes her head. "What's happening to you, Teddy? I did not raise my son to behave like this, like a barbarian. This is all your uncle's fault, teaching you that it's sport to kill small animals. I should never have let you have that gun."

"Jesus, Mother, that was six years ago. This has nothing to do with Uncle Martin. If it's anyone's fault, it's yours. You want to know why I got that C in seventh grade? Because Freddy Waseleski ripped up my science project, that's why. He ripped it to shreds and threatened to shove a ruler up my ass if I ever told anyone. And then you made me go to his mother's funeral. Not because he was my friend, but because you cared about what other people might think if I didn't go. You've always cared more about what other people think than about me."

His mother looks stunned. "I'm sorry, Teddy. I didn't know. How could I have known? You never told me."

But Mead is on a roll. He can't stop, every slight he ever felt bubbling to the surface. "And then he poisoned Mr. Cheese. Not that you gave a damn about that either. You hated that mouse from day one. And now..." Mead turns away from his mother. He has said enough. He has said too much.

She grabs his arm. "What, Teddy? What happened up at

college? Has someone threatened to harm you? Is that why you came home?"

"It isn't your concern, Mother. I took care of that problem and I'll take care of this one too. On my own."

"But you didn't take care of it, Teddy, you got a C. I'm the one who spoke to your teacher. I'm the one who fixed it. And you want to know why? Because I do care about you. I care about you more than I care about myself. So please, let me help."

Mead yanks his arm out of her hand. "No, it's too late. I'm a grown man now. I don't want or need my mommy's help anymore."

"So what're you going to do, walk away from a college degree? After all the years of hard work you've put into earning it? You're proud of your accomplishments, Teddy. You put your heart and soul into your studies. I know it. I know you. And I know how much it means to you to graduate. To get credit where credit is due. If someone is threatening you, Teddy, you have to tell me. Because you don't belong here in High Grove, you belong at that university. You owe it to yourself to tell me, Teddy. Please. Tell me so I can fix it."

"You don't get it, Mother, do you? I don't want your help. I don't want you to fix my life, I just want you to leave me alone." And he gets up off the bed and storms out of his room.

IT'S LEANING AGAINST THE BACK WALL behind a cardboard box. Mead's old banana bike. Sky blue with tassels hanging off the ends of the handlebars. He moves a ladder out of the way and rolls the bike into the middle of the garage. The tires are flat but hold air when he pumps them up. He raises the seat as high as it'll go and gets on, but his legs are still too long. It takes him a minute or two to find his balance but then he's off and pedaling through the streets of High Grove. He bikes past the cemetery and out of town toward Snell's Quarry. There isn't much of a shoulder on the two-way road, just gravel, so the speed limit is posted at forty. But no one pays attention to it. Most of the cars swing wide around Mead's bike but a few come close to side-swiping him, sending him headlong into the brush. Mead doesn't care. Even when his legs begin to cramp up, he keeps pedaling. Eager to clear his head, to get away, to escape the voices of his mother and his uncle and his father, not to mention Bernhard Riemann and Grampa Henry. Too many voices. Mead has too many voices in his head telling him what to do and not a single one of them does he trust. Only when he gets to the parking lot does he stop.

She's here. Just as he had hoped. Mead rests his bicycle against her blue Dodge coupe and reaches inside the passenger side window—which has been rolled down a few inches to let the hot air escape—to unlock the door, then crawls inside and pops open the glove box. He takes out a bottle of suntan lotion and slathers the stuff over his arms and face even though the sun is low on the horizon and the shadows long. Even though the day is almost over. Then he puts the bottle back and gets out.

He spots her right off, swimming across the quarry. Her blond hair trailing behind her like a veil. When she reaches the far side, she turns around and looks straight at Mead. As if she were expecting him. But she doesn't wave and neither does he. She rests a moment and then starts back. When her hands next touch rock, Mead is standing over her. She squints up at him, breathing hard from the exertion, and says, "Theodore, you really shouldn't be out here, not with that sunburn of yours."

"Those swimming trunks don't belong to your brother."

"Excuse me?"

"The ones you loaned me, the ones that were drying on the shower rod in my parents' bathroom when my aunt came over for supper the other night. She claims they belong to Percy and I believe her."

Hayley gives Mead a noncommittal look. It is a look he knows well. A way to buy time. To give your accuser an opportunity to fill in the blank with the answer he most wants to hear. So Mead chooses his words carefully because he is tired of always giving the other guy the upper hand. He's tired of always supplying the wrong answer, the one that allows him to hold on to the false notion that he is dealing with a friend when perhaps he needs to own up to the fact that he may be dealing with just the opposite.

"You dated him, didn't you, Hayley? He was your boyfriend."

"Yes," she says. "He was."

"So why didn't you just tell me? What's the big deal?"

Hayley pulls herself up out of the lake, water pouring off her body. Wrings out her hair. "Sit next to me, Theodore," she says and pats the rock.

"No, I prefer to stand."

She squints at him, sizing him up. So Mead makes himself a little taller.

"You remind me of him."

"Of Percy? You're crazy. We aren't the slightest bit alike."

"Not on the surface, no, but scratch just below it and you're exactly the same. Same dogged determination, same intelligence, same stubbornness. And neither of you takes disappointment very well either. It's not personal, you know, it's just life."

"You still haven't answered my question," Mead says. "Why the big secret?"

Hayley stares out across the lake. "I thought he'd come back. I thought he'd get homesick and come back and I didn't want him to be mad at me when he did, so I kept my word and didn't tell anyone where he'd gone. But he didn't come back. He traveled around the country and sent me postcards from Florida and Kentucky and Ohio." She shakes her head, remembering. "When I realized that he wasn't going to come home, I went after him. But Percy had changed. I mean, he was nice and all when he saw me, said all the right things, but he was distant. I think..." She takes a deep breath and exhales as if fighting back more tears. "I think I reminded him of his past. And he didn't want to be reminded. It was almost as if he feared being sucked back in. As if I were a vacuum and he was a piece of lint hiding under the bed." She stares down at her feet, which are moving in circles under water, slowly stirring the lake. "And then, of course, he did come back. But he still had about him that sense of distance. You know, like he was here but at the same time he wasn't here." She looks up at Mead. "You have that same look about you, Theodore. You say you've come back to stay, but your eyes say different."

"He sent them to me too," Mead says. "Postcards." He looks out over the lake then back at Hayley. "Do you know, by any chance, why he drove up to Chicago?"

She nods.

"Why?"

She looks down at her feet. "I loved Percy. Still do. He's stubborn and proud and I would've married him in an instant if he'd asked." She shakes her head again. "He had so much life in him. But he had other plans. He'd decided to become a sportswriter. That's why he drove up to Chicago, Theodore. He had an interview with this guy at the *Tribune*, someone he met while he was playing in the minors. He called me afterwards. He said—" She chokes up as if she's going to start crying, takes a deep breath, and exhales, starts again. "He said it had gone really well. He called me from a bar. He'd been celebrating and sounded kind of drunk and so I told him not to drive home, to stay up there overnight and sleep it off." She looks up at Mead, tears rolling down her face. "That's when he mentioned you. He told me he was going to crash with you for the night. At the dorm."

"So it was my fault."

"No," she says and swipes her hand across her wet cheek. "It was his fault, his choice to get back behind that wheel. Not yours, Theodore, his." But it doesn't sound like something that even she herself believes, it sounds like something she is trying to talk herself into believing.

"Why didn't you tell me all this before, Hayley?"

"I don't know. Because he told me not to tell anyone. And because talking about it makes it real and I'm not ready for real yet. I keep telling myself that he's still up there. In Chicago. That he got the job. That he's living in some cockroach-infested apartment that looks out onto an airshaft and that he'll be coming back to get me any day now. Maybe tomorrow. Maybe next month. When he's making enough money to get us a nice place." She looks at Mead. "It sounds stupid when I say it out loud."

A bloodcurdling scream pierces the air as a boy jumps off Dead Man's Leap, his body plunging into the lake like a rock. Like dead weight.

"It's not stupid," Mead says.

"Yes, it is. He's not coming back. I'm stuck is what it is. I'm stuck and I don't know how to get unstuck."

Mead kneels down and takes hold of Hayley's hand. Squeezes it. "Percy isn't coming back, but I'm here and I'm not going anywhere."

Hayley squeezes his hand back. "Your eyes say different."

"Would you stop with the eyes already? The sun's in them. I'm squinting. All my eyes are saying is will someone please make the goddamned sun set already."

"If you really believe that, Theodore, then you're in more denial than I am."

Mead pulls his hand away. Why is she being like this? Why is she being so mean when he's sitting here trying to be nice? She's really starting to piss him off. "Stop calling me Theodore," he says. "My name is Mead now. Not Theodore, not Teddy. Mead."

"My point exactly."

"Point? What point? No, don't tell me. I've heard enough. More than enough." Mead's chest feels tight, as if it's going to explode. How dare she act as if she knows him better than he knows himself. The girl doesn't know a goddamned thing about him. Or about Herman. Especially not about Herman. If she did know about Herman, then she would know that Mead had no other choice but to do what he did. Namely, leave.

Another scream pierces the air, echoing off the walls of the quarry.

"So do it," Hayley says.

"Do what?"

"Prove to me that you can change: Jump off the cliff."

"Oh, changing my name doesn't prove a thing, but jumping off a cliff will?"

"Yes, I can see it in your eyes." And she says it real serious-like.

"No," Mead says, stands up, and stomps back to his bike. He's had enough.

"Theodore, come back. I'm sorry. You don't have to jump off the cliff, okay?"

But Mead is too mad to go back. Instead he hops on his bike and pedals out of the parking lot, spraying gravel in his wake. And as he pedals furiously back into town, he wonders why it is that the people who claim to care the most about you are the ones who always inflict the most pain.

12

BREAK A LEG

Chicago
Two Weeks Before Graduation

MEAD TAKES SHIRLEY TANAPAT TO THE COVE, an eatery in the student center where your meal ticket buys you a hamburger and a Coke. Or, in this instance, two cups of coffee and a slice of carrot cake. It is their fourth such date in as many weeks. "I love carrot cake," Shirley says when she sees it listed on the mimeographed menu, so Mead orders it for her. The girl working the counter places two forks on the tray along with the slice of cake and Mead carries the whole thing to an empty table near the back. The rest of the tables are occupied by other students boycotting the college cafeteria although Mead suspects that both eateries get their food from the same wholesale distributor.

"Why aren't you having any cake?" Shirley asks. "It's delicious."

"I don't like carrot cake," Mead says. "Too sweet."

Shirley frowns. It's not a real frown, it's the fake kind people put on to let you know they feel bad about what just happened or what was just said, but not that bad. "You should've said something. We could've ordered something else."

"It's all right. I'm not hungry. I had a big lunch today. In Baylor Hall."

"Baylor Hall? Where the elite meet to eat? I'm impressed."

"I didn't bring it up to impress you, just to explain why I'm not hungry."

Shirley looks at Mead's hands, which causes him to look at them too. The left one is wrapped around his mug of coffee, the right one stirring a spoon round and round inside of it, betraying his nervousness. Mead lets go of the spoon and the mug and tucks both hands under his legs and out of sight.

"You don't like coffee either, do you?"

"No. Too bitter."

Shirley crosses her legs and her right foot bumps into Mead's suitcase. His lunch with the dean ran late. A review of his outline turning into a dress rehearsal of his presentation. It wasn't supposed to, it's just that once Mead gets started talking about the Riemann Hypothesis, he can't stop. Mead moves his suitcase over a few inches to give Shirley more room. "I've never met anyone quite like you before," she says. "You must have very interesting parents."

"Not really," Mead says, "I'm much more interesting than my parents."

Shirley smiles. But whether she is reacting to the piece of cake she just put in her mouth or Mead, it is impossible for him to know.

THE BIKE RACK IN FRONT OF EPPS HALL IS EMPTY. Mead checks his watch, thinking that he is early, but he is right on time. He shakes out his umbrella in the vestibule and heads up to Dr. Alexander's office to wait. But the door is cracked open so he must be here. Mead peeks his head inside. The professor's chair is empty. And on his desk is a rough draft of Mead's presentation, the one he dropped off a couple days ago for the professor to read over.

"Dr. Alexander? Hello? It's me, Mead."

He waits for the professor's gray crown to rise up over the edge of the desk, like a moon over the horizon, but it doesn't. Mead glances at the blackboard. Several 4x4 matrices have been drawn on it, along with their characteristic polynomials and traces, and then the whole thing partially erased. As if the person doing the erasing was interrupted by a ringing phone or some other urgent matter. "Dr. Alexander?"

Mead steps into the office and around the desk, expecting to find the professor stretched out on the floor, eyes closed, a pair of headphones clamped over his ears. But no one is there.

A real and an imaginary axis has been drawn below the matrices, the resulting graph a series of dots that looks utterly random. Like birds on a telephone wire. Or rather, several telephone wires. But the Riemann Hypothesis says they are not random, despite their appearance. That their position can be predicted. But how? Maybe that is what Dr. Alexander was thinking about when he was rudely interrupted.

"Oh good, you're still here," a voice says. "I was afraid you might've already come and gone."

Mead turns around. Dr. Kustrup is standing in the doorway.

"There's been a change in plans," he says. "I'm going to be working with you from now on, Mr. Fegley, instead of Dr. Alexander."

"Why? Where is he?"

"I'm afraid he's been in a bit of an accident. Someone sideswiped his bicycle with a car. Don't worry, though, he's going to be fine."

"Who hit him? You?"

Dr. Kustrup gets all huffy-looking. "That's not very amusing, Mr. Fegley."

"It wasn't meant to be."

The chairman of the math department glances around the

office as if for help but none is forthcoming. He looks back at Mead. "This attitude of yours is going to have to change, Mr. Fegley. You have a very important presentation coming up. All eyes are going to be on you, not to mention this university, so it is imperative that we make a good impression. As a team. That's what I'm here for. To help. As a member of the team. I understand that you and Dr. Alexander have been working together and I think that's great. But we can't stop playing simply because one man got knocked out of the game. That's why I'm here, Mr. Fegley, to take up the professor's position on the field. So please, if we could just proceed." And he picks up an eraser and wipes the board clean, wipes away all evidence of Dr. Alexander, then he sits down in his chair, folds his hands together behind his head, and flashes a smile that would make the sleaziest snake-oil salesman look sincere. "Why don't you start by giving me a dry run-through of your presentation and I'll tell you whether or not I see any errors in your logic."

"Where is he?" Mead says.

Dr. Kustrup pretends he hasn't heard and waits for Mead to begin.

"I said, where is he?"

Dr. Kustrup sighs. "He's at home, Mr. Fegley, resting peacefully. He fractured his right fibula and will probably be confined to a bed for the rest of the quarter. Now, show me the number fields you used to plot these zeros on the function plane."

Mead snatches his presentation off Dr. Alexander's desk and hugs the papers to his chest. "I'll be happy to show them to you, Dr. Kustrup, at my presentation." And he heads for the door.

The professor leaps out of the chair, bracing his arm against the doorjamb to block Mead's exit. "Don't leave," he says. "I must advise you, for your own benefit, to stay. Do not resist me, Mr. Fegley. This is for the best. This way everyone wins."

"Are you threatening me, Dr. Kustrup?" Mead says, then looks down at the chairman's brown shoes and sees again the two pairs of shoes in the bathroom stall. "Or are you propositioning me?"

"What? No," he says and drops his arm.

"You had your chance to work with me, Dr. Kustrup, and you gave it up."

"That wasn't my choice, Mr. Fegley, my hands were tied."

"No? Then whose choice was it, Mr. Chairman-of-the-Department?"

"I'm sorry, Mr. Fegley. I made a mistake. What else can I say?"

"Excuse me. I have to go," Mead says and pushes past the professor cum chairman and out the door.

MEAD HAS TO TRANSFER BUSES TWICE to get to Dr. Alexander's house. The rusting VW Rabbit is parked in the driveway just as before, the professor's bicycle leaning against the side of the house in its usual spot. Only now the front wheel is crumpled, bent into the shape of a pretzel. Mead steps past it to the front door and rings the bell.

"You're soaked through to the bone," Mrs. Alexander says.

"I forgot my umbrella."

"As bad as my husband," she says as she steps back to let him inside. "He won't use one either." She gets Mead a towel and a dry shirt. A new one still in its original packaging. "I can't accept this," he says. "I'll just take an old shirt."

"This is old," Mrs. Alexander says. "It's been in my husband's dresser drawer for nearly ten years. A gift from one of his students. He'll never wear it, though."

"Why not?"

"It has long sleeves. He hates long sleeves."

So Mead peels off his wet shirt and puts on the dry one. And it's a perfect fit.

The professor is in the living room, propped up on a chaise longue that has been outfitted with bed pillows and sheets and blankets. The cats are nowhere in sight, having been displaced from their favorite napping spot. Dr. Alexander's right leg is in a plaster cast that extends from his toes all the way up to his knee. His gray hair has been freed from its rubber band and fans out over the pillows, giving him the appearance of a cartoon character with his finger stuck in an electrical outlet. A gash on his forehead has been covered with a bandage. A scratch on his cheek has not.

"It's not as bad as it looks," the professor says. "It's worse."

Mead sets his presentation on the coffee table next to a pitcher of water and a prescription bottle of painkillers. Some of the pages are wet, but all are still legible. "You forgot this," Mead says, "in your hurry out the door."

The professor raises his eyebrows. "How did you know I was in a hurry?"

"The chalkboard. It was only half-erased."

Mrs. Alexander enters the room carrying a tray with two steaming cups of soup on it. "I hope you like cream of cauliflower," she says as she places one of them in front of her husband and the other one in front of Mead.

"I hate it," Dr. Alexander says.

"I wasn't talking to you, dear," she says. "I was speaking to our guest." But she says it in a teasing way, not all hostile the way Mead's mother would.

The professor winces as he lifts his maimed leg off the chaise longue and leans forward to pick up his cup of soup. "I lost track of time," he says as he sips the soup. "I had an appointment to meet with the dean and the chairman of the math department to further discuss my retirement plans. I was running late."

"I thought you didn't want to retire," Mead says.

"I don't." Dr. Alexander takes a second sip, slurping his soup like a child. "The car hit me on my way over there. I should've just walked."

"I knew Dr. Kustrup was behind this," Mead says. "He was in your office, you know, when I went up there to meet with you today. He offered to help me with my presentation."

"Did you tell him to go to hell?"

"No, I accused him of attempted vehicular manslaughter."

"Even better."

The professor tries, rather painfully, to get his leg back up on the couch. Mead comes around the table to help him. "Easy there, Mead," Dr. Alexander says. "I've still got a few good years left in that appendage."

"Dr. Kustrup says you're going to be laid up for the rest of the quarter."

"Poppycock. I'll be back next week. He's not getting rid of me that easily."

Mead is relieved to hear this. He sets down the professor's leg and walks back to his side of the table. Sits. "Has anyone ever complained about him?"

"Dr. Kustrup? All the time. He's a wretched teacher, as you well know."

"No, I mean his behavior outside of class."

"Outside of class? He's a bull in a china shop. Crass. Obnoxious. Opportunistic."

Mead shakes his head. "No, I mean I saw him in the men's room. In one of the stalls with another man. A student, I think."

"Are you talking about sexual harassment? No. There's never been a complaint of that nature that I know of. The man is a leech, yes, but a predator? Unlikely. Are you sure it was him?"

"All I saw were shoes. I might be wrong."

"Nonetheless, you should go to the dean and report what you saw."

"But I'm two weeks away from graduation. I don't want to make waves."

"Still."

"All right," Mead says, then nods at his presentation. "So, what do you think?"

Dr. Alexander takes another sip from his cup of soup. "The work is thorough and fully comprehensible."

"But?"

"I'm sure it'll impress the socks off the dean's distinguished guest list."

"But?"

"It proves nothing."

Mead slouches. "I know. Maybe I shouldn't present it at all."

"Poppycock," Dr. Alexander says. "It's a well-researched paper with impressive data. If you don't present these findings, someone else will. Eventually. And take all the credit. It shows that you're someone to be reckoned with. I say do it, Mead. Announce yourself to the mathematical community. Dazzle their socks off."

HERMAN EMERGES FROM THE STUDENT CENTER and walks toward the dorm. In one arm he is holding a stack of books, in the other he cradles Cynthia Broussard. She seems to hang on his every word, gazing into his face as he yammers away. Mead watches from his second-story window until they disappear beneath the sill.

But how can this be? Why would Cynthia continue to go out with Herman after what he did to her? Unless, of course, it wasn't Herman who caused those bruises. But Mead saw the scratches on his neck. Could they really have been caused by a staple? Mead abandons his post by the window and crosses his room to the door. Cracks it open and listens as footsteps come up the stairs. They get louder as they cross the landing on his floor, softer again as they ascend to the third floor. One pair, not two. Which means Cynthia is no longer with Herman. Mead waits for the second hand on his watch to make a full sweep around the dial. Waits to make sure Cynthia isn't lagging behind. Then he steps out of his room, closes the door, and follows Herman up the stairs.

Mead is about to knock when he hears two people talking on the other side of the door. His hand freezes in midair. But Mead could have sworn he heard only one set of feet on the steps, not two. Now he isn't so sure. The voices continue talking. Arguing, really. Two males voices. "I can no longer tolerate this kind of behavior," one of them says. "Calm down and let me explain," the other answers back. More heated words are exchanged but Mead cannot make them out. Then the voices stop.

Mead drops his hand and retreats to the stairwell. He shouldn't have come up here. It was a bad idea. He thought he had something to say to Herman. He thought he finally understood what had taken place in the bathroom stall that day. Thought he would tell Herman what he saw before going to the dean. In case the guy wants to come along. But now Mead isn't so sure. Maybe he got it wrong. Again. Because apparently he got it wrong with Cynthia.

Mead has just started back down the stairs when Herman's door opens. He steps out into the hall and says, "Hey, Fegley, where you going? Why didn't you knock?"

Mead stops and looks back, wondering how Herman knew he was there.

"I saw your feet," Herman says. "Under the door."

"It's not important," Mead says. "You're busy. I'll come back later." And continues down the stairs. But Herman comes after him. He leans over the railing like a prince over the ledge of a balcony and says, "I was just watching the TV, Fegley. But I'm not anymore. Come back up and tell me what's on your mind."

"Do you prefer Coke or Pepsi?" Herman asks and digs a can of each out of the miniature refrigerator that sits like a nightstand between his two beds.

"Coke," Mead says and Herman tosses him the can. Mead then perches on the edge of the spare bed, pops the tab off, and glances at the closet door. Herman usually leaves it hanging open but now it's closed. Watching TV, my foot. That wasn't the TV Mead heard; someone is in that closet. Hiding. Someone by the name of Dr. Kustrup. Shit. Mead wishes he had never come up here, wishes he had never told Dr. Alexander about what he thinks he saw that day, wishes he could just forget about the whole thing.

Herman sprawls across the other bed—his bed—and says, "So? What's up?"

Mead has to think of something else to say, make up some other reason for this unexpected visit. He sips his soda and glances at the closet door again. "Are you?" He clears his throat. "Are you and Cynthia still dating?"

Herman appears to give the question a lot of thought. And the longer it takes him to answer, the more idiotic Mead feels for having asked. He should just get up and leave. Walk out of here before he embarrasses himself any further. In front of Herman. In front of Dr. Kustrup. And he is about to do just that when Herman says, "If you mean have we been sleeping together, the answer is yes."

"And by sleeping together," Mead says, "you don't actually mean sleep, correct?"

Herman smiles, a cocky smile that further underscores the lack of good judgment that brought Mead to his room in the first place. "What's this all about, Fegley?" he says. "Why the sudden interest in my love life?"

Mead glances at the closed closet door. "Never mind. It's none of my business. I shouldn't have come up here." Mead puts down the soda can and stands up. "I'm sorry to have bothered you. I'll leave."

Herman grabs his wrist. "Did Cynthia say something to you?"

Shit. Why did Mead have to go and mention her? That's not even why he came up here. What is wrong with him? "No," he says. "I...I met a girl."

Herman looks surprised. He lets go of Mead's wrist and says, "Who is she?"

"Her name is Shirley Tanapat."

"Tanapat. Can't say I'm familiar with that name. Is she in one of your classes?"

"No, she's a librarian. Over at the library."

Herman smiles, all cocky again. "An older woman. I'm impressed, Fegley."

"They're all older women to me, Weinstein. I'm eighteen." Then he grabs his Coke off the top of the fridge and knocks back a slug. Belches. Decides that since they are on the subject anyway he might as well go ahead and ask. Realizes that he has, in fact, been wanting to ask Herman this question for a while now. One friend to another. "So when did you first know? About Cynthia, I mean."

"Know what?"

"Come on, Weinstein, don't make me spell it out, you know perfectly well what I'm asking."

"When did I first know that Cynthia wanted me to fuck her?"

"Jesus," Mead says. "Do you have to be so crude?"

"No, but I love the reaction it gets out of you."

Mead feels like a total idiot for having come up here. For bringing up Shirley. But, well, since he has gotten himself in this deep, he might as well keep going. After all, he can use all the advice he can get. And if he can't ask his best friend these kinds of questions, then whom can he ask? And that's when it dawns on Mead that he actually has one. A best friend. The first best friend Mead has ever had. "So, what're the signs?"

"Signs? You mean aside from hard nipples and wet cunts?"

Mead sets down his Coke and stands up. "That's it, Weinstein. I'm leaving."

"All right. I'm sorry. Cool your heels, Fegley. You want another soda?" And Herman rolls across the bed to the fridge and removes another can, holding it out to Mead as a peace offering. And it suddenly dawns on Mead that he might also be Herman's first best friend. That neither of them are very good at this. And so he forgives Herman for his crude behavior, knowing that he himself has a lot to learn when it comes to extending kindness to his fellow man.

Mead accepts the proffered soda can, even though the one he is holding is still half full, and sits back down. Herman smiles and pulls another can out of the fridge, pops off the tab, and slurps the foam that bubbles up out of it. He licks the lid with his tongue all suggestive-like and says, "I'm gonna tell you the biggest secret there is to know about love, Fegley. You ready?" Then he leans forward, as if what he is about to say is really important and highly confidential, and says, "If someone really likes you, there isn't a whole lot you can do to fuck it up."

"I don't follow."

"You can't make someone love you, Fegley; they either do or they don't. But if they do, you can be the biggest scumbag in the world and they'll bend over backwards to explain away your behavior just so they can keep on loving you."

"So what you're trying to tell me, in your own crude manner, is that if a girl likes me that eventually she's going to want to sleep with me?"

Herman flops back on the bed. "Have you asked this Shirley Tanapat out yet?"

"We've had coffee four times."

"But you don't drink coffee."

"I know."

"Does she know?"

"She does now."

Herman smiles.

"What?"

"I don't know why you're wasting my time with all these questions, Fegley. It's obvious to me that you've already won her over."

Mead smiles; it's just the answer he was hoping to hear.

"Did you have something else you wanted to ask me, Fegley?"

Yes, Mead thinks, and looks over at the closet. No longer able to bear the thought that Dr. Kustrup might be hiding inside of it, he sets down the two cans of soda, gets up off the bed, and, heart pumping wildly, throws open the closet door.

"I think I'm probably a couple of sizes bigger than you," Herman says. "But sure, go ahead. Borrow whatever you want. The girls love anything Armani."

Clothes. The closet is stuffed full of clothes, but Dr. Kustrup is nowhere in sight. Mead thinks again to ask Herman about that day in the men's bathroom. To tell his best friend what he saw. To tell Herman that he is prepared to go to the dean and offer himself up as a witness. He is about to open his mouth and say just that when Herman says, "The Beaumont Theater."

Mead turns around. "Excuse me?"

"It's this old movie house off campus with velvet seats and chandeliers. It's a great place to make out. You should take Shirley there. They show only year-old movies but the tickets are half-price."

"Won't that make me look cheap?"

"Nah. A girl likes it when a guy takes her someplace she's never been before. Someplace he discovered on his own that he wants to share with her. Besides, you'll seem more mature taking her to a theater off campus rather than to the student center. And that's what you want, right? To appear as mature as possible?"

Mead decides to bring up the Dr. Kustrup thing another time.

MONDAY IS SHIRLEY'S NIGHT OFF, so that is the night Mead takes her to the movie house. They meet in front of the library and walk over to the theater Herman suggested. Only he neglected to mention one minor detail: It plays adult movies only. The XXX-kind. Which is a little more "mature" than what Mead had in mind. Four months ago, he wouldn't have even been able to get inside the place. Not legally, that is.

Needless to say, it makes Shirley uncomfortable. As if she just discovered she is out on a date with a pervert. As if she wishes she had worn sweatpants and a pair of running shoes instead of a skirt and high heels. "I'm sorry," Mead says. "I didn't know."

"I'll bet your roommate recommended this place, didn't he?"

"Do you know Forsbeck?"

"No, but I know boys. I have three brothers. Listen, it's okay, Mead. An honest mistake. We'll just go someplace else." And she suggests this bookshop she knows that is a couple of blocks down and a few blocks over from the theater. A store that stocks rare periodicals in areas of special interest, including mathematics.

"Sounds like my kind of bookstore," Mead says. And it is. The shop is small. Taller than it is wide. It resembles a library in a private home, its bookshelves extending all the way from the floor to the ceiling with no way to get to them except by ladder and catwalk.

"The owner's a retired professor," Shirley says. "I don't think he cares as much about selling books as he does about just being surrounded by them."

"Wait a minute," Mead says. "I know about this place. Dr. Alexander told me about it. The retired professor is a physicist, right?"

"Yes," Shirley says. "That's right."

Despite the small square footage of the store, the retired physicist has managed to squeeze a table up front. By the window. And installed a coffee machine next to the register. Shirley orders a double espresso and sits. Mead inquires about mathematical periodicals and is sent up the ladder to the ceiling.

Dozens of back issues of *American Mathematical Monthly* and the *Mathematical Intelligencer* crowd each other for space on the shelf. A cornucopia of knowledge, just like Dr. Alexander's basement. Mead also finds a copy of *The Theory of the Riemann Zeta-Function* and *An Introduction to the Theory of the Riemann Zeta-Function*, both of which Dr. Alexander introduced to Mead a couple years ago. He even finds a few periodicals he hasn't read before. He selects one or two to take home, and is tucking them under his arm, when he comes across a periodical that appears to be mis-shelved. A paper written by a physicist. Mead pulls it out with the intention of placing it in the correct section but something about the title—*Dynamical Systems: A Model for Theoretical Chaos*—grabs his attention and he flips it open, skims through a few pages, and comes across an expression that is familiar to him. $1-(\sin(\pi u)/\pi u)^2$. It's the distribution function for the spacings between zeta zeros. Only in this periodical it's called the form factor for the pair correlation of eigenvalues of random matrices. Pair correlation is a term Mead has never heard before, one that makes his heart start beating faster and his face grow flush. It's warm all of a sudden, and Mead begins to sweat inside his double-breasted vest.

Discarding the other periodicals, he backs down the ladder and buys the physics paper, then realizes that he has no money left to pay for Shirley's espresso. She doesn't seem to mind, though, and graciously pays for it herself, saying, "I'm just glad you found something you like."

Mead pores through the periodical on the way back to campus, is so absorbed by it, in fact, that he would have walked straight past the dorms and on into the park, where he probably would've gotten mugged or worse if Shirley wasn't here to stop him.

"Well, I guess I should be heading home," she says and Mead realizes that he has barely spoken two words to her all night.

"Come up to my room," he says.

"Excuse me?" Shirley says.

"I want you to hear something."

She glances at her watch. "I don't know. It's getting pretty late and I have to be at the library when it opens first thing in the morning."

"This won't take long. I mean, you introduced me to your favorite bookshop so now I'd like to introduce you to my favorite musician."

Shirley stares at the sidewalk, as if the answer to her dilemma might be found in the cracks of cement. "All right," she says, "but just for a few minutes."

Mead cannot believe his luck when he opens his door and Forsbeck isn't there. He clears away the zeta zero papers strewn across his bed — to make room for Shirley to sit — and fetches the CD player off his roommate's desk. Removing Forsbeck's Pink Floyd disc, Mead replaces it with Bach's Suite No. 3 in D Major, slips the headphones over Shirley's ears, and presses PLAY. When the first few notes touch her ears, she smiles, then lifts her hands and begins to play the air as if it were a piano. She looks at Mead and yells, "I performed this for my final recital in school," because the music is loud and she cannot hear her own voice.

"You play the piano?" Mead yells back.

Shirley nods. "I'm pretty good at it too."

SHIRLEY TANAPAT STAYS for more than a few minutes. She kicks off her shoes, crosses her legs yoga-style, and listens to Bach with her eyes closed. When Suite No. 3 ends, she doesn't get up to leave but continues listening to Suite No. 4. Mead sits at his desk and reads. Every once in a while he sets aside the periodical to riffle through his own papers, looking for a specific function or expression or number field. At one point, he looks over and sees that Shirley has rolled onto her side, her head cradled in his bed pillow, her stocking feet tucked up under her skirt. When he looks again, she has fallen asleep, her breathing slow and even. And he doesn't know what to do about it: wake her up and send her home or let her sleep. Then he notices the time. It's after midnight. And Shirley has to be at the library at nine. But he can hardly send her home now. Send her out into the streets of Chicago in the middle of the night. What if she got mugged? He should probably walk her home. But what if he got mugged coming back? Besides, Mead has no idea where she lives. Whether it is nearby or far away. So he decides to leave her be.

It is close to two when Mead finishes the periodical. He can hardly wait for the sun to come up so he can tell Dr. Alexander about it. Math and physics. Bernhard Riemann would have made no distinction between the two areas of study. Not in his time. So neither should Mead.

Forsbeck still isn't back. Which is highly unusual for a weeknight. Perhaps he is spending it with his new girlfriend. Which frees up his bed. But Mead does not much relish the idea of sleeping in it. Especially since Forsbeck hasn't changed the sheets since the girlfriend last stayed over. So Mead considers his other options—sleeping in his chair or on the floor—but dismisses them both as too uncomfortable. He could go upstairs and crash on Herman's spare bed—again—but Mead does not feel comfortable with that option either. Which leaves him with no other choice but to get into bed with Shirley.

Mead takes off his shoes and crawls in beside her, trying to jiggle the mattress as little as possible, but Shirley stirs and rolls over. Mead freezes, afraid to take a breath until she settles back into sleep. She looks lovely lying on his bed. Like a nymph in a Shakespeare play. Mead removes the headphones from her ears and lies down behind her, tucking his knees into the crook of her legs. Her hair smells like shampoo. He pictures her in the shower washing it, soap suds cascading down her neck and over her breasts, and grows hard. He wraps his arm around Shirley and cups one of her breasts in his hand. His dick begs for attention and he obliges, reaching down into his pants with his other hand to give it some relief. Moans when he comes. Shirley stirs and he drops both her breast and his dick. Embarrassed. Ashamed of his hedonist behavior. He starts to remove his arm from around her body when she grasps his hand, intertwining her fingers with his. Mead holds his breath in an attempt to make time stand still. There are no words to describe what he is feeling at the moment. It is beyond anything he has ever experienced before. All he knows is that he wants it to last forever—this moment—even though he knows it cannot. But still he holds his breath. Holds it in as long as he can. Until Shirley, half-wake, says, "Hold me tighter, Kevin."

MEAD PACES BACK AND FORTH. Glances at his watch. Paces some more. Finally, the door to the classroom opens and students begin to file out. But Mead cannot wait a moment longer and pushes his way inside, pushes against the flow of departing students like a salmon swimming upstream against the current. "Hey, buddy," someone says, "watch where you're going." But Mead knows exactly where he is going.

Dr. Alexander is standing at the chalkboard, eraser in hand, a crutch tucked under one arm. He looks up at Mead and says, "Are you here to help me? Because it isn't necessary. As I have told all my other students, I can get around just fine on my own."

"I found it, Dr. Alexander. You were right."

"Right about what, Mead?"

"Physics," Mead says and waves the periodical in the air. "I found this in that bookstore off campus. The one you told me about. The one the retired professor opened. It's all about quantum-scale dynamical systems. About the periodic orbits that underlie a classical chaotic system. The Riemann Hypothesis models itself after one of these systems. A chaotic system. I'm sure of it. They have the same characteristic polynomials. The same eigenvalues."

"Wait a minute. Slow down, Mead. What does the Riemann Hypothesis have to do with the theory of chaos?"

"I don't know, I just know that it does."

Dr. Alexander looks pale, as if he might faint. Reaching for the edge of the desk, he lowers himself into a chair. "My leg," he says. "It needs to be elevated." Mead helps him lift it onto the desktop then runs out into the hall to refill the professor's water glass. Dr. Alexander washes down one of his pain pills. "Okay now," he says, "let me see this periodical that has you all hot under the collar." Mead hands it to him and points to the distribution function. The professor studies it for a moment, then flips through the rest of the pamphlet. He reads some of Mead's notations in the margins, looks up with a grin on his face, and says, "Close the door."

MEAD MAKES IT TO THE LIBRARY with five minutes to spare, having run all the way, afraid he wouldn't make it before closing time. But now he cannot get himself to go inside. Shirley is standing at the front desk peeking into backpacks and shoulder bags. She smiles at this one tall, lanky, towheaded boy and says something that makes him smile back. Could that be Kevin?

When Mead woke up this morning, she was gone. And Forsbeck was sleeping in the next bed. It was almost as if Shirley had never been there. A figment of Mead's imagination. And yet he knows she was. He has the bags under his eyes to prove it.

All night he fell in and out of sleep, wondering who Kevin was. An ex-boyfriend or a current one. A fellow pianist, perhaps. He wanted to run outside and scream at the top of his lungs. Scream out in frustration. But he couldn't because Shirley would not let go of his hand. She held on to it as if on to a lifeline as she slept. Then sometime around dawn, as the sky outside Mead's window began to grow bright, he fell into a deep sleep. When he woke up, she was gone.

The last student pushes through the turnstile and exits the library. Shirley follows him to the front door — to lock it — looks up and sees Mead on the other side of the glass. She does not look happy to see him. Does not look like someone who had a good time last night. She looks like someone who woke up and found herself sleeping next to the wrong man.

"I've been wondering what happened to you," she says. "Why you didn't come by the library as usual tonight. If you were going to avoid me for the rest of the year."

"I've been behind closed doors all day with one of my professors."

"I see," she says in a way that suggests she does not.

"I know about Kevin," Mead says, hoping she will fill him in on all the missing details. But she doesn't, she just says, "I see," again and looks down at her hands, which are twisting themselves one around the other. "I guess that would explain it then."

"Explain what?" Mead says.

Shirley cocks her head to one side, like a robin listening for worms in the soil, and says, "I thought you'd be different, but you aren't. You're just like all the rest."

Mead blushes. She must have been awake after all. Must know he masturbated while holding her breast. "I'm not like that," he says. "I swear. I've never done anything like that before."

"I guess that's not what you told your friend, though, is it? You made me sound so good he wanted a taste for himself."

"Who? You mean Forsbeck? My roommate? What did he do?"

"It's all right. My mistake. I'm a grown girl and take full responsibility for my own actions. I shouldn't have gone up to your room. It was stupid. It's just that I'd been having such a nice time and I thought..." She shakes her head. "I should've known better."

"You did? You had a good time?"

"Good night, Mead," she says and closes the door, the deadbolt dropping into place with all the finality of a period at the end of a sentence.

* * *

The door to Mead's room is closed. He opens it and finds Forsbeck in bed with his new girlfriend. They aren't having sex or anything, just sitting there. Talking. Both fully clothed. Mead lunges at Forsbeck, grabbing him by the collar and pinning him down to the bed. "Jesus fucking Christ," Forsbeck says. "What the hell's gotten into you?" But Mead is not in the mood for words; instead he takes his fist and slams it into Forsbeck's face. The pain that follows can only be described as excruciating. "Shit," Mead says and shakes out his hand. "Shit, shit, shit."

"Sonofabitch," Forsbeck says, blinking away tears. "What the hell did you go and do that for, Fegley?"

"For propositioning Shirley," he says and hopes his hand isn't broken.

"Shirley? Who the hell is Shirley?"

"She won't even speak to me now," Mead says, "thanks to you."

Forsbeck's girlfriend gets all angry-looking. "Who is this Shirley he's talking about, Charlie? Is she that girl in economics class who wears the short skirts?"

"No," he says. "I have no idea who the hell he's talking about." Forsbeck looks at Mead. "I swear I don't know any Shirley."

"She's the girl who was sleeping in my bed last night," Mead says. "When you came stumbling in at dawn. Is it clearer now?"

Forsbeck's bewildered face softens and he begins to laugh.

"What's so damn funny, Forsbeck?"

"A girl?" he says. "In your bed?" Forsbeck grabs his stomach and rolls onto his side, overcome with hysterics. He is laughing so hard that his girlfriend forgets she is mad and starts laughing with him. It's a convincing act. But if Forsbeck did not proposition Shirley, then who the hell did?

13

LEFTOVERS

High Grove
Three Days Before Graduation

MEAD'S MOTHER MAKES A GREAT DEAL OF NOISE removing the coffee tin from the freezer. Measuring out several spoonfuls. Plugging in the percolator. As it starts to gurgle and snort, she walks over to the table where Mead is sitting and stands over him. She does not speak, just stands over him passing silent judgment. And so he does his best to ignore her. To pretend she isn't there. To focus his attention on the newspaper crossword puzzle instead. Eight across asks for the name of an ancient city of southwest Asia with seven letters in it, the fourth being Y. Mead fills in the empty spaces with a B-A-B and L-O-N.

The percolator goes silent and his mother walks away, her heels *click-clacking* against the linoleum floor. She fills a cup with hot coffee and comes back to the table, pulls out a chair, and sits down to stare at him some more. She is waiting for Mead to confess. To tell her why he came home. To tell her who is threatening him. She thinks she can stare it out of him but she is going to have a long wait. What good would it do to tell her anyway? Herman is not Freddy. He's a lot smarter. A lot more savvy. Within ten minutes the guy would have Mead's mother eating out of his hand, convinced that he was right and Mead was wrong. And how could Mead argue? After all, he has brought this on himself. Maybe he should just give in to Herman and let the guy have his way. Put this whole sordid mess in the past and move on. The same way Mead gave in to Freddy. Only Freddy has never gone away. He has been lodged in the back of Mead's head like a bullet from a drive-by shooting for years.

The phone rings, trilling like a fire alarm going off. Mead's first thought is that it's for his dad. That someone has died. His second, that it is the dean. Or maybe it's Dr. Alexander calling back to check up on Mead, to make sure he's okay.

The phone rings again. His mother sets down her cup and gets up to answer it. And suddenly it dawns on Mead that it might be Herman calling to tell Mead's mother that her son is a greedy, self-centered egotist and not the innocent genius she thinks he is. And so Mead reaches in front of her and snatches up the receiver. His mother glares at him and Mead glares back, the two of them locked in a staring contest.

"Hello?" the voice at the other end says. "Is anyone there?" It's a female voice. Not Herman. Not Dr. Alexander. Not the dean. And so Mead says hello back.

"Who is this?" she says.

"Aren't I supposed to ask you that?" Mead says. "After all, you called me."

"No, I didn't. I called my husband and you are definitely not my husband."

Mead's mother reaches for the receiver but Mead holds it away from her. "It's Aunt Jewel," he says. "She's looking for Uncle Martin."

"Teddy, is that you?" his aunt says on the other end of the line.

"Yes, Aunt Jewel. It's me."

"Well, I'll be goddamned. I must've dialed wrong. I didn't even know I had your number up there in Chicago."

Oh boy, here we go again. Must be one of her bad days. "You don't, Aunt Jewel. I'm home. Here in High Grove. Remember? We ran into each other over at the A & P. I walked you home. Then you and Uncle Martin came over for supper."

"We did?"

"Yes. Two days ago."

Mead looks at his mother, covers the mouthpiece of the phone, and says, "Now do you believe me?"

"Hand me the phone," she says and tries to grab the receiver but Mead ducks and all she grabs is air.

"I better hang up and call the store," Jewel says.

"He's not over there, Aunt Jewel. Uncle Martin went into St. Louis to pick up some embalming supplies. Didn't he tell you?"

"St. Louis? Oh. Oh my, that is a problem. The drain. It's all stopped up and I need him to fix it so I can take my shower."

"Why don't you call a plumber?"

"Oh, no. Martin told me not to call anyone except him. He says they charge too much money. Besides, he likes to do this kind of thing himself. He's a real handyman, my husband, a real fixer-upper."

"Well, it's probably just hair, in the drain. You can clear it out with a snake. It's really quite easy."

His mother makes another grab for the receiver. "That's enough, Teddy, let me talk to her." But he holds the receiver out at arm's length. Away from her. He is not giving up the phone; he likes his aunt too much to subject her to his mother.

"A snake?" Jewel says.

"Yes. It's a long metal coil that you feed down the drain and—"

"Oh, no. I can't do that," she says. "I wouldn't even know where to find such a thing. Oh, my. I don't know what I'm going to do. Martin's gonna be so mad. He doesn't like it when I don't take my shower."

"Well, what do you say I come over and unclog the drain for you?"

"Would you? Would you be a dear and do that for me?"

Mead's mother is waving her hands around in the air, the international sign for hand-over-the-phone-before-I-bop-you-on-the-head.

"I'd love to," Mead says. "I'll be right over."

HE RINGS THE FRONT DOORBELL and waits but no one answers. He checks the number on the house, even though he knows he's at the right address, then rings the bell again. Then he knocks on the door and says, "Aunt Jewel? It's me, Teddy. I just spoke with you on the phone a couple minutes ago. I've come by to fix the tub. Aunt Jewel?" But still no one answers. Maybe she isn't here. Maybe she wandered off to the hardware store to buy a snake. Or to the grocery store for another half-gallon of peppermint stick ice cream dressed in her robe and slippers.

Mead abandons his post at the front door and walks around to the back to try the kitchen door. And stops up short. He remembers his Uncle Martin mentioned a vegetable garden but what the guy neglected to say is that the entire backyard was overturned to plant it. Not one square inch of lawn left. And no evidence—at least not as of yet—that anything other than weeds has taken root. Perhaps Mead should offer up his services as a gardener. Clearing their backyard of unwanted weeds might be kind of cathartic and one heck of a lot easier than weeding the evil out of mankind.

Mead stands on his toes to peer through the kitchen window, hoping to catch a glimpse of his aunt, but it is covered over by a gingham curtain. At the back door, he knocks again. "Aunt

Jewel? It's Teddy, let me in." Then grasps the knob—to see if it is locked—and the door pops open. Easing it wider, he steps into the kitchen and stops up short yet again.

The room is filled with dirty dishes. Literally. Every square inch of the table and counter, including the stovetop, piled high with dishes. Plates with hardened egg on them, bowls with dried bits of oatmeal glued to the bottom, glasses with orange pulp stuck to their sides. And the sink is even worse. Pots and pans and more plates and cups sit half-submerged in a pool of gray water. A line of scum runs around the inside of the basin about four inches above the water level, an indication of just how long these dishes have been sitting in their own filth. For weeks, if not months.

The cupboard doors have been left open and the shelves are empty except for one bag of A & P Eight O'Clock coffee and a box of filters. Mead peeks inside the refrigerator and finds a half-eaten wheel of Gouda cheese, a box of saltines, and, in the freezer, the half-gallon carton of peppermint stick ice cream.

No wonder Uncle Martin doesn't want Aunt Jewel to call a plumber.

He closes the door and stands transfixed. Mead has inadvertently walked in on something he would rather not have. He pictures his uncle standing in the sterile environment of the preparation room in the basement of Fegley Brothers, where every surface shines and the air reeks of ammonia, and wonders how he can stand living in this mess. How it could have gotten this bad without anyone (i.e., Mead's parents) finding out. And why Uncle Martin hasn't told anyone—not even Mead's dad who is probably the least judgmental person on the whole planet.

Mead steps into the dining room. Its table, too, is buried under platters and dishes and bowls. Only these are still filled with food. Green beans almondine. Beef stroganoff. Chicken noodle casserole. Macaroni-and-cheese. Chicken salad. Fruit salad. Cucumber salad. Tomato salad. The whole thing is swarming in ants. Hundreds of black ants. And in the middle of all this chaos is a wreath of brown, wilted flowers—what used to be white lilies—and a card. Mead picks up the card and reads: MAY GOD BE WITH YOU. WE LOVE YOU, PERCY.

A chill runs up Mead's spine. Shit. This is the food from his cousin's wake. Three months ago. Mead feels like throwing up. He had no idea. He knew his aunt was acting all nutty and stuff but he had no idea her depression had gotten so out of control. Mead is not sure who the crazier one is here: his aunt, for walking around town in her bathrobe; or his uncle, for walking around acting as if everything is okay.

Mead steps back into the kitchen. He is in over his head here. He needs help. He'll go to the store and tell his father. He won't believe him, of course. He will think Mead is exaggerating, he will pray to God that his son is making the whole thing up for some sick, perverted adolescent reason beyond the comprehension of his middle-aged years. A bad, bad joke. Because that will be easier to believe than this.

A noise comes from somewhere deep inside the house, as if someone has dropped something. Mead stops at the kitchen door to listen and hears it again. That must be his aunt. She must be here after all. He turns and walks toward the noise—around a corner and down the hall—and finds the door to the basement open. A bare bulb at the bottom of the steps lit. His armpits begin to itch. What if she's down there hanging herself right now? What if her misdialed number was really a cry for help? Shit. Mead should have just called a plumber, to hell with what Uncle Martin wants. Or at least called his father. He could still call him now. There's a phone in the kitchen, not twenty feet away. But what if, while he is dialing, she steps off the chair.

Then, for the rest of his life, Mead will have to live with the fact that he could have saved her. That he came this close and failed. That he was indirectly responsible not just for his cousin's death but his aunt's as well!

Thump.

Holy shit. Was that a chair falling over? Or maybe Aunt Jewel is trying to shoot herself, her hands got all sweaty and she dropped the gun. In which case there is still time. Now or never. Mead starts down the stairs, grasping the railing as if for courage, and says, "Hello? Aunt Jewel? Is that you down there?"

"Teddy? Is that you, Teddy?"

Relief sweeps over him like a cool breeze. "Yes, Aunt Jewel, it's me," he says and continues his descent. "I rang the doorbell but I guess you didn't hear. What're you doing down here?" And at the bottom of the stairs, he sees her. She's dressed in an ankle-length nightgown, her hair up in rollers, standing next to Uncle Martin's workbench. Her hands are buried in an open drawer and again Mead thinks gun.

"I'm looking for that snake you told me about," she says. "I thought I'd try and find it myself but all I've found is this." And she holds up a roll of electrical wire.

Mead laughs with relief.

"What's so funny?"

He shakes his head. "I'm just glad to see you, is all."

Jewel clasps her hands over her hair rollers in an attempt to hide them. "Don't tell your uncle you saw me like this. Before my shower. He'll have a fit."

Mead zips his mouth shut with his index finger and thumb. "You've got my solemn promise, Aunt Jewel. I won't say a word."

The snake is hanging in plain sight on a Peg-Board above the workbench. Mead takes it down and follows his aunt back upstairs. The living room is just as bad as the rest of the house, with crumpled napkins and lipstick-stained coffee cups littering every flat surface. Clothes are draped over the banister that leads to the second floor. They hang from every doorknob. But among all this chaos and disarray is one sign of sanity. An ironing board. It's set up in the middle of the hall, two button-down shirts on hangers dangling from one end of it, pressed and ready to wear. The door to his aunt and uncle's bedroom is open, their bed unmade. More clothes draped over everything. But the next door—the door to Percy's room—is closed. At the end of the hall is the bathroom.

The tub has not been cleaned in a while and soap scum is clinging to its sides like rust. Mead gets right down to work, feeds the snake down the drain and dislodges a ball of hair that looks like something a cat might cough up, only bigger. He wraps it in bathroom tissue and drops it into the wastebasket, which is overflowing with facial tissues as if someone in the house has been suffering from a bad cold. Or crying.

"Oh, what a dear you are," his aunt says when he tells her the problem has been cleared up. "How about I fix us both a little something to eat after my shower?"

"That's all right, Aunt Jewel. I just had breakfast." This is a lie. Mead is actually quite hungry. Would, indeed, enjoy having something to eat but can think of nothing in his aunt's kitchen that he would feel safe putting down his throat.

"Oh, but you can't leave, Teddy. I haven't seen you since you got home. You have to tell me what you've been up to. I'll only be a minute. Please stay."

How do you say no to a woman in pink curlers whose son has just died and whose funeral you missed?

Aunt Jewel closes the bathroom door and, as soon as the shower turns on, Mead hurries downstairs to call the store. To call for backup. "You've got to get over here, Dad," he says into the receiver. "You've got to see this with your own eyes to believe it. Aunt Jewel needs help and she needs it now."

AUNT JEWEL ENTERS THE KITCHEN looking no different than before her shower. She is wearing the same nightgown and the same pink rollers in her hair, the only indication that she has taken a bath at all being the ringlets of wet hair at the nape of her neck.

"My, my, my. Look how you've grown," she says and takes hold of Mead's hand. "Why, you were just an itty-bitty thing when you first went off to that big-city university. I was so worried. I was afraid you wouldn't manage up there all alone."

"You were?"

"Sure. And I aired my concerns with your mother too. Told her I thought it'd be better if you waited a year. Grew up a little."

"I'll bet she took that advice really well."

"Wouldn't speak to me for six months."

Mead laughs. If not for the dirty dishes, unwashed clothes, and tumbleweed-size dust balls in every corner, he would think his aunt just as sane as the next guy. Maybe even more.

"Come. Sit down," she says and pats the seat of a kitchen chair, then opens the refrigerator and takes out the half-wheel of cheese and box of saltines. To make room for them on the table, she has to stack a few of the dirty dishes one on top of the other—a real juggling act at this point—then cuts a slice of cheese off one end of the wheel, places it on a saltine, and hands it to Mead. The cheese is dry and hard on the side that was exposed to the air inside the refrigerator. Mead hesitates, but only for a second, then pops it in his mouth and chews and coughs when a fragment of saltine lodges in his airway. He coughs a second time but the damned thing just won't budge.

"Let me get you some water," his aunt says and walks over to the sink. She lifts a glass out of the pool of gray sludge, fills it under the tap, and hands it to Mead. Dysentery. That is the word that goes through his mind. He sees himself in a couple of hours, rolling around on the floor in pain, running to the bathroom every fifteen minutes. But he takes the glass from her anyway. From his nurturing aunt. The mother with no child left to pamper. He takes it from her and sips it so she can feel like a mother again. Even if just for a moment.

"There now, isn't that better?" she says and pats his hand.

Mead nods, then starts to cry. Not from choking on the cracker but because he realizes that he has been acting as crazy as his aunt, pretending that everything is fine when in fact it is not. Sitting here in her fucked-up house drinking toxic water when he should be sitting at the desk in his dorm room writing his valedictory address. It's just so unfair. Life is so unfair. Why did Percy have to choose that day to come visit him? Why did Mead have to cross paths with Herman? If only he *had* waited another year before going off to college, grown up a bit first as his aunt suggested to his mother, then maybe he wouldn't have even run into Herman Weinstein in the first place. Simple as that. But he didn't wait. And Percy did choose that day. And Mead did run into Herman. And so here he sits in his aunt's fucked-up kitchen, both their lives in shambles.

A WHITE HEARSE IS PARKED at the curb, FEGLEY BROTHERS inscribed across the side of it in gold lettering. A middle-aged man is seated in the front seat, on the passenger side. "Who's that sitting in the hearse?" Mead asks his father.

"Dr. Breininger. He's a psychiatrist. And it isn't a hearse, it's an ambulance."

Mead studies the doctor's silhouette. Stern. Impassive. His

thoughts a secret from the world. A man like Mead's father who has seen more than his fair share of what the rest of us go out of our way to avoid. "Did he bring along a straitjacket?"

"Yes, but I doubt we'll have to use it. Jewel doesn't seem to be in much danger of hurting herself."

"Actually, I was thinking more along the lines of Uncle Martin, about how he is going to react when he comes home and finds us here."

Mead's father gives Mead an I-don't-think-that's-very-funny look and steps past him into the house. But Mead didn't mean for it to be funny. He is dead serious.

His father takes a tour of the house, walking from room to room, assessing the situation, weighing his son's comments over the phone against his own perceptions. By the time he enters the kitchen, where Jewel is helping herself to a cheese-and-saltine sandwich, he has seen enough to know that Mead was not exaggerating. Not even a little bit. She rises to her feet and says, "Lynn, what a pleasant surprise. Teddy and I were just enjoying a little snack, would you care to join us?"

"Jewel," Mead's father says, "when was the last time you did the dishes?" But he might as well have said, "Jewel, have you lost you're frigging mind?" Because his straightforward question changes the atmosphere in the kitchen from one of ignorant bliss to one of uncomfortable self-consciousness. Jewel looks around as if seeing the kitchen for the first time in weeks.

"And the dining room," Mead's father says, pouring salt into an open wound. "It looks as if you haven't cleaned up in there since the funeral."

Jewel's eyes fill with tears. "Martin said I didn't have to, he said I could wait until he gets back. But he hasn't gotten back, Lynn, and I'm beginning to get worried."

Mead's father wraps his arm around Jewel and eases her down

into a chair. "He just went to St. Louis, Jewel. He'll be back later this afternoon, don't worry." She pops back up and says, "Really? You have no idea how relieved I am to hear that, Lynn. I've been waiting so long. Too long."

"Okay, well, you just sit here and relax," he says and eases her back into the chair, "and Teddy and I will start cleaning the house up, how does that sound?"

"You can't!" Jewel says and pops up out of the chair again. "Not until after he gets here. All those people. They came to his party and brought all that food. They were so thoughtful and generous. He has to see. He has to see how much everyone loves him. If you clean it all up before he gets here, Percy will never know. And he's got to know, Lynn, he's got to know how much people love him."

Talking rationally to an irrational person is a waste of time. Mead's father knows this all too well from working for so many years with so many people in mourning. So instead of talking, he pats Jewel's hand, nods as if he understands, and eases her into the chair yet again then sits down himself. He looks exhausted. As if he is trying to wrap his head around the size of this one. Mead places his hand on his father's shoulder, as a way of showing his support, because for the first time in his life he understands—really understands—how hard his father's job is. How brave and fearless the man is to do what he does for a living: to deal with people in their most vulnerable state.

"Dad," Mead says but his father doesn't respond. "Dad," he says again and shakes the man's shoulder. His father snaps back from wherever it is he goes at such times and looks up. "Maybe now would be a good time to go," Mead says and nods in the direction of the waiting ambulance.

His father reaches into his breast pocket and pulls out two blue pills—pills that look like the ones the hospital gave Mead after he hit Forsbeck—and places them in Jewel's palm. Then he picks up the glass of gray water and says, "Drink these down, Jewel. They'll help you sleep." And even though Mead is pretty damned sure his aunt has done little but sleep and dream about Percy for the past three months, she swallows them down and then allows herself to be eased out of the chair and up the steps to bed.

"How come you didn't just put her in the ambulance?" Mead asks when his father returns.

"Because that is a decision only your uncle can make."

"You're kidding, right? I mean it's not like the man hasn't known what's been going on around here all this time. Do you really think he's the best one to judge?"

His father pulls a pair of rubber gloves out of a kitchen drawer and offers them to Mead. "Would you prefer to wash or dry?"

"What I would prefer to do is to get the hell out of here before Uncle Martin comes home and blows his stack, that's what I'd prefer."

The gloves hit the floor with a loud smack. "My god, Teddy," his father says. "Do you really think every problem in this world can be solved by running away?"

"What? No, of course not."

"Well, that sure as hell comes as a surprise to me."

Mead has never before heard his father swear, never before seen him throw anything on the floor, never before been the target of the man's anger. "Dad, why're you yelling at me? This isn't my fault."

"Take a look around you, Teddy," he says and waves his arm through the air. "Do you see this? Do you know what this is? This is what happens when you try to run away from your problems. They pile up all around you, one filthy dish on top of the other. Sure, you can walk around pretending you don't see them, but the rest of the world will, Teddy. The rest of the world will see your mess even if you can't."

"What're you saying, Dad, that I've made a mess of my life? Is that what you think? What the hell do you know about my life anyway?"

"Nothing. I know absolutely nothing because you won't tell me. You won't reach out for my help even though you so obviously need it. I mean, how the hell are your mother and I supposed to help you if you won't talk to us? My god, Teddy, don't you realize that we love you more than anyone else in this world?"

Mead stares into his father's red face that can't be more than twelve inches from his own, then turns and storms out of the room.

"There you go again," his father says. "Running away."

Mead stops dead in his tracks, his father's tongue as sharp as a knife to his back, spins around and stomps back into the kitchen. "You of all people should talk," Mead says. "I mean, who really has his head buried in the sand around here, huh? Your own brother is completely fucked up, his wife half out of her mind, and you didn't have a clue. They were right under your nose the whole time and you didn't have a clue. Even when I told you I saw her dressed up as if for Halloween in the freezer section of the A & P, you still chose to look the other way. God forbid someone around here should admit that there's a problem that can't be fixed by doing extra credit. God forbid someone should show any signs of weakness. What a horrible embarrassment that would be, right? It'd only bring shame upon the family to admit human failure, to admit to being anything less than perfect. Best to sweep it under the rug and keep going. Strap on a pair of blinders and pretend everything is fine. Don't look left, don't look right, just plow straight ahead. Well, guess what. Surprise, surprise. I'm the only one around here who isn't wearing fucking blinders."

His hand strikes like lightning, slapping Mead across the face. It doesn't hurt so much as surprise. Mead had no idea his father was capable of such emotion; it's a side of the man he has never seen before. He wasn't sure it even existed and is relieved to know it has not been lost altogether. But then, like a popped balloon, his father's anger deflates, replaced by a look of regret, a look that adds years to his face. He stares at the floor, the house so quiet Mead swears he can hear the ants in the next room. Chewing. A million of them all at once.

"You're right," his father says. "I screwed up. I admit it. I sensed that something was wrong and didn't pursue it. I told myself that time was all Martin and Jewel needed to heal. Obviously, I was wrong." Then he lifts his eyes and adds, "So now it's your turn, Teddy. Tell me what happened up there at that university."

Mead meets his father's gaze. Eye-to-eye. He has never before looked at him like this. Straight on. Man-to-man. His heart thumps in his chest, so loud that Mead can barely hear himself when he says, "I befriended the wrong guy, Dad. I made a deal with the devil and now I'm going to have to pay the price."

"What guy?"

"Herman Weinstein."

"You mean that boy your mother and I met? I thought he was your friend."

"So did I. Or so I told myself. But really I just used him."

"Used him? That doesn't sound like you, Teddy, that doesn't sound like you at all. Tell me what happened. I want to hear the whole story. From the start."

But before Mead can utter even a single word, the front door flies open and Uncle Martin comes sailing through it.

* * *

"GET OUT OF MY HOUSE." This seems to be the only thing Uncle Martin knows how to say. "Get out of my house." Mead's dad tries to explain what happened. The chain of events that led up to now. How Jewel called his house by mistake, trying to get a hold of Martin at the store. How Teddy answered the phone then came over here to help her unclog the drain in the tub. "Get out of my house," Martin says and Mead's dad explains that Teddy then called him at the store, concerned about his aunt. (Concerned, that's the word his father uses. Concerned.) That Jewel is now sleeping upstairs. "Get out of my house," Martin says and Mead's dad explains how ashamed he is, that he had no idea what was going on over here. "Get out of my house." That he wishes Martin had felt he could reach out to his brother for help. "Get out of my house." That he believes Jewel needs more than just time to heal. "I SAID GET THE HELL OUT OF MY HOUSE!"

Mead's dad then tells his brother that he thinks Jewel should be admitted to a mental hospital. "Where she can get counseling so she can get better," he says, all calm and cool. As if he were trying to talk Martin in off a window ledge.

Mead's uncle goes all silent, like the eye of a hurricane. He looks into the living room to his right and then into the dining room to his left. The front door is still open, and behind him, out by the curb, Dr. Breininger emerges from the white ambulance, slides a gurney out of the rear of the vehicle, and begins to make his way toward the house. He's about halfway up the walk when Martin explodes, his right arm sweeping across the dining room table and sending the green beans almondine, the beef stroganoff, the chicken noodle casserole, the macaroni-and-cheese, the fruit salad, and hundreds of black ants sailing through the air. The walls become an instant work of abstract art. Jackson

Pollock would be in awe. Bowls and plates shatter into pieces. Tupperware bounces and rolls across the floor. Martin winds up for a second assault on the table but before he can inflict any more damage Mead's dad jumps into action and wraps his arms like a straitjacket around his brother. A struggle ensues. Martin scoops up a handful of whipped potatoes and mashes it into his brother's face. But Mead's dad refuses to let go and both of them end up on the floor, his uncle pinned under his father. And then it ends. Just like that. Martin stops fighting and goes limp, his anger having suddenly converted into tears. Mead turns away then. Not because he is embarrassed by his uncle's display of emotion but because he understands, intuitively, the importance of maintaining one's dignity at a time like this.

While the two grown men are still lying on the floor, Dr. Breininger sticks his head through the open front door and says, "Excuse me, but can someone please come help me get this gurney up the steps?"

Mead's mother goes with them, with Aunt Jewel and Uncle Martin and Dr. Breininger to the mental hospital in St. Louis. Mead's father called her while, upstairs, Martin and the good doctor roused Jewel from sleep and got her onto the gurney. She arrived in what seemed like seconds. Didn't even put on lipstick first. She held on to Jewel's hand as the gurney was rolled across the front lawn, then sat in the back of the ambulance and wouldn't let go. Mead tries to remember the last time his mother held his hand like that and, for a second, feels jealous. But only for a second. Then he picks up the rubber gloves his father threw on the floor and turns his attention to a more important matter. Namely, cleaning up the mess that used to be his aunt and uncle's home.

He starts where he and his father left off: with the kitchen sink. The drain belches a few times as murky water pours down its throat, then Mead refills the basin, squirting pink liquid detergent into a stream of clear tap water. Hot water. Hot enough to scorch bare skin. He soaps up a plate, rinses it off, and sets it in the drying rack.

His father steps up beside him, lifts the plate out of the rack, and begins drying it. Mead grabs a second dish, soaps it up, and waits for his father to ask him to expound on his earlier confession. To spill his guts. To confess his sins. Only his father doesn't say a word. He just sets the clean plate in the cupboard and waits for the next one, waits for Mead to start talking when he is good and ready.

God, how Mead hates that. How his father always has to play the role of Mr. Patience. Mr. Sensitivity. Mr. Understanding. Mr. Holier-Than-Thou. A bubble of anger wells up in his chest but Mead fights to keep it down because it is inappropriate. For another time or place. Not now. Not when his father is still upset about his brother. And Jewel. Mead is being petty. Childish. He knows this but he can't help it. He tells the bubble to go away but that just makes it grow bigger. Mead feels as if he is going to burst. As if he can't breathe. Rinses off the plate and throws it into the drying rack.

"Easy there," his father says. "You don't want to break it."

"Why!" Mead yells. "Why didn't you just accept the fucking scholarship? There isn't another human being on the face of this earth who would turn his nose up at free money. Why you? Did you do it to make me feel indebted to you? Was that your way of getting back at me for not becoming an undertaker? Would it really have been such a goddamned terrible thing to do? Why? Tell me why you did it!"

His father sets down the dishtowel. "That's what you think? That I refused the university's offer of a scholarship to punish you?"

"Yes. No. I don't know what to think, not anymore."

Mead's father pulls out a chair and sits down at the kitchen table as if he is suddenly very tired. As if the wind has been knocked out of his lungs. Mead feels horrible. Why did he just say that? Why is he tormenting the poor man? After all it isn't his father who betrayed him; it's Herman. He should apologize. Take it back. Beg his father for forgiveness. But he does none of these things. He just stands, frozen in place, waiting for a response.

"I suppose that I was upset," his father says. "At first, when I first realized that you wouldn't be following in my footsteps. It's every father's dream, of course, to have a son just like himself. But I knew better. You see, it was my father's dream too. He wanted me to be a carpenter. My very first memory is of whacking my thumb with a hammer. I think I was three at the time." He shakes his head, remembering. "I never got the hang of it. Never much enjoyed that kind of thing. Martin had an easier time of it. He was more like our father. Good with physical things like hammers and saws. They got along great. That is until Martin hit his teens, when he got it in his head to become a ballplayer."

"What?" Mead says. "You mean Uncle Martin wanted to be a baseball player? Like Percy?"

His father laughs. "Ironic, no?"

"Don't tell me: Henry Charles wouldn't let him."

"It never came to that. Martin wasn't as good as Percy. But it was a bone of contention between them for quite a few years. And, I am ashamed to say, I took advantage of that fissure in their relationship. I ingratiated myself with my father the only way I knew how, by taking an active interest in the other half of his business."

He stops talking and rises out of the chair. Picks up the discarded dishtowel and gestures for Mead to continue washing.

Which Mead obediently does. Picks up another plate, soaps it, and hands it to his father, wondering where this is going, impatient for an answer to his question. But he keeps his mouth shut—for a change—because Mead hasn't spoken with his father like this in years. No wait, make that ever.

As his father dries the plate, he continues to talk.

"I hated everything about it: the formaldehyde, the dead bodies, and all those sad people. I was throwing up every day. I must've lost ten pounds that first year. But I never let on to my old man how miserable I was because that was the only way I knew to get his nod of approval, by working alongside of him." He places the plate on the cupboard shelf. Nods at the sink. Mead washes another dish and hands it to him. "I guess what I'm trying to say is that I never wanted you to think you had to be a certain way to gain my approval. I guess that's also why I turned down the scholarship. Because it was important for me to pay for your education myself. To prove to myself that I could be a better father to you than my old man was to me. That I could fully support my son no matter what vocation he chose." He sets the dried plate in the cupboard and waits for the next one.

"I wish you would've told me all this three years ago."

"I didn't realize it was necessary."

"It wasn't," Mead says and picks up another dish. "It just would've been nice to know."

WHEN THE PHONE RINGS, Mead's father answers it expecting Martin or Mead's mother to be on the other end with an update on Jewel. But as it turns out, it's neither of them. "I have to go out," he says after hanging up. "Mrs. Schinkle just passed."

"Now?" Mead says. "She couldn't have waited until tomorrow?" But he is only kidding. Or at least half-kidding.

"I'd like you to stay here," his father says as he pulls on his jacket. "I'd like someone to be here when Martin gets home. To stay with him overnight."

"Sure thing, Dad," Mead says.

His father starts out the front door, then turns back and says, "I still want us to sit down and talk, Teddy. I want to know everything."

"Okay, Dad."

His father looks at him a moment longer, then steps outside and closes the door.

MEAD IS CLEANING THE LIVING ROOM when his uncle comes through the front door. He waits to see if his mother will come in behind him but she doesn't. Mead pulls back the curtain and looks out just as she is driving away. A wave of anger rolls over him. Surely she knows that he is still here. Mead's father must have told her. She could've at least poked her head inside and asked how he was doing. If he needed any help. But no, she's still mad at him for coming home. If Mead wants to get her sympathy, he will first have to graduate from college.

He drops the curtain and glances at his uncle, who is hanging his jacket in the front closet. Not knowing what to say—or if he should say anything at all—Mead goes back to doing what he has been doing for the past four hours. Cleaning. He empties an ashtray into a lipstick-stained coffee cup then sets the ashtray back down on the table.

"That's not where that goes," his uncle says.

Mead looks up. "I'm just cleaning. You can put everything back where you want tomorrow." But as soon as he starts for the kitchen, Martin steps over to the table, picks up the ashtray, and moves it six inches to the left. It irks Mead but he lets it go. After all, this is his uncle's house and he can put his stuff wherever he damn well pleases.

After emptying the ashes into the garbage can, Mead soaps, rinses, and then sets the coffee cup in the drying rack. Martin comes into the kitchen and sits at the table. Mead thinks to ask his uncle how it went but he already knows the answer. Not well. Nothing like that ever goes well. And since Mead can think of no good reason to make his uncle relive the experience, he says nothing. Instead, he picks up the dishtowel and starts putting away the remaining dishes.

"That's not where those go," his uncle says. "You're doing it all wrong. The cups go over there and the plates are supposed to go over there." And he gets up and starts emptying out the cupboard, stacking the clean, dry dishes on the dirty, wet counter.

"Leave it be," Mead says. "It's late. We can move stuff around tomorrow."

But Martin ignores him and keeps pulling dishes out of the cupboard, stacking them on the counter. "You're getting everything all dirty again," Mead says, growing more and more annoyed even though he knows he has no right to. "Stop, please." But Martin keeps going. Even when he runs out of room. He stacks the dishes too high and then one of them falls into the sink of soapy water. "Uncle Martin," Mead says. "Stop. You're making a mess. I just cleaned all these dishes." And he grabs his uncle's wrist. Martin yanks it free and, when he does, the dish in his hand falls to the floor and shatters. "Goddamn it, Uncle Martin. I just finished cleaning this place up!"

The instant the words are out of his mouth, Mead regrets them. Shit. He waits for his uncle to get mad, to call Mead an ungrateful spoiled brat. Instead, he looks up and says, "It's all wrong. The room they put her in, the walls are white. Pink. The walls should be pink; Jewel loves the color pink. And there are no curtains on the windows. It's cold. It was a cold room. How is she supposed to get better in a cold, white room?"

"I don't know," Mead says, a cold sweat breaking out across the back of his neck. Shit. His uncle should have checked into the room next to his aunt. Why didn't Mead's mother make him? He thinks to call his father, to call for help. But he can't. The man already has his hands full. And Mead sure as hell isn't going to call his mother. Shit. He's just going to have to deal with this on his own; something Mead feels woefully underqualified to do. But this isn't some rich, spoiled kid at school he's dealing with here. It's his uncle. And so Mead takes a deep breath and lunges ahead. "It's a hospital, Uncle Martin. I'm sure she'll be fine."

His uncle loses interest in the dishes then and sits back down at the table. "I should've gone to one of his games."

"Excuse me?"

Martin stares at his hands. "He sent me tickets, you know. Me and his mother. She never knew because I threw them out. I think that's why he performed so poorly, because he didn't have our support. It's my fault he got released at the end of the year, my fault he came home, my fault he hit that tree." Martin looks up. "Do you know where he should have been that day? In Arkansas for spring training. He could've been a professional ballplayer. He was that good. If only I had given him my support. It's all my fault."

He's thinking about Henry Charles. That's what it is. He's thinking about how his own father didn't support him as a young man. He's beating himself up because he didn't do better by his son than his father did by him.

"Percy had a job interview, Uncle Martin. That's why he was up in Chicago. He'd decided to become a sportswriter. It wasn't your fault. He was okay with how things had turned out. He was moving on. It wasn't your fault, it just happened."

Martin continues to stare at Mead.

"Hayley Sammons told me. Yesterday. She's the only one he told."

Martin pushes back his chair and stands up as if he is mad. As if he is going to hit someone or something again. But he doesn't, instead he walks out of the kitchen. He walks over to the staircase, turns around, and beckons with his hand for Mead to follow.

"I'll come up later," Mead says. "After I finish with the dishes."

"Forget about the goddamned dishes, Teddy, this is more important. Come. Now." And he proceeds up the stairs.

Reluctantly Mead takes off the kitchen gloves and follows his uncle, stands at the base of the staircase and looks up. Martin waves again then disappears down the hall. This can only come to no good, but Mead ascends the stairs anyway. At the top, he finds his uncle standing in front of Percy's closed bedroom door. "Come on," he says, opens it, and disappears inside.

Shit. Now Mead is sure this is a bad idea. Nonetheless he follows his uncle.

Percy's room looks pretty much like the rest of the house. Untouched, it appears, since the day he left for that job interview in Chicago. His clothes are lying about on the floor and draped over furniture. Posters of baseball players are taped to the walls. The bed is unmade. It is a typical teenage boy's room. It appears as if he has just stepped out and will be coming back any minute. How many times have his aunt and uncle come into this room and had that exact thought?

Martin waves Mead over to the dresser against which a baseball bat is leaning. A mitt hangs from one of the drawer pulls. Martin picks up a framed picture that is sitting on top of the dresser. It contains a photograph of three rows of men dressed in baseball uniforms. "That's him, right there," Martin says and points. "See?"

Mead takes the photograph and gives it a closer look. In the back row, all the way off to one side, is his cousin, squinting more than smiling into the camera, his left shoulder cut off by the picture frame, but he's there, all right: a member of the team.

"Every time I look at this picture," Uncle Martin says, "I wonder who that boy is. I mean I know he's my son. I know he grew up in this house. I know I clothed and fed and educated him, but I don't know who he is because I never took the time to get to know him; I was too busy seeing who I wanted him to be and not who he really was."

Mead doesn't know what to say, so he says nothing.

"You know where I was today?" his uncle asks.

"In St. Louis. Picking up supplies."

"I went to Busch Stadium. I sat in the bleachers all the way up near the top and watched them play." He taps the photograph. "When Percy didn't get re-signed, I thought it was God's way of making things right, of telling my son it was time to come home and fulfill his family obligations. I thought Fate was on my side. I thought He wanted what I wanted." Martin shakes his head. "I come in here five, six times a day to look at this picture, to look at that face, to look at the son I never knew."

"So stop," Mead says.

Martin looks over at him. "Excuse me?"

"Stop. I mean, what's the point? It seems to me that you're just torturing yourself for no good reason at all. Coming in here, looking at this photo, thinking about all the things you could've done differently. But it didn't happen that way. Things happened the way they happened. So what's the point? It's not going to bring him back, Uncle Martin. Nothing is going to bring him back so you might as well think about all the good times you two had together instead because, either way, he isn't coming back. I hate to be so blunt about it, Uncle Martin, but he just isn't."

His uncle looks dumbstruck, as if Mead just slapped him across the face. In a moment he is going to come around, though. In a moment he is going to pick up the bat leaning against Percy's bureau and bring it down over Mead's head. Blood splattering everywhere. Another death in the family. And in two months Martin will be staring at a photograph of his dearly departed nephew, regretting that he made the wrong decision yet again.

"I think I better go back downstairs," Mead says, "and finish the dishes." But as he goes to set the picture on the dresser, something falls partway out of it. At first Mead thinks it's the photograph, that it has slipped through the frame. But then he looks more closely and sees that it is a fifty-dollar bill, folded in half and tucked behind the picture. Shit. Percy never spent it. He kept it all these years. Half the prize money. He saved it the way one saves a birthday card: not for the cash value but for sentimental reasons. And suddenly it hits Mead how stupid he is. How he wasted all those years feeling jealous of his cousin when the whole time he was the one thing Percy wanted more than anything else in the world: the closest thing he would ever have to a brother.

"I'm so sorry, Uncle Martin," Mead says. "I don't know what else to say except that I'm so very, very sorry." And then he leaves. He's halfway down the hall when his uncle sticks his head out the door and says, "Hey. Mead."

He stops and turns around.

"That's what you like to be called now, isn't it? Mead?"

"Yes," he says.

"So, Mead, how would you like some help with those dishes?"

14

REAL VERSUS IMAGINARY

Chicago
Nine Days Before Graduation

MEAD'S HAND SWELLS UP OVERNIGHT and in the morning it looks more like a catcher's mitt than a human appendage. Forsbeck's face has fared better, partly because his girlfriend made him apply an Icy Hot pack to it right away and partly because his face is a lot more solid than Mead's hand.

"You oughta get that hand checked out," the girlfriend says to Mead. She spent the night sleeping in Forsbeck's bed. Not having sex, mind you, just sleeping.

"Yeah," Forsbeck says. "And it's your right hand too. I feel bad."

"Why?" Mead says. "I punched you, remember?"

"Yeah, but I still feel bad."

"I didn't make it up, Forsbeck. There really was a girl in my bed."

"Whatever you say, Fegley," he says and exchanges a look with the girlfriend.

It takes twice as long as usual to shower and dress, what with one hand not working at all. Then Mead heads over to the student infirmary. The nurse takes one look at his mitt and orders a university van to transfer him to the city hospital, where X-rays confirm that his hand is not broken, just bruised. "What did you do," the technician asks, "punch some guy in the face?"

Mead does not dignify her question with an answer and instead says, "How long am I going to have to wear this Ace bandage?"

She gives him a non-answer along the lines of "however long it hurts" and a prescription for pain relievers that Mead fills at the hospital pharmacy. Taking orders from his body instead of the instructions, Mead swallows two in the bus on the way back to campus and two more before heading into Epps Hall. As if they were aspirin. Despite it being a beautiful spring day, the building is stifling hot, its radiators not yet turned off. Mead roams the first floor, peering into one classroom after another, making his way from the front of the building to the back. At the far end is the auditorium—the room where Mead is to give his presentation, the largest classroom on campus with a blackboard that extends all the way to the ceiling of the sixteen-foot-high wall, the Madison Square Garden of academia—Mead removes the now well-worn copy of *Dynamical Systems* from his back pocket and rereads his notes in the margins. This is what his presentation should be about, not the statistical study of zeta zeros that the dean has been advertising. It's good, that study, very convincing, but this is great. Or could be great, if Mead had more time. But he doesn't. The presentation is only two days away now and the dean is counting on him. His final grade is counting on it too.

He rolls up the periodical and tucks it back into his pocket, then presses his nose against the small window in the auditorium door and scans the faces of the students seated inside. They look confused, which can mean only one thing: Dr. Kustrup is lecturing. Mead keeps scanning. Row by row. Seat by seat. But before he can get through all the faces, class is dismissed and the students start flooding past him into the hall, faster than he can check out all their faces.

"Mr. Fegley," Dr. Kustrup says. "What an unexpected surprise. To what do I owe this great honor?"

"I'm looking for Herman. Have you seen him?"

"Why, yes, I have. His father's in town visiting. We had breakfast together this morning, the three of us." Then he notices Mead's bandage. "If I may ask, Mr. Fegley, what happened to your hand?"

Mead stares at his bandaged mitt as if seeing it for the first time, as if it belongs to somebody else. "Oh, this. I punched somebody for screwing with me but it seems that I punched the wrong guy."

Dr. Kustrup studies Mead, trying to decide whether or not he should take him seriously. Mead is probably the last person on earth Dr. Kustrup would imagine hitting anyone. And he is right. But apparently they are both poor judges of character.

The professor gathers up his lecture papers, placing them in a spanking new leather briefcase gold-stamped with his initials. It doesn't really go with the rest of his elbow-patched, tweed-jacket ensemble, looking more like something a CEO would carry into a boardroom. "Is it your birthday today?" Mead asks.

"No, why do you ask?"

Mead nods at the briefcase.

"Oh, this. Isn't it a beauty? Genuine cowhide. Imported from France." Dr. Kustrup clasps the briefcase shut and lifts it off the desk, then says, "I'll be introducing you at the presentation on Friday, Mr. Fegley. Are you excited?"

"I haven't thrown up this much since I was four."

Dr. Kustrup laughs. "I'm glad we've patched up our differences, Mr. Fegley. For both our sakes. Don't worry, you'll do a great job. I'll see you on Friday."

Mead waits until the professor has left, then follows him down the hall and around the corner to the men's room, like a bloodhound following the scent of an escaped convict. Mead hesitates for a moment outside the door, his heart racing with anticipation, then pushes it open and steps inside.

No one is standing at the sinks or at the urinals. Mead steps over to one of the sinks, pulls open the faucet, and lets the water run full blast as he peeks under the doors of the four stalls. A pair of men's brown oxfords is visible in the stall on the end, trouser cuffs bunched down over them, and a spanking new leather briefcase sits next to them. One pair of shoes, not two. But that doesn't necessarily mean Dr. Kustrup is in there alone. Herman would have heard Mead walk in. He could be crouching on the toilet.

It's a gift from Herman. The briefcase. There is no doubt in Mead's mind. A little something the guy picked up the last time he was in Paris, a bribe for his mentor. It's all beginning to make sense to Mead why Dr. Kustrup picked Herman. The professor is probably in there right now thanking him. How many other gifts has Herman given Dr. Kustrup? Does he slip a couple hundred dollars to the professor every quarter, buying himself a spot on the honor roll the way he bought his way out of that speeding ticket?

Mead shuts off the tap and steps into the stall next to Dr. Kustrup. The predator waiting for his prey. Or is it the other way around? It's eerily quiet in here. Too quiet. The professor unrolls some toilet paper from the dispenser and falls silent again.

Mead stares at his bandaged hand. The hand Shirley held on to while she slept, the hand he used to defend her honor. He flexes his fingers and pain shoots up his arm.

Mead cannot believe how stupid he was to have given Herman the benefit of the doubt. To have thought even for a second that Weinstein was the innocent victim in that little bathroom duet. Herman is not a victim; he's just as culpable as Dr. Kustrup. A user of people. But why go after Shirley? What could she possibly have that Herman wants?

The professor flushes and exits the stall. Mead peers through the crack in his door as Dr. Kustrup washes his hands, then combs his fingers through his thinning hair, adjusts his belt, and leaves, taking his spanking new briefcase with him. As if he doesn't have a care in the world. Mead sits tight, his heart thumping loudly, and waits. He's got Herman right where he wants him. Trapped in a bathroom stall, unable to come out. Mead is not sure what he's going to say, how confronting Herman about his alleged consensual activities with Dr. Kustrup and his alleged abuse of Cynthia—neither of which Mead has any proof—is going to make the situation with Shirley any better. An apology, that's what Mead wants. An apology and an explanation as to why Herman would tell Shirley that Mead had bragged about sleeping with her. Why he propositioned her as if she were the campus slut. And a retraction. He wants a retraction too, because an apology to Mead won't do much good if Herman doesn't tell Shirley that he made it up, that he was just kidding around, that his warped sense of humor and Mead's behavior have nothing in common.

A minute goes by, then two. He's good, that Herman, so silent Mead could swear he isn't even in there. A real pro. But Mead knows that the best hunter is a patient hunter and so he sits tight and waits. And waits. Leans down to peer under the divider. No feet. So he waits some more and then gets an idea and stands up on the toilet seat to peer over into the next stall, sure he will find Herman perching on the edge of the toilet bowl like an urchin on the edge of a fountain, water spurting forth from his stone penis. Only the stall is empty. Shit. And Mead was so sure he was right.

The door to the men's room opens and a student steps in. When he sees Mead peering over the top of the stall, he backs out again. As if Mead were the crazy one and not Herman. He almost runs after the boy to explain, to proclaim his innocence, but decides it more important to save his explanation for somebody else.

MEAD WALKS DOWN THE BARREL-VAULTED HALLWAY past portraits of deans come and gone. A century's worth of oil-painted eyes staring down at him, judging him. Impassive faces that hide secrets that were buried along with the men who knew them and told no one, secrets that were necessary to uphold not only their reputations but the reputation of the institute they represented. They scowl and frown and shake their heads as Mead passes by. "Who let him in here?" one of the bearded men says, his voice booming off the arched ceiling and echoing down the limestone passageway. "We don't like squealers," says another. "You have to play the game by the rules," says a third. But Mead ignores them all and keeps walking. It must be the pain pills he's taking. They're playing tricks with his head. He needs to lie down and rest but first he needs to speak with the dean.

At the end of the hall is a mahogany door with a brass plaque that reads: OFFICE OF THE DEAN. Mead goes through it and up to the secretary. Only it isn't the dean's regular secretary, it's Mead's mother. And she's wearing a suit of armor. Mead blinks and rubs his eyes. Damn, those pills are strong. He looks again and the suit of armor is gone, as well as his mother, and sitting in her place is a middle-aged woman Mead has never before seen. "Hello," she says. "How may I help you?"

"Where is the dean's regular secretary?"

"She's on vacation. May I help you?"

"I'd like to speak with Dean Falconia."

"And you are?"

"In a bit of a hurry."

She frowns, displeased with Mead's response. "Do you have an appointment?"

"It's urgent."

"I'm sorry, young man, but Dean Falconia is busy at the moment. I suggest you make an appointment and come back later."

Mead stares at the door to the dean's inner sanctum. Sealed shut. Closing the man off from all the unscrupulous activity taking place right under his nose. The dean needs someone to tell him what has been going on, to raise his awareness before things get any worse. An ambassador of truth: This is the position to which Mead has elected himself. To make a wrong right, to make several wrongs right. Mead would have happily kept his mouth shut, taken his diploma, and quietly slid out of Dodge, so to speak. But too much has happened. Too many injustices, too many lies, Shirley was just the last straw. Dean Falconia has to know the truth about Dr. Kustrup and Herman. About their extracurricular activities. And about the grave mistake he would be making if he were to allow Dr. Kustrup to force Dr. Alexander—the best intellectual mind in his mathematics department—into retirement. It is time to set the record straight, to open the dean's eyes to all the rats in his kitchen.

"I'll only be a minute," Mead says and reaches for the doorknob to the dean's office with his good hand. The secretary, defying her age, springs up out of her chair to try and stop him. "Excuse me, young man," she says. "You can't go in there." But it's too late; Mead already has the door open.

Behind the dean's broad oak desk sits a deep-cushioned chair, its leather upholstery worn smooth. A chair where decisions that change people's lives are made every day. A chair that is, at the present moment, empty. Shit.

"When will he be back?" Mead asks.

The secretary crosses her arms under her breasts, peering at Mead over the top of her reading glasses. "Not until this afternoon. Why don't you come back at four."

"Fine. I'll be back at four," he says and pushes his way out of the office and down the hall, the periodical falling out of his back pocket.

"Young man," the secretary calls after him. "You dropped something." She picks up the thin pamphlet and waves it in the air. "Young man, you didn't give me your name." But Mead cannot hear her over the din of all those past deans casting disparaging remarks upon him.

SOMEONE SHAKES HIS SHOULDER and Mead wakes up. His mouth is dry, his throat parched. He didn't mean to doze off like that. It must be the damned pills; they're making him drowsy. He goes to raise himself up on his arm but a shockwave of pain shoots through his body, causing him to fall back on the bed. Shit. He forgot all about his maimed hand.

"How did you get in here?" Herman asks.

Mead looks up at his best friend. He sounds mad. Mean even. It is a side of Herman that Mead has never before witnessed firsthand, although he has amassed plenty of secondhand knowledge of it. "The resident advisor let me in," Mead says. "I told him I left one of my books in here."

"That's trespassing, you know. I could have you arrested."

Mead swings his feet over the side of the bed and sits up. And that's when he sees Mr. Weinstein, standing in the doorway behind Herman. Shit. Mead came up here to confront Herman about propositioning Shirley. To ask his so-called best friend why he would do such a rotten thing. To give the guy a chance to convince Mead that it was a poorly thought out joke that, in hindsight, he regrets terribly. He wanted to make the guy squirm a little, to make Herman grovel his way back into Mead's favor. He forgot all about Mr. Weinstein being in town.

"Relax, Herman," Mr. Weinstein says. "The boy is your friend. I'm sure he didn't mean any harm by coming in here, did you Mead?"

"No, sir," Mead says and wonders why Herman's father is in town this week as opposed to next week. For graduation.

Mr. Weinstein nods at Mead's bandage. "What happened to your hand?"

I hit the wrong guy. This is what Mead would like to say to make Mr. Weinstein aware of the immoral things Herman has been doing as of late. He wonders how well the elder Weinstein knows his son. Whether or not the man would be shocked to learn that Herman bribes his professor and beats up his girlfriend. Mead does not feel, however, like being the person to open the man's eyes. Even if Mr. Weinstein were to be receptive to such knowledge, he might not feel grateful for it. He might harbor some misdirected anger at the messenger. And it would not exactly be to Mead's benefit to antagonize Mr. Weinstein at this point, to possibly jeopardize the man's good feelings toward him, to muck up the best chance Mead has of getting into that Institute in Princeton. Better that Mr. Weinstein learn of his son's misdeeds through a neutral third party. Like the dean. Mead would prefer to leave himself out of it altogether since none of these matters concern him directly. All are just observations he has made. He would, however, like to clear up another matter. One first touched upon in Princeton. The one regarding Mead's work on the Riemann Hypothesis and the misconception that the elder Weinstein appears to have about the degree of his son's involvement. Mead let it slide before. As a favor to his friend. But in light of what Herman said to Shirley, he feels that now would be a good time to set the record straight.

"What happened to my hand," Mead says, "is not important. What is important, sir, is that I clear up a misconception that you appear to have made about—"

Herman snatches the vial of prescription pills out of Mead's breast pocket and says, "This is strong stuff, Fegley. How many have you taken?"

"Not enough," Mead says and snatches it back. "I still feel pain. As I was saying, sir, I—"

"You still haven't told me why you broke into my room."

"I'm trying to, Weinstein, but you keep interrupting me."

"Quiet, Herman," Mr. Weinstein says, then, "Go ahead, Mead."

"It's about the Riemann Hypothesis, sir. Herman and I are not now, nor have we ever been, working together on it. I don't know where you got the impression that we were, if you came up with that on your own or somebody fed it to you, but it isn't true."

Herman raises his arm and Mead flinches, waiting for the sting of impact, certain that the guy is going to strike him. But instead Herman places his palm on Mead's forehead and says, "You're burning up, Fegley, did you know that? I think you might be delusional." Then he points to his own head and twirls his index finger around in a circle as if to indicate to his father that Mead is crazy.

"I am not the delusional one here, Weinstein," Mead says. "You are." He turns back to Mr. Weinstein. "Your son has had it in for me since day one of college. And he stole Dr. Kustrup away from me, did you know that? Your son is a thief."

Herman laughs. "Listen to yourself, Fegley. Do you realize how paranoid that sounds? I think you better lie back down; you're all hopped up on painkillers."

"I am not all hopped up," Mead says. "I have never felt more clearheaded and sober in my life." And he steps away from Herman, to distance himself from the enemy, to prove to Mr. Weinstein that he is speaking the truth. But when he steps away, he trips over one of Herman's feet. *Can you see the floor, Theodore?* The phrase goes through his head as Mead falls, a fall that seems to happen in slow motion. A fall during which he relives every humiliation ever hurled upon him. By the time Mead hits the floor, he has shrunk to the size of his former self. He feels as lonely as that ten-year-old boy in a urine-soaked shirt lying half-naked next to a babbling brook behind the school.

"Jesus, Fegley, you're in even worse shape than I first thought," Herman says and kneels down to help him up. But Mead pushes the guy away. "I'm fine," he says and gets up on his own, then perches himself on the edge of the spare bed and holds his throbbing head in his throbbing hand.

"I should be going," Mr. Weinstein says to Herman, then turns to Mead. "If I were you, son, I'd rest up. You have a big day ahead of you. I'm looking forward to hearing the presentation on Friday." Then he turns back to Herman. "If I could have a word with you in the hall?"

"Sure thing, Dad," Herman says. "Just a sec." And pulls from his mini-fridge a Coke, pops off the tab, and hands it to Mead. "Drink this, Fegley. It'll help clear your head. I'll be right back."

Mead takes the cold can and holds it to his forehead. Shit. He blew it. He finally had his chance to set the record straight with Mr. Weinstein and he blew it. What could Mead have been thinking? He just accused the man's son of stalking, assault, and theft. No matter that it's true, that's not the point. The point is his story came off as lacking credibility. And it's all Herman's fault. If the guy hadn't propositioned Mead's date then Mead wouldn't have hit Forsbeck and he wouldn't be sitting here in Herman's room with his hand wrapped in a bandage all hopped up on medication. Double shit. At this rate Mead is never going to get into that damned Institute in Princeton.

They have started arguing. In the hall. Mead cannot make out their words but it is obvious that neither Herman nor his father is very happy. Could it be that Mr. Weinstein believes Mead after all? Or is that just wishful thinking? The argument is short. Perhaps it is not about Mead at all. A pair of hard-soled shoes retreats down the hall making a *slap-slap-slap* noise as their owner trots down the stairs. Silence follows and Mead begins to fill with anxiety. Shit. Now he is going to have to deal with a truly angry Herman, someone Mead is not much looking forward to meeting for the first time.

The guy steps back into his room looking as if he came up on the short end of the argument. His face is ashen; his shoulders, slumped. Mead drops his eyes and knocks back a slug of Coke, rubs his temples, and tries to remember why the hell he came up here in the first place. Oh, right. Shirley.

Herman sits down on his bed, leans back on his elbows, and stares at Mead. "You upset my father, Fegley, with that little outburst of yours. And he doesn't much like to be upset. I'm trying to understand what just happened here. I'm trying to convince myself that you didn't just try to screw me over with that little speech of yours — that it was the pills talking, not you — but I'm having a hard time. Help me. Help me to understand."

"I'm trying to screw you?" Mead says. "You're kidding, right?"

"No, I'm not kidding. I've never been more serious in my life."

"He believes me, doesn't he? Your father knows I'm telling the truth."

"I thought we were friends, Fegley, I thought I could trust you."

"Trust?" Mead says, not quite believing his ears. "How can you sit there and talk to me about trust? Jesus Christ, Weinstein, you propositioned Shirley. You lied to her about me and then you propositioned her. Why? For what insane reason would a person who claims to be my fucking friend do a thing like that? You've got a serious problem, Weinstein. You really ought to seek professional help." Mead sets down the can of Coke. He has got to talk to Shirley. He has got to explain to her what happened and warn her to stay as far away from Herman as possible. And then he will go back to the dean's office and tell the man all the crazy things Herman has been doing. Tell him that Weinstein may very well be a madman. Mead stands up, eager to make right all that has gone so horribly wrong, but his knees give way and he slumps to the floor.

Herman jumps off his bed, grabs Mead under the arms, and props him up against the bed. "Jesus, Fegley, you really are a mess. You're in no shape to be going anywhere. I think you better lie down and sleep it off."

Mead knows he should leave. Knows he should go talk to Shirley and then to the dean and he wills his body to do just that. To get up and leave. But it doesn't obey. And truth be told, Mead is not the least bit sure he trusts his legs to get him downstairs to his own room, let alone across campus to the dean's office. So he lets Herman lift him off the floor. Lies back on the bed and closes his eyes. Just for a minute. Just until his head clears. Then he will go talk to Shirley. And then he will go to the dean's office and tell the man everything.

MEAD AWAKES WITH A START. The room is dark so he cannot read the face of his watch but he doesn't need to see it to know that he has missed his four o'clock appointment with Dean Falconia. Shit. He might still have time, though, to get to the library before it closes.

His foggy mind has cleared but his throbbing headache is worse than ever. And there is this terrible weight pressing on his chest, making it difficult for him to breathe. Mead goes to sit up and discovers that the weight is an arm, glances over his shoulder and sees Herman lying next to him. In the same bed.

His heart starts racing. Mead looks down to make sure his pants are still on. They are. Then he looks over at Herman and, thank god, his pants are on too. Mead remembers lying in bed next to Shirley, holding her breast and masturbating while she slept. He remembers the two pairs of shoes in the men's room. Shit. Could Herman have done the same thing to Mead?

He gets a sick feeling in the pit of his stomach. Like a rabbit in an open field, Mead senses danger, every cell in his body telling him to get out, to run for cover. He wraps his hand around Herman's wrist with the intention of lifting it off his chest when the guy stirs. Mead lets go and lies still, hoping that Herman will drift off again. But he doesn't, he sits up and says, "Hey there, sleepyhead, you feeling any better?"

"Yes," Mead says in as calm a voice as he can muster. "You were right. All I needed was a little nap. I feel much better now. Thank you." Then he attempts to get up out of bed, but Herman grabs his arm and pulls him back down.

"What's your big hurry, Mead? Relax. This is nice, isn't it?"

No, he wants to say, it's creepy. You scare the hell out of me, Weinstein. And why are you suddenly calling me Mead? What happened to Fegley? I was more comfortable with Fegley. But he doesn't say any of this because he has said too much already. Mead should not have spoken to Mr. Weinstein in front of Herman. He should have gone to the dean and told him everything instead. Mead fears that he has become Herman's next victim. Or maybe Mead has been the real victim all along. Maybe Dr. Kustrup and Cynthia and Shirley were merely for practice. Collateral damage. Mead needs to play it cool. To be quiet, make no assumptions, and look everywhere always. So he says, "Yes, it's been real nice but I really have to go now."

Herman rolls halfway on top of Mead, pinning him down with his leg. His face within inches of Mead's face. "I gave you the option to leave. Remember? On the way to Bell Labs. I would've taken you to the airport. I would've let you off the hook but you didn't accept my offer, Mead. You already had the bait in your mouth and you didn't want to let go. You didn't want me to throw you back in the ocean. You made the choice and now you'll have to live with it."

"What are you talking about, Weinstein? What bait?"

"Access to the supercomputer."

"I didn't ask you to fly me out there, Weinstein. I didn't even know the Cray X-MP existed. It was your idea. You bought the ticket and then you goddamned nearly had to kidnap me to get me to go."

"You remind me of my little brother," Herman says. "I used to think that he did it deliberately. I used to think that he deliberately set out to humiliate me in front of my father by outplaying me on the piano." He laughs. It's not a real laugh; it's the fake kind that sounds like a curse word. "But I have recently come to the conclusion that he is simply oblivious. Talented and oblivious like you. So you see, I don't hate you, Mead, because it isn't your fault: You're simply oblivious."

Great. So now Herman is comparing Mead to the little brother. The very one he tried to kill in his parents' garage. This has gone too far, gotten too weird. Mead has to leave. Right now. And so in one swift motion he pushes Herman away and rolls out of bed, landing on the floor with a loud thud, landing on his maimed hand. Pain shoots up his arm and Mead screams out then curls into a fetal position and moans.

Herman gets up off the bed and stands over him like a hunter over wounded prey, as if he is trying to decide whether to put him out of his misery or let him go. "Jesus, Fegley," he says. "Why did you go and do that? You'd think I was trying to rape you or something."

His voice has changed. A moment ago it was soft and warm, now it has a hard edge. Mead doesn't move, partially because he is in so much pain and partially because it just seems a whole lot smarter not to. Perhaps if he plays dead, his tormentor will go away.

"Take my hand," Herman says and extends it to Mead, who does not respond. "Take my hand, Fegley, so I can help you up off the floor."

Not wanting to further infuriate the guy, Mead reaches up and takes hold of it. Herman lifts him to his feet then shoves him back on the bed, sitting down on top of him and holding his wrists so tightly that Mead fears the blood to his hands will be cut off, that his skin will bruise. And again he thinks of Cynthia.

"Tell me, Fegley," Herman says. "Have I not been the best friend you ever had?"

"What?"

Herman rests one of his knees on Mead's chest. "You're being terribly ungrateful, Fegley, after all the things I've done for you: taking you to the symphony, giving you that CD player, flying you out east to use the supercomputer."

Mead begins to sweat under his arms and across his back. "Yes," he says.

"Yes what?"

"Yes, you're the best friend I've ever had."

Herman smiles. A mean smile. "I wish you would take a minute to ponder that thought, Fegley, to really think about how generous I have been. And to think about how ungrateful you have been in return."

"That's not true, I've been grateful."

"How grateful?"

"Very grateful."

"Prove it."

"Prove it? How?"

"By making me coauthor of your paper."

"What? No way."

Herman presses down with his knee, making it hard for Mead to breathe. "Come on, Fegley, admit it. Without my help you wouldn't even have a paper. You'd have nothing at all to dazzle the dean and all those visiting mathematicians. So this is how it's going to play out: Tomorrow you are going to make an appointment with Dean Falconia. Then you are going to go to his office and tell him that you lied to my father, that you have not been working on the Riemann Hypothesis alone, that you have decided to come clean and reveal the identity of your coauthor, the individual who made it all possible, your silent partner: me."

"You're out of your mind, Weinstein, I will do no such thing."

Herman releases Mead's wrist and grabs his throat. "Don't make me look bad in front of my father, Fegley. I need this. And so you are going to do as I say. You are going to do this for me out of the goodness of your heart the same way I gave you access to the Cray X-MP out of the goodness of my heart. Because we're best friends, Fegley, and that's what best friends do: They help each other out. Like brothers."

Mead stares up at Herman in disbelief. He feels cornered. Trapped. Not because the guy's hand is wrapped around his windpipe but because he brought this on himself. Mead knew from the get-go that Herman was someone to be avoided at all costs and yet he ignored all the warning signs and let the guy befriend him anyway. Because of what Herman could do for Mead. Because of who his father is. And because he thought himself too smart to succumb to the fates that befell both Dr. Kustrup and Cynthia. And he hates himself for it. Hates himself for being such a willing victim. For so easily setting aside his moral compass for material gain. So he could outshine his cousin. So he could impress the dean. So his mother would have something to crow about back in High Grove. But mainly, he hates himself for having been so foolish as to have thought that Herman was his friend.

"So tell me, Fegley, are you ready to prove to me how grateful you are?"

Mead nods.

"I didn't hear you, Fegley, speak up."

"Yes. I'll talk to the dean. Tomorrow. I'll make you coauthor of my paper."

15

CHAOS AND ORDER

High Grove
Thirty-Six Hours Before Graduation

By the time the last dish is dried and put away, the day is long gone. A few ants continue to circle the dining room table. The stragglers. The ones not quite able to grasp the sudden change in their reality. But the rest of the house has been returned to normal, at least in appearance. Mead flops down on the sofa, exhausted. He is half asleep when Uncle Martin taps him on the shoulder and says, "You'll rest better in a real bed. Follow me."

"I'm fine right here, Uncle Martin."

"In an hour you'll wake up stiff as a board. I insist. Upstairs. Now."

Mead has absolutely no desire to move. He could sleep on the floor and be comfortable he is so tired, but he gets off the sofa and follows his uncle up the stairs anyway because he is too tired to argue. And because he understands that this is his uncle's way of saying thanks for all of Mead's help, by putting him in a real bed for the night. It isn't until Uncle Martin leads him back into Percy's room that Mead realizes that the man has something else in mind altogether. He grabs Percy's blue down quilt and yanks it off the bed, then tosses Percy's pillow at Mead and strips off the bedsheets. "Give me the pillowcase," he says to Mead and stuffs everything into the hamper in the bathroom. Digs a clean set of sheets out of the linen closet and remakes the bed. Mead helps him tuck in the corners and fits the pillow with a new case as Uncle Martin smoothes out a fresh bedspread. A green one. The color of resurrection. "There," he says. "That's better. Now you'll get a good night's sleep." Then he marches off down the hall to his own room.

Mead glances at the dresser. The team photo is gone. His uncle did it; he put the picture away. He's ready to accept Percy's death and move on. Mead lies down on his cousin's bed and tries to fall to sleep. But despite his utter exhaustion he can't. His mind is wide awake. Racing. All he can think about are all the lost opportunities he had with his cousin. How he never thanked Percy for looking after him at school. How he never told his cousin how much he enjoyed their afternoons together in the cornfields. How he never thanked Percy for helping him build the maze. Mead did give him half the prize money but that isn't the same. He doesn't even know what happened to the maze after the science fair. Is it still sitting around somewhere or did his mother set it out on the curb along with Mr. Cheese's wire cage?

Mead sits bolt upright. He has to know what happened to it and he has to know right now. He hops out of bed, tiptoes down the hall, and peeks in through his uncle's open bedroom door. The man is sound asleep. He'll never even know Mead is gone. Then he trots down the stairs and out the front door, closing it quietly behind him. The night air is chilly so he stuffs his hands deep inside his jean pockets and it doesn't hurt, his sunburn having finally subsided. He walks fast, fighting back tears that keep trying to push to the surface. He pictures Percy knocking on the door of his dorm room, waiting, looking at his watch, knocking again and then finally leaving. Getting back in his car. Maybe he sat there awhile waiting for Mead to come back from the library. Maybe he sat there and started to question his decision to drop in on his cousin unexpectedly. After all, it isn't as if they were all that close as kids. Maybe he thought his cousin wouldn't be that happy to see him since Mead never in three years asked Percy to come up and visit. Maybe he decided it was a stupid idea, started up the engine, and got back onto the highway.

Mead rounds the corner onto his street and sees a strange car parked in front of his parents' house, the lights on in the living room. Shit. His mother must be entertaining. So this is the reason she dropped off Uncle Martin at the house and sped away without so much as a hello to her son. Nice, real nice. Mead sneaks up to the living room window and peeks inside to see who the mystery guest is but all he can see through the crack in the drapes is his mother pouring a cup of coffee and talking animatedly. She must have dragged another innocent bystander over to the house to try and talk some sense into her son. To waylay Mead as he comes in through the front door all tired and exhausted after a long day of caring for his aunt and uncle. To catch him at his most vulnerable. A last-ditch effort to get her son back to college in time to graduate. Who is it this time? The county librarian? One of Mead's mentors from science camp? Or maybe it's the high school counselor who first told him about Chicago University.

Mead steps away from the window pissed off at his mother for once again putting her cold heart so blatantly on display. How she could be so insensitive as to take Aunt Jewel to the mental hospital one moment and the very next moment resume her campaign against her son is beyond Mead's comprehension. Did it ever cross her mind that he might be upset about his aunt?

That he might prefer his mother put her arm around his shoulder and ask him if he was doing all right rather than cross her arms over her chest and demand that he go back to school right now? No. Because when she looks at Mead she does not see a young man with thoughts and feelings of his own; she sees only an extension of herself.

Well, she can entertain whomever the hell she wants. Mead could really care less. Actually, it's better this way because if she's in the living room she'll be less likely to hear him. Mead circles around the house to the garage. The door is open, his father still at the store. He's probably down in the basement of Fegley Brothers right now with Mrs. Schinkle. Mead should head over there and offer his father a hand. But the man would probably just yell at him for having left Uncle Martin alone. And Mead really doesn't feel like being yelled at any more tonight.

He starts his search in the garage. One by one he opens up the cardboard boxes stacked between the lawn mower and the lawn chairs. In one he finds a bunch of old clothes that never quite made it to the Salvation Army, in another a set of dishes his mother received as a Christmas present one year and never used, in another an assortment of carpentry tools inherited from Henry Charles that his father doesn't have the heart to throw out. But no maze. So he decides to look for it in the basement. But the only way to get there is through the kitchen.

A tray of canapés is cooling on a wire rack next to the stove. His mother has gone all out for her latest guest, laying the charm on thick. She's probably feeling pretty desperate, the clock ticking down fast now, the deadline frighteningly near. But whom could she have convinced to come over to the house at eleven at night? Who would be crazy enough to comply with such an invitation? Then the answer comes to Mead. Shit, could it be Herman? Could she have called him up at the dorm and begged him to come to High Grove to drag her son back to school?

Mead boils with anger. But of course, she thinks the two of them are friends. She thinks the best thing her son ever did was befriend Herman Weinstein. And that is exactly the kind of thinking that got Mead into this mess in the first place. No wonder he is such a poor judge of character. No wonder he let himself be taken in by Herman. None of this is Mead's fault; it's all on his mother. This whole fucked-up mess happened because of his stupid mother!

"Here, let me freshen up that cup of coffee for you," Mead hears her say to her guest, then her heels start *click-clack*ing toward the kitchen.

Mead hurries down the hall and ducks into his bedroom, standing stone still in the dark as she patters around in the kitchen waiting on Herman, sucking up to the rich boy from Princeton who is probably in the living room right now having a good laugh at her expense. Only when his mother has returned to the living room does Mead tiptoe back into the kitchen, pull open the basement door, and slip down the stairs.

A rack of clothes in dry-cleaner bags stands next to the furnace. The rollaway bed on which Henry Charles wasted away sits next to the water heater. Two card tables and eight folding chairs are stacked up against the far wall. And sitting on the never-used workbench next to them is the maze. It's still here; his mother never threw it out. Mead runs his finger over one of the bridges and it comes away covered in dust. And he starts to cry. For all the things he never said. For all the things he should have done differently. For not being at the dorm when he was supposed to be. For not making it to Percy's funeral. For putting his trust in the wrong person. For disappointing the dean. He screwed up. He screwed up so royally that he doesn't even know where to begin to make it all right again. Everyone thinks he's a genius but Mead knows the truth: He is the stupidest person ever to have walked on this planet. Ever!

He swipes his sleeve across his face to dry his cheeks and catches sight of something blue sticking out from under the maze. Curious, he grasps the edge of it and pulls and out comes a folder with the words "The Life of a River" written across the front of it in the neat penmanship of a ten-year-old boy. Inside is the science report he handed in to Mr. Belknap, the letter C scrawled on the upper right-hand corner in red pencil and circled. But what is it doing here? Mead distinctly remembers burying it in the bottom of the garbage can on the morning of trash collection day eight years ago. He remembers because he was so grossed out from having come in contact with rotting leftovers that he ran to school and washed his hands all the way up to his elbows in the boys' lavatory. Mead now flips through the pages of the report until he finds evidence to back up his memory: a brown-rimmed stain that long ago soaked its way through the last four pages.

But that isn't all he finds. Tucked behind the report Mead handed in is his original science report, the pages taped back together as if by an archaeologist trying to make heads or tails out of some unearthed ancient text. But on the same day he buried his C-grade report in the trash, Mead put the pieces of his original report in a shoebox and then stowed the box on his closet shelf because he didn't have the heart to throw them out. Who found the box? Who reassembled these pages?

"Chin up, Fegley," Herman says. "It can't be that bad."

Mead spins around. Herman is standing at the bottom of the stairs.

"Go away," Mead says. "I'm not in the mood to deal with you right now."

"It's good to see you too."

"I mean it. Get lost," Mead says and swings his arm through the air as if to dismiss his vision of Herman once and for all, but instead he hits flesh and bone. "Shit," Mead says and cradles his not-yet-fully-healed right hand in his left hand.

"Ouch, Fegley," Herman says, "that hurt. I think I deserve an apology."

Which just makes Mead even angrier. He drops his hand and says, "Listen, Weinstein, I don't know what little scheme you and my mother are cooking up together to try and make me go back to school, and frankly I don't care, so why don't you just sneak back up the stairs as quietly as you snuck down and go tell my mother that I'm not going along with it. I've had it with the both of you."

"You've got me all wrong, Fegley."

"No, I don't. I've got you just right. You use people, Weinstein. You used Dr. Kustrup and when that didn't turn out so great you decided you'd use me. I must have looked like some damned easy target to you. Fresh off the hay truck. A naïve, young kid with brains but no social skills who spent every Saturday night sitting alone in the library reading math books, easy pickings for a sophisticated prep school kid like yourself who doesn't think twice about breaking the law because he knows he'll get away with it. Well, I'm sorry to disappoint you, Weinstein, but I guess it turns out that I'm not as much of a sad sack as you first thought. I happen to know what real friendship is because I once had a real friend. He built this maze right here for me and never asked for a thing in return. So screw you, Weinstein. Now get the hell out of my basement."

"Your mother didn't invite me here, Fegley."

"So you invited yourself. Big surprise. Now leave."

"I think you better shut up and start listening. Are you listening?"

And then Mead hears it. His mother is still talking to someone in the living room. But if she isn't entertaining Herman then who the hell is she entertaining?

"What do you say we get out of here and go for a ride," Herman says. "We don't have to go back to Chicago, we can go anywhere you'd like: California, Florida, Mexico. We don't even have to pick a destination, let's just take off. Two buddies on a road trip together. Like Jack Kerouac and Neal Cassady."

"They were unemployed bums with no future."

"Exactly. It'll be fun."

It has its appeal, it really does. It's even better than a cello player who couldn't cut it with the local garage band. Mead could work for cash and sleep in the back of a car. It doesn't get more anonymous than that.

"That was you in the cemetery, wasn't it?" Mead says. "I wasn't seeing things. You've been here all week stalking me."

"I don't like that word, Fegley. Stalking. It sounds so psychotic."

"I'll take that as a yes."

"Well, I was hardly going to hang around campus. My father came this close to throwing me back into that mental institution after you made your big declaration of independence to him in my dorm room. This close," he says and holds his thumb and forefinger within inches of Mead's face. "I could have talked him out of it, though. I could have convinced him that you were wigging out from the pain pills and the pressure and all, but then you had to go and take off. You're a lousy friend, Fegley, but I forgive you. I forgive you because I know you didn't do it deliberately, you did it because you were oblivious to the consequences. That's why I'm here now. I'm here to give you a second chance. To make things right. I'm here to tell you that I'm willing to put that little incident behind us. I'm here to work on rebuilding our friendship. Because that's what friends do, they forgive each other their shortcomings."

"What're you, deaf? We are not friends, Weinstein. Got it? You and me: not friends. And how dare you stand there and talk to me about second chances. I didn't screw you over, I simply told the truth. You screwed me. If anyone owes anybody an apology around here, you owe me."

"You're right."

"Damned straight I'm right."

"I'm sorry."

"You should be."

"Now you apologize to me."

"For what?"

"I can't go back there empty-handed, Fegley. You gotta give me something."

And even though Mead doesn't think he owes Herman a goddamned thing, he feels like doing the guy a favor anyway. Maybe because he knows his father is a dick. Maybe because he never thanked Percy for the maze. Maybe because, despite being so screwed up in the head, Herman did do Mead a huge kindness by flying him out east and getting him access to the supercomputer. And even if he did it for the wrong reason, at least he's willing to stand here now and admit it. And so Mead says, "I'll make things right with your father. I'll tell him you were helping me out and got carried away in your enthusiasm."

"So the road trip is on?"

"I'll get my suitcase and we can go."

Mead gets to the top of the steps before he realizes he's still holding the blue folder. He sets it down on the breakfast table—he'll deal with *that* later—and heads for his room. Herman follows, standing in the doorway like a prison guard as Mead drags his suitcase out of the closet and tosses in a clean pair of socks, an undershirt, and some boxers, then shadows Mead back down the hall. They are just entering the kitchen when they hear Mead's mother say, "The bathroom is through that door and down the hall to your left." And a second later the kitchen door swings open and Dr. Alexander steps through it. At first Mead does not react, unsure of whether it is the actual professor standing in front of him or just another one of Mead's many hallucinations, so he says, "Is that really you, Dr. Alexander?"

"Mr. Fegley," the professor says. "How would you apply the basic prime finding process to all real numbers up to 701,000?"

"With a pen, a pad of paper, and a list of primes up to 829."

The professor then proceeds to pull something from his back pocket. "I believe this belongs to you," he says and hands him the periodical Mead found in the bookshop off campus. "The dean asked me to return it to you."

Mead sets down his suitcase and takes the pamphlet from Dr. Alexander. A note is paper-clipped to it. "My door is always open," it says. And it's signed *Dean Falconia*. "Ohmygod," Mead says. "It is you. You're really here. But what are you doing in High Grove?" Mead looks down at the professor's cast. "And how did you get here?"

"Your mother picked me up at the train station in Alton a few hours ago."

"My mother?"

And as if on cue, the door swings open again and she steps through it.

"Teddy," she says. "When did you get home?"

Mead looks at his mother all neat and prim and perfect standing next to the rumpled professor and says to her, "But you wouldn't even shake his hand. In Chicago."

"I've already apologized to your professor for that, Teddy. And he graciously accepted my apology. I can only hope that you will do the same."

The last time Mead's mother apologized to him was at

Mr. Cheese's funeral. It didn't seem like enough back then, so is it enough now? But then it has to be, doesn't it? Because she cannot take back what she did any more than Mead can take back what he did. Shit. He ditched his presentation. He wasn't thinking about anyone but himself. Not the dean, not all those visiting professors, just himself. If Mead cannot find it in himself to accept his mother's apology, then how in hell can he expect the dean to accept his?

Mead's mother looks at Herman, as surprised by his appearance in her kitchen as Mead is by Dr. Alexander's, and says, "What is he doing here?" As if Herman is trying to steal her thunder. As if she suddenly suspects that the rich boy from Princeton is not the good friend she first thought he was to her son.

"Herman's taking me back to school, Mother. We were just leaving."

"Now?" she says. "In the middle of the night? When did you make these arrangements, Teddy? How come you didn't tell me?"

These are all good questions, none of which he has any good answers to. But he does have a few questions of his own. Mead picks up the blue folder and says, "You found this in the trash, didn't you? And you found the shoebox in my closet. You knew my original science report got destroyed and yet you still punished me for getting that C. Why? Why did you take me to Wessman's if you knew the whole time?"

"Because," she says in a tone that suggests that she has rehearsed the answer to this question a million times over the past eight years, "I was afraid of the consequences if I didn't."

"Consequences? What consequences?"

Mead's mother looks from Dr. Alexander to Herman to Mead. "When you were a toddler I used to take you over to your aunt and uncle's house to play with your cousin. Percy was always yanking whatever toy you were playing with out of your hand. It made me so mad. But what made me even madder was that you never cried or complained about it, you just let him take whatever he wanted, and I thought: Throughout his whole life, people are going to take advantage of my son." She shifts her eyes to the blue folder. "When I saw you burying that in the trash, I knew something was up and searched your room looking for an explanation. I didn't know who did it, only that it had happened. *Who* wasn't important. I wasn't going to be able to follow you around for the rest of your life and protect you." She looks back up at Mead. "You weren't a physically strong boy, Teddy, but you were exceptionally smart. I had to make sure that you would utilize that god-given talent to its fullest extent. And if taking you to Wessman's that day meant you might end up hating me for the rest of your life, it was a gamble I was willing to take in order to ensure my son the best possible life."

Mead sets the blue folder back down on the table. "I'm a grown man now, Mother. You're going to have to trust me to take care of things in my own way." And then he picks up his suitcase and steps out the back door.

"You handled yourself admirably back there, Fegley," Herman says as they walk toward the strange car parked in front of the house. "I almost believed it myself, you know, that you've suddenly grown up. I hope it's really true."

It's a nondescript rental sedan. The car. The kind gangsters drive in movies. And it gives Mead a moment of pause. He thinks about turning around and going back into the house but pride won't let him. Instead he tosses his suitcase onto the backseat, crawls into the front, and slams the door. To let Herman know that he doesn't appreciate the comment. Only when Herman has crawled in behind the wheel and started up the car does Mead bother to utter his own sarcastic response. "I'd give you directions to the highway," he says, "but I don't suppose you need them."

"You're right," Herman says. "I don't." And pulls away from the curb, winding his way through the streets of High Grove as if he's been living here his whole life. He's not in a big rush the way he was out east, the aura of tension around him gone. He's like a farmer waiting for the corn to grow. And it makes Mead uneasy.

Herman makes a right and a left and then another right and passes by the cemetery on his way out of town. The streetlights drop away and the surrounding homes and trees fall into darkness, the headlights of the sedan carving a tunnel through the night. Then Herman makes another left.

"Where are you going?" Mead says. "The highway is straight ahead. I thought we were heading back to Chicago."

"I never said anything about Chicago, Fegley."

"It was implied. In our agreement."

"Was it?"

"You know it was, Weinstein, now turn around. I thought you said you knew your way around here. This is a dead-end road. There's nothing out this way but Snell's Quarry."

"I know," Herman says and keeps driving.

A prickly sensation creeps over Mead's scalp. This is not good. This was not part of the plan. At least it wasn't part of Mead's plan but maybe it's what Herman has had in mind all along. To get Mead out on a deserted road. In the middle of the night. Alone.

The sedan rolls off the pavement, its tires crackling over gravel. Herman slows to a stop a few feet shy of the water and shifts the car into PARK but doesn't turn off the engine. The headlights illuminate a path of light that dances across the surface of the lake and then stops up short against a sheer face of rock. Against Dead Man's Leap.

Herman pulls a pack of cigarettes out of his breast pocket and shakes one free then pushes in the lighter on the dashboard and waits for the coil to heat up, as if the whole reason he drove out here was to sit by the lake, have a smoke, and look up at the full moon that is just now lifting itself over the horizon. But Mead isn't buying it. He thinks Herman has something else in mind altogether. And unless the guy has brought with him an affidavit for Mead to sign swearing that Mr. Herman Weinstein is in fact the coauthor of Mead's paper on the zeros of the zeta function, then Mead is in serious trouble. Panic rises up in his chest, making it hard for him to breathe. He cannot believe he did it again: suspended his better judgment and trusted Herman. He should have stayed at the house with his mother and Dr. Alexander. What the hell is wrong with him? Mead rolls down the window for fresh air but it doesn't help. He considers bolting from the car but knows that Herman would only come after him. Running isn't working anymore. Mead needs to try a new tactic and so he says, "Why did you pretend to be surprised that Cynthia and I knew each other?"

"What're you talking about, Fegley?"

"The first time I came up to visit you in your room, Cynthia was there. You started to introduce us and when she said we already knew each other you acted all surprised and jealous. But you weren't surprised, Weinstein. You were stalking me even back then. You knew I liked her and so you went after her."

"I suppose that is what attracted me to her: the fact that she could like a guy like you. That she could see below the surface; that she could see the value of the person inside." Herman looks over at Mead. "She liked you too, you know. I even think she would've gone out with you if I hadn't come along. She couldn't stop talking about you after you dropped by that night. I think maybe she was having second thoughts."

"Is that why you hit her?"

Herman looks surprised. This is news to him, that Mead knows.

"And is that why you fucked Dr. Kustrup? Because he liked me better than he liked you?"

"You seem to have me all figured out, Fegley. I'm curious, if you knew all those things about me, though, why you never turned me in."

Because I'm an idiot, Mead says to himself. Because I thought it would be easier to keep my mouth shut. Because I thought I could graduate and slip out of town without causing any waves. But obviously I was wrong. "I don't have you figured out, Weinstein. I may know who and what you have done stupid shit to but I am utterly clueless as to why. I mean I get it: You hate your brother and you're taking it out on me because I remind you of him. I get it. What I don't get is how you could possibly think that forcing me to make you my coauthor or killing me or whatever other crazy shit you have in mind to do is going to change any of that. I hate to be the one to break it to you, Weinstein, but it isn't. You'll still be a lousy excuse for a human being and your father will probably still despise you."

"I know."

"You know. You know? Then what the hell are we doing out here? I've changed my mind. I don't want to drive to Chicago or California or Mexico or wherever the hell else it is you think I agreed to go. Take me back to the house."

Herman places the unlit cigarette between his lips, shifts the car into reverse, and starts to turn around. Only he does not head back out to the main road, instead Herman starts driving around the lake, the sedan lurching about as its tires try to find their footing on the uneven rock, scrub brush scraping against the sides and along the undercarriage of the car. And the prickly sensation returns to Mead's scalp.

"What are you doing, Weinstein?" he says, but Herman does not respond.

The full moon has risen completely above the treetops now, the landscape bright enough for Mead to get his bearings. And he can see where Herman is headed. Up the hill to Dead Man's Leap. Mead's window starts rolling up on its own. The lock on his door thunks into place. Shit, Herman *is* going to kill him.

"You can't drive back here, Weinstein. It's illegal."

"The law doesn't much concern me right now, Fegley. It's like you just said: I can't do anything to change who I am or what my father thinks of me so what's the point in even trying?"

"That's not what I meant. You *can* do something, just not something stupid. And I don't think I have to tell you that whatever it is you have planned to do right now most definitely falls under the category of stupid."

The headlights of the sedan light upon a sign that reads: DANGER. DO NOT GO BEYOND THIS POINT. Herman drives right over it.

"I'll help you write another paper," Mead says. "One for which you really are my coauthor. How about that?"

"I don't want your charity, Fegley. I'm a Weinstein. We help those in need, not the other way around."

"It's not charity if you work for it, Weinstein."

"But it'd feel like charity, Fegley."

The top of the cliff is within sight now, the moon hanging directly over it. The tires of the car hit a patch of loose rock and the sedan skids sideways. Mead almost shits in his pants.

"Okay," he says. "You win. I'll make you coauthor of my paper. *This* paper."

Herman brings the car to a stop and looks over at Mead. "You say that now, Fegley, but what is to stop you from changing your mind an hour from now when you're sitting in the safety of your parents' cozy little house. I'm afraid I can't take the chance."

"I won't change my mind, I swear."

Herman pulls the lighter out of the dashboard, holds it to the end of his cigarette, and lights up, inhaling deeply. "You know, you are the most unique person I have ever known. You don't care about what other people think; you just care about math. I admire you, Fegley. I just want you to know how much I admire you. You were the closest thing to a friend I ever had." The lock on Mead's door thunks again. "Go on, Fegley, get out."

He's letting him go. Thank god. Mead cracks open the door then looks back at Herman. Were, he said. You *were* the closest thing to a friend I ever had. Past tense. Mead pulls the door closed again and says, "No."

Herman smiles. "There you go again, Fegley. You say we aren't friends but then you go and act like the best friend in the world. You're amazing, Fegley, truly amazing. Now get out."

"No," Mead says and crosses his arms over his chest.

"Then I'll get out." And he puts the car in PARK and does just that: gets out and walks up to the edge of the cliff and looks down. He sucks on the cigarette and exhales a large plume of smoke then turns back toward the car and, squinting into the bright headlights, says, "Now I see why you were so hesitant to jump. It's quite scary from up here. How many stories above the water do you think we are: Four? Five?"

Mead does not answer; instead he crawls over the gearshift into the driver's seat. It is a new feeling for him, sitting behind the wheel. Exciting and scary at the same time.

Herman sucks on the cigarette. "You want to hear something

crazy? I never learned how to swim. My father tried to teach me once but I got hysterical when he put me in the water. He thought I was acting out, he thought I was deliberately being difficult to embarrass him in front of all the other men at the yacht club." Herman takes another puff. "What can I say? It was a lot less embarrassing to let him think that than to know the truth, than to know that his bastard son was a spineless wimp who was scared to death of drowning."

Mead leans his head out the window. "Get back in the car, Weinstein. Now."

"I can't go back, Fegley. There's nothing for me to go back to."

Mead looks at Herman looking at the moon and remembers something Uncle Martin once told him about why men hunt. He said they are propelled by an atavistic impulse to reconnect with nature, that they are seeking a way to get back in touch with their basic instincts, to escape, even if just for a few hours, from the pressures of their day-to-day lives. So that must be why Herman has been stalking Mead—hunting him, really—for the past three years: He has been trying to get back in touch with something he lost. Or maybe never had at all. But death is the goal of the hunt, not the hunter.

"Come on, Weinstein, it'll be fine. You're a smart guy. If you don't want me to help you write a paper, fine, write one on your own. Trust me, if you put as much time and energy into studying as you put into stalking me, you'll do just fine. And don't do it for your father, do it for yourself. Find a subject you love. Maybe it isn't math; maybe it's something else. Maybe it's something that'll really piss your father off. You know, a two-birds-with-one-stone kind of thing. Think of the possibilities."

Herman inhales on the cigarette, then drops it to the ground and stamps it out with the toe of his shoe. "That sounds great,

Fegley, that sounds really great. In theory. But I'm not much interested in proving or disproving it." And then he jumps off the cliff.

Herman doesn't scream but Mead hears his body hit the water as he scrambles out of the car and rushes toward Dead Man's Leap. He peers over the edge and down into the black hole that is the lake, waiting for Herman to pop back up to the surface. Only he doesn't. Shit. A wave of nausea rolls over Mead. He thinks about the quarryman who jumped off this same cliff a hundred years ago. He thinks about Percy driving into that tree. No one could save that quarryman and Mead wasn't there to save Percy. But the quarry is now filled with water and Mead is here. *Boys as young as eight jump off this cliff in the belief that when they hit the water they'll be men.* Mead sure as hell hopes that's true, closes his eyes, holds his nose, and steps into the air.

ACKNOWLEDGMENTS

ONE DAY I GOT IT IN MY HEAD to write a novel. It would be my life's purpose. My family most likely thought me crazy: the middle kid seeking attention again. But a college friend sent me her copy of *The Artist's Way.* I taped a couple of its inspirational passages over my desk, then sat down and wrote my heart out. The result wasn't great but it wasn't terrible either. I was hooked. Over the intervening years, a few special people have read and reread and reread and reread my numerous attempts to sculpt a publishable story. Without them I could never have done it. And so I want to extend thanks to my sister, Mary Jacoby, and to Meredith Reed, Mary Keane, Gary Brozek, and Jaya Miceli for their honest feedback and unflagging support. I also want to thank Barney Karpfinger for plucking my novel from the hundreds that have passed through his hands over the years and Jamie Raab for believing in me and giving me the benefit of her sharp editorial eye. I would like to extend an intellectual debit to *Meditations on Hunting* by José Ortega y Gasset and *Prime Obsession: Bernhard Riemann and the Greatest Unsolved Problem in Mathematics* by John Derbyshire. They taught me, respectively, the language of hunting philosophy and of math. And lastly I want to thank my college friend, Amy Muir Stevens Sternberg, who passed away before I managed to get published. I still have your book, Amy. And if it's all right with you, I think I'll keep it.